FOREVER WITH YOU

Book 3 in the Fixed Trilogy

by Laurelin Paige

© 2014 by Laurelin Paige

ISBN-13: 978-0-9913796-1-3

First edition January, 2014.

The following story contains mature themes, strong language, and sexual situations. It is intended for adult readers.

Forever With You

Forever With You

Chapter One

I took a deep breath and stared at the door of apartment three-twelve. Whether or not I wanted to go any further, I hadn't decided. Actually, I couldn't remember deciding to come this far. But here I was—my heart pounding and hands sweating, debating the pros and cons of raising my fist to the wood and knocking.

God, why was I so nervous?

Maybe more deep breaths were in order. I took several—*in, out, in, out*—and examined my surroundings. The hall was long and empty. Gold-framed abstract art lined the walls. Though the building was nice and in a good part of town, the carpet was old and threadbare. Rose petals were strewn across the floor in front of the threshold a few doors down. Must have been left over from someone's romantic gesture. *Sweet.*

To the other side of me, the elevator opened. I looked over and saw a couple walking in the opposite direction. The man, dressed in a nice suit, held his hand to the small of the woman's back. Her blonde hair was tied up in a perfect bun. Even from behind, they were beautiful to look at. It was obvious they were in love.

Funny how I was seeing romance everywhere. Perhaps it was my state of mind.

I turned back to the door in front of me. It was plain and ordinary, but something about it felt ominous.

Well, might as well get this over with.

I pulled my bag higher on my shoulder and knocked.

Nearly a minute went by and no one answered. I leaned my ear against the door and listened. It was quiet. Maybe I had the wrong unit. I checked my hand where I'd scribbled the address in red pen, but it had rubbed off from my sweat.

It didn't matter. I knew I was in the right place.

"Try the buzzer," a man said from down the hall.

"The buzzer?" I asked, but he had already gone into his own apartment.

I hadn't noticed a buzzer, but I searched the wall by the doorframe anyway. There I found a small circular button. Strange I hadn't seen it before. I brought a trembling finger up and pushed.

A loud bark ripped through the air, and I nearly jumped out of my shoes, my heart pounding in my chest. I wasn't usually afraid of dogs, but I was already so anxious that it took very little to set me off. Movement sounded from inside and a voice talking sternly to the animal. Seconds later, the door opened.

Stacy stood in the entryway, her face more welcoming than she normally was with me. Her overly bright smile sent a chill down my spine. She was dressed casually in a faded t-shirt and jeans—not at all the attire I was used to seeing her in when she worked at Mirabelle's boutique. She was barefoot and her toes were painted with a pale pink polish. She looked relaxed. Comfortable.

I felt just the opposite.

Her grin widened. "You came."

"I guess I did."

She didn't move to let me in, so I stood where I was, awkwardly shifting my weight from one foot to the other. Did she hear my knees knocking? I was sure she must.

"Oh, sorry! Come on in." She stepped aside and let me move past her.

I took a tentative step inside, scanning her apartment. It was nice. Not nice like Hudson's apartment—Hudson's and *my* apartment, rather—but nicer than the studio that I used to reside in on Lexington Avenue. The space was sterile and cold, though completely immaculate except for the kitchen table to my left. It was covered with stacks and stacks of papers, reminding me of the top of the file cabinets in David's office back at The Sky Launch.

"This way." Stacy gestured to a couch in her living room. It was a twin to the sofa in Hudson's office—brown leather with oversized arms. I'd admired the design so much that I'd ordered a similar, less expensive one for the office at the club. Hudson and I had christened that couch, actually, with a round of heated sex. Stacy's version was not the cheaper variety, and with as prudish as the woman seemed, I doubted that she'd christened it with anyone.

Weird, though, that we all had similar taste.

Actually, what was weird was that I was there finding out Stacy's taste at all. Why was I there? The tight knot in my gut said this was the wrong decision. I should leave.

Except, I couldn't. Something kept me there with an intense force. Like my shoes were metal and the floor a super magnet. I knew it was all in my head—that I could physically walk out the door anytime I wanted. Yet there I stayed, compelled against my better judgment.

I threw my shoulders back, hoping it would make me feel more confident, and took a seat. I sunk lower than I'd expected, my knees sticking up higher than my thighs. I looked and felt ridiculous. So much for being self-assured.

"So sorry," Stacy apologized. "The springs are broken. Scoot down further and you'll bounce back."

Awkwardly, I lifted myself from the concave spot and moved further down the sofa. I sat slowly, testing for firmness. Thankfully, the springs were indeed intact. My poise, on the other hand, was not.

Stacy settled into the armchair next to me. A large gray cat rubbed against her leg, hissing in my direction. The unfriendliness of the cat reminded me of the barking from earlier. I looked around, but found no sign of a dog. Stacy must have locked it up in another room. It was odd that she'd have both pets in such a small apartment. I'd never figured her for an animal lover.

But I'd never figured her to wear jeans and a t-shirt either. It was all the unexpected that had me on edge, I told myself. That's all.

"Can I get you anything? Water? Iced tea?"

"No, thank you." I crossed my legs. "Actually, I'm sort of on a schedule. Do you mind if we get this over with?" It was a lie. I had nowhere to be. I didn't even have a driver waiting for me. I'd taken the subway instead of asking Jordan to bring me. Jordan reported to Hudson, and I didn't want him to know about this visit.

"Yes. Of course." She stood and crossed to her television. I noticed her computer was plugged into it, and when she turned on the set, her desktop showed on the large flat screen.

Having lost its leg to rub against, the gray cat moved over to my leg.

Great. Now I'd have gray fur all over my black pants. How would I explain that to Hudson? Maybe I could change before he noticed.

Stacy chatted as she scrolled through files on her computer. "Honestly, I wasn't sure if you'd come. You hadn't seemed interested before. I was surprised to get your text."

"Yeah, I wasn't sure I'd come either. Curiosity won out." Maybe it was because of the animal at my feet but I couldn't stop thinking about the *curiosity killed the cat* adage.

Fuck, what was I doing? Was it too late to change my mind about this?

It wasn't too late until she actually started the video. But I couldn't turn back now, could I? I'd never be able to stop wondering what secrets Stacy held about Hudson.

Maybe I should have asked him about it instead of showing up here.

"Well, I set up in case you did come. I just have to load the file. Hold on. It's here somewhere."

It seemed to take hours for Stacy to search through her computer. Each second that passed felt like agony. Thoughts of what could be on her video nagged at the edges of my mind—Hudson betraying me in various forms. I tried to shake the images away, but they clung, nipping at me, begging for my attention.

I'd chewed half of my nails ragged before I finally sought to relieve the tension. "Perhaps you could tell me what's on it while we wait."

"Oh, I couldn't do that." She gave me another warm smile. "You won't believe it until you see it. But trust me. It will change everything you know about Hudson. He's a liar, you know." She never smiled this much. It was as if she took pleasure in my discomfort. As if she were delighted to destroy my relationship with Hudson.

"He's not a liar. I trust him." I was the one who'd lied to him. Hudson had done nothing but proven himself over and over.

"You'll see."

Her certainty sent goose bumps down my skin. There was no way she was right. I knew Hudson. He didn't have secrets from me.

"Ah! Found it!" Stacy said in a sing-song voice. "Are you sure you don't want anything before I start this? Water? Iced tea?"

I gritted my teeth, the knot in my belly tightening with every passing second. "I said, no thank you."

"Popcorn?" She laughed. "I always like popcorn when I'm watching TV. Popcorn and M&M's."

"Look, Stacy, this isn't entertainment for me. You say you have something that will make me feel differently about Hudson. Do you think I'm looking forward to this?"

This was ridiculous. What was I doing here, behind Hudson's back no less? I should be talking to him, asking him about this stupid video instead of sneaking off to watch it. I didn't even know if I could trust the woman in front of me. Maybe this whole video thing was a trick.

I stood to leave. "I shouldn't be here. I have to go." I headed toward the door.

"No! Wait! It's already playing."

Again, curiosity got the better of me. I turned back to the TV. The screen was dark, but there was a muffled voice in the background. Little by little, the voice became clearer. It was Hudson.

"I want you, precious. Whatever it takes to make that happen. Whatever I have to do. Whatever I have to say. I have to have you in my life."

The screen was still dark, but I recognized the words. He'd said them to me—earlier. At the club.

"Is this some kind of a sick joke?"

"Just be patient." Stacy giggled.

The screen began to lighten and the picture came into focus. Hudson lay on a bed facing away from the camera, completely naked. I glanced at Stacy, furious that she had seen my boyfriend without clothing, but Hudson's next words drew me back to him. "Whatever I have to say, precious. I have to have you in my life."

They were familiar words, but I'd never seen this scene before. I didn't know that bed or that room. I hadn't been there when this had been filmed. I shook my head—*no, no, no.* Those were *my* words. *Precious* was *my* name. Whom was he sharing my words with?

The camera began to move, zooming around Hudson. I held my breath, waiting to see whom he was speaking to, not wanting the confirmation.

But as the camera zoomed closer, the focus blurred. So much so that it was impossible to make out what was going on or who was on screen. It was like looking through a dirty windshield or a cloudy contact lens. I blinked over and over, hoping to clear the blur, to bring the picture into clarity. I was desperate to see what was going on, desperate to see who was there. Even though I didn't want to, I was compelled.

I went to the TV and slapped my hand on its side, trying to sharpen the image. "Show me, dammit," I screamed at the picture. "Show me what you're hiding!"

I hit the television again and again, my hands red from the force, my breath ragged from the effort. I had to see, had to know. My gut told me the truth—the video held the answers. What I needed, what I was meant to see was here on this screen. Beyond the blur was what I dreaded most, my deepest fears, my darkest imaginings—the thing that could ruin everything.

The thing that could tear me and Hudson apart for good.

Forever With You

Chapter Two

I awoke in a panic, sweat beaded along my brow, my heart racing. I knew it was a dream, but the feeling it left was intense and vivid. Stupid, really. It wasn't real.

But it wasn't the dream video that had me in a panic—it was what might be on Stacy's real life video. She'd said it was some sort of evidence about Hudson and Celia. I'd blown it off earlier in the night, but maybe I shouldn't have because now it was seeping into my subconscious thoughts.

I glanced over at Hudson asleep next to me. Usually we remained in constant contact while we slept. His missing warmth exacerbated the "off" feeling that still clung to me after my nightmare. Not wanting to disturb my lover, I ignored the pull to snuggle into him and instead climbed out of bed, grabbed my robe, and headed to the bathroom.

Splashing cold water on my face, I took deep breaths and tried to calm down. I'd never been prone to nightmares. Even when my parents had died, my dreams had remained sweet and calm. My obsessive mind did enough work during the waking hours—sleep wasn't where I fleshed out my problems.

I wasn't obsessing like I had in the past, though. And there were problems still to be worked out. Yes, I was happy and in love. But the past week had been heartbreaking and stressful with Hudson in Japan and our relationship in limbo. I'd kept secrets that I wasn't sure he could ever completely forgive me for. And he'd betrayed me in his own ways—going behind my back to remove David as the manager of The Sky Launch. Then, the worst, he hadn't defended me. He'd chosen to listen to the lies of his childhood friend who was playing her own game where I was the pawn.

I knew our love outweighed the heaviness of those mistakes. He proved he knew it too when he arrived at the club earlier that evening, surprising me with his declaration of commitment to our relationship. Though he still hadn't said the three words I longed to hear, I didn't *need* them. I felt his love in every fiber of my being. Felt it as he'd made love to me on the dance floor with care and attention that spoke volumes. We were together for the long run, through thick and thin—it was apparent now and with that knowledge there should be a freedom from anxiety.

Except we still hadn't worked out all our trust issues, and that had me feeling edgy. Plus there was this video that Stacy claimed to have. What did it show? Did I want to see it? Was it simply a trick? Or was it actually significant?

It bothered me enough to make me restless and unsure. Make me obsess while I slept.

It's nothing, I told myself. *It won't affect anything with Hudson.*

But the unease that encased me said differently.

"What's wrong?"

Hudson startled me, but the tempo of my already accelerated heartbeat barely registered the shock. I peered over my shoulder at him standing in the bathroom door. He looked as he always looked—sexy and aloof. The sight of his naked body caused my breath to intake—every time—even when thoughts of jumping him weren't on my mind. I bit my lip as my gaze traveled down his body. Well, maybe thoughts of jumping him weren't as far away as I'd assumed.

He came behind me, his gray eyes probing mine in the mirror. "Are you okay?"

It crossed my mind to lie, but I wasn't doing that anymore. I'd gotten a second chance with this man, and if we were going to make things work, I'd have to be better at sharing.

I needed to tell him about Stacy's video.

And I would. But I needed a few minutes to regroup. "I just had a bad dream, and now I can't sleep."

His brow creased with worry. "Want to talk about it?"

I shook my head. Then changed my mind. "Yes. But later."

"Hmm." He wrapped his arms around my waist and kissed my head. "How about I get a hot bath going for you in the meantime?"

"That sounds heavenly."

He let me go and started to the task. I leaned against the shower stall as Hudson bent over the large soaker tub and turned on the faucets. It was impossible not to admire his hard body, not to want to lick along the muscles of his abs, to bite the tight curve of his ass.

He glanced up at me. "Those are naughty thoughts clouding those brown eyes."

My lips curved up into what I hoped was a suggestive grin. "Are you joining me?"

"In the naughty thoughts or in the tub?"

I swatted at his luscious behind. "The tub."

"I'll join you in both." It was three in the morning on a weeknight. He had work in the morning. And the man had jet lag from a week overseas. But he never faltered at caring for me. He was always there. Even when I kicked him away to Japan, he still made sure I was looked after—sending his sister to check in, calling the doorman to deliver messages. When would I stop being surprised by his attention?

Never. That's when.

I undid my robe and hung it on a wall hook, enjoying the lust in Hudson's gaze as I stood naked before him. I stuck a toe in to test the heat. The water was perfect—almost too hot, just like I liked it. I stepped in and leaned forward so that Hudson could slide in behind me. It dawned on me that we'd never bathed together. How could it feel like we'd been through everything yet there was so much we had left to experience? It was a comforting thought—to realize that we were still only in the new, that we could look forward to more.

When he was settled, I leaned back against his chest.

He nuzzled his nose along my cheek. "This is nice."

"The temperature is perfect." My muscles were already loosening in the warmth, the tension of my dream easing.

"I meant holding you." Hudson's voice was soft, as though his words were difficult to admit. "I've missed this."

God, I'd missed it too. That was one of the reasons I felt so uneasy—I was still recovering from the time we'd been apart. My mind was still processing what I'd almost lost—everything.

I'd almost lost everything.

That was surely why I was so worried about Stacy's supposed evidence. The questions that remained between us didn't help my anxiousness. We still had so many things left undeclared.

We soaked in silence for long comfortable minutes. When the water began to cool, Hudson reached for a bottle from the built-in ledge behind the marble tub. He poured a dab of soap into his hand from my cherry blossom body wash—a new favorite scent of mine—and worked it into my skin with deep massaging strokes. When he'd finished with my arms, he nudged me forward to continue the treatment on my back. Then he pulled me against him and bent my legs so he could reach every part of my body.

Last, his fingers splayed along my belly and up my chest. He spent a sweet amount of time on my breasts, kneading them with just the right amount of pressure until my nipples perked up. He nibbled at my earlobe and one hand began its descent to my lower regions. The thickening of his cock against my lower back told me exactly what was on his mind.

But first there were things to say. I didn't believe there was anything worrisome enough to crush our potential future together, but big enough that things had to be said.

I turned to straddle him, the water sloshing at my sudden movement.

Lacing his hands in mine to keep them occupied, I began. "We have stuff to work through."

His eyes stayed pinned on my breasts, as he raised an eyebrow. "We do?"

"We do." I bent my head to catch his gaze. "Who's going to run your club?"

His smile was mischievous. "You."

I smirked but didn't agree. I also didn't disagree. He claimed he wanted me to take over The Sky Launch, but I was convinced it was only an excuse to get rid of David Lindt. Hudson achieved part of his agenda—David was leaving in a little more than a week to take over one of Hudson's clubs in Atlantic City. I'd been pissed, but as the idea had settled over me, I'd realized it had been the right move on Hudson's part. Working every day with my ex wasn't exactly a good idea. I wouldn't want Hudson working with one of his exes, after all.

It didn't mean I was ready to run the club myself.

I also wasn't quite willing to give it to someone else.

Perhaps that would have to be tabled for a time when Hudson's cock wasn't pressing against my core. His cock could make me say *yes* to anything.

His fingers still linked with mine, Hudson began to seduce me with his lips, leaning forward to take my breast in his mouth.

I sighed with pleasure, my body yielding to him. My head, however, was still wrapped up in details. "And what happens next with Celia?"

His lips left my breast. "Really? You want to talk about Celia now?"

"I never *want* to talk about her. But I need to know that she isn't a threat to me." I swallowed the unexpected lump that formed in my throat. "To us." I hadn't realized how scared I still was about her possible influence on my relationship with Hudson.

"Hey." Hudson cupped my face in his hands. "She's not a threat. She has no solid proof of her claims, and she's not pressing charges. Even if she did, I'd still be here with you. You know that."

I nodded weakly. "But what about going forward?"

"Simple. We don't see her. We don't speak to her. We don't answer her emails."

"*We* don't?" Of course *I* wouldn't see her—I hated the bitch. But what about Hudson?

"Yes, *we*. I don't have room in my life for anyone who is against us."

Another wave of tension rolled off of me. "Your mother is against us too, you know." I was pressing my luck. Sophia Pierce, monster that she was to both her son and me, would likely always be a staple in Hudson's life. I would never ask him to cut her off. Though I disliked her, I recognized the importance of family.

"I know." Hudson sighed, his hands leaving my face. "At least she hasn't tried to sabotage us. If she does, I'm done with her. You're the only one that matters."

"Thank you." I kissed him softly. "But I hope it doesn't come to that. It would be nice to believe that there could one day be reconciliation where Sophia is concerned." It had only been a few days since I'd reconciled with my brother Brian. It had relieved a constant knot in my belly that I hadn't even been aware of. The same scenario wasn't likely to happen with Hudson and Sophia, but, hey, what did I know?

My thoughts travelled back to Celia, her reasons for playing me still unclear. "But why did she do it, Hudson? Why was Celia against us?"

"Not *us*. Me." His jaw tightened. "She's mad at me."

"Still? For what you did all those years ago?" My heart panged at his obvious torment. Hudson wasn't proud of his past and how could he be expected to move on when it kept coming back to haunt him?

Then anger took over. "I don't care what you did to her—she's a bitch. It was awful and terrible and horrible to do what she did. Especially when she claims to be your friend. Is she still in love with you? Is that her problem?"

Hudson lowered his eyes. "If she thinks she loves me, hurting you isn't the way to win my affection."

"Well, she certainly acts like a jealous lover."

"Without reason." He brushed his hand across my cheek. "Celia and I have never had anything together. Nothing. Except for…" His voice softened. "Except for what I made her believe I felt for her."

"She knows that wasn't real." I hated that this still tormented him. "And that was forever ago, now. If she's trying to get you back, it seems she already did that when she slept with your father and trapped you into claiming to be the father of her baby instead of Jack. Why didn't you tell me about that, by the way?"

"I should have." His tone was filled with regret.

"Yes, you should have." It would have made things much clearer to me about his relationships with both Celia and his father. And it had been yet another thing that stood as a wall between us— though most of the secrets keeping us apart had been mine. That was my regret.

Hudson released his hands from mine and swept them down my ribs. "It didn't feel like it was my secret to tell."

"Okay, that's fair." I shivered as his fingers kneaded the skin at my hips. He was getting restless, wanting more, wanting me. The time for talking was nearing an end. I had to jump to the meat of my concerns. "But some things have to change between us. We have to be able to share these things with each other. You could have at least told me you had good reasons not to trust her, reasons *I* shouldn't trust her."

"And you could have honored my wishes when I said *don't see her*."

"Yes, I could have." I let out a sigh. "We both have to change. We have to put everything on the line, Hudson, as much as possible. We know now that we're together, thick and thin, right? We have to trust that more than anything. We can't be afraid of our secrets and our pasts. Both of us. Honesty, open doors, transparency."

He cocked a brow. "Nakedness?"

Yep, I was losing him. "You're such a perv."

"I agree." He leaned forward again to lick a bead of water from my nipple. "I am a perv where you're concerned."

I smirked. Which was difficult considering how his tongue on my breast made me crazy. "Hudson, stop. I'm serious."

"I know." He leaned back against the tub. "And I agree with everything else you said. We need to be honest."

"Good." I put my hand up to stop him before he resumed his seduction. "Hold on. I have one more thing."

"Okay, what?"

He was getting impatient but trying not to show it. I almost decided to leave the rest of our conversation for later. But the memory of my nightmare and the cold foreboding feeling that lingered in my chest pushed me forward. "What happened between you and Stacy?"

"Stacy?" He seemed confused. "Mirabelle's Stacy?"

"Yeah."

"Nothing happened." He was bewildered by my question. "What do you mean? Like did I date her? I took her to a charity event a year or so ago. But after that, nothing."

"And I didn't sleep with her," he added before I had to ask.

That was comforting. But that wasn't the reason she concerned me. "Is there a reason she'd have a vendetta against you? Or reason to distrust you?"

He shook his head slowly. "Not that I can think of."

"She wasn't one of your past victims?"

"Victims?" His eyes narrowed. "Is that what you call the people I played with?"

I cringed. "Maybe that wasn't the best choice of words?"

"No. It probably *is* the best choice. That doesn't make it pleasant to hear."

"I'm sorry."

His features darkened. "Don't be. It's my past. I have to live with it. Why are you asking?"

I took a deep breath. We were putting everything on the line, after all. This was part of it. "The last time we were at Mira's, Stacy told me that she had some sort of video. A video that proved something or other about you and Celia. She didn't have it with her, so I gave her my phone number so she could contact me later."

"The last time we were at Mira's together?"

"Yeah. She cornered me while you were finding me shoes. Do you know what she's talking about?" I studied his face, trying to pick up on anything he might be hiding.

"No idea." Either he was really good at acting or he truly had no clue. I'd never seen him so perplexed. "She didn't tell you what the video was of?"

"No. Just that she had it and that it would show me why I couldn't trust you." I bit my lip. "And she texted me again tonight. Or sometime this past week when I didn't have a phone, and I didn't get the message until tonight."

I expected him to ask why I hadn't told him earlier, but he didn't. "What did her text say?"

"That the video was too big to send over the phone but to contact her if I wanted to see it."

He considered. "Do you want to see it?"

"No." But I kind of did. "Yes." Unless I didn't. "I don't know. Should I?"

"Well." He rubbed his hands up my arms. "You know that Celia can't be trusted already. And there is nothing that Stacy could have on me that you don't already know. You know more about my secrets and my past than anyone. You know me, Alayna."

"I do."

"Then unless you don't trust me…"

"I do trust you. If you say there's nothing I should be concerned about…"

His eyes locked on mine. "There isn't."

I paused. The minute I said my next words, I couldn't take them back. I'd have to put the video out of my mind and move on. It went against all my obsessive tendencies—could I do it?

I believed I could. For Hudson. I smiled. "Then I don't need to see it." It was easier to say than I would have imagined. And I meant it. I didn't need the proof of other people to know who Hudson was, what he meant to me.

It was amazing how much better I felt having the subject of the video off my chest. It no longer felt like a weight on me, though there was still some lingering edginess that probably just needed time to distill.

Hudson leaned forward and kissed my chin. "Thank you."

"For what, exactly?"

"For being open with me." He tilted his head. "You didn't have to tell me about that, and you did anyway."

"I'm serious about being more open and honest."

"I see that. I'm serious about it too. The only way we can move on is to decide that we're committed to each other first and foremost." His eyes rose to meet mine. "Are we?"

They were only two short words, but the weight of the question was heavy—heavier than when he'd asked me to be his girlfriend or to move in. And yet it was with ease and certainty that I responded. "I am."

"So am I." He captured my mouth with his, sucking lightly on my bottom lip before his tongue flicked inside, twisting with mine in an erotic dance of foreplay. I threw my hands around his neck, pulling myself closer into him. His cock thickened between us and my pussy clenched in reaction, wanting and needing him as much as his kiss said he needed me.

Without releasing my mouth, Hudson moved a hand to my breast. He was such an expert at handling me in the way I needed, his touch never too gentle, always just the right amount of rough. I cried against his lips as he squeezed my tit, driving me mad. I was so concentrated on his attention to my chest, I didn't notice his other hand traveling lower until his thumb was rubbing against my clit. I jolted at the exquisite pressure, my knees clutching his hips. I was already feeling the tight sensation in my lower belly building toward eruption. So soon, too soon.

I was on top, and wanting to delay my explosion until we could go together, I pushed away his hand from my core. Hudson's eyes closed slightly as I circled my grip around his thick erection. I stroked him once before shifting my weight forward onto my kneecaps. Positioning myself over him, I slid down his hard length, moaning as he filled me.

I sat atop him, sitting still for several seconds as my body adjusted to his size, my walls expanding to make room for him. Damn, he felt good. Just like that, without any movement—he felt made for me, as though his penis had been carved to fit my pussy and mine alone. I shuddered at the carnal thoughts that intensified the heavenly sensation of him inside me.

He shifted beneath me, his impatience evident. So I moved, riding him. Slowly at first, then more determined. My hands braced against his shoulders, pushing me off with the force I knew Hudson desired, the force *I* desired. It wasn't long before his hands were wrapped around my ass, augmenting my movement. And then, he held me still as his hips thrust up and forward in a circular pattern, driving into me with long deliberate strokes.

"Do you always have to take over?" I asked, breathless. Not that I minded. I enjoyed being on the other end of his control.

23

His lip curled at the edge. "If you want us both to come, then yes."

I laughed, the action causing him to twitch inside me, bringing me to the brink. When I could speak again, I asked, "And who is it that wouldn't come if I stayed in control?"

"You." His fingers tightened at my hips and, as if to prove his point, he pushed deeper into me, brushing against a spot—*that* spot, the one that always did it for me, the one that only he could find and that he found each and every time.

My orgasm came suddenly, taking me by surprise. I gasped, digging my fingernails into his skin as I rode the wave of ecstasy that passed through my every nerve, shooting down my limbs and clouding my vision.

Hudson's tempo didn't abate as I crumpled on top of him. He continued to thrust towards his own climax, driving toward that intangible goalpost. And then he was crossing the finish line, grinding against my clit as he spilled into me, causing another shudder from my already limp body.

While he settled, he kissed along my neck, along my jawline, finally making it to my lips where he sweetly lingered, adoring me with his mouth until our heart rates returned to a more normal pace.

Then he pulled away and met my eyes. His brow furrowed. "Alayna." Hudson cradled my face. "What is it, precious?"

It took me a beat to understand his question. Then I realized that tears were leaking down my face. And then they were more than tears. Uncontrollable sobs broke through me as though a great well of grief had been released.

Embarrassed and unable to explain my outburst, I pushed away and climbed out of the tub.

"Alayna, talk to me." He was behind me, wrapping a towel around my body as he dripped onto the floor.

I shook my head and ran to the bedroom.

Hudson followed. He grabbed my upper arms and turned me toward him. "Talk to me. What is it?"

My body heaved with the anguish. It wasn't a new pain, but one that had been with me for the better part of a week. I just hadn't fully expressed it yet—not to Hudson, not to myself.

"You. Really. Hurt me," I managed. The words were broken and hard to get out between sobs.

"Just now?"

"No." I swallowed and tried to calm myself enough to speak. "You really hurt me. With Celia. When you believed her. Instead of me." The pain was so raw, so fresh. Even though he'd made amends and we were together, the remnants of that betrayal still clung to me. I'd tried to move on before the scar had formed, and now, unexpectedly, the wound reopened.

"Oh, Alayna." He pulled me into his chest. "Tell me. Tell me all of it. I need to hear it."

"It hurts, Hudson. It hurts so much." I took a ragged breath. "Even though you're here. Now. And we're together. There's a hole." My sentences were short and broken. "A deep, deep hole."

His body tensed around me and I felt the degree to which he shared my grief. "I'm sorry. I'm so sorry. If I could take it back, if I could change how I reacted...I would have chosen differently."

"I know. I do. But you didn't choose differently. And you *can't* take that back." My voice strengthened as the ache inside surfaced. Like I was throwing up. Once it started, there was no stopping, and the process was uncomfortable and suffocating.

I pulled away from him, still in his arms, but no longer buried in him. "You can never take that back."

"No. I can't." He pushed my wet hair off my shoulders.

"And that changes things. It changes me."

He paused, worry etching his face. "How?"

"It makes me vulnerable. Exposed." I suddenly became aware that he was wearing nothing. It was fitting. Because, even though I was wrapped in a towel, I'd never been more naked in front of him. "And you know now. That you can hurt me." I choked as my tears returned. "You can hurt me real bad."

"Alayna." He pulled me back into him, his voice thick with emotion. "My precious girl. I never want to hurt you again. Will you ever be able to…forgive me?"

I nodded, unable to respond verbally. Yes, I could forgive him. I already had. But it didn't change how much it hurt. It didn't change how much healing still had to occur.

Hudson rocked me in his arms as I cried, intermittently kissing my head and apologizing. After a while, he swept me into his arms and carried me to the bed. He curled up with me, holding me against him.

When I'd finally finished with the tears, I sat up against the headboard with a hiccup. "Huh. I don't know where that came from."

He sat up next to me, wiping my cheeks. "You needed to let it out. I understand."

"You do?"

"I do." He put a tentative arm around me. "Is it okay that I'm here?"

"Yes! Please, don't leave." I clutched him, afraid that he would go.

"As long as you want me, I'm here."

"Good." I relaxed, letting my heartbeat return to a normal pace. "All that?" I gestured abstractly, referring to my sob scene. "That was just…"

"Healing?"

"Yeah. Cathartic. The last step of all that before stuff. I think I have some closure now." I felt cleansed—inside and out. I smiled as I traced Hudson's lips with my finger.

"I admire your optimism, but old pain has a way of showing up from time to time, even when life is going well." He caught my finger in his hand. "I'm sure we'll both feel this way every now and then."

I took a long breath in. I couldn't stand that I'd hurt him too. It almost pained me as much as his betrayal.

"Don't dwell on it." His voice was soft. "We have the future to make up for the hurts we've caused each other."

Right then, I was ready to dedicate my life to making up. Was I really thinking of us as forever? Well, at least long term.

I twisted my lips at the thought. "This is a new beginning for us, isn't it?"

He leaned forward to brush my nose with his. "No. This is better than a beginning. This is what happens next."

"I like that."

He leaned in and kissed me, sweetly and luxuriously, with promises of all the other things that would happen next. As if there was nothing in the world to do but lavish me with love.

Chapter Three

Hudson called into the office the next morning, deciding to work from home. I'd already made arrangements to be gone from the club for the next several days so I didn't bother going in either. We spent our time in the library, each of us working on our own projects, not talking much, which was fine. Exhausted from jet lag and lack of sleep, Hudson was in a mood. Even grumpy, I was glad for his presence. It was comforting just to be with him.

I did leave the apartment but only to get a wax and attend my group therapy that evening. When I returned, Hudson was passed out in our bed. I let him sleep.

Before I joined him, I got a run in on the treadmill and texted Stacy. *Thanks, but no thanks*, my message said. I probably didn't need to respond at all, but it gave the issue finality. I slept soundlessly the whole night through.

The next day was a holiday—the Fourth of July. Hudson surprised me by taking me to brunch at the Loeb Boathouse in Central Park. Afterward, we walked through the park, holding hands and enjoying each other's company. We were good—it felt right being with him. Easy.

Yet there was a tangible fragility between us. We were cautious with each other, handling one another with kid gloves. Hudson's lingering fatigue didn't help the situation.

Later, getting ready for the evening's fireworks display, Hudson came up behind me as I primped in the bedroom mirror. He wrapped his arms around my waist and kissed along my neckline. "We've been pussy-footing around each other all day," he said at my ear. "I'm warning you now that I'm done. It's time for me to start treating you like what you are: Mine."

My breath caught sharply.

"And yes, that means that you'll be fucked later. Hard."

Just like that, our tentativeness was over. And I needed a change of panties.

***

Except for a few casual strokes and caresses, Hudson kept his hands to himself during our ride to the Firework Cruise. I had a feeling the minimal contact was purposeful. He was building the anticipation.

And, god, was it working.

The air between us was charged. His sexual promise remained ever present in my thoughts, turning me into a powder keg waiting for that one spark to light me on fire. He, on the other hand, seemed completely unaffected—as though he hadn't uttered those carnal words to me only an hour earlier.

It was late evening, the sun just beginning to set, when we arrived at the pier. Hudson didn't wait for Jordan to open our door. He stepped out of the Maybach and reached for my hand to pull me out behind him. He was striking in his tan pants and dark suit jacket. He'd forgone the tie, leaving his white shirt unbuttoned to expose the top of his chest. The wind blew across the river that shared his name, mussing Hudson's hair into sexy chaos. As always, he took my breath away.

The moment was short lived. Cameras clicking and people shouting Hudson's name interrupted the reverie. Having been to only one other event with him where media was present, I wasn't used to the attention.

But Hudson was.

Like he had the last time when I'd gone with him to his mother's charity fashion event, he put on a show, pulling me into his side to pose for the cameras. He tactfully ignored many of the questions, only answering some with a simple *yes* or *no*.

"Is it true you've bought back your old company, Plexis?"

"Yes."

"Are you planning to break the company apart?"

"No."

"Is this your current girlfriend? Alayna Withers, is it?"

"Yes."

"What about Celia Werner?"

This was one Hudson didn't answer. The only betrayal that he'd even heard the question was a twitch of his eye. The man had stoicism down to a science.

I did not. The mention of Celia's name threw a shiver down my spine. It hadn't only been his mother who thought he and Celia should be together. Even the press had thought they were more than friends. Hudson, not caring what people thought or said about him, never bothered to correct the assumption.

I realized then that the media would never let her out of our life. She'd always be asked about, always be linked to him in the tabloids. I'd have to get used to it if I planned on staying with Hudson long term. And I planned on exactly that.

But just because I had to live with it didn't mean I couldn't fight back.

Forcing a smile, I did something that surprised even me—I spoke to the onlookers. "Don't you think it's rude to ask that when I'm standing right here?" I paused but didn't let the reporter get a word in before continuing. "He's with me now. Bringing up another woman in front of me is completely distasteful. If stirring up gossip is the only way you can write a decent story, I feel quite sorry for you. Don't bother rebutting. We have a party to attend."

Hudson's eyes widened. "You heard the lady." He took my hand and pulled me with him toward the dock where *The Magnolia*, a two hundred and fifty foot yacht, waited for us.

I squeezed his hand. "That wasn't so bad." I needed his reassurance. Needed to know I hadn't pissed him off.

"It was mostly terrible," he hissed.

Immediately I felt guilty for my outburst. "I shouldn't have said anything. I'm sorry."

"Why? You were the only reason it wasn't all terrible."

"Well, then." My smile widened. "Maybe I should talk to the press more often."

"Don't push it." Hudson's smile was brief. He quickly returned to his somber mood. After our pleasant day together, I had hoped that his crabbiness was over. Not the case. It was understandable. Dealing with the press and having to attend a big social event were not Hudson's favorite ways to pass the time.

I, on the other hand, didn't mind parties. Though I would have been just as happy to watch the show on TV from our bedroom. Or skip the viewing altogether. "Why are we going if you hate these things so much?"

He paused, mid-stride. "Good question. Let's not go."

"Hudson…" I tugged at him. Now that I'd gotten all dolled up, we might as well go through with the evening. Besides, even though he didn't want to be there, I sensed he wouldn't abandon the Firework Cruise so easily.

He sighed and let me pull him toward the ship. "I'm here because Pierce Industries sponsors this event. I have to go. If I don't, it reflects poorly on the corporation."

I put on an exaggerated frown. "Poor Hudson Alexander Pierce. Born into responsibility and obligation. Oh, and money and opportunity."

He looked at me, an eyebrow raised. "Really?"

"A little, yeah. If you're going to throw a pity party, H, I'm not planning to attend." Frankly, I was tired of his cranky mood. I wanted fun Hudson for the evening.

The edges of his mouth relaxed ever so slightly. "I'm not throwing a pity party. It's impossible for anyone to feel sorry for me when you're at my side." He pulled me closer to him so his arm could circle my waist.

"Yeah, that's why people envy you."

This got me a smile. "If it's not, it's the reason that they should."

At the end of the dock, a man dressed in naval attire stood waiting by the plank leading to the yacht.

"Good evening, Mr. Pierce. We're ready to cast off whenever you are, sir."

Hudson nodded. "Then let's go." He motioned me ahead of him, but I heard the man, who I assumed was the captain, whispering something else to Hudson behind me.

I stepped off the plank onto the boat deck then looked back to see Hudson's expression had grown grim.

"I'd rather not cause a scene," he said, his voice low. "But have the crew keep an eye out for any trouble."

"Yes, sir."

Hudson climbed aboard, putting his hand at the small of my back when he'd reached me.

"Is everything okay?"

"Fine." His tone was terse.

Dammit. Whatever the captain had said to him seemed to have undone the progress I'd made at ridding Hudson of his bad mood.

I knew from experience that pressing the matter would only make him grumpier. But I couldn't help myself. "Hudson, honesty and transparency…remember?"

He glared at me for three solid seconds before his features softened. "It's nothing. An uninvited guest arrived. That's all."

I suddenly felt guilty for teasing him about his obligations. Even on a holiday night when he should be enjoying himself, he couldn't relax. He'd always have to take care of something, manage someone. No wonder these events were such a pain in the ass.

Making up my mind to try to give him the best night possible, I let the subject of the uninvited guest go, even though I was itching to know more of the details. The last thing Hudson needed was me badgering him.

Instead, I worked again to make him more amiable. I leaned into him and whispered, "By the way, I meant to tell you that I got waxed yesterday." Since he'd been asleep when I got home, I hadn't gotten a chance to show him. Which was probably best since the recommendation was to wait twenty-four hours after waxing before having sex.

"Waxed?" Hudson said too loudly, his brow furrowed in confusion. Then understanding set in. "Oh." Immediately his expression lit with interest.

Behind us, a crew member that was helping the captain draw the plank into the ship looked up, obviously also getting my meaning.

Hudson glared at the man, and ushered me further onto the deck with him. "Tell me more." This time his volume was appropriately quieter.

"I'm talking *waxed*. Like, all the way. Bare." Normally, I kept a little more than a landing strip. This was the first time since I'd been with Hudson that I'd gone clean.

Hudson's eyes narrowed as he adjusted himself. "Are you trying to make this the most uncomfortable night of my life?"

"I was trying to give you something to look forward to, Mr. Grumpy Pants."

"Mr. Strained Pants, I think you mean."

I laughed. "Is that going to be a problem?"

"For you." He pulled me against him so that I could feel his erection against my belly. "It's going to be a long evening. By the time I finally get to be inside you, I'm going to need to be there for a long time. And I don't expect that I'll be able to be gentle."

Okay, wow. "No complaints here."

"Good girl." He stared longingly at my lips, but he didn't kiss me. Finally, he said, "I'll try to improve my mood. Let's go. The sooner the socializing is over, the sooner I can bury my face between your thighs."

Hudson led me up the stairs to the main deck. I'd never been on a yacht before, but I was pretty sure this one was more luxurious than most. I looked up the side of the boat and counted four decks, plus the mini one that we'd entered on. The deck furniture was simple but in good taste. Amazing taste, actually. At least what I could see of it. Most of it was covered by bodies. Dozens and dozens of bodies. There were at least forty people already in full party mode on this deck. Above me, more people leaned on the deck railings. And we hadn't even gotten to the inside yet.

I followed Hudson through the throngs of people and inside to a grand lounge. This area was even more packed then the decks. "How many people are here?" I asked.

He nodded at a server across the room who immediately headed our way. "There were two hundred invited. They were each allowed one guest. We only take this many people out for the annual Macy's fireworks. There are fourteen staterooms, so we'd never actually travel with this many aboard."

Hudson took two champagne glasses from the server and handed one to me. He clinked his glass to mine before taking a swallow. "Except for a few other important people, we'll be the only ones sleeping here tonight."

"Hopefully there won't be much sleeping." The bare skin between my thighs was aching for the attention it had been promised.

"You'll pay for your teasing later."

Just then, the boat launched smoothly into the river. I grabbed Hudson's arm to adjust to the motion as the crowd erupted into cheers. The place was utter chaos. Definitely not my boyfriend's usual type of scene. No wonder he'd been anxious.

We made our way up the grand staircase to an upper level, stopping every so often so that Hudson could greet a guest. He introduced me to all of them, sometimes as his girlfriend, sometimes as the promotions manager of his club. I guessed he chose my title depending on how it would benefit me and my career. Always looking out for me.

The next room we ended up in looked like a large living room. A bar curved around the wall and an abundance of couches and armchairs filled the space. A giant flat-screen TV graced one wall. It was turned onto the telecast of the pre-fireworks show though no one seemed to be paying attention. This room was also crowded, but I heard my name called through the buzz of conversation.

I turned toward the voice and found Hudson's sister sitting on a couch in the corner. She stood as we approached her, and I bent to embrace the petite woman I'd grown to love nearly as much as her brother. It was amazing how tightly she could hug with her pregnant belly between us.

When she released me, I checked out her dark blue maxi maternity dress. "Mira. You look adorable!"

"Ugh, thanks. I feel like a whale." She reached to give Hudson a hug, which he tolerated. "Hello, brother. Glad to see you back in the States, though you ruined all my amazing planning."

Before Hudson had shown up at The Sky Launch on Sunday night, I'd planned to fly to Japan and surprise him. Mira had helped make all the arrangements.

"Not that I'm complaining," she added before Hudson could respond. "You did good. I'm proud of you."

Hudson glowered at his little sister. He wasn't the type to accept praise. And Mira was the type to give it anyway.

I decided to come to Hudson's rescue before Mira could continue. "Did Adam abandon you?" I looked around for her husband.

"Nah, he's finding me something nonalcoholic to drink. It's surprisingly difficult."

"Ah." More like he was probably hiding from the crowd. Adam was another antisocial member of the family. At least Hudson knew how to fake it.

Mira sat back down on the couch, hitting the spot next to her. "Come. Sit. How did you manage to get a holiday off from the club?"

I shrugged as I took the seat next to her. "I'm sleeping with the owner."

"Nice." She shook her head like she was frustrated with herself. "I'm such a dummy! You were supposed to be in Japan. I guess you already got your shifts covered."

"Yes. David and another manager are covering the next few days." I should have felt guilty mentioning David. I didn't. In fact, for some reason I decided to poke at Hudson. "But I won't be able to count on David after this week."

Hudson scowled down at me.

"Why?" Mira asked.

I set my empty glass on the end table next to me. "Hudson transferred him to Adora in Atlantic City."

Mira looked from me to her brother. "Seems like there's a story there."

Hudson perched on the arm of the sofa. "You actually have him for *two* more weeks. I asked him to stay a little longer while we look for his replacement."

Well, that was news. Good news. It gave me longer to figure out my role at the club.

Mira's face twisted in confusion. "Look for his replacement? Why Laynie, of course. Duh."

"Um…" I'd brought it up. I should have been prepared to be put on the spot. I did want the position, and each day I grew more and more comfortable with the idea. But I still wasn't ready to make the commitment.

She must have read the complexity of the situation in my face. "Another story, I'm supposing."

"Yeah. Let's not go there." I patted Hudson's knee. "This guy's cranky as it is. Jet lag and everything."

"Got it. You look gorgeous, by the way. That's not one of mine though." She pursed her lips.

"Whoops." Pretty much my whole wardrobe these days was from Mirabelle's boutique, but wanting to be patriotic, I'd chosen a simple red flare dress with a nearly bare back from my club wardrobe.

She smirked. "You're coming to my Grand Reopening, right?"

I'd only recently found out she was remodeling. I had no idea an event was attached. But this was the social butterfly, Mirabelle. Of course there'd be an event attached. "Sure. When is it?"

"You didn't tell her?" She reached over me to swat Hudson.

"It slipped my mind."

"Hudson, you are such an ass!" To me, she said, "The twenty-second. It's a Saturday."

"I'll have to make sure someone else closes the night before, but that shouldn't be a problem." I was already thinking in terms of being responsible for The Sky Launch. Who was I kidding? I'd totally decided the job was mine.

"Oh!" Her eyes widened. "Will you be one of my models? Please say yes. Please, please, please."

"Um, sure?" It was nearly impossible to say no to the girl, but modeling was not something I had any interest in. Wearing pretty clothes, on the other hand… "What does it involve? Like, do I have to walk a runway?"

"Don't be silly. I didn't remodel that much. Okay, it's a small runway but not like what you're thinking. It's almost nothing. I'm simply showing off a few of my favorite looks for publicity. So I just need you to stand there and look gorgeous in one of my outfits while people take pictures of you."

Except for the pictures part, it sounded fabulous. "Okay. I'm in."

"Awesome! Can you come by sometime to get fitted? Like next Monday? Around one?"

My schedule was up to me and I didn't have any appointments set since I had planned to be overseas. But going to Mira's meant a good chance I'd see Stacy. She hadn't responded to my text, but did that matter?

"Why are you hesitating?" Mira looked offended.

"Sorry. I was running through my schedule in my mind. Yes. I can be there then." What was Stacy going to do anyway? Force me to watch her video? That was ridiculous.

"Yay!" Mira made pom-poms with balled-up fists and shook them in the air.

Beside me, I felt Hudson tense. Then a familiar voice said, "Ah, here's where the party is."

"Jack!" I stood to give Hudson's father a hug, careful not to knock the drinks he held, one in each hand. "I didn't realize you'd be here."

"He wasn't invited." Hudson bit out.

Aha. The uninvited guest from earlier. As if Jack would cause a scene. Or maybe it was Hudson that would disturb the peace. He seemed less than pleased to see his father aboard the yacht.

Jack only smiled at Hudson's displeasure, his eyes gleaming like they often did when he was about to be contrary. "I'm a Pierce. My invitation's standing."

Leaning toward me, Jack said, "Hudson isn't speaking to me."

The last time Jack and Hudson had seen each other was the day that Jack admitted fathering Celia's baby. It had been a secret that Hudson had been determined to keep from his mother. He was not happy that Jack had spilled the beans. "Oh, I suppose he isn't." And while I was thinking of the horrid woman… "Is Sophia with you?"

Jack scratched his temple. "She's not speaking to me either."

"Serves you right." Mira's words were more sassy than chiding. The girl didn't have it in her to be volatile.

Jack nodded toward his daughter. "Can't figure out what I have to do to get this one to stop speaking to me."

"Daddy!"

He winked at Mira. "I'm teasing, pumpkin. You're the light of my life, and you know it. Here, I brought you a virgin daiquiri."

Mira harrumphed but took the drink from her father's outstretched hand. "I'm not exactly happy with you these days myself, you know."

Jack sighed. "I know. Chandler's keeping your mother company tonight so she's not alone. You're a sweet girl to be worried about her. I'll try to make it up to you sometime."

"It's not me you need to make up to," Mira said under her breath.

Either not hearing or decidedly ignoring his daughter, Jack turned his attention back to me. "How are you?"

"I'm good. And I'm so glad to see you. I wanted to thank you. For being my support when all that went down." Jack had been one of the few people on my side when Celia had accused me of harassing her. Bringing it up now, I felt that small pang of betrayal. Hudson was right—it wasn't so easy to forget that kind of pain.

"It was nothing, Laynie. I knew whom we were dealing with. I would have thought others here would have too." He didn't bother to look at Hudson, but his words hit their mark just the same.

I hadn't meant for the conversation to go that direction. Despite the hurt he'd caused, Hudson had valid reasons to think Celia's accusations might be true. "To be fair, you don't know me quite as well as others here do either. But anyway, thank you." I took Jack's hand in mine and squeezed.

"Alayna…" Hudson warned.

I let go of Jack's hand and turned to look at my man who was now standing. His stance was foreboding, even with his hand tucked casually in his pocket. His jaw flexed and his eyes darkened with warning. It was surprisingly hot.

"Jealousy doesn't look good on you, son."

I disagreed. Jealousy *did* look good on Hudson. Quite good indeed.

A low grumble came from the back of his throat.

Jack cocked his head. "Did he just growl?"

Though Jack was clearly not Hudson's competition, I understood his reasons for feeling that way. It wasn't worth it to try to convince him otherwise. "Obviously I'd love to talk more, Jack, but it doesn't seem like it would be a good idea."

He took a sip from the clear drink in his hand as he eyed his son. "No, it doesn't." Again, he addressed me, his free hand on my shoulder. "I'm glad you're still here. In his life, I mean. Even though he's a stubborn oaf that blames me for all the wrongs in my relationship with his mother—"

"Are you saying that you aren't at fault?" Hudson challenged.

Jack's face lit up. "He's speaking to me!"

Hudson wiped his brow. "Ah, Jesus."

"Anyway, I'm glad you're with him, Laynie. He needs you more than he probably realizes. And there's no doubt he recognizes your worth. That boy has real feelings for you." His eyes drifted to Hudson. "Look. He's blushing."

"He is!" Mira exclaimed excitedly. She was a hopeless romantic and never pretended otherwise.

"I am not." But Hudson's protest only darkened the red in his cheeks.

Jack laughed. "See? His love for you is written all over his face."

Hudson stepped forward and put his arm possessively around my waist. "Could you stop pawing my girlfriend?"

Jack rolled his eyes but removed his hand from my shoulder.

The whole scene was amusing, not to mention a big a turn-on. I didn't at all mind when Hudson got all alpha male on me. In fact, I may have even provoked it in him. "I'll have to tell you more how appreciative I am when we get together sometime."

"No, no, no. Not happening," Hudson fumed.

Jack chuckled. "Look at you rile him up on purpose. You're a wicked little woman, Alayna Withers." He looked us over, as if taking in all of who we are and what we meant to each other. "Perfect."

"That's it. We're done here." Hudson turned me away from his family.

"Talk later," I called over my shoulder.

"Monday!" Mira reminded after me.

Yes, Monday. At the boutique. With Stacy.

A knot formed in my gut. The thought crossed my mind without permission—what was on that video? Was there actually something I should be concerned with?

I wouldn't watch it, whatever it was. I'd said I didn't need to.

But wondering about it still—that I couldn't help. I was only human, after all.

Chapter Four

Hudson escorted me out to the deck and I let thoughts of the video float away in the breeze.

I turned into him and surprised him with a deep kiss.

"What was that for?" he asked when I came up for air.

"No reason." Except that I needed it. He seemed to need it as well. "You know there's no reason to be jealous of me and your father, right?"

"Uh huh." He pushed out of my arms and took my hand, leading me up the deck.

"He's attractive. I won't deny that."

"Not helping."

He was in front of me and couldn't see my smile. I was only teasing him, but he needed to know that I'd never betray him with Jack. "There's nothing between us. No chemistry at all. And if you stopped wanting me, I'd never retaliate against you like that. I'm not Celia."

He spun toward me. "I know you're not Celia. You don't think I fucking know that?"

His heated reaction threw me off guard. "I...didn't..."

He pulled me back into his arms, clutching me tightly. "And don't talk about me not wanting you. Ever. It's not even a breath of a possibility."

I wrapped my arms around him, shocked by his desperate tone. "Okay. I won't."

He kissed my temple. "Thank you." He held me like that for a long beat before he relaxed his grip on me. "The fireworks are getting ready to start. I have a spot reserved for us at the bow."

"The bow?" I was so not a boat person.

"The front of the yacht. We'll have an excellent view." Though his eyes were perusing my body, and I wondered if he wasn't talking about the view of the sky.

"Awesome." I let my own eyes graze his perfect form before shaking myself out of my lustful stare. "I need to use the restroom before the show starts. I'll meet you there?"

He reached in his pocket and pulled out a key. "Use the one in our stateroom. No lines. Number Three. It's just in there." He nodded toward an entry back into the ship. "Oh, and when you come back, I'd like you not to be wearing any panties."

I grinned as I took the key from him. "You got it, H." I knew what that was about. He'd felt threatened by his father and by talk of not being together. Having me at his beck and call was another way for him to feel reassured. Silly man with his insecurities. How did he not know that I completely belonged to him?

It only took a few minutes to find our stateroom. It was beautiful and grand like the rest of the ship and as large as our bedroom back at The Bowery. I didn't linger, eager to get back to the show and, more importantly, Hudson. I used the bathroom, leaving my underwear hanging off the side of the tub, and returned to the deck just as the sky lit up with the first explosion of light.

Hudson was waiting for me at the front—*the bow*—of the ship. He'd acquired a spot at the railing between two small caterer stands where partiers could set empty glasses. Though there were still people everywhere, it gave us a little bit of seclusion, as bodies weren't pressed right up against us like they were around the rest of the yacht.

Not that I minded a body pressed up against mine. As long as it was Hudson's.

His eyes lit up when he saw me. I handed him the stateroom key, which he pocketed, then he held out his hand for mine. "Come here." He tugged me in front of him.

I waited for his arms to circle around me, but instead he grabbed my ass through my dress, squeezing my cheeks. A breeze blew over the river and the feel of the air against my very bare pussy, plus Hudson's massage of my behind, had me feeling aroused.

"Good," he whispered. "You obeyed."

Ah, so the butt rub was simply a panty check. Whatever the reason, I'd take it.

Hudson propped his leg on the lower rail and continued caressing my behind while, overhead, the sky lit up again and again. Each time the sparks caused cheers from the crowd, drowning out the sound of the music blaring from inside the ship. I'd never been so close to the Macy's Annual Fireworks, and I was mesmerized. They shot above the river from at least seven different barges, simultaneously turning the darkness into a flash of color—magical.

Things got even more magical when Hudson's arms wrapped around me. And then his hand made its way under my skirt, hiking the fabric up around my waist, flirting with the skin above my pubic bone.

I was exposed to the night. Though Hudson's propped leg covered the view on one side of us, the crowd on the other side of me only had to move their interest from the sky to us, and they'd see.

I inhaled sharply. "What are you doing?"

"Setting off fireworks." His mouth was at my ear, rumbling with the rockets in the sky.

Fuck, I didn't care who could see—I was turned on.

My eyes burned from the blaze overhead, my nerves lit from Hudson's touch, my lower belly sparking with need.

"Spread," he commanded.

I obeyed, lifting my left foot onto the lower rail, mirroring his stance. It gave more privacy, blocking the view from the other side of us. Yet it wouldn't take a genius to figure out what he was doing to me—all anyone had to do was pay attention.

With full access, Hudson stroked over my pussy, sweetly grazing the newly exposed area. "Ever since you told me you were bare, I've been thinking about touching you." His breath at my neck drove a shiver down my spine.

Then his fingers slid between my lips, finding the sensitive nub, and I thought I might burst—burst with the fireworks above me. He settled his thumb on my clit, circling with expert pressure. "God, precious, I couldn't keep my hands off you if I tried. You're so slick already."

"Hudson." It was barely a word, more of a cry, really. Louder than I'd intended, drawing a glance from a couple not far from us.

Hudson's hand froze. "If you want to come, Alayna, you have to promise me you can be quiet."

"Okay." *Anything.* Anything to make him keep touching me.

He started his movement again, his thumb dancing over my clit as his fingers went lower. "Do you know what it does to me to see you come apart?" he taunted, his touch now spiraling around my hole. "Do you?"

How did he think I could talk? "No," I managed on a breathy exhale.

"It drives me fucking insane." He jabbed two fingers inside. At least, it felt like two fingers. It was difficult to be certain. All I knew for sure was that it felt amazing.

He plunged again as his thumb resumed whirling over my clit. Swirling and plunging, he fucked me with his hand, right there, in the open air, as the crowd around us stared upward in a patriotic daze.

So. Fucking. Hot.

The tension was building, tightening in my womb.

Then his lips were moving at my ear again. "Sometimes it's all I think about. Taking you to the edge. Watching you spill over. It's the most goddamned beautiful thing there is."

I was close. So close. About to explode. I leaned back against him, rubbing his erection with my ass. I felt incredible. Sexy. On fire. Small grunts formed at the back of my throat.

"Bite on your hand to stifle your screams if you need to."

I wanted to challenge him—to say, *oh you're so sure I'll be screaming*—but then he bent his fingers and stroked against a particularly sensitive spot. A moan escaped from my lips.

"Hand," he ordered.

Just in time, I flung my hand to my mouth, biting down on my finger as I came. My orgasm flared through me, erupting in tandem with a spectacular sequence of fireworks. I couldn't tell what parts of my blinded vision were from the display and which were from Hudson. It was glorious.

But I wasn't nearly sated.

I wanted more. Wanted him.

I spun into him, kissing him with frenzy. My hand rubbed his cock through his pants. He was so hard. He wanted me as much as I wanted him. More, maybe.

The fireworks show wasn't over. I didn't care. "Take me to bed," I demanded against his lips.

It was Hudson's turn to groan. I swallowed the sound with another wet kiss, licking into his mouth with deep strokes. God, he tasted good. I couldn't get enough of him, was ready to fuck him right there on the deck.

Somehow Hudson found the strength to untangle from my embrace. "Jesus, woman." His eyes were nearly black with desire. Then he turned toward the entry to the staterooms, pulling me behind him.

The crowd cheered at that moment. For the fireworks, of course, but it drew my gaze up.

That's when I saw her.

On the upper deck, looking down at me was Celia Werner. My mind flashed back to my dream and the terror that accompanied it sparked through me. Her eyes met mine, piercing through me, and I suddenly understood the phrase "shooting daggers." Anger emitted from her cold stare. Hudson had said it was he that she was mad at, and maybe she was mad at him. But she *hated* me. It was evident in her entire posture.

A chill ran down my spine as, again, I realized she'd always be there. She'd always be threatening at the periphery of my life with Hudson.

The realization only fueled my need for Hudson to be inside me.

I pushed Hudson onward, determined to recapture the mood from a moment before, to remind myself that I was the one with him, not her. Me. Only me.

As soon as we were in the hallway leading to the staterooms, we were kissing again. He pushed me against the wall, his hands reaching under my dress to fondle my naked ass.

Desperate to make his groin meet mine, I curled my leg around his thigh. He relaxed his pressure so that I could jump up and wrap my legs around his waist. He sucked and licked along my neck as he carried me to our room. There, he braced me against the other wall so he could fumble with the key and the lock, swearing as he did until we were finally inside with the door shut behind us.

Panting, we both broke into a laugh. Hudson's serious demeanor made outbursts like this rare, and I swam in the sound of his unbridled amusement.

Until our eyes met.

Then we were lip-locked once again.

With me still wrapped around him, he sat—more like *fell*—onto the bed. I didn't hesitate, scrambling down to the floor to my knees so I could undo his belt. He toed his shoes off and lifted his hips so I could pull his pants and briefs down.

As soon as his cock sprang free, my eyes were glued. I wanted to lick it, to take it in my mouth, to feel it filling me, twitching in me.

But there were still clothes in the way, and I needed to be naked. Needed *him* naked.

I reached my arms up so Hudson could pull my dress over my head. The backless nature of the outfit hadn't allowed for a bra to be worn. Thank god. One less item to be removed. While he worked on unbuttoning his shirt, I circled my hands around his penis. Damn, it was steel. I only had time to stroke him a couple of times before he was pulling me with him onto the bed.

Both of us naked, we pressed into each other with a frantic need to be skin-on-skin in as many places as possible. Our hands explored like it was the first time, like we might never have the chance again—caressing and touching while we kissed with fevered passion. Hudson's fingers eventually made their way to my lower regions where I wanted him most.

He slid through my wet folds once before tearing abruptly away. "Turn around and kneel above my face. I have to lick you."

I shook as I clambered into the position. Hudson had gone down on me plenty of times, but never with me hovering over him in such a carnal way. It felt dirty and base and so, so sexy.

When I was bent over his face, he put his hands on my thighs and slid my knees further apart so that my cunt was a half an inch above his mouth. I was squirming before his tongue ever touched me. And he took his time before it did, blowing across my clit first, sending delicious little sparks through my limbs.

I peered down at the erotic sight of him between my legs and watched as he buried his nose in my lips and inhaled. "You smell so fucking good," he groaned.

Holy. Fuck. I almost came right there.

Then—*finally*—his tongue flicked across my already excited clit. My body lurched and I cried out, fingernails digging into his hips. *Amazing...so amazing.*

How could it always be so amazing?

As I struggled to hold on, to not go over too quickly, I saw his cock twitch below me. There was no question that I had to have him in my mouth. Immediately. I grasped my hands around the base of his shaft and slid his crown past my lips like I was sucking on a Popsicle. Only Hudson was much yummier.

His whole body shifted underneath me, his grasp on my thighs tightening. "Fuck, yes! Suck it."

It was what I loved the most about sucking Hudson off—that I could have power over him. I was always the one who fell under his spell. I enjoyed the way he molded me, manipulated my body, bent me to his will—I *craved* it. But when I had his cock in my mouth, I finally understood why he liked being in control. It was quite heady to be the one making him twist and writhe. Making him succumb to me.

And while I bobbed over him, he continued to suckle at my core. The ecstasy warred with my solemn intention to give to the man who was always giving to me. My insides tightened and I felt close to coming, but I held on, focusing on him. He thickened as I hollowed my cheeks and increased my tempo. My free hand ran up and down the inside of his thigh, then moved to cup his balls. He groaned and that was when I knew he was as close as I was. It was a battle—who would get there first? And who would the winner be? The one who came or the one who didn't?

I considered it my victory when he pushed me away. "That's enough. On your back. I need to come inside you."

I swiveled to do as he commanded. I bent my knees, planted my feet on the bed, and spread my legs as Hudson scooted toward me. But instead of covering me with his body, he stayed kneeling. Lifting me under my ass, he urged me up into an arch. One hand moved to support me under my thigh. The other moved to rub my still-throbbing clit.

Talk about a view. I had the perfect vantage point to see his cock knocking against my bare pussy.

"I'm so turned on right now, Alayna. It's going to be rough."

He was asking my permission. Crazy, because I trusted him implicitly with my body. Trusted him with all of me.

My eyes met his. "Please."

He groaned. Then he plunged in, deep and hard, just as he'd promised.

I cried out, fisting the sheets. I had already been on the brink and the minute he entered my channel, my orgasm ripped through me.

Hudson wasn't slowing at all as I clenched around his cock. He drove into me with single-minded fury, over and over. His thighs slapped against mine, the sound driving me mad, stirring up another climax within me. He talked to me—crazy sex talk that I could barely make meaning of in my haze. Each word punctuated as he thrust in, in, in. "You're. So. God. Damn. Hot. You. Make. Me. Come. So. Hard."

And then we were both coming. So hard. He pushed into me with a long groan. My eyes were glued to him, and I watched his entire torso stiffen as his hips bucked against my pelvis. Then my own vision went white, clouding with the intensity of my release. His name was on my tongue, both a curse and a prayer as I surrendered to the convulsions that begged to overtake me.

God, oh, god.

It seemed ages before I recovered enough to speak—to *think*. When I could, Hudson had already fallen on the bed beside me. He was equally affected, I knew. If he weren't, he'd be holding me. Instead, we lay side by side, our shoulders the only parts of our bodies touching, yet the connected feeling was palpable.

I took a final deep breath. "That was incredible." Incredible was an understatement. There weren't words for what it really was. I looked over at the glorious lover beside me. "Seriously. How does sex with you just keep getting better and better?"

Hudson didn't pause in his answer. "We've learned to trust each other."

"Is that what it is?" It meant a lot that he trusted me after the things I'd done. In many ways I didn't deserve it. But I would never betray him again. I'd grown past that.

"Yes. That's what it is." He turned his head toward me, his eyes narrowed. "Did I hurt you?"

"In only the best ways." He had been rougher than usual. But I'd loved every second of it, even though I now felt raw and a bit tender. "I had no idea you were so into a shaved pussy."

He smiled, his shoulder lifting as if in a half-hearted shrug. "I've never really cared. It's you I'm into. Shaved, bushy—I'll take you."

I giggled. "I've never been bushy with you." Bushy had never been my style. But if it was something Hudson wanted…

"But you could be and I'd be turned on." His eyes darkened and I could tell he was imagining it. "Jesus, now I'm hard again."

"Are you kidding me?"

"No. I'm not." He nodded down toward his penis.

I had to look. Sure enough, it was hard. "You're such a horn-dog."

"Perhaps." Except he'd always said it was me that made him crazy, no one else.

Could that be true? Could it really only be me that turned him on to no end, transforming him into a greedy lover?

It had been true for me. Until him, sex had been fun, but that's all. Sometimes it could even begin an unhealthy obsession. But my addictions had never been about the physical. With Hudson it wasn't exactly about the sex, either. It was more about wanting to be as close to him as possible. And, because it was Hudson and he communicated best with his body, being as close to him as possible involved being naked.

He'd never let anyone in before. Maybe sex really had only been for sport in the past. With us, it was speech.

Which might have something to do with why we still had such trouble talking to each other.

We were working on that though. So I brought up the subject that I knew neither of us wanted to broach. "I saw Celia."

Hudson groaned. "And now I'm soft."

My eyes flicked downward. "No, you're not."

"It feels like I should be. Come on—Celia?"

"Sorry. I thought you should know."

"I suppose I should." He sighed. "Did she bother you at all?"

"No. I didn't talk to her. It was as we were coming down here. I think she was watching. On the deck above. When...you know." How come I could do completely nasty things with the man and still be so embarrassed about mentioning them outright?

"When I made you come all over my hand?" Leave it to Hudson to say it bluntly.

It was quite the turn-on, actually.

"Yeah, then."

"Hope she enjoyed the show." His expression was proud.

Like I'd said before—total horn-dog.

I started to tease him back but then I realized he hadn't been surprised by her presence. "It wasn't Jack you were referring to who was the uninvited guest, was it? It was Celia. How did she get here?"

Hudson ran both his hands through his hair. "She came with one of the men in my advertising department. He's always been interested in her and she's never given him a second look. I'm sure she used his crush simply to get on-board tonight."

It was obvious he didn't want to talk about her, but he was willing so I pressed on. "Why does she want to be here so badly?"

"Maybe she wanted to see if we were still together. I don't know. You know more about that kind of obsession than I do." He didn't say it to be hurtful. It was honest. I did know about that kind of obsession. Very well.

I let myself remember the reasons I'd been attracted to the men I'd stalked. "Somehow your attention validates her. Makes her feel alive." I felt my tone get heavy with years of sadness. Recalling those emotions of my past was not pleasant.

Hudson narrowed his eyes, trying to read me. "Do you think I'm being too cruel to her by cutting her out of my life?"

"No." Though if I were right—if she really did feel the way I suspected she did about Hudson—then I understood the pure devastation that she had to be going through at his dismissal. "Does that make me a shitty person?"

"No."

Whether he was right or wrong, I accepted his absolution without debate. Besides, just because I understood how she might feel didn't mean I could soften the blow in any way. Even if she had Hudson, she'd never really think she did. I'd never believed the men who were with me were really with me. Believing Hudson actually cared for me had taken a great deal of healing on my part. Those were steps Celia would have to take on her own.

But if Celia truly were obsessed with Hudson in the ways I used to be…

I shuddered to think of the lengths she might go to in order to win him. I voiced the nagging concern that had been tugging at me the entire night. "She's never really going to be out of our lives, is she? She's always going to try to destroy us."

Hudson rolled to his side to face me. "It doesn't matter." He cupped my face, lining his eyes with mine. "You belong to me, precious. You belong *with* me. I won't let anything come between us. I won't let anything hurt you. Especially not her."

The man couldn't say *I love you*, but somehow he knew how to make declarations that struck right into the core of my heart. And his eyes—they backed up every word he said. I had no doubt that he would fight for me, fight for us. He hadn't before. Now was a different story. Warmth spread from my chest throughout my body and I felt dangerously close to tearing up.

But I didn't want to get emotional. I wanted to tell him how I felt in the way he understood best. With my body. I flashed a suggestive smile. "Now *I'm* turned on again."

Hudson's jaw relaxed and he pulled me flush with him. He leaned in until his mouth was a mere inch from mine. "So we can stop talking about her?"

He smelled of sex and champagne and Hudson, and my desire flamed instantly. "We can stop talking period."

He covered me with his body, teasing me with flicks of his tongue along my jaw. At my neck, he nibbled and sucked, likely leaving a glaring hickey. Which was fine. Perfect, actually. He could mark me in any way he wanted. I was his. I wanted to be *known* as his.

I arched my back and pressed my breasts to his chest. God, I loved the feel of his skin against mine. My hips writhed underneath him, urging him to stop teasing and get on with it already.

He lifted his head to meet my eyes. "Stop rushing me," he chided. He was always very conscientious about varying the moods of our lovemaking. The last time had been driven and furious. This time would be slow and sweet. Always, it was he that decided how it would go.

I didn't prefer one tempo over another. Didn't care if he made it fast or if he took all night. But as it was occurring, whichever way we were fucking, I always thought it was the best.

At his own pace, Hudson took me to where I wanted and needed to go. Loving me thoroughly with his body. Loving me entirely without words. Loving me completely.

And as we spun into the intoxication of our passionate interlude, I said to myself, *this time. This time is the best.*

Forever With You

Chapter Five

The boat docked while we'd been lost to each other in our stateroom. The drunken crowd had dispersed and *The Magnolia* was quiet—as if we were the only ones on Earth. Enveloped in Hudson's arms with the gentle rocking of the water underneath, I slept better than I had in ages. I guessed he did too, if his mood had anything to say about it. His jet lag seemed to have finally been relieved. Oh, the power of great sex and a good night's sleep.

We left before dawn, slipping off soundlessly. Jordan was waiting at the Maybach when we reached the top of the boardwalk. This time there were no reporters, no flashing bulbs—it was just the two of us and our driver as Hudson and I climbed into the back of the car.

Once on the road, I sidled up to Hudson, or as close as the restraints of the seat belts would allow. With his improved spirits, it was time to talk about the future. "I've been thinking about who's going to manage The Sky Launch."

"You."

My head was tucked under his chin, but I could hear the smile in his voice.

I chuckled. "No pressure."

"Yes, pressure. Lots and lots of pressure." He stroked his hand down my hair. "I want you to run the club. I've always wanted you to run the club. I've told you that."

I sat up to look at him. "I know. And that's what I've been thinking about."

"Go on."

"I want to do it. I do. And I think I have the ideas and the marketing sense to pull it off."

"You do."

I'd only received my MBA a little more than a month before. I'd never been in charge of an entire business by myself. Hudson was being overly optimistic about my qualifications, especially when he intended to have very little to do with the day-to-day operations. "I adore that you think so highly of me, H, but I'm still lacking practical experience. Which was what I was looking forward to learning from David."

Hudson rolled his eyes—an odd gesture on such a solemn face. "David would have held you back. You have more genius in your little pinky than—"

I cut him off with my finger to his lips. "Stop it. Your perception of my abilities is tainted."

He kissed the top of my finger before he covered my hand with his and moved it to his lap. "It's not."

"Anyway." There was no use arguing the subject. It was partly what had kept us at a standstill since he'd first brought up the idea. He believed I could do more than I believed I could do. It was endearing and empowering, but also overwhelming.

Still Hudson's faith in me had worn me down. "I *want* to run the club. And I'm telling you yes to running the club—"

His eyes lit up. "Yes?"

"But on one condition."

"That I also give you my body and soul? If you insist..."

I smiled but otherwise ignored his flirting. "I want to hire another full-time manager to share the load. Someone with the experience I don't have."

He considered. "I don't see a problem with that. But I'd still want you to be the point person. And, hell, I'll still throw in my body and soul."

"Fine. That's what I want." I corrected myself before he could turn my words on me. "I mean I want to be the point person."

"You don't want my body and soul?" He twisted my words anyway. Of course.

"Shut up," I scolded. "I already have that."

"That you do." He wrapped his arm tighter around my waist and kissed me on my forehead. "Go ahead and put an ad out today. Unless you already have someone in mind?"

"That's just it." It was hard for me to ask this. I'd been so insistent about me doing my job without Hudson interfering, but now I needed him to.

"What?"

I pulled away. It felt too odd to be in his embrace while discussing business. Too much like some form of nepotism. "Well, there's no one at the club qualified. No one who knows more than I do. And if I put an ad out and got resumes…I just don't think I'm going to find the type of person I'm looking for. Especially not as quickly as I need them. But maybe you, with your connections and everything…"

"You want me to find someone?"

I bit my lip. "Yes."

"Done."

"I haven't even told you the type of person I'm looking for."

He sighed. "Then tell me."

This was hard for him too. I recognized that. He wanted to assume he knew what was best for me. Maybe he did. But if I was going to be his point person, I needed to have some control. "I'm thinking someone who has a history of managing a club or a restaurant, even. Someone with a resume. Someone who would know the right numbers for what should be incoming and outgoing and could handle the staff. I'd want to do most of the marketing and behind-the-scenes business while he or she would work more of the day-to-day operations. Or night-to-night operations, I guess is a better way to put it. Would you be able to find someone like that?"

"When would you want them to start?"

"Immediately. That way David could help with the training."

"Like I said before, done."

"Really?" I had expected more of an *I'll-see-what-I-can-do* response. Hudson was powerful, but part of his effectiveness came from not making promises he couldn't keep.

"Yes, really. I already have someone in mind. I'll set something up."

There. I'd done it. I'd agreed to run the club and it was happening under my terms. "Perfect."

Hudson traced my cheek with his finger. "You know all you have to do is ask and it's yours."

A sudden wave of anxiety rolled through my belly. I turned to face the back of Jordan's head. "Actually, I don't know that, and honestly, that sort of makes me uncomfortable."

Hudson put his hand on my neck. "Why?"

There were lots of reasons. But I settled on the most obvious. "I don't want to be the floozy manager who only gets things because she's fucking the owner."

My eyes were still on Jordan. He was so good at his job—he didn't even flinch at my crass language.

Hudson, it seemed, preferred that the conversation remain between us. He leaned in to whisper in my ear. "First of all, I love that you're fucking the owner. Please don't stop. Second, that's not why you get things. You get things because you're qualified. If you'd shown up to the interviews after the symposium, you would have had people fighting for you. But third, and most importantly, you get things from me because you're my other half. Everything that is mine is yours. My connections, my money, my influence—it's all half yours."

I shivered. While I adored the sentiment—craved it, in fact—it also made my panic buttons go off. Those were the kinds of words that could make me think things I shouldn't think. That I was more important than I was. That we were closer than we were. They were trigger words for me, and though I'd been healthy with Hudson, it had only come from diligence on my part.

But how I wanted to wrap myself in his declaration…

I swallowed. "I don't know how to respond to that."

Hudson nuzzled his nose against my earlobe. "You aren't ready for that, I know. But I needed to tell you. As for your response, how about you say you'll run our club?"

"I'll run your club."

"Ah—"

I knew my mistake immediately. Funny, how strongly I wanted to correct myself. I turned to meet his eyes. "I'll run *our* club."

"Now kiss me because you've made me a very happy man."

He didn't have to ask me twice. He didn't even really have to ask me once, because his lips were covering mine as I opened my mouth to agree. His tongue slid in immediately, and he kissed me thoroughly until the car came to a stop in front of The Bowery.

Reluctantly, I released myself from his embrace. "Thank you, Hudson." *For the chance to run the club, for helping me be successful at it, for loving me in the best way you know how, for finding me in the first place.*

He swept my hair away from my shoulder. "No. Thank you."

***

I spent the rest of the day at the club. After I'd realized I wouldn't be in Japan, I'd arranged to meet with Aaron Trent to discuss an advertising plan. Our meeting was at one-thirty that afternoon and preparations took all morning. Throwing myself into work was energizing. I loved marketing and scheming. For the first time since I'd learned David was leaving, I felt really good about The Sky Launch's future and my part in it.

Because of all my prep, and because Aaron Trent had the best ad team in town, our session went well, and we finished up earlier than I'd expected. It was just after three when our meeting concluded. Suddenly exhausted, I curled up on the couch in David's office to chill out.

"Great meeting," David said, as he entered the office. "I'm bummed I won't get to see the fruit of all your work today."

"Don't worry. I'll keep you updated." I stretched my arms in front of me. With the things Hudson had me doing the night before, it was no wonder I felt tired and sore. The memory brought a smile to my lips.

"What's up with you today?"

I looked up to see David perched on the far arm of the couch, his eyes pinned on me. "What do you mean?"

His brow creased. "I don't know if I can explain it. You're different today. More on fire, if that's possible."

I thought for a moment. I'd always been passionate about my job, but that morning's decision had instilled me with renewed vigor. "Well, I did tell Hudson this morning that I'd take your place when you leave."

He beamed. "Finally! Now I can actually feel good about leaving."

"Whatever. You've been excited about Adora since Hudson gave you the job."

"Mostly because I'd thought Pierce was going to fire me. The promotion instead was a nice surprise."

My smile faded. I'd convinced myself that David was eager to leave The Sky Launch. It made it easier to accept that he'd been pushed out because of my jealous boyfriend. Though I'd rather continue the illusion, the truth was more important.

I shifted my body to face David. "So you only agreed to take Adora because you thought you'd be fired from here if you didn't?"

"Come on, Laynie. Let's be honest. Pierce wasn't going to let me stay here."

David's words may have been true, but I hadn't gotten a chance to fight as hard as I would have liked to for him to stay. If he didn't want to leave, if he really wanted to stay on at The Sky Launch, I'd go back to Hudson and duke it out. "But if he did—if that wasn't the issue—would you have still said yes? Or would you have stayed here?"

David took a deep breath. "I'm not really sure, to be honest. Adora is the pinnacle of nightclubs. I'd never have an opportunity like that on my own. And I think I'll do a good job there. There's a whole team of managers I'll be joining. I'll have flexibility and support that I've never had before. It's sort of my dream job."

I relaxed some.

He moved from the arm to the cushion. "But it's hard to leave the things you love. The move means leaving my home and my friends. This place." He met my eyes. "You."

"David…" I knew he had feelings for me, but now he was alluding to love. Dammit, that was closer than Hudson could get to saying I love you. I didn't want to hear it.

He ignored my warning. "Don't laugh, but I used to have this fantasy that we'd eventually run this place together."

I couldn't help but smile at that. "I used to have that same fantasy." I'd pictured that we'd get married and be this really cool duo who ran the hottest club in town. That dream vanished when I met Hudson.

"Really?"

"Yes, really." Immediately I regretted the confession. David's expression said it meant more than I wanted it to mean.

I swung my legs around so I was no longer facing him. "I mean, seriously. This place needs two managers. It was silly that you did it alone for so long."

"I wasn't really alone. The staff is full of great assistant managers."

I smirked. "That's not the same. Full-time commitment is what you need. I asked Hudson to find a partner for me today." I looked down at my lap. "I don't want to do it alone."

David scooted closer. He lifted my chin with his finger. "Say the word and I'll stay."

"I can't ask you to do that, David." My voice was practically a whisper.

"You could."

"No, I couldn't. And you know why."

He dropped his hand to his lap. "I do. But in answer to your earlier question—if it weren't for Pierce, I'd never leave. You can pretend to interpret that any way you need to, but you know what I'm really saying."

"I...I'm...um." I bit my lip. David had been such a great friend when I'd had very few. And for a while, he'd been more. I was heartbroken that he was leaving. But I in no way returned the feelings he seemed to be declaring.

"You don't have to respond. I get it. You're with him." He wouldn't even say Hudson's name.

"I am with him. Completely."

"And if you're ever not..." David had told me before that he'd be there if I decided things with Hudson weren't working out. It was a ridiculous thing to promise. Especially because I was over him, and, even without Hudson, I wouldn't fall back to David.

But I wouldn't be that blunt about it to his face. He was already leaving. I didn't need to hurt him further. So instead, we sat in awkward silence for several thick seconds while I debated what I could say that would be a gentle letdown.

Fortunately, I was saved by the ringing of my phone. I rushed to pick it up from the side table next to me, not even bothering to look at whom the call was from.

"Laynie!" Mira's voice bubbled through the earpiece. "Are you busy? Can you talk?"

I stood and distanced myself from David. "Of course I can talk. What's up?"

"I was wondering if I could ask a favor."

"On top of being a model at your event?" I was only teasing. I'd do practically anything for the girl. She'd welcomed me into her family even before Hudson had. I owed her.

"A different favor. Man, I'm kind of needy these days, aren't I?"

"How about I refrain from answering that until you tell me what the favor is?" Absentmindedly, I paced the room as we talked.

"Fair enough. Dad wants to have lunch with me tomorrow. And I don't really want to be alone with his sorry ass. And I'd love to see you. So would you consider joining us?"

"I'd love to!" Thinking about Jack put a smile on my face. There was no way Hudson would approve of me seeing him on my own, but what could he say if I was with Mira? I'd be honest about it, tell him upfront and it would be fine. "But why don't you want to be alone with him?"

"He's trying to make up for all the crap with Celia. He doesn't get that I'm not the one he needs to make up with. I don't really give a flying fig what he did or didn't do or should have done. I just want him and Mom to grow up and act like adults for half a second. I mean, wouldn't that be so nice?"

Sophia and Jack grow up? "Keep dreaming."

"I know, I know. Anyway, we're meeting at Perry Street at one. I'll call and add you to the reservation. Yay! You turned something dreadful into something I'm looking forward to!"

"I'm looking forward to it, too."

I hung up and stuffed my phone in my bra then glanced over and saw David working at his desk. Or, rather, pretending to work. He kept sneaking looks at me and I wondered if he wanted to say more than he had. I hoped not.

Instead of waiting to find out, I announced that I had a few errands to run. They weren't pressing, but after his declaration, the office felt stifling.

I stepped out into the summer heat and pulled my sunglasses on. Since I'd left spur of the moment, I didn't have a chance to call Jordan for a ride. The stops I wanted to make were nearby anyway. I could walk everywhere I planned to go. Besides, it was a beautiful day and it was nice to be out in the fresh air.

I didn't notice my follower until I'd nearly reached the first place I needed to go—a graphics shop a few blocks away from Columbus Circle. Perhaps I'd been too preoccupied with thoughts of David and the club. And Hudson—always Hudson. Otherwise, I'm sure I would have spotted her earlier. When I finally did notice her, I knew immediately it wasn't a coincidence that she was walking down Eighth Avenue at the same time I was. I also knew that she meant to be seen. I was an experienced stalker, after all. With a little effort, it's not that hard to remain unnoticed.

Celia wasn't trying to remain hidden at all.

She stopped when I stopped. Started again when I started. All the time her eyes were pinned directly on me. My heart beat furiously, but I remained cool, keeping an even pace to my steps. When I went into the graphics shop, she thankfully didn't follow. But she took her place outside the front window so that I could see she was there.

Celia hadn't exactly done anything to me, hadn't spoken to me, but her presence wrapped me in a blanket of fear. I knew without a doubt she was making a statement—*I'm here. I see you. You can't escape me.* Was this what Paul Kresh had felt when I'd followed him around for weeks at a time? It was an awful feeling and the regret for my past actions had never been so heavy.

There was a line at the counter, so I was able to take a few minutes to collect myself before my turn at the cashier. My thoughts raced to Celia's motive. Maybe she wanted to talk to me. But she could text or email. And if she'd wanted to talk, why hadn't she approached me?

No, she had a different intent with her stalking. First on the boat, now here—would she ever leave me alone? Was this another trick that she meant to somehow turn back on me later? Or did she simply mean to scare me?

If scare was the goal, she'd achieved it. But unlike the last time she'd screwed me over, I was prepared. Now she didn't have my trust. After I texted Jordan telling him where I was and asking him to meet me, I used my phone to click a picture of her—I wanted proof. She saw me take the picture, I was certain, but she didn't leave or seem concerned. Next, I called Hudson's office.

"He's in a meeting," Trish, his secretary, informed me. "I'll have him call you as soon as he's finished."

That wasn't good enough. I knew he'd want me to interrupt him for this, but Trish would never do it herself. Hoping he'd check his cell phone, I shot him a text. *I'm on my way to your office. I need to see you.*

I was calmer when it was my turn at the cashier. I collected the table cards I had ordered, took a deep breath, and headed out of the store. I was terrified to walk out with Celia so near the entrance, but I wouldn't let her see that. Thankfully, just as I put my hand on the door to push it open, Jordan pulled up. Celia took off at a brisk pace down the sidewalk. If all it took to send her away was Jordan, I'd never go anywhere without him again.

I slid in the car before Jordan had a chance to get out and open the door for me. "Up ahead, on the sidewalk," I said pointing toward Celia's back. "Do you see her?" She was walking fast and I wanted someone else to see her before she disappeared in the New York City crowds.

Jordan was quick with a good eye. "I see her. Was she following you?" He didn't seem to be surprised.

"Yes. How did you know?"

"I spotted her this morning when I dropped you off at the club, but I wasn't certain it was her. We need to tell Mr. Pierce."

"I plan to right now. Can you take me to his office?"

He answered with a nod.

I sat back and buckled my seatbelt as he pulled out into traffic. Celia was still in sight and I watched her as we drove closer. She stopped walking when we passed, and even though she couldn't see me through the tinted windows, she smiled and waved.

It was a good thing I was a pacifist, because otherwise I'd have started planning her murder.

Chapter Six

Hudson hadn't responded to my text by the time I'd arrived in the lobby, so I sent another. *I'm getting in the elevator. I'll be in your office in 2.*

I still hadn't received a reply when I stepped onto his floor, but I breezed by Trish as if Hudson were always available for me.

From the way he usually talked, he *was* always available for me.

"Excuse me," Trish called after me. "Mr. Pierce is still with his appointment—"

"He knows I'm coming," I called over my shoulder.

The door opened before I even touched the handle. Hudson stood there, concern etched on his brow. "It's okay, Patricia." He ushered me in.

As soon as the door shut behind me, he cupped his hands around my face and searched my eyes. "I got your text. What's wrong? Are you hurt?"

"No, not hurt." I was shaking, and now that I was with Hudson, I wanted to cry.

"Alayna, what is it?"

I pulled my phone out and began to cue Celia's picture. "I need to show you something. Can I—"

A rustle behind us caught my attention. I peered around Hudson and saw a woman standing by his desk. Her auburn hair was tied loosely at her nape, the color accentuated by the pale cream of her suit.

My back straightened, warning bells sounding in my head. "Oh, I'm sorry. I didn't realize you weren't alone."

Hudson put a hand at my back and gestured toward his guest. "Alayna, you remember Norma."

"Yeah, I do. Norma Anders. We met at the Botanic Gardens event." The same knot of jealousy I'd felt at meeting her formed now. Or rather, her presence tightened the knot that had been in my belly for the past half hour.

Norma had an obvious interest in Hudson. It bothered me. She worked with him daily, touched him casually, used his first name— he rarely let people use his first name, particularly not his employees. And here she was alone with him in his office midday. And he had ignored my texts.

"We did meet then." Norma looked me over, sizing me up. When we'd met before, she'd barely given me a second glance. She'd been too focused on my man. "It's good to see you again, Alayna." Her terse tone said otherwise.

She delivered her next line to Hudson. "If you two need to talk alone, we can step out."

We? My eyes traveled the room and I noticed another woman sitting in the other armchair facing Hudson's desk.

Ah, he wasn't alone with Norma. A wave of relief ran through me, followed by a wave of guilt. I was being ridiculous and paranoid. The events of the day had me off balance. Hudson was simply meeting with two of his employees. No midday trysts. Nothing inappropriate at all.

Still, the knot persisted. I was eager to talk to Hudson about Celia, but it would have to wait. I stuffed my phone back in my bra. "No, no. I apologize for bursting in. It's not like me to interrupt."

Hudson scooted past me toward his desk. "Actually, Alayna, this is perfect timing." He nodded to the woman still sitting and she stood. "This is Norma's sister, Gwen. She's one of the managers at Eighty-Eighth Floor."

"Oh." Not an employee after all. The Eighty-Eighth Floor was a popular nightclub in The Village owned by a rival businessman.

It took a second longer than it should have for me to click things into place. "Oh!"

I kicked myself into gear and approached Gwen, my hand extended toward her. "Alayna Withers," I offered as she shook my hand.

Her grasp was firm. A good first sign for a possible co-manager. "Nice to meet you."

She had a good smile too. Nice teeth, not too flirty. Her features were very similar to Norma's, except lighter. Her skin tone was pale, her hair either dark blonde or light brown depending on the lighting. Her eyes were gray-blue. She was pretty like Scarlett Johansson—the type of pretty that some people might overlook and other people would over-acknowledge.

I wondered which kind of people Hudson was in this instance.

I quickly chided myself for the thought. What was wrong with me? It had been typical for me to be unnecessarily jealous with past boyfriends, but I'd never been that way with Hudson.

Hudson stepped nearer to introduce me more properly. "Alayna's currently the Promotions Manager at The Sky Launch, but, as I told you, she'll become the General Manager once the current manager leaves."

"Hudson told me you're looking for an Operations Manager." Gwen addressed me confidently and completely. It was refreshing considering her sister's knack for forgetting I existed.

I nodded. "Is that something you might be interested in?"

"Definitely."

A co-manager who worked at Eighty-Eighth. With all the insider information she'd have, plus the experience...I had to admit, Hudson had done good.

And he knew it. Though his face remained businesslike, his eyes twinkled with the pride of a job well done. "She has all the qualifications I believe that you're looking for, Alayna. Perhaps you want to set up an interview for yourself?"

"Yes. Definitely." I pulled my phone from my bra. When I unlocked it, Celia's picture was there, ready to show Hudson. I froze at the sight and another chill ran through me.

"Alayna?" Hudson prompted softly.

"Sorry. Rough day. I'm a bit flustered." I flipped through my schedule for the next day. I had lunch planned with Mira and Jack, but my evening was free. "Would you be able to come into The Sky Launch tomorrow? I think calling it an interview is a little too formal. I could show you around and we could talk then."

"Sounds perfect. I'm off tomorrow so I'm wide open."

It crossed my mind that I should ask why she wanted to leave Eighty-Eighth Floor, but it could wait until we met again. My earlier anxiety was overtaking me and all I cared about was finishing the conversation and getting Hudson to myself. And not for the reasons I usually wanted him alone.

"Great. Then you can come by at eight." I entered the info into my calendar. "You can see the club when it's open."

"I'll be there."

"See, Norma?" Hudson winked at his employee. "The kids didn't need us after all. They worked everything out on their own."

Hudson's playful jab at Norma fueled my angst. Why had she been invited to this meeting anyway? Just because Gwen was her sister, Norma didn't have to be included. And how had Hudson even known that Norma had a sister that managed a club? Were Norma and Hudson closer than he'd led me to believe?

At the height of my obsessive disorder, I suffered greatly from paranoia. Sure, it returned from time to time, but not to any significant extent since I'd met Hudson. Was I being paranoid now or were my questions valid? And if it was just paranoia, why was it returning now?

It was Celia and her fucking mind games getting to me. It had to be that. I couldn't backslide because of her. Otherwise she'd win and I wasn't having that. I had to get a grip.

I stepped out of the way while Hudson ushered the Anders sisters out of his office. Mentally I tried to calm myself, taking deep breaths and reminding myself to communicate rather than jump to conclusions. Perhaps I needed to pencil in another group therapy session for later in the week. Anything to end the rising panic.

When we were alone, I couldn't hold back any longer. "Why exactly was Norma here?" I added a smile and a light tone so that it didn't come off harsh, but how could it sound like anything other than an accusation?

Hudson locked the door before turning toward me. "She arranged to have Gwen meet with me. I'd never met her and Norma wanted to be here to acquaint us. Why do you ask?"

"Just curious." I leaned against his desk, needing the support. "How did you know that Gwen worked at Eighty-Eighth?"

He walked over to me in several easy strides. "Norma's mentioned it."

"Just in casual conversation. Between a boss and his employee?" I folded my arms in front of me. Not the best pose for remaining aloof.

Hudson put his hands on my elbows. "Alayna, you're acting unusually jealous. While it's always a turn-on, I have a feeling it's a symptom of something else today. What's going on?"

I shrugged, not wanting to jump into the Celia issue until I'd cleared up the Norma issue. "It just seems strange that you would know such personal details about one employee when you have hundreds—thousands—of people working for you."

"Hundreds of thousands."

I didn't even crack a smile. "Even stranger then."

Hudson released me and put his hands in his pockets. "What exactly are you asking me, Alayna?"

I already hated myself. The person standing here facing the man I loved was not the person I wanted to be. I didn't want to question or worry or be paranoid.

But my gut was twisting and churning and the words flew out of my mouth like vomit. "I'm asking why you know personal details about Norma Anders' family."

"You're asking what kind of relationship I've had with Norma. The answer is strictly working."

"Have you ever kissed her?" My voice shook and I had a feeling if I uncrossed my arms, my hands would be trembling as well. My mind was already filling with images of them together. It was crazy what I could conjure up—detailed scenes of passion. The only thing that could possibly stop the flood of imagination would be his assurance that it never happened. Even then, there was a chance the images would remain.

"I don't make it a habit to kiss people I have working relationships with."

He'd kissed me when I worked for him. "Yes or no, please?"

"No, Alayna. I've never kissed her. I've never fucked her. I've never anything with her." His tone was smooth but emphatic.

I returned his level expression even though I was an irrational mess inside.

My seeming composure egged him on. Or he sensed that I was a thread away from falling apart. He ran a hand through his hair. "Since she's in the Financial Division, Norma handled the transaction when I purchased The Sky Launch so she knew I had the club. The other day she asked if there were any management positions available there. I told her no, but that I'd keep Gwen in mind. I didn't want to tell you about her because I was afraid if you knew, you'd take that as a reason not to be the manager yourself. It's as simple as that."

"That makes sense." And the slightly manipulative way he kept it from me was totally typical Hudson. In my heart I knew he was telling the truth, but my head—it was in overdrive.

So which did I believe? My heart or my head?

He met my eyes and held my stare for several seconds. "There's nothing with her, Alayna. I'm with you. Always. Okay?"

My heart. I believed my heart. *Always.*

This was Hudson. He loved me, even if he stubbornly couldn't say the words. I trusted him. What had he ever done to tell me otherwise?

I shook my head, ashamed of myself. "I'm sorry. I'm being stupid."

Hudson tugged me into his arms. Finally, I felt calm. I breathed him in—the scent of his soap and aftershave filled me with a soothing balm. There was nowhere that I'd rather be than right there in his embrace.

He ran his hands up and down my back and kissed along my temple. "I know you wouldn't be like this if something hadn't happened. And you came in here upset. What's going on, precious?"

I clung to him, my hands digging into his jacket. Now that he was holding me, I didn't want to let him go. This was where I was safe.

"Alayna, talk to me."

I turned my head so my words wouldn't be muffled in his clothing. "It's Celia."

Hudson pushed me away to meet my face. His eyes were wide with concern. "What did she do?"

"She's following me."

His brows furrowed. "What do you mean, *following you*?"

"Like, showing up where I am and going wherever I go. Following me." I showed him the picture on my phone and explained how I'd spotted her tailing me while I ran errands and added that Jordan had seen her that morning. Plus, she'd been on the boat the night before.

I feared he'd say I was overreacting, that he wouldn't believe me like the time before. I had a picture, but what did that show? Would he think I was the one who'd followed her?

75

But his response this time made up for his previous doubts. "Fucking bitch!" He spun away from me and ran his hand through his hair. "I swear to god if she does anything to you…"

Tears sprung to my eyes, half from terror, half from relief that he was on my side. "What does she want from us? From me?"

Hudson circled around to the other side of his desk. "It doesn't matter. She can't do this. I'll call my lawyer. We'll get a restraining order." Before I could interject, he'd pushed his intercom. "Patricia, get Gordon Hayes on the phone."

"Yes, Mr. Pierce."

I shook my head and sunk into one of the armchairs. "It's not that simple."

"I don't care if it's simple or not. I'm getting a restraining order."

I'd never seen him so worked up. His calm aloofness had vanished and in its place was a wild passionate man.

It was me who was the voice of reason. "Hudson, you can't get a restraining order for simply being followed. She had a measurable distance, didn't approach me, didn't threaten me or pull any crap at any of the places I stopped. We have nothing on her."

His eyes were pinned on the phone, as if he could make it ring by staring at it. "That's ridiculous. She has you scared. I can see it on your face."

"Yes, she has me scared. But there's nothing you can do about it." Again, I was reminded that I had done this same thing to other people. Paul Kresh had filed a restraining order against me. It had been the first one I'd received. He hadn't been the first person I'd stalked. "Trust me. I'm well-versed in the art of terrorizing someone while evading police involvement."

"Don't talk like that." Hudson's tone echoed the pain I felt.

"It's the truth. I used to do this to people, Hudson! It's horrible. How could I be this horrible to other people?" The tears that had been just at bay broke through.

Hudson rushed to me and pulled me from my seat into his arms. "Hush now, Alayna." He stroked my hair as I sobbed on his shoulder. "This isn't the same. You were searching for love. Celia's actions are quite different."

I pushed him away. Though I wanted and needed his touch, I didn't feel like I deserved it. "Are they? Isn't she doing this because she wants your love? How is that different?"

He sighed and perched on the edge of his desk. "I don't believe that's why she's doing this. She means to keep me unhappy. She knows that hurting you would destroy me. This is payback for my past. This has nothing to do with yours."

I swiped the tears off my cheeks. Dammit, Celia had screwed with both of us so easily. Here we were, regretting our pasts, hating ourselves, undoing years of progress—*fucking bitch* was right.

I sat down again and laid my head against the chair back. "I really don't care why she's doing it. She'll keep on doing it, though, because she's winning. You're down on yourself and I'm a mess. I'm paranoid and anxious and I'm afraid I'm reverting back to my old self." My voice cracked as a new set of tears threatened to fall.

Hudson moved to kneel in front of me. He put his hands on my upper arms as if he meant to shake sense into me. "You aren't. You have valid reasons to feel this way today. She's thrown you off balance, but you'll get ahold of yourself. You're stronger than her."

I wiped at my eye with my knuckle. "I'm strong with you."

"And I'm not leaving you. I'm here. We're in this together. Do you hear me?"

I nodded weakly.

The phone beeped. Hudson stood and reached across the desk to push the intercom. "Did you reach him?"

"No." Trisha's voice filled the room. "I'm sorry but Mr. Hayes has gone home for the evening. It's after five."

Hudson glanced at his watch. "Shit," he muttered. He paused and I suspected he was toying with calling his lawyer's cell. "I want him on the phone first thing tomorrow."

"Yes, sir. Anything else before I leave?"

"No. Thank you, Patricia." He turned the intercom off and turned back to face me. He studied me for long seconds. "She won't win, Alayna. You kept it together in front of her, didn't you?"

"Yes." There was no way in hell I'd have let her see that she got to me.

He beamed with pride. "Of course you did. You're incredible like that. Stronger than you give yourself credit for."

I didn't feel incredible. But his assurance bolstered me.

Hudson leaned against the desk, his expression glazed. I recognized it as his calculating look—the one he got when he was considering a big business deal. "Celia has no idea if she hit her target or not. That puts us at an advantage."

I hated to interrupt whatever he was planning, but I couldn't stop the thought that bubbled to the front of my mind. "What if she doesn't stop at stalking?"

His eyes came back into focus. "Jordan is ex-military. Special ops. He can protect you. You can never go anywhere without him in the future. Promise me."

"I rarely go anywhere without him now. Today was a fluke."

"Just promise me." His tone was insistent.

"I promise." I'd known Jordan was more than a driver but hadn't known the specifics of his background. Knowing it now wasn't what prompted me to agree—I'd have agreed to anyone being charged to me, just to ensure I'd never be alone with Celia again.

"Good. I'll hire another bodyguard for when Jordan's not available. I know you didn't want one—"

I cut him off. "I'll take it."

He nodded a thank you. "I'll bring someone in to check the security cameras at the club and make sure they're sufficient. The penthouse is already monitored. And I'll talk to my lawyer—"

I interjected again. "He can't do anything."

"I'm talking to him anyway. I want to know our rights. If I have to throw money at the situation, I will."

I chuckled. I'd never heard Hudson talk so candidly about what his wealth could buy. It was a foreign concept to me—that solutions to problems could simply be bought. It's why I'd always feared someone else would be more suited for Hudson than me. Someone like the blonde we were currently discussing. "Celia has money, too."

Hudson shook his head dismissively. "Money is only good in the right hands. I have no doubt that my power extends beyond her and the Werner family."

I nodded as I brought the knuckle of my index finger to my mouth and sunk my teeth into the skin. It was either that or let out the scream that had been building the last few minutes. Though Hudson was performing with the take-charge attitude I needed, he couldn't make the promises I wished he could make.

He read my anguish. "Alayna, I'll take care of this."

"I know…"

He leaned forward and pulled my hand from my mouth, lacing my fingers through his instead. "But…?"

"She's never going to be out of our lives, is she?" Even if she were on her best behavior, she'd still be there. Her life was so intertwined with Hudson and his family. I couldn't imagine any scenario that would remove her from being a constant presence.

Hudson rubbed his thumb gently across my skin. "She will. I'll figure something out. Do you trust me?"

"Yes." *With my whole heart.*

"Then believe me—I'll take care of her." He squeezed my hand once more before he let it go. "In the meantime, stay with Jordan. No more outside runs for a while."

Running was one of my favorite ways to calm myself. It was a necessity for my mental health. The treadmill worked, but it wasn't the same as being outside with the sun beating down and the breeze blowing across my sweaty body. "I'll just have Jordan run with me. I'm sure he won't mind. I know he's in good shape, and if he's Special Ops, he must do some running."

"No. Not good enough. He can't be on his best game when he's exerting himself physically."

"I don't know," I mumbled. "You're on your best game when you're exerting yourself physically."

"What was that?"

"Nothing. I just don't want to live in a prison." I hated giving up one of my only sources of solace because of Celia.

"Alayna, please." His eyes were soft but determined. "Just until I get a better plan together."

What was I thinking? Hudson was my true solace. I could give up everything else if I had him. "Okay. Fine. I'll keep my runs to the treadmill. For now."

"Come here." Hudson pulled me out of my seat and into his arms. "I only want you safe. I couldn't bear it if anything happened to you."

I nuzzled into his neck, breathing in his scent and warm words, hoping they'd envelope me in calm.

But as soon as I'd start to relax, a new haunting thought would make its way to the forefront of my mind. I let myself ask the worst. "Do you really think Celia would do something besides scare me?" I'd suggested she might earlier, but I didn't know if I really believed it. I'd never done more than stalk. Well, nothing harmful, anyway.

Hudson's grip tightened around me and he buried his face in my hair. "I don't know what she'd do. I'm not willing to find out."

The edge in his voice coupled with his uncertainty caused another spike in my blood pressure. "Hudson, I'm scared."

He pushed me away enough to cup my face in his hands and meld his gaze with mine. "I'm not, Alayna. Not in the least." It was a one-eighty from his last declaration, and I suspected his words now were only for my benefit, that he was more worried than he was letting on. He couldn't fool me.

But it felt good to hear him try.

"Trust me." He placed a kiss on the tip of my nose. "I'll take care of it." He kissed the side of my mouth. "I'll take care of you."

He licked along the seam of my lips. When I parted my mouth, he eased inside, mesmerizing me with sensual strokes along my teeth and tongue. He kissed me slow and deep and with careful attention. With his lips he did the thing his words had failed to do—he made me feel better. Or he distracted me, at least. Either way, he gave me what I needed.

In fact, I needed more.

I pushed into him, lifting my breasts to meet his chest.

Hudson smiled against my mouth. Then he wrapped up the kiss with a final peck on my lips and pulled away.

My fingers curled into his jacket, drawing him back to me. "Don't stop. I need you." I pressed my body against his, my desire growing with an intense urgency.

"Alayna…" His eyes traveled to the phone on the desk behind him. He wanted to be making calls, setting things in motion. It's what he needed to do to feel better. To feel safe. I got that.

But what I needed to feel safe was much simpler. More tangible. More within reach. "I need you, Hudson." I moved my hand to stroke against the ridge in his pants. "Please. Please make it better."

"Dammit, Alayna," he growled. "You're making it hard for me to do what I should be doing."

I continued rubbing his crotch. "I'm trying to make it harder." God, I'd never had to beg, but if he wanted me to, I would. "Hudson…please!"

"Fuck." In one swift motion, he turned me so that the desk was pressed against my behind. He leaned down, and with the length of his arm, pushed aside the files that lay on top. Then he lifted me so that I sat on the edge of the mahogany surface. "Take off your panties," he commanded, as he undid his buckle.

He didn't have to ask me twice. Hudson had his cock out by the time I'd slid my panties off and kicked them to the floor. I watched as he stroked himself, his shaft thickening with each pump.

I ran my hands along his chest and squirmed, spreading my legs further apart. I ached to have him moving inside me—ached with an intensity that I couldn't recall having ever felt before. I was desperate. Frantic. "Hudson." I couldn't stop pleading. "I need—"

He cut me off. "I know what you need. Trust me to give it to you." With one hand still wrapped around his cock, he placed his other hand between my folds and swirled his thumb across my bud.

I moaned and tilted my hips to increase the pressure.

Hudson leaned his forehead against mine. "You're so eager, precious. It's going to hurt if you don't let me get you ready first." He slid his finger along my lips and back to dance across my clit.

"I don't care if it hurts." It hurt *not* having him inside me. I tugged at his tie. "Come on!"

He swore under his breath. Then he let himself go. Tangling his hand in my hair, he pulled me roughly toward his lips. "It's hard enough to control myself around you as it is. If you give me permission, then you better believe you're going to get fucked."

I wanted to reply, *Thank god*, but his mouth had claimed mine with frenzied passion and speaking was no longer an option. At the same time, he drove his cock into me with a deep, forceful jab. I cried out at the pleasure/pain. I'd been wet, but he'd been right—I hadn't been quite as ready as I could have been.

And it didn't matter. I loved him inside me, and my snug channel let each of his short stabs rub against every wall. I cried into his mouth at each stroke. God, oh god, oh god.

Still it wasn't enough. I wrapped my legs around his waist and bucked against him, meeting his thrusts. I closed my eyes. I was aroused and insane with needing the release I knew would come if I could just get there.

He let go of the lip he'd been sucking on. "Jesus, Alayna. Slow down."

"No. Can't. Want you." I couldn't even speak in complete sentences.

"I know. I know what to give you." He nipped at my jaw. "But if you don't let me take care of you, you aren't going to get where you want to go."

"Need," I corrected. And I couldn't slow down. I was crazed.

Hudson huffed my name in frustration. Wrapping a handful of hair around his fingers, he pulled my head back until I gasped. His strokes slowed to a steady pulse. "Listen to me. Are you listening?"

I nodded.

"Look at me."

I opened my lids and met his gaze. Immediately, his gray eyes soothed me.

"You need to let me take charge, Alayna. You need to trust me. I'm going to take care of you." He wasn't talking about achieving an orgasm. He was speaking about much more. "Okay?"

I did trust him. Implicitly. I'd told him over and over.

But even with my declarations, I was still recovering from his recent abandonment and the pain of it lingered. Saying I trusted him was easier than actually letting myself go to fully act on that trust.

He was calling me out on that now.

And I wouldn't let him down. "Okay," I said.

"Good. Now let's do this." With one hand still pulling my hair, he moved his other to my clit where he rubbed with expert circles. "Hold on to the desk."

I moved my hands to grip the edge of the desk. He picked up the tempo of his thrusts, his tip knocking against the same spot on the inside that his thumb massaged on the outside. The sensation in that one concentrated area built quickly. Soon, I felt the tightening in my lower belly, and my limbs began to tingle.

And Hudson was feeling it too. "God, Alayna. Your pussy feels so good. So tight. You make me so hard. I'm going to come so hard." He quickened the pace again, and the sound of our bodies slapping and his sex words pushed me higher and higher and higher.

When I was about to orgasm, he urged my hips up and drove into me with staccato jabs that sent us over together with a shared moan. He rubbed into me for several long seconds, spilling everything he had, my own fluids mixing with his.

"Better?" he asked before I'd even caught my breath.

"Yes. Much." But even as I was still soaring on the tails of my climax, I recognized that I'd just done the thing I'd always accused him of—used sex to solve a problem. "I, um, I'm sorry about—"

"Shh." He put a finger to my lips and smiled. "It's nice to be on the opposite side for once."

"Well, thank you." I kissed his finger then laced my hands around his neck.

"Anytime you need it, I'm happy to fuck away your woes."

I laughed. After cleaning up and putting my panties back on, I left him to begin the tasks he felt were necessary for our protection.

Celia was nowhere in sight as I climbed into the back of the Maybach, but I shuddered, still feeling her eyes on me from the last time I'd been in the car. Hudson believed he could rid her from our lives. And I had total faith in him.

But I loved the man more than I'd loved anyone. It was totally plausible that my faith was biased.

Chapter Seven

Instead of going back to the club, I decided to call it a day. Besides, Hudson and I had planned that morning to be home to eat dinner together, and even though the new developments of the afternoon were keeping him at work late, I didn't want to waste the cook's efforts.

At the penthouse, I put our dinner trays in the warmer and sat at the dining room table nibbling on my salad while I tried to concentrate on a new book. I'd picked *Lady Chatterley's Lover* by D.H. Lawrence, hoping it would help me focus on the romantic and sexual aspects of my life rather than the dread Celia had instilled.

But reading required more attention than I was able to devote to the task. Giving up, I tossed the book on the table. A blank business card poked out between the pages at the bottom. I hadn't seen it before—throwing the book must have jostled the card from where it was lodged inside. I flipped the book open to the page the card marked and then turned the card over to see if the other side was also blank.

It wasn't. And the name on the back almost made me drop the card.

With a hand on my chest, I talked myself down from my panic attack. Hudson had ordered the books from Celia and her design company—it was only natural that she'd stick her business card between the pages.

Except the books were new. And the page that the card had marked had a quote highlighted in yellow: *"She was always waiting, it seemed to be her forte."*

Had Celia marked that quote? And had she meant it for me or for Hudson? And whoever the intended target was, what did she mean by it?

"Good book?"

I jumped at Hudson's voice behind me. I'd been too absorbed in the book and Celia's mark on it to hear him come in.

He leaned down to kiss my neck. "Sorry, I didn't mean to sneak up on you."

"It's not that. Look." I showed him the card and held the book up for him. "I found this business card in this book—it's one of the ones you got me. And this quote is highlighted."

I felt Hudson's body heating with rage. He crumpled the card in his hand and threw it across the room. "Goddammit!"

"What does it mean?"

"Who knows?" He took a deep breath and reined in his fury. "You know what? Don't even think about it. That's what she wants. She wants it to mess with you." He grabbed the book from me and took it with him to the kitchen. "Have you eaten?"

"I waited for you. It's in the warmer." I sat quietly until he returned with our dinner plates. "You took her key away, right?"

Hudson set our plates down. "She didn't just leave that in your book now. This has to be from before. When she had the boxes delivered." He disappeared again into the kitchen.

That hadn't been an answer to my question and his avoidance made me nervous. I waited until he came back, this time with a bottle of wine.

"Hudson—her key?"

"Yes. I took away her key." He poured me a glass and then one for himself. He had his half finished before I'd even taken one sip. "The day after she made the delivery."

He hadn't told me about seeing her then. But I'd seen Celia many times without telling him so I supposed it was fair.

Instead of dwelling on why he'd never mentioned it, I thought about what else he'd said—that she must have put the note in the books before they'd been delivered. There were hundreds of books. How had I happened to find the one with the note? Unless there were more. "So there could be secret notes and messages in all of the books."

Hudson took another swallow of his wine—a swallow that finished off the glass. "I'll replace them all."

"You don't need to do that." Truthfully, I was already planning to search them. Curiosity was pretty much my middle name, after all.

Hudson refilled his drink. "I'll do it anyway."

He had made up his mind and when he made up his mind, there was no arguing with him.

I glanced at the clock on my phone. It was after eight. "You got home late. Does that mean you came up with ideas on how to deal with her?"

Hudson didn't look at me as he took a bite of his fish. "I have something in the works," he said when he'd swallowed. "But I'd rather not talk about it, if you don't mind."

"Um, yes, I do mind. This affects me and I want to know what's going on." If he thought he was doing this on his own, he had another think coming.

"You know what you need to know. I've hired security, the new cameras are being installed at the club tomorrow, and I have some preliminary ideas to try to make Celia lose interest in her game." His entire demeanor was dismissive.

And my demeanor was getting pissed off. "Ideas that you aren't going to share?"

"No. I'm not."

I set my fork down, a little more forcefully than I'd intended. Or maybe exactly as forcefully as I'd intended. "Hudson—transparency, honesty—remember? Are you hiding something from me? Is it illegal?"

"No. And no. And you said you trusted me." He raised a brow. "Remember?"

"I do trust you. But we're supposed to be in this together and this is not together. This is you keeping me in the dark while you go play superhero. Or I assume you're playing superhero, because I don't really know."

He sighed and closed his eyes. When he opened them again, he looked at me directly. "We are in this together, Alayna. And I'll tell you. Just not now." He covered my hand with his own. "I'd rather spend my evening with you. Alone."

It hadn't occurred to me that he needed a rest from the subject. It was how he dealt with things—internally and on his own. We both needed to learn to work things out as a couple. But he'd said he'd tell me later. Maybe tonight I could let it go too.

I turned my palm up to lace my fingers through his. "Okay. No more talk of Celia."

We exchanged smiles. Then Hudson let go of my hand to continue his meal.

We sat in silence for several long minutes. Hudson finished most of his plate while I poked at my food, my appetite long gone. I could agree not to talk about Celia, but that didn't mean I could stop thinking about her. She'd penetrated so deeply into our relationship—did she realize that she consumed our thoughts? That our time together was now so intertwined with her that we were practically a threesome?

Hudson swirled his wine in his glass and watched me. "Now you're quiet."

I chuckled. "I don't know what else to talk about."

He ran his hand across his face and I knew he was thinking the same thoughts I'd been thinking—about how we couldn't even have a simple meal without Celia there. He opened his mouth to say something, and for a moment, I thought he was going to go ahead and let her win.

But then his face changed and he became resolved. "Well, let's see. I know how today went. What's on your agenda for tomorrow? You're interviewing Gwenyth, right?"

"Her name's Gwenyth? Hmm." That was the first time I'd heard her full name. And it bothered me. Hudson was not one to use nicknames.

"What's that supposed to mean?"

"Nothing." I was probably making a mountain out of a molehill. But I couldn't help myself from pursuing it. "I've heard you call her Gwen."

He shrugged. "That's what she goes by."

"You never call people by their nicknames." My irritation was showing.

And so was his. "Are you suggesting it means something that I use hers?"

"No." Why did this bother me so much? "I don't know." It was Celia. The mood had been set and now, even as we tried to move past it, we struggled.

It was my turn to sigh. "I'm just tense. I'm sorry."

"I know. I am too." Hudson took another swallow of his wine. "I don't know why I call her Gwen. I knew her as that first. I suppose it's in my brain now."

"You don't need to explain." But I was glad he had.

I took a sip from my own glass, trying to focus on something that wasn't going to piss either of us off. He'd asked about my agenda for the next day...*fuck*. I remembered something we needed to talk about. But it was definitely not going to be a pleasant conversation. Might as well get it over with.

"About tomorrow…" I began tentatively. "I do have plans I should tell you about."

"You better not be planning a run in Central Park. Your new bodyguard will tackle you down." His tone was light, but his eyes said he was serious.

"I said I wouldn't run outside. *Trust me* works both ways, you know. Do I get to meet this bodyguard? Is he also very attractive but unavailable because he's gay?"

Hudson smirked. "That's not even a little funny."

I knocked his knee playfully under the table. "It totally is and you know it."

"I'll introduce you on his shift tomorrow. He's not gay. And I trust you so I'm not worried about whether or not he's attractive."

"Good boy."

"Now what do you need to tell me?" He took a bite of his risotto and pinned his attention on me.

I paused, hating to destroy the lighter mood. "I'm, um, having lunch with Mira tomorrow. And Jack."

Hudson froze, his fork mid-air. "What did you say?"

The look on his face said he'd heard me fine. But I played along, trying to sound more confident the second time around. "I'm having lunch with your sister and father."

"Like hell you are." His eyes blazed with fury.

His reaction wasn't a surprise, but I fought not to get immediately defensive. "I'm guessing it's the Jack part that has you upset and not the Mira part."

His jaw twitched. "I'm not upset about any of it because you are not having lunch with my father."

With as much lightheartedness as I could muster, I said, "I'm not sure you can tell me what I am and am not doing."

"Oh, yes, I can."

I groaned, running my hands through my hair. "Hudson, this is ridiculous. I've told you before, I'm not Celia. I'm not going to sleep with your father—even if he comes on to me. Which he won't because your baby sister will be there."

He wiped his mouth with his napkin and tossed it on his plate. "Why do you even need to spend time with him?"

"I don't *need* to. I didn't plan to. Mira didn't want to be alone with him, and so I offered to be a buffer."

"She doesn't need a buffer. Cancel your date and have coffee with her later. Just Mira."

I considered for about half a second. Then I abandoned that and started to get angry. "I don't want to cancel. I want to have lunch with Mira. And Jack. I like him. Not because I'm into him, but because he's your father. And I don't have a father anymore and bonding with Jack makes me feel good." My voice cracked, but I kept on. "Maybe he's not a great replacement, but he's the closest thing I have. Plus, knowing him helps me feel closer to you. And when you keep things from me, H, I need all the access to you I can get."

"Alayna…"

Immediately I felt bad. "That last part was uncalled for. I'm sorry."

Hudson pushed his chair away from the table. Then he reached over and pulled me into his lap.

This was better. The tension that had hung thickly in the air began to dissipate.

He ran his hand up and down my arm. "I'm not keeping things from you, Alayna. Really, I'm not. I just want a night without…her."

"I know," I said, burrowing deeper into his chest.

"And please, don't use my father to get close to me. He's not the road to my heart."

"Where is the road to your heart?"

With one finger, he lifted my chin to meet his eyes. "Don't you know? You're the one who paved it."

I bit back tears, not wanting to spoil the moment with crying. "Don't think I'm going to cancel my lunch because you're being sweet."

He laughed. "Don't worry. I don't think that at all. Have lunch with him if that's what you want. At least I know you'll be safe from

Celia with him around. They aren't friendly anymore. And I wouldn't deny you something that makes you feel good."

Desperate to hold on to his lighter mood, I chose to respond playfully. "It's not your right to deny me anyway."

He pretended to sigh. "I hate that."

A rush of emotion swept through me. God, this man...he stopped his whole world to look out for me, to take care of me, and now he'd accepted my decision to meet with his father—a decision that had to be tearing him apart inside. Maybe he wasn't perfect, but he was pretty darn near.

I wrapped my arms around his neck and held on to him tight. "I love you."

"And that's why I'm letting you win this conversation."

I pulled back to meet his eyes, my brow raised. "*Letting* me?"

"Please, indulge me a little."

"How about this—" I shifted so I was straddling him. "How about we cease conversation altogether and indulge in an activity where we can both win?"

"Can we both win twice?"

"Honey, we can win three times if you're up for it."

The growing bulge beneath me told me what he thought about that before he even spoke. "Now that sounds like a plan."

***

Mira tapped her pursed lips with a French-manicured finger. "I just don't understand why he wouldn't tell you what he's planning. It makes no sense."

When I joined Mira for lunch the next day, I hadn't meant to tell her about Celia's stalking, but the words poured out the moment I'd seen her. If Jack had been there, I knew I wouldn't have shared as much, but his tardiness had me spilling everything, including Hudson's deflection when I'd asked him his ideas for dealing with the bitch. He'd had a valid reason for not giving me more information, but it continued to nag at me.

Perhaps I was being unfair. "Maybe he really didn't want to talk about it anymore. He just seemed more elusive than that." I opened a packet of pink stuff and stirred it into my iced tea.

Mira frowned. "You're afraid he's keeping something from you on purpose?"

"No." Though, I wasn't quite sure. "I don't know."

She shook her head, her hair bobbing against her shoulders with the movement. "I don't know either. I'm sorry."

Her apology took me by surprise. "Why are you sorry? You have no reason to be sorry."

"He's my brother." When she realized that didn't exactly explain anything, she went on. "I feel like I should understand him better, and I don't."

"No one does." Would anyone, ever? Sometimes I thought maybe I would, but really, could I?

"Are you ladies ready to order?" The waiter's question drew my eyes back to the menu I'd tossed aside. I still hadn't decided on a meal, having been too preoccupied with chatting.

The waiter saw my hesitancy. "Or would you prefer to wait for your other guest?"

Mira glanced at me. She already knew what she wanted to order. "We'll wait."

"Very good." The waiter left us to attend to his other tables.

I picked up my menu and scanned the lunch items. But my mind was still on the conversation at hand. I lowered the menu and leaned toward Mira. "Here's the thing—I'm afraid the real reason he won't tell me what he has planned is that he doesn't have anything planned."

"Wouldn't he just admit that?"

"No." There was no way Hudson would let me believe he didn't have complete control over the situation. "He wants me to feel safe."

Mira beamed. "Of course he does." There was never any doubt that the girl had faith in her brother. "Laynie, he'll come up with something. I know it. And whatever it is, he'll do a good job. He'll be committed and he'll go to great lengths. This is probably a horrible comparison, but look how devoted he was to keeping Celia's secret. All to protect her."

"He wasn't protecting Celia." Jack sat down in the chair between me and Mira. "Sorry, I'm late. Traffic. I didn't realize you were joining us, Laynie. What a nice surprise!"

Mira spoke before I could give my own greeting. "Are you suggesting Hudson was protecting you? Because that makes me sick." She roughly handed him her menu.

"Oh, I know what I want," he said, setting the menu to the side without acknowledging Mira's hostility. "He was protecting your mother. He didn't want her to get hurt from my infidelity."

Mira looked to me. "Still a valid comparison—Hudson will do far more for you than he'd do for Mom." Again, before I had a chance to speak, she turned back to her father. "And you say that as if it were unreasonable that she would be hurt."

"It's unreasonable that he cares." Jack circled his shoulders, probably trying to release the building tension.

Mira's jaw tightened—the same way her brother's tightened when he was upset. "Thank god he didn't inherit heartlessness from you."

"No, he inherited that from Sophia."

Her eyes widened. Leaning forward, she whispered harshly, "Would you just stop?"

My eyes danced from one to the other as they volleyed their attacks. So much for me being a buffer at the meal. Hudson was right—Mira definitely didn't need one.

Jack set his palms on the table and turned to face his daughter. "Mirabelle, I'm not heartless. You think it's cruel that I cheated on your mother. It was. It is. I'm not perfect."

Mira's eyes filled and I suddenly recognized her anger as pain.

"But you have to understand, sweetie, that Sophia is also culpable. She's not an easy woman to love."

Mira dabbed at a stray tear that had spilled over. "And do you love her, Daddy?"

Jack reached over to take Mira's hand in his. "Yes. I do. Of course, I do."

"Do you tell her?"

"Every day."

Mira smiled. But it was brief. She pulled her hand away from his. "Actions speak louder than words, you know."

I'd been silent, letting the father and daughter say the things they needed to say, while I sat feeling like a voyeur. But I couldn't let her last comment go by without reacting. "Sometimes."

Jack and Mira looked at me as if they'd just remembered I was there.

Or maybe they wanted clarification. I wasn't about to turn the meal into a Hudson-hasn't-said-he-loves-me conversation, so I simply said, "Sometimes it would be nice to have both."

The waiter's return saved me from saying more. Since everyone else knew what they wanted, I went last, settling on a Chef Salad.

"And can I get a Manhattan?" Jack asked before the waiter left.

"For lunch, Dad? Seriously?"

"Hey, I'm not the one with the drinking problem."

I braced myself for Mira's reaction. Generally, no one spoke about Sophia's alcoholism. I wasn't even sure if Mira acknowledged it or if she was in denial.

Her dark eyes didn't even flinch. "But you certainly facilitate it." Apparently, she wasn't in denial. "Can't you just have tea? Or water?"

"Oh for the love of Pete. Your mother isn't even here." Jack's eye twitched—another of Hudson's traits when he was upset. "Is it too tempting for you, my dear? Because it doesn't look like you've touched your water. I'm sure you'd rather have something stronger."

Mira folded her arms over her belly and huffed. "I don't care what you drink. I'm not thirsty. I'm saving room for my meal."

There was finally a break in their bickering, and I searched for a new topic to discuss, but before I could think of one, Jack did.

"Now what is this about Celia and Hudson?"

I cringed at the sound of their names together. Like they were a couple.

Mira's eyes lit up. "Can I tell him?"

"Oh my god, no." Though he'd never said so, I had a feeling Hudson preferred to keep his father out of his private life.

Mira had no such barriers. "I'm telling him." Without waiting for my consent, she told a condensed version of the story I'd told her—Celia following me, the notes in the books, Hudson trying to formulate a plan.

When she finished, I realized I was flushed. All the attention focused on me was embarrassing. "It's really not a big deal. I was overreacting to bring it up."

"No, you're not!"

Jack met my eyes, his expression tight. "Mira's right. Celia isn't a threat to take lightly."

"See that guy over there?" I pointed to a man sitting alone a few tables away. "He's my new bodyguard. Believe me, we aren't taking this lightly." Remembering this new addition to my life renewed my anxiety about the situation.

"Good. Hudson's taking her seriously. That makes me feel better."

Jack's concern wasn't helping me. "Why?"

He seemed surprised by the question. "I care about you, Laynie."

I stiffened, afraid of where his declaration was going.

If he noticed, it didn't stop him. "You're family now. You're an important part of Hudson's life and he—and I—would be devastated if anything happened to you."

"Thank you, Jack. I really appreciate that." Of course his affection was innocent. I kicked myself for momentarily thinking otherwise. And his words were an unexpected balm. "I care about you too." I darted my eyes to Mira. "All of you." Maybe not Sophia, but that didn't need to be said aloud.

I swallowed back the lump of emotion in my throat. "What I meant though, is why does Celia worry you? Why does she care so much about hurting me? She acts like a jealous lover. Were she and Hudson together?"

"No way," Mira said at the same time Jack said, "They were never together."

"But Hudson's so secretive. He might not have told either of you. You can't know for sure."

"I know for sure. There's no way he was with her." It wasn't the first time Mira had stated her opinion on the matter.

Jack agreed. "He's been disgusted with her ever since she seduced me."

Mira scowled. "*Seduced you*? As if you weren't part of it."

"Yes, I was part of it." Jack grinned devilishly. "But there are very few men who would turn down a naked woman in their bedroom, no matter what their marital status."

"Oh, I don't know. It's not unheard of." Paul Kresh came to mind. I'd been naked in his office once. All it earned me was an arrest.

The waiter delivered Jack's drink. Mira rolled her eyes but didn't comment on his beverage choice again.

When the waiter left, she asked, "If Hudson's so disgusted with Celia, why are they even friends?"

Her question was one I'd asked myself many times over the past few weeks. It never occurred to me that Jack might be the one with the answer.

He took a swallow of his drink and sat back in his chair. "Hudson blames himself for who she is now. He feels a sort of responsibility for her."

Mira's forehead twisted in confusion. "I don't get it. Why would he be responsible for who she is?"

Apparently Mira didn't know about the true history of Celia and Hudson—how he'd manipulated her into falling for him and then slept with her best friend. It was that betrayal that had driven her to sleep with Jack in the first place. As some sort of revenge.

Jack met my eyes, confirming he knew more than his daughter. "It's a long complicated story. If you want to know more, you're going to have to ask Hudson. Or Celia."

"Yeah, that's not happening." Using her spoon, Mira fished out an ice cube from her still full water glass and stuck it in her mouth. Surprisingly, she didn't pursue the *long complicated story* further.

While hearing from Jack had been insightful, my one haunting question remained unanswered. "Okay, they're friends and he's supported her and he's never been into her and she knows that—so why is she after us?"

Jack sighed. "Beats me. It's probably another one of her games. She's fond of them, you know. And she's good at them. I put nothing past her. She's a calculating, conniving woman, and she hates to lose."

"Great." I rubbed my hand across my forehead, trying to ease the headache that was quickly approaching. "How the hell are you supposed to get out of her grasp?"

"Let her think she's won."

Our meals arrived then, and the conversation turned lighter to talk of Mira's baby and her decision to not find out whether she was having a boy or a girl and what colors she was planning for the nursery. Despite the earlier tension between her and Jack, they settled into an easy groove, and I found myself more relaxed than I'd been in days. Lunch with the two was just what I'd needed.

When we were finished, Mira talked us into crème brûlée and coffee. We lingered over our dessert, enjoying each other's company. Finally, she shoved away her plate. "God, I'm stuffed. And I have to go to the bathroom. Again."

I'd gone with her the first time, but now I chose to stay behind, eager to get a few private words in with Jack. This would probably be my only opportunity, after all.

When Mira was out of earshot, I dove in. "Jack, I have a personal question for you, if you don't mind."

"About six and a half inches. But it's not size that matters; it's what you do with it." Hudson's dirty sense of humor obviously came from his father.

I rolled my eyes. "I'm serious."

He looked as if he might be preparing a comeback, but perhaps the glare on my face changed his mind. "Okay. Shoot."

"Sophia once told me that Hudson was a sociopath. Do you believe that too?" It was blunt perhaps, but I knew Mira would be back soon, and I didn't know how honest Jack would be with her around.

"Sophia's still claiming that bullshit?" Jack shook his head, his expression a combination of disgust and exhaustion. "*One* psychiatrist suggested it *one* time a handful of years ago. Hudson's never been clinically diagnosed as such, and no, I don't believe it. That boy cares. A lot. He just isn't always able to express it. Blame that on Sophia too."

I let out the breath I didn't know I'd been holding. No matter what Jack's answer, I already knew what Hudson was and wasn't. But hearing the details of Sophia's claim—and knowing his father didn't agree—was a relief.

But his words brought up another question, one that had plagued me from the moment I'd met Hudson's mother. "Why do you blame Sophia for his lack of expression? I don't think you mean just her drinking. What did she do to him?"

"Well, if I'm going to explain that then you're going to realize that I'm to blame too."

"I can handle that."

"But can I?" Jack considered a moment. Then he sighed. "Sophia wasn't always hard like she is now. When I married her she was refined and serious, but she could be fun. But then I started building Pierce Industries. I didn't have the money that Sophia came from. Her parents were convinced that she married beneath her. I wanted to prove them wrong, prove that I could be the man she should have married."

"And you did." Though Hudson had taken Pierce Industries to the top, it had been Jack that had built a solid foundation.

"I did. And Sophia wanted that too. But she hadn't expected how lonely it could be, being married to a man who was married to his work. She decided I was cheating long before I ever did."

His eyes glossed with sadness, or perhaps regret. "Not being around—that was my mistake. Her loneliness drove her to drinking. Alcohol made her more closed off. So it became a cycle—I wasn't around because of work and when I was around, I didn't want to be because my wife was a coldhearted bitch. I'd throw myself more into work, just to avoid her."

I hid my smile. If I'd had to live with Sophia, I'd have done the same thing.

Reading my mind, Jack winked, but his somber tone remained. "Eventually, she realized the one person I would come home for was Hudson. He was my son. My firstborn. I made time for him whenever I could." Jack's eyes beamed with a love that only existed between a father and his child.

It made my heart soar—I really did love this man who loved my man as much as I did.

Jack swirled his finger around the rim of his coffee cup. "Sophia used my son to get to me. She dangled him in front of me to get my attention and pulled him from me just as quickly. Hudson was always a smart kid. He learned pretty early on that his mother used him as bait. Poor guy got caught in the middle of so many games. It's no wonder he became good at them himself."

My chest ached, picturing Hudson as a little boy, only wanting to be loved by his parents, instead being used as a pawn. "Was it the same with Mira?"

"No. Hudson had already become Sophia's rival by the time Mira came along. Sometimes I think he fought his mother just to keep his sister out of her focus." This idea seemed to make Jack proud. "Now does that sound like the actions of a sociopath?"

"No. It doesn't. But I already knew he wasn't. He has too much love in him." Or was I just fooling myself? If he really loved me, why couldn't he say it?

I felt a presence come up behind me, and I turned, expecting to see Mira.

"What the fuck are you doing here with her?"

It wasn't Jack's daughter.

It was his wife.

Chapter Eight

Sophia's fingers clutched the back of my chair. "Celia wasn't enough? Now you have to steal this one from Hudson too?" Her voice was too loud, and people nearby were already starting to murmur.

Jack's face said he was as surprised by his wife's presence as I was. "Sophia. What are you doing here?"

"Spying on you, osbiviously." She meant obviously, but her words were slurred and hard to understand. I'd never seen her that way. Never seen her that intoxicated.

"You're drunk."

"That's illeverant. Irreverant." Sophia slumped into Mira's empty seat. "That doesn't matter."

"How did you even know to come looking for me here?"

Sophia smirked. "Mira. She told me she was having lunch with you. I decided to come to the lie. To see the lies. To hear your lies about me this time. Now the whole thing is a lie. You got your daughter covering for your cheating ass as well?"

"Mom?" This time the person behind me was who I was expecting.

Sophia reached for her daughter's hand with both of hers. "Mira! Look who I found your father with now. Hudson's new girl."

Mira glanced around at the onlookers as she patted her mother's hand. "Mom, Dad's not with Alayna. He's with me. I told you I'd be here. I was the one who invited Alayna." She spoke to Sophia like she was a child.

Memories of helping my own drunken father swam to the surface of my mind. Public situations were the worst. At home, Dad could scream and cry and make a fool of himself. We'd let him pass out in his mess and clean him up later. When there were others around, we had to be responsible and hope he wouldn't be completely humiliating.

Mira's expression said she was hoping pretty damn hard for the same.

"*You* invited this whore?"

Too late—Sophia had already crossed to embarrassing. Though her attacks on me were fairly routine.

"I did invite her. I didn't invite you. Why are you here?" Mira waited only a second before going on. "Never mind. Mom, you're drunk. We need to get you home. Did you take a cab to get here?"

"No."

"How did you get here?" Mira signaled to the waiter to bring our bill. It was admirable how take-charge she was. I guessed it was a role she was used to.

"Frank?" Sophia paused as if not sure that was the right answer. "Yes, Frank's outside somewhere."

"I'll call him." Jack was already pulling out his phone.

Mira bent down to her mother. "I'm going to walk you to the curb, okay?"

Jack stood. "No, Mira. Let me. Frank?" he spoke into his cell. "Sophia and I are ready to go home. Fine. We'll be out there." He pocketed his phone then moved to help Sophia stand.

"Did you drive yourself, Daddy?" Mira's words were mundane, but her eyes were filled with gratitude.

"Yeah, my car's with the valet."

Sophia fell against Jack. She was passing out.

Mira gently slapped her mother's face. "Mom, you're almost there. Hang on 'til you get to the car." When Sophia roused, Mira said to Jack, "I took a cab. I'll drive your car home for you."

He reached in his pocket and pulled out a valet ticket. "Thank you, babydoll."

Mira took the ticket and nodded. Then she collapsed in her chair.

I watched as Jack led Sophia out of the restaurant. There was love in the kind way he held her up, the way he supported her journey.

When I turned back to Mira, I found she was crying.

"Don't mind me." She waved at her face as if she could fan away her tears. "I cry at everything these days."

"I think this was a valid thing to cry over." I shifted in my chair. It wasn't that I was uncomfortable with Mira's emotion, but I wished I knew how to soothe her. The best I could come up with was putting a hand on her knee.

"Why? I should be used to this by now, shouldn't I?"

I didn't say anything. I knew she didn't really want an answer—she wanted someone to listen. As for myself, I'd never gotten used to it. But Mira was older than I was when my father died. I probably would have expected to be used to it by then too.

Mira looked out toward the restaurant entrance. Even though her parents were long gone, I knew she was picturing them there. "I just keep thinking, this is going to be the grandma to my baby. Do I want my child to be exposed to this?"

God, I'd never thought about that. If Hudson and I had a kid…

I shook the thought off. "I can't imagine what that must be like. I do know how hard it is to have an alcoholic parent—how embarrassing it is. Has she ever been to rehab?"

"No." She laughed, like it was an inside joke of some kind. "She won't even talk about it."

"Have you forced her to talk about it? Like an intervention? I'm not saying they're fun, or easy, but they can work. I've seen them work firsthand, actually."

"With your father?"

"No. No one ever staged an intervention for him. I regret it often. I wonder if things would be different if…" How many times had I wondered if my mother could have changed something? If his boss and his friends and Brian and I and our mother had sat him down and demanded change. Could that have saved his life? Saved my mother's life?

I'd never know the answer. "Anyway. That's the past. But I was talking about me." I cleared my throat, surprised that I was sharing something so personal with someone I admired. "I had an intervention pulled on me."

"What? When? For drinking?" My confession seemed to shock Mira out of crying.

"For obsessing over relationships, actually. I didn't have many people in my life that cared for me at the time, but I'd gotten arrested, and—"

"Wait a minute—for *obsessing*?"

I watched my hands wringing in my lap. "For stalking." I peeked up to see Mira open-mouthed. "I know. Embarrassing." I swallowed my humiliation and focused on the goal of sharing my story. "Anyway, my brother and a couple of friends I had back then that have since all abandoned me because I was a total shit to each and every one of them, well, they sat me down and convinced me to seek help. Honestly, I only went because if I didn't agree, it would have been jail time. But having them gathered like that—hearing that people cared what I did and what happened to me—it meant a lot."

Mira put a hand to her mouth. "Alayna, I didn't know." Her eyes glistened still from her tears, but I could see something else as well—not disgust, like I would have expected, but compassion. "You've hinted at a rocky past, but…I didn't know."

"Of course you didn't. Why would you?"

"I guess I wouldn't."

"My point in telling you is that I've learned through all my therapy that most addictions are really just a cry for love. And the crazy thing is that the more you're addicted to something, the harder it is to look up and see all the love there is around you. For the one outside, it can be tough to break through. But sometimes you *can* break through. As long as you're willing to try."

I watched the wheels turn in Mira's head as she processed all I'd said. But she didn't say anything else. And then the waiter was there, telling us that Jack had paid for our bill on the way out, and our lunch was over.

"Monday for your fitting?" Mira asked as we parted.

"Yep. I'm looking forward to it."

I pulled out my phone, ready to text for my ride when I saw Jordan waiting for me across the lobby. With my bodyguard in tow, I walked to meet my driver. "Jordan, is there something wrong?"

"Not exactly, Ms. Withers. But I wanted to warn you that Ms. Werner is outside. She's been here throughout your lunch."

"Fuck." So much for thinking bodyguards and Pierce family members would protect me from Celia. "What is she doing?"

"Nothing. Sitting on a bench down the street is all. She even waved at me."

"Yeah, she's a very friendly stalker, isn't she?" I chewed on my lip, thinking. "Did you tell Hudson?"

"I texted him, yes."

"Would you take me to him?"

"Of course."

Maybe Hudson would share his plans for my stalker now. I just hoped he actually had something in the works.

***

My new bodyguard, Reynold—who was only mildly attractive— insisted on coming with me into the Pierce Industries building. Having only had him around one morning, I hadn't yet gotten used to always having a shadow. Fortunately, Reynold was good at his job. He tailed me inconspicuously and made it easy for me to forget he was even there.

Reynold stayed in the lobby while I took the elevator up to Hudson's floor. As soon as I saw his secretary, I realized I hadn't called or texted ahead of time. I had a feeling my unannounced visits irritated her, but Hudson had never claimed to mind so I smiled and pretended my presence was no big

deal. "Hi, Trish. Could I possibly stick my head in to chat with Hudson for just a minute?"

Trish returned my smile. "I'm sorry, Ms. Withers, but Mr. Pierce isn't back from his lunch date." She seemed a little too happy to really be apologetic.

I glanced at the clock on the wall. It was after two. Still at lunch? "Oh. Okay. Thanks."

Disappointed, I pushed the elevator call button to go back down. While I waited for it to arrive, I pulled out my phone and texted Hudson that I'd stopped by.

I had just pushed send when the elevator doors opened. Standing there was Hudson. With Norma Anders.

Immediately I tensed. They were the only two people in the elevator—was that who Hudson had been on a lunch date with so late in the afternoon?

"Alayna. I didn't expect to see you here." Hudson didn't seem put off by my presence, at least.

"I almost missed you."

"I'm glad you didn't. Come with me into my office." He began to usher me toward his door. Then he stopped. "Norma—"

She cut him off. "I'll email you."

Hudson nodded. "Good. Thank you."

Norma took off down the hallway, I guessed to her own office. I hadn't realized she shared a floor with Hudson. I'd never thought about it, really, but now that I did, it bothered me how close they worked together.

Once the door was shut behind us, Hudson put his hands on my upper arms. "Why are you here? Did something happen?"

The original reason I'd come to see him seemed like nothing compared to how I now felt at the sight of him and Norma together. My blood was boiling and my stomach was knit tight. "I don't know—*did* something happen?" Jealous accusations had always been one of my fortes.

Hudson leaned back, confusion on his face. "What do you mean?"

I wrapped my arms around his neck, hoping I'd sound less bitchy if I was in his arms. Also, I was sniffing for women's perfume. "Let me rephrase—was Norma your lunch date?" The only scent I came up with was the usual Hudson smell that tended to set my pheromones on overdrive.

"More like lunch meeting, but yes."

I'd hoped the evidence had been misleading. "Did you dine with her alone?"

Hudson withdrew from my embrace and pinned me with a stern stare. "Alayna, keep this up and I'm going to have to put you over my knee. Except I know how much you like that." He bopped my nose with his finger and headed toward his desk.

His patronizing attitude made me all the more infuriated. "I don't like that you had lunch with her. Alone."

He shuffled some papers, his attention obviously elsewhere. "Well, I don't like who you had lunch with either, so we're even." Before I could react, he looked up at me. "And no, that's not why I had lunch with her. It was business. We're working on a deal and we needed to hammer out details."

Of course it was business. Did I have any reason in the world to think otherwise?

I didn't.

I still didn't like it.

I walked over to the other side of his desk. Memories of our last encounter here helped take the edge off my emotions, leaving me sounding less accusatory but whinier. "Did you have to do it in a social setting?"

Whinier seemed to work in my favor. Hudson's eyes softened, though his tone was still straightforward and aloof. "I chose a lunch meeting with you in mind, Alayna. Would you rather that we'd stayed in my office with the doors closed and no one around?"

With the lingering images of the things I'd done with Hudson in his office behind closed doors, the question made me a bit ill. I slumped into an armchair. "You are not helping the situation."

Hudson sat across from me. "You know that Norma is one of my key employees. My business frequently requires me to interact with her. In person. Sometimes, we're alone."

The explanation of his working relationship with Norma made sense. And sounded familiar. I decided to suggest a one-size-fits all solution. "Maybe you could transfer her."

"With what reason?"

"The same reason you transferred David." It was the exact same deal, after all. In reverse.

Hudson pinched the bridge of his nose. "While I understand your comparison of the situations, I'm not transferring Norma."

I stood with a shriek of frustration. "This is really unfair you know." I paced as I spoke. "I can't work with someone you don't trust but you can work with someone I don't trust? And since you're the big business owner in this situation, you were able to just take care of things with David, transfer him, and if he refused, fire him. What can I do? Nothing. I'm helpless." I paused my walking and shook a finger at him. "Norma has a big fat crush on you, Hudson. I can see in her eyes that she's not afraid to make a move."

Hudson jiggled his mouse and focused on his computer screen. "She is quite aware that I don't return her feelings."

"How does she…?" The only way she'd know that was if he'd told her and the only reason he'd tell her…"Has she already made a move?"

"Alayna, this conversation is going nowhere. I have appointments—"

"Hudson!"

With a deep sigh, he leaned back in his chair and met my eyes. "She's told me that she wishes there were more between us. If that counts as making a move, then yes, she's made a move. But, as I've said, I'm not interested. And she knows it."

I gritted my teeth to insure my next words didn't come out in a scream. "Can you explain how this is different than me working with David?"

He blinked. Twice. "I can't. You're right. It's not different."

"But that's all I get? You won't change it?" It wasn't going to be much of a victory if he answered the way I suspected he would.

"I can't lose Norma. She's too valuable to my company."

And that was what I'd expected he'd say.

I leaned on the back of the armchair. There was nothing to say. Nothing I could say. He agreed with my point but was unwilling to do anything about it. Now we were at an impasse. Our eyes locked on each other as we each silently refused to back down.

After several long seconds, Hudson swore under his breath and looked away. When he turned back, he asked, "Do you want David to stay?"

My heart flipped in my chest. "Would you let him if I said yes?"

His eye twitched. "If that's the only way to make this right, then I would."

A thrill of happiness ran through me.

Until I remembered all the reasons why David staying wasn't a good idea.

"Dammit, Hudson." I couldn't believe I was actually going to say what I was going to say next. "No. I don't want David to stay anymore." I refused to meet Hudson's eyes. "It wouldn't be good for him. He's…he's in love with me."

"I know."

I already knew Hudson knew. It was me that was just now admitting it.

I turned away from the desk and plopped myself down on his couch. Hudson came and sat down next to me. I rubbed my hand across his cheek. "Thank you for offering, though. I know that wasn't easy for you."

"No. It wasn't." He ran his fingers up and down my arm, leaving goose bumps in their wake. "But it would be worth it to make you happy."

Man, he'd grown up in the last few weeks. I had to give him that.

But maybe I hadn't, because I still wasn't quite ready to let the subject of Norma Anders go to rest. "Have you considered that maybe it's not good for Norma to work with you either?"

Hudson chuckled. "No, I haven't. And I'm sure it's not."

I shifted to face him. "Could we make some sort of concession here?" I took his hand in mine, playing with it as I talked. "Like, could you not have meetings alone with her? Is there anyone else on your team that could join you in the future?"

With his free hand, he brushed a piece of hair out of my face. "On the project we're currently working on—no. But it's almost done, and I don't expect that this level of secrecy would be necessary in the future."

And on top of their private meetings, they were sharing a secret. Fucking great. "What project are you working on?"

"Nothing you'd be interested in." Before I had a chance to scowl, he corrected himself. "I'm trying to purchase a company from someone who would never sell if they knew I was the purchaser. Norma's the only person I can trust not to leak the information."

"Fine." I hated that there was no way around their working relationship. *Hated it*. But what could I do? "Fine," I said again, more for me than him. "Social settings only, please. Where there are people around. And when this deal's over, you won't need private meetings with her anymore?"

"No. I won't."

"I'm going to still ask about her. Like, all the time. Because I can't just let it go."

He nodded. "I understand."

Though I was pleased that we'd worked through our argument constructively, the resolution was still a bitter pill to swallow. "Do you know how much this hurts to let you keep her employed?" I squeezed his hand hard, digging my fingernails into the back of his hand to accentuate my pain level.

Hudson narrowed his eyes, tolerating my assault. "Believe me, I do."

"Okay then. As long as we're clear." I released his hand.

"Was there another reason you stopped by?" He rubbed the back of his hand. "Or was Norma the intended subject all along?"

I laughed as I recalled the ridiculousness of my day. "No. I came by because I just wanted to see you. Lunch was…interesting…and then Celia was there again."

His brow shot up. "Celia was there?"

"Jordan said he texted you."

Hudson reached in his pants pocket and pulled out his phone. He flipped through a few screens. "Damn. I left my phone on silent. I didn't know. She didn't try anything?"

"Nope. Just let me know she was there."

"Alayna. I'm so sorry." He pulled me so I was half on his lap and wrapped his arms around me from behind.

I sighed, settling into the warmth of him.

Hudson kissed the top of my head. "Maybe you should take some time off. I could send you out of town. Would you like another week at my spa?"

I stretched my head to see if he was serious. He was. "I can't leave now. Not with everything at the club. And she'll know she scared me off. I can't let her have that victory."

"That's a very brave response. I just hate that you're in this position." He tightened his arms around my breasts.

It was then that I remembered my other reason for stopping by. "Do you have a plan to deal with her?"

He was silent for a beat. "I talked to my lawyer today," he said finally. "As you said, there's nothing we can do legally. But we're looking into some other options."

"Illegal options?"

"How about you let me handle this? I'll fill you in when everything's sorted out."

I didn't have the energy at the moment to push him. Besides, it seemed he really didn't have anything worked out at all, and forcing him to admit that would be unkind.

So I let it go. "You require an awful lot of trust these days."

He placed a light kiss at my temple. "Too much?" His voice was strained and his body tight—it was his turn to need my reassurance.

So I said, "No. I trust you." Though sometimes my trust was more of a work-in-progress. I turned to kiss his cheek. "I know you'll take care of me."

"Always." His lips met mine just as his intercom buzzed. He sighed against my mouth. "I'm sure that's Patricia letting me know my next appointment is here."

I stood and then offered my hand to help him up. "Guess my blowjob plans are shot to hell then."

His eyes darkened. "Maybe I could make them wait."

Laughing, I swatted at his shoulder. "Shut up. I didn't have blowjob plans. For all that I'm conceding to, I think I'm the one who deserves the sexual favors."

"Tonight."

"I'm holding you to it, H." I reached up to give him a final peck on the lips. "Meanwhile, you should know that I hate you a little."

"You do not. You love me."

I shrugged. "Same thing."

Hudson walked me out so he could welcome his next client in as I was leaving. I'd almost made it to the elevators when Trish called after me.

I walked back to her desk, wondering if she meant to scold me for keeping Hudson occupied.

"This was delivered for you while you were with Mr. Pierce." Trish handed me a simple white envelope with my name written in block letters on the outside.

It didn't occur to me that I should have given the envelope to my bodyguard until after I'd opened it and found the same business card that had been stuck in my books at home. *Celia Werner, Interior Design.*

The knot in my belly tightened. She'd been on foot when I'd left her at the restaurant. How could she possibly have followed me so quickly? Did she simply guess that I'd come here? Why hadn't Reynold seen her coming up in the lobby?

"Who gave you this?" I asked Trish, aware that my voice was more demanding than would be deemed polite.

"I don't know. A courier. I didn't pay attention."

"Was she blonde, blue-eyes—"

Trish cut me off. "It was a he."

That explained why Reynold hadn't seen Celia—she'd had someone else deliver it. As for knowing I was at Hudson's office, well, wasn't that predictable of me too?

I closed my eyes and took a deep breath. All she'd left was a silly business card. It didn't hurt me. It was meant to scare me, that's all. Meant to warn me that she was watching. That she knew how to get to me.

Resolving to *not* let her get to me, I opened my eyes. I quickly scrawled a note to Hudson on the white envelope and put the card back inside. "Thank you, Trish. When Hudson is free, can you give this to him?"

I really wanted to burst through his doors and show him personally. Then convince him that both of us should leave it all behind and go to his spa.

But that would be running away. And running away never solves anything. Or so, that's what everyone always says.

Forever With You

Chapter Nine

After I left Hudson's office, I decided to try to forget my tension by wrapping myself in work. I was successful for most of the afternoon, but the anxiousness and stress of the day lingered just under the surface. I had to be at the club to meet Gwen by eight and imagined it would be a late night. I longed for a run, but decided instead on a group therapy session. Thursdays weren't the day I usually went, but there was a session at six led by my favorite counselor. I could grab a bite to eat, hit the group, and be back in time to work that evening.

I shifted in my rusty folding chair in the Unity Church basement as I focused on listening to the others share. Most of the Thursday night regulars were strangers to me, and it seemed most of their addictions were hard to relate to mine. One person was a shopping addict. Another was addicted to social media. There was a gamer there too, a guy who was just as consumed with buying the latest system and game as he was with playing them. The only person that I felt even slightly connected to was the tattooed sex addict that I'd seen on other nights as well. I'd heard her speak before and recognized a lot of her same fears and frustrations as my own.

"Would you like to share anything, Laynie?"

I was more than a little surprised when the group leader called my name. Members weren't required to speak at each meeting—or ever, if they didn't feel comfortable—so it was odd for Lauren to call on me specifically. She knew me, though, having counseled me since the early days of my recovery. And if she couldn't tell from my demeanor that I had something on my mind, the fact that I'd shown up twice in one week had to be an indicator.

I gave the customary history of my illness and then paused. Since I hadn't planned on speaking, I wasn't quite sure what I wanted to say. After a breath, I said, "I've had some extra stressors in my life recently, and I'm here because I feel like it's causing me to backslide."

Lauren nodded, her long braids clicking with the movement. "Very concise identification of emotion, Laynie. Let's first talk about what kind of stressors you're dealing with. Is there anything you can eliminate?"

"Not really." I guess half of my stressors would be removed if I broke up with Hudson, but that wasn't an option I was willing to consider.

"And that's perfectly fine. Sometimes you can't eliminate stressors." Lauren turned her words to the whole group, using it as a teaching moment. "Most times you have to deal with them. Or we choose to deal with them because the reward is greater than the impact of the stress."

Boy, had she nailed it. "Yes. That's it."

"So what are these stressors?"

"Um." Now that I thought about it, I realized I'd had a lot in the last few weeks. "I recently moved in with my boyfriend." I didn't add that the relationship was still fairly new. At least not out loud. Internally, I marked it as another factor in my anxiety level.

"You have a new living situation." It was customary for the leader to acknowledge the information shared. "That's an adjustment."

"Yes. And I just took a huge promotion at my job."

The room buzzed as people shared congratulations. "Kudos to you," Lauren said. "But yes, another stressor."

"And my boyfriend..." How to bring up my current situation when I wasn't quite sure why I was in it in the first place was tricky. "He has baggage that I'm having some trouble dealing with."

Here Lauren took notice. "What kind of baggage?"

"Well, his ex—" Celia wasn't really his ex, but it was easier to call her that. "She's decided for whatever reason that it's her mission to destroy our relationship. She's been terrorizing us. Me, really. First, she accused me of harassing her—which I didn't do." I looked around at the other group members. "Honestly."

"Hey, no one's judging you here," Lauren reminded.

Which wasn't exactly true, because I was certainly judging myself. Admitting the next part was especially hard. I was about to complain about the thing people usually complained about me for. "And now she's harassing me. Following me places. Leaving me notes and things."

"Oh my god," the shopping addict exclaimed. "Have you been to the police?"

A few other people mumbled the same concern.

I shook my head, halting the talk. "She hasn't done anything worthy of reporting." I could go on about what was and wasn't worthy of reporting, but it wasn't relevant.

"That kind of harassment would be stressful to anyone." Lauren leaned toward me, her forearms braced on her thighs. "But I'm going to take a guess that it's been harder on you. Does it bring back emotions from your past?"

"Of course it does. I used to do these same things to other people. It's awful. It makes me feel awful." I'd been afraid I might cry, but surprisingly, the tears were absent. Perhaps, I was growing stronger or had become more reconciled with the situation.

With my emotions in control, I was able to delve further into analysis. "Also…I kind of feel like I deserve it now. Like it's my karma for the shit I pulled."

The red-haired sex addict piped up, "You know that's not how life works, right?"

"I guess." But hell, I didn't really know anything.

Lauren let us sit silently for a moment. She believed in a lot of quiet moments of reflection. They were often the worst and the best parts of the session.

I chewed on my lip as I processed. "Honestly, I know there are things that I need to work through in the area of self-worth. I'm journaling. I'm doing some meditation—yes, I need to do more. But really, those aren't the emotions that I'm concerned with."

"Okay," Lauren conceded, "as long as you recognize that you have some work to do there, we can move on. So you have these stressors—some of them good—that can't be eliminated. And you say they're causing you to backslide. How so?"

I ticked the list off on my fingers. "I'm agitated. I'm anxious. I'm paranoid. I'm accusatory."

"That sounds like me on my period." Again from the sex addict.

"Yeah, I call that being a woman." This came from the compulsive shopper.

I couldn't decide if they were attempting to relate or invalidating my feelings. Paranoid that I was, I assumed the latter. "You're saying these are normal emotions, and I need to just chill the fuck out."

"Maybe," sex addict said.

"Not necessarily." Lauren tapped her index fingers together. "They are normal emotions. But if they are impacting your daily life and relationships, then you need to deal with them."

"They aren't...yet. But only because I'm fighting them." At least I was trying. "The paranoia is the worst and it's unfounded. I'm suspicious of a woman my boyfriend works with. And I have no reason to be. Fortunately, he likes it when I'm jealous." I delivered the last part for the sex addict who winked in appreciation.

"Do you think you'd like to try medication?" Lauren preferred to stay away from drugs, but she always offered it as a solution.

I'd hated the numb zombie I'd become on the anti-anxiety pills I'd taken in the past. "No. No meds. I'd rather handle this on my own."

"Well, you know the drill."

"Yes. I do. Substitute behaviors." Though two of my go-to substitutes were running and reading—both had been compromised by Celia.

Lauren pointed a stern finger at me. "And communication. Make sure you talk through all the feelings you're having, no matter how unreasonable."

I tried not to roll my eyes. "That's why I'm here."

She smiled in a way that made me think she understood I'd felt patronized. "Being here is a great step, Laynie. Don't get me wrong. But it's not just us you need to talk to. Make sure you're communicating with your boyfriend too."

Communicating with Hudson...

God, I was trying. We were both trying. But if I really went there, really told him all the paranoia that lived inside, about the knot of dread that permanently occupied my belly—would he still be interested?

As she often did, Lauren addressed my unspoken concerns. "I know, it's scary. You're afraid other people can't deal with your thoughts and your feelings. And I can't promise that they can. But this is who you are. It's not going away. If you can't share who you are with the people who love you, then maybe they don't really love you."

That was the biggest question of all, wasn't it? Did Hudson truly love me? He'd shown me that he did, but he'd still never really said it. And I'd never really asked. Maybe there were still things left to be said—by both of us.

***

Gwen showed up to The Sky Launch fifteen minutes early, which would have been impressive if I wasn't running in just she arrived. And because of everything else on my mind, I felt off my game.

Fortunately David was there with me to help fill in the gaps as we walked through the club and talked about what role Gwen might fill.

It turned out Gwen Anders knew her stuff. At every turn she had appropriate questions and innovative ideas. She was no-nonsense, enthusiastic, and forward-thinking. Though most everything she said was right on, I inexplicably bristled a few times at her suggestions. Maybe because she was tough. Maybe because she challenged me. Maybe because I was on edge in general.

After the tour, Gwen helped us open for the night. Then we moved back to David's office to wrap things up. More accurately, *my* office, since David was leaving. Maybe *our* office if I decided Gwen would be the one to help me with The Sky Launch.

"So," Gwen began, "right now the club is open from nine p.m. to four a.m., Tuesday through Saturday?" Gwen and I were settled on the couch. David had pulled the desk chair around to make an easy conversational area.

"Right," David confirmed.

"But we're moving to expand the hours and be open seven days a week." That had been one of my goals since I'd gotten my promotion to assistant manager.

Gwen frowned. "That doesn't seem the best idea right now. Eventually perhaps. But right now you aren't filled to capacity when you are open."

I tried to hide my scowl. It was refreshing that she was so direct, but attacking one of my ideas so blatantly didn't sit well.

Apparently not noticing my reaction, Gwen went on. "Why would you extend your hours? First step is to bring more people in, fill the club, then expand."

David looked hesitantly to me. "There's actually some good reasoning in that, Laynie."

There *was* good reasoning. Still, did I want to work with someone who was always so forthright?

I wasn't sure.

124

"Expansion was your idea, wasn't it?" Gwen finally caught on. She shrugged. "I stand by my opinion."

She was good. Real good. "Gwen, I have a feeling we're either going to be very close friends or bitter enemies."

"Do you want this job, Gwen? Because I'd suggest the close friends angle and then you're a shoe-in." It was sort of cute how David tried to smooth the tension over. He'd never been one to like conflict. He was more of a people-pleaser.

"Oh, I don't know." Gwen crossed her long legs. "Alayna's a smart woman. She strikes me as the type to know the value in keeping your enemies close."

I narrowed my eyes. The last time I'd heard that phrase it had been from Celia. Keeping her close hadn't benefitted me at all. Of course, I hadn't been aware she was my enemy at the time, and I wasn't sure that Gwen was my enemy either. I just didn't know enough about the woman yet.

"Tell me something, Gwen." I put my elbow on the arm of the couch and propped my chin in my hand. "Why do you want to leave Eighty-Eighth Floor?" The question had crossed my mind before, but I hadn't gotten around to asking until just then. "You seem to be an integral part of that club's success, and, not that I wouldn't love to steal you away from them, but why would you let me?"

"Sometimes a woman just needs a change of scenery." She ran a hand over her leg, smoothing out her pantsuit with deliberate focus.

"I don't buy it." If she could be hard-nosed, so could I.

"Touché." She sighed then met my eyes. "Personal reasons. Forgive me for not being more forthcoming, but it really doesn't have any bearing on why I should or shouldn't be hired. My boss at Eighty-Eighth knows I want to leave. He'll give me a good reference. Other than that, I'd rather not share."

People and their damn secrets. I wondered if Hudson knew Gwen's reasons. I wondered if he'd tell me if I asked.

Then, paranoia snuck in, and I wondered if it wasn't the reasons she wanted to leave Eighty-Eighth Floor that were important, but the reasons she wanted to work at The Sky Launch. "It's not because of Hudson, is it? That you want to work here."

"I'm not sure what you're asking. If you mean, do I want to work here because this club is the only one in town owned by the powerful business exec Hudson Pierce who also runs the hottest restaurant in town—Fierce—and the hottest club in Atlantic City—Adora—then the answer is yes. I want to work here because Hudson Pierce has the power needed to make this place live up to its potential. The Sky Launch is one of the few places that could rival what Eighty-Eighth is."

Of course that's why she'd want to work here. What other reasons would there be?

I scolded myself for thinking the personal reason had to do with Hudson. *Trust.* I had to remember trust.

Blowing a piece of hair out of my eye, I made my decision. "Then you're hired. Not because you're my friend or my enemy but because you're exactly who I need. I reserve the right to pass judgment on you personally in the future."

Gwen smiled slightly. "Fair enough."

David stood and held out his hand. Gwen stood up to shake it. "Welcome aboard," he said. "Sorry I won't be here to watch you kick ass. Or kick Laynie's ass. Either way, I think you're going to knock her off her feet."

"Hey, now. I can kick ass, too." I stood and put my hands on my hips, feigning indignation.

The look on Gwen's face said she doubted my statement.

"What's that expression for? You can't doubt me. You don't even know me."

"No, I don't." She narrowed her eyes. "But you have to be lacking something—or you *think* you're lacking something. Otherwise, you wouldn't have come looking for me."

Maybe we'd be enemies then. "I just don't want to do it all alone." My voice came out meek and I regretted defending myself. I didn't owe her anything.

To make matters worse, Gwen pointed out my unnecessary words. "No need for explanations. All I need to know is when I start."

"You'll accept the position then?" I was already somewhat regretting my decision.

Gwen raised a brow. "You accept that I might be a bitch to work with?"

"For some crazy reason, yes, I do." We had to work together, after all. Not be friends.

"Then I'm all yours." This time her smile reached her eyes.

"Fantastic."

***

Hudson was asleep when I arrived home hours later. It was disappointing—not just because he'd promised sexual favors, but because, after therapy, I'd been eager to connect with him. I considered waking him, but a part of me couldn't help feeling like he might be avoiding me. There was no reason to believe that. Just that he rarely went to bed without me and my insecurities were on high alert.

Instead of giving in to them, I sat on the edge of the bed, closed my eyes and ran a few mantras through my head. The repetition settled me, but I longed for more. From his breathing pattern, I knew he was sound asleep behind me. Still, I was eager to start the communication that Lauren had suggested. Without bothering to undress, I stretched out next to him and ran my fingers through his sleep-tussled hair.

"I'm scared, H."

His breathing didn't alter.

"About lots of things. Little things. Mostly, I'm worried about Celia—that I'm not strong enough to not let her get to me. Especially because she's always been the girl that you should be with. In my head, she's the one I picture you with. Everyone does. She's perfect for you, from her manicured nails to her pedigreed upbringing. And, at the moment anyway, she doesn't have a police record." I smiled to myself, fantasizing about Celia pushing far enough that she'd possibly get a restraint against her.

Of course, she was a Werner. Her money and connections would never let that happen. I shared that fear with Hudson too.

It was so simple to tell him these things when he was sleeping. Not because it was difficult to talk to him when he was awake, but because his presence dominated so completely that I didn't feel the need. It was when I was away from him that my thoughts tortured me most.

"I believe in us, H. More than anything. But do you? You used to tell me you were incapable of love. Do you still believe that? Or do you love me as much as I believe you do?" He curled into me, but it seemed like a reflexive move, not a conscious one.

As he turned, his phone fell into my lap. He must have fallen asleep with it in his hand. Had he been waiting for my call? I'd texted around midnight saying I'd be late. Had he gotten that message?

Curious, I swiped his screen to unlock it. My text message had been marked unread—he must have fallen asleep before that. No wonder he hadn't texted back.

It was mostly accidental that I hit the recent calls button. At least, I told myself it was an accident. Immediately, the name on the last call caught my eye—*Norma Anders*. They'd talked for twenty-seven minutes, the call ending at nine-fourteen.

I reached over Hudson to put the phone on the nightstand then settled into his arms. He'd probably been talking to Norma about Gwen and her new position at the club, I told myself. Except Gwen hadn't left the club until ten. She hadn't made any calls or dismissed herself during that time, so Norma and Hudson couldn't have known I'd offered the job to Gwen at the time of the call.

And the thing that really didn't fit into the equation—why was Hudson the one who called Norma?

They work together. They were discussing business, of course. Because wasn't nine at night exactly the time that a typical executive talked to his female financial manager? On a cell phone? From his bed?

Chapter Ten

I woke up with Hudson's head between my thighs.

"Mmm." His breath along my folds sent chills down my spine. I peered down at him through half-open lids, wondering how he'd gotten me bare and spread without rousing me until now.

He caught my gaze. "You didn't wake me up last night." He licked along my seam. "And I owed you." His words were gravelly. I loved that I was the first person he spoke to most mornings—that his just-woke-up voice belonged to me.

And I loved what he was doing with his tongue.

I shivered as he caressed my clit with a long velvety stroke.

His head popped up suddenly. "Or would you rather I let you sleep?"

"No! Don't stop." I pushed him back down and stretched my arms above my head.

Hudson chuckled lightly. Then he attacked my nub with earnestness, in turns sucking and licking and swirling his tongue, exciting every nerve in my body. My insides clenched, and a trickle of moisture pooled in my channel. Overcome with pleasure, I wriggled underneath him, but his hands grasped under my thighs, keeping me still and at his mercy.

My breath came out in soft, jagged moans, and then in a gasp as his tongue moved lower, plunging into my hole. "Oh god, Hudson." My hands flew to his hair. Though I'd never dream to control his actions—he'd do a much better job than I would—I loved pulling and tugging at his strands while he drove me mad with oral attention. While he fucked me with his tongue.

Then his mouth was back at my clit, flicking and dancing along my tight ball of nerves, and it was his fingers inside me, rubbing along my wall, stroking me in just the right place.

"Fuck yeah, right there." My leg muscles tightened and my lower belly tensed as the pleasure built within me. The first wave of climax washed over me unexpectedly, much faster than I wanted it to.

"It's not enough," Hudson growled. "I need you quivering and out of your mind."

I couldn't argue if I wanted.

He renewed his assault with invigorated passion, adding a third finger, stretching and filling me with skilled strokes. He reached his other hand up to massage my breast through my clothes. I ached to feel him skin-on-skin but didn't want to interrupt his rhythm to undress. Instead, I arched into his kneading palm while my hips bucked under his artful ministrations.

Damn, I was soaring again, so soon. My legs shook, my knees knocking against Hudson's head as I tried to hold on. Then, with a half-sob, half-yelp, my orgasm burst through me. Stars shot across my vision and my entire body trembled while I came and came over Hudson's hand.

He fed on me while I settled, teasing my pussy until the last waves of my release shuddered through my system.

"You're welcome." Hudson was up and off the bed before I could regain thought process.

I reached after him. "Where are you going? I need to return the favor." Though my limbs were mush, and my mind already skirting the line between consciousness and post-orgasm coma.

"That wasn't part of the deal. And besides, as incredible as that sounds, I have an early meeting to get to." He leaned down and kissed me on the forehead. "What time did you get in last night?"

"Three-ish," I mumbled, still in a haze.

Hudson pulled the covers over me. "Go back to sleep, then. I'm sorry I woke you."

"I'm not."

I must have dozed because Hudson had already showered when I finally got up and padded into the bathroom. I yawned a, "nice view" as I passed Hudson shaving in a towel at his sink.

"You slept in your clothes."

"But I somehow seem to be missing my panties." I flashed my bare ass to remind him. "And yeah, I was too tired last night to get undressed."

He grinned. "You should have woken me. I would have helped."

"Nah, you looked so peaceful. I didn't want to disturb you."

"Trust me, it wouldn't have been disturbing. It's disturbing now because I can't have you the way I want you." His dark gaze met mine in the mirror. "I thought you were going back to sleep."

"I will. Nature called." And I wanted to see him. His phone call to Norma nagged at me, and, in an effort to take Lauren's advice, I thought I should communicate my feelings about it. Hell, even without Lauren's advice, I'd still be eager to confront him.

I started past him, figuring I'd talk to him when he was done in the bathroom. Or at least when he was dressed and the sight of his body with a measly towel around him wasn't such a distraction.

But Hudson reached his arm out and caught me. "Hey."

I could never resist his touch. I settled into his embrace, inhaling his just-washed smell.

He lowered a clean-shaven cheek to my head. "I missed you."

I smiled against his chest. "I missed you too." So much. Missed being in his arms, missed touching and cuddling, missed feeling like we were completely together and safe from the world.

My fingers trailed against his bare skin, and I felt the towel tent up between us.

"Christ." Hudson pushed me away with a reluctant groan. "I want you, but I really don't have time to deal with you properly this morning."

"I wasn't the one who woke me up." I sighed, recalling the good-morning delight. "Not that I'm complaining."

Hudson looked after me with clouded eyes. "Maybe I can be late."

"No, no. You be on time like a good businessman." I waggled a finger at him. "How about I follow you around while you get ready and we can just talk?"

"I'd like that. I've missed talking to you too." He returned his focus to the mirror, applying cream to the still unshaven cheek. "Oh, I got your note you left with Celia's business card. My lawyer said we should save anything we find like that. As potential evidence. So if you get anything else, let me know."

"Believe me, I'll tell you." I sat on the edge of the tub and braced both of my hands on the porcelain at either side of me. "There's nothing he suggests we can do about it, though?"

"No. Not yet." His tone was more serious than I liked. "Are you sure you don't want to leave town?"

"I'm sure." But I did think about it for half a second. Getting away had its appeal. But being apart from Hudson was the last thing I needed at the moment. Especially with all the women in his life that wanted me gone.

My thoughts flashed again to the name I'd seen on his call log. "Though I bet Norma wouldn't mind if I wasn't around."

"Norma again?" He grimaced. "What's brought her up?"

"You're going to laugh." Or he was going to be pissed off. Taking a deep breath, I let it spill. "You fell asleep with your phone and I checked to see if you had gotten my text. Then...oh god, don't hate me."

"What did you do?" His tone was curious.

I lowered my gaze. "I checked your recent calls. I saw you talked to Norma."

When I peeked up, I found he was smiling. "Let me guess—that bothers you?"

His amusement erased my hesitation. "You called her at eight-something at night. From your bed."

This time, he laughed. "Come here."

I didn't move, infuriated by his response.

He composed himself and turned to face me, holding his hand out as he had before. "Alayna, come here."

Sighing, I went to him. "I told you I was always going to ask about her."

"Yes, you did." Hudson wrapped his arms around my waist and settled his forehead against mine. "It was business. I needed to get some figures together for the meeting this morning, and the ones she'd sent me earlier in the day didn't add up."

"It was business," I repeated, relaxing into him. "Always business. Always the excuse." Asking him didn't really make a difference. I knew what he'd say. But it would nag at me whether I voiced it or not. Speaking up gave me the chance to hear his story stay the same, one of the bonuses of communicating.

I pulled my head back to see his face and found his grin was back. "Why are you smiling at me?"

"Because I adore it when you're jealous." He circled my nose with his. "You know this."

"Shut up. I hate it. I can't believe you like seeing me crazy."

"I like seeing that you care."

I didn't know if I should laugh or be concerned. Why would he need my reassurance? "I love you. You know that." Hadn't I proven that time and again?

"Yes, I know." He tightened his grip around me. "Your jealousy shows me your words are true. It's nice. Keep being jealous. Or crazy, if that's what you want to call it."

"You're so weird." I ducked away as he bent to kiss me. "You're going to get shaving cream all over me."

"I don't care." This time when he came toward me, I met his lips. He kissed me sweetly and tenderly, yet I could feel he was holding back, trying to not get carried away with his passion when he had a schedule to keep.

I wasn't on a schedule though, and I liked kissing him. I put my hands around his neck and pulled him closer, deeper, moving my tongue in further to play with his.

He had to push me away. "I can't have you this close anymore." He swatted my behind as I walked back toward my spot at the edge of the tub.

"I'm sorry I snooped." But I wasn't all that sorry. Not anymore. It had earned me a fabulous make-out session that I didn't regret in the least.

Hudson turned back to the mirror. "Don't be sorry. You know I have no secrets." He paused. "Well." He kept his eyes down as he washed his razor. "You know I don't care if you snoop."

My stomach dropped, as if I was coming down the hill of a roller coaster. "What do you mean by that?" I moistened my suddenly dry mouth. "Do you have secrets you aren't telling me about?"

Without looking up, he shook his head. "Of course not." He turned to face me. "I simply meant that we can never know everything about each other. Can we?"

"But we can try."

"Yes. We can try."

We sat a few seconds in awkward silence with him leaning against the back of the counter and I on the edge of the tub. There was something more beneath his statement. Something dark and heavy. I was both drawn to it and turned off all at once. Maybe he was referring to the details of the things he'd done to people in his past. I'd heard some of his stories—none of them pretty. I never expected he'd share each and every past guilt. It would be cruel to want him to relive his pain. I certainly hadn't told him every one of my past indiscretions.

But what if there was something else…something new, something present. Were there secrets that he kept from me that were relevant to us?

How could I ever know?

"Speaking of Norma—" He was the one to end the weirdness. "How did your interview with Gwenyth go?"

Talking business was the perfect escape from the worry that was edging into our pleasant morning. I jumped right in. "I offered her the job, and she accepted. She's leaving Eighty-Eighth Floor without notice. They knew she was trying to leave, it seems, so she's working today as her last shift there and will be at The Sky Launch tonight."

I hadn't realized how excited I was about having a partner until right then. Wow. I was going to be the manager of The Sky Launch. And I wouldn't fail because I had a good team—Hudson, Gwen, and a slew of other great assistants. Why hadn't I let this sink in before now?

"Congratulations!" Hudson caught my enthusiasm. "I'm glad you hit it off."

I thought back to the strange interaction Gwen and I had the night before. "I wouldn't say we hit it off, exactly. Challenged each other is more like it. But she'll be good for the club. Do you know why she wanted to leave Eighty-Eighth so quickly?"

"I don't." He turned back to the mirror and wiped off the remaining shaving cream from his neck with a face towel. "Did you ask her?"

I kept my eyes down and traced the floor's tile pattern with my big toe. "She said it was personal. I thought you might know more. Because of Norma." Was she the source of his secret?

"If Norma knows, she didn't share." He set down the towel and turned toward me. "Or if she shared, I wasn't paying any attention."

I grinned, somewhat mollified. "I like to hear that you don't always pay attention to Norma Anders." I slid my gaze over him. He was so hot. I didn't think I could ever get tired of how delicious his body was. And he was all mine. Wasn't he?

"Stop looking at me like that or I'll definitely be late."

I instantly longed for him to forget his meeting. He could stay and warm me up, fuck me good morning until the sun was high in the sky. There couldn't be room for doubts as long as he was in my arms.

But unfortunately, we couldn't live our lives in bed.

With strength I didn't know I possessed, I tore my eyes away. "Get dressed. It will help."

"Good plan." With an evil grin, he tossed his towel aside.

My eyes were glued to his naked behind until he disappeared into his closet. *Such a tease.*

While Hudson dressed, I undressed, trading the clothes I'd slept in for a t-shirt of Hudson's from the hamper. It smelled of him and I needed that—needed his presence to cling to me even as he was preparing to leave.

When he met me again in the bedroom, he was wearing one of my favorite suits—a dark gray Armani two-piece that intensified the color of his eyes. He looked sharp. Extra sharp. His meeting was obviously an important one.

"You look good."

He glanced at me in the mirror where he was straightening his tie. "Do I?"

"Mm-hmm." In one of my more passive-aggressive moves, I added, "I'm sure Norma will agree."

But though Hudson was good at games, he only played them when he was the one in control. His didn't say a word as he filled his pockets with his phone and wallet, didn't acknowledge if my guess was right.

Communication, I reminded myself. *This is who I am. I need to know.* "She will be there, won't she?"

Finally, he turned to me. "She will." In three quick strides he was at the bed, pulling me roughly to my knees. He wrapped his hand around the back of my neck, forcing my eyes to meet his. "And whether she thinks I look good in this suit or not is none of my concern. I only care that you'll be the one to take me out of it later tonight."

My breath caught. "Okay."

He brushed his nose down the side of mine. "You'll be home to undress me this time?"

I nodded. "I promise." I couldn't remember everything on my agenda for the day, but if there were a conflict, whatever it was, I'd rearrange it to be home.

"Good." He inhaled deeply and I sensed he was warring with himself. "I have to go. This meeting—"

"I know, I know. You're late."

He paused. "Kiss me goodbye?"

I moved in to give him a peck, not wanting to kindle any flames when he was running behind. But Hudson wouldn't settle for that. He plunged in between my lips, fucking my mouth with aggressive strokes of his tongue the way he'd fucked my pussy earlier. When he'd finished, I was breathless.

"That seemed a lot like a promise of some sort," I panted. "Whatever do you have up your sleeve, Mr. Pierce?"

"Now I can't give away all my secrets, can I?" He kissed my nose. "Going now. Get some rest. You're going to need it."

I climbed back into bed with the taste of him still on my lips and the smell of him on my clothes and the warmth of him in my heart.

***

I made it into the club around eleven. With David training Gwen on most of the night shifts, I was alone with my bodyguard for most of the afternoon. It made it easier to be productive, but it was also lonely. If Jordan had been on duty, I'd at least have someone to talk to. But it was Reynold, and he wasn't the chatty type. It was silly to have him while I was at work. Hudson's money, though, not mine. If he wanted to pay for the guy to sit outside my office and play Candy Crush on his iPhone, then so be it.

Around four, I decided to get some coffee at the shop nearby. Reynold was talking on the phone this time so rather than bother him with my plans I let him think I was going to the bathroom and slipped out the back door. Stepping into the light of day, I remembered how much I loved the outdoors. Sure, I preferred the earlier hours before the heat and humidity became sweltering, but if it weren't for my recently acquired stalker, I'd definitely be in the fresh air more often. *Damn, Celia.*

Thinking of her made a trickle of sweat bead at the back of my neck. Perhaps I should have brought Reynold along after all. Traffic rushed around the circle next to me. A cab was idling at the curb. A limo pulled up behind it. I was surrounded by people—why did I suddenly feel so anxious?

As if spawned by my anxiety, a strong arm wrapped around my waist, while another covered my mouth, stifling my scream. I was hoisted and pulled into the back of the limo and onto the lap of Hudson Pierce.

"What the fuck?" I scrambled to a sitting position, my heart beating at a rapid pace. "Hudson! You scared the shit out of me!"

"Where's your bodyguard?" he asked pointedly. "You on the sidewalk without him scared the shit out of me."

I scowled. "Terrifying me isn't any way to prove a point."

"It isn't?" He grinned, pulling me into his arms.

I struggled, still fuming about his prank, but I wasn't a match for him. He easily restrained me against his chest. Besides, in the end, I enjoyed being in his arms. "What are you doing here, anyway?" I nestled into him.

"I'm kidnapping you. Obviously." His hand slid up and down my bare leg, leaving gooseflesh in its wake.

I wrapped my arms around him and beamed. A night out with Hudson was exactly what I needed. "Awesome. Are you taking me to dinner or something?"

"Or something." With his elbow, he nudged the intercom on. "Let's go," he said, and the limo pulled out into traffic.

My concern for the unattended club outweighed my usual concern about riding without a seat belt. "Wait! I haven't locked up the club or anything."

Hudson tightened his hand around my waist, holding me in place, and moved a finger up to my lips to shush me. "I was talking to Reynold when you left. He's taking care of securing the building. Why were you sneaking away?"

I stuck my tongue out and licked the length of his finger, the salty taste lingering on my lips. He pulled it away with a stern look. It seemed he wanted answers before he was willing to play. "I wasn't sneaking away." Okay, maybe I was. "I was only running next door for coffee. No big deal." The crease in his forehead said that he didn't agree with my assessment of the situation. "All right, I won't do it again." I leaned up and pecked him on the lips. "So seriously, where are you taking me?"

He smiled mischievously. "I said I wanted you out of town."

"What?" I bolted upright, straining against his hold. "I can't leave town, H. I work tomorrow night. And I don't want to leave town. We talked about this."

He grabbed my wrists and held them as if he feared I would push the intercom and ask the limo driver to stop. Which I was considering.

"Settle down, precious." He pulled my hands up to his mouth and placed a kiss on each one. "I simply thought a weekend away might be good for us."

"Both of us?" I'd been very much opposed to the idea of running away, but a weekend away with Hudson was an altogether different idea. Sweet. Romantic.

"Yes, both of us. I'd send you away if you'd let me, but I'm glad you won't because I can't bear to be away from you." He circled my nose with his before settling a kiss on the tip of mine. "I arranged for David and Gwen to cover The Sky Launch tomorrow. We'll be back Sunday night."

"I'm the main manager now. I can't just take off whenever I want." There wasn't any fight in my protest though. I was only pointing out the facts so that I wouldn't feel guilty.

Hudson had no such guilt. "I'm the owner. Yes, you can."

"I feel like I should be irritated at you about this." I grinned. "But I'm not. Thank you. I'd love to be away with you for the weekend."

"I think you need it. *We* need it."

"You've never been more right. And that's saying something since you're right an awful lot. But don't let it go to your head." I wriggled out of his arms, eager to get into my own seat where I could buckle up.

I snuggled as close to him as I could with my belt on. "Where are we going? Are we stopping at the penthouse so I can pack some clothes or did you take care of that, too?" Knowing him, he probably did.

"You'll see when we get there." He fastened his own belt, likely for my benefit, then threw his arm around my shoulder. "And precious," he whispered at my ear, "you aren't going to be needing any clothes."

***

"Wake up, precious. We're here."

I must have fallen asleep leaning against Hudson, because the next thing I knew, we were stopped and he was gently nudging me.

I blinked several times, letting my eyes adjust to the light. "Where's here?" I yawned.

"Come on out and see." He tugged me out of the limo.

We were by a log cabin surrounded by lush green woods. A line of wildflowers bordered the stone walkway, butterflies dancing from blossom to blossom. The blue sky was clear and free from smog. Birds sang and a pair of chipmunks scurried up a tree nearby. A little way beyond the house, I could see a lake. The scene was so remote, and the limo and Hudson's two-piece attire were out-of-place. It completely satisfied the yearning for nature that I'd been experiencing.

"The Poconos?" I guessed. He nodded, his eyes watching mine as I took in the beauty. It was perfect. "It's absolutely gorgeous."

Hudson's face relaxed into a smile. He turned to the driver of the limo who was unloading a small suitcase from the trunk of the car. "Seven p.m. on Sunday."

"Yes, sir."

I watched as the driver got back in the car and drove off, leaving us alone in what I was calling paradise. Hudson picked up the suitcase with one hand and took my hand in the other, leading me to the door of the cabin.

I gestured toward the luggage. "I don't need clothes, but you do?"

He laughed. "It's essentials. For both of us. I assure you, if you're naked, I will be as well."

At the door, Hudson pulled a key from his pocket. "This cabin's been in our family for years," he offered before I could ask. "We have a hired manager that opens the place up once a week to keep it from getting musty. Other than that, Adam and Mira are the only ones who come up here on a regular basis. I thought it was time to get my own use out of the property."

"As I said before, H, good thinking."

He opened the door and swept his hand for me to go in first. The interior was as perfect as the outside. The design was rustic and homey—not typical of the Pierce's usual gravitation toward luxurious spaces. I could see why it wasn't a place that Sophia would hang out, or even Jack for that matter. The front room had large comfy sofas and leather armchairs. Two log columns separated the space. A stone fireplace broke up the floor to ceiling windows that overlooked the deck and the lake beyond. It was peaceful and breathtaking.

And we were alone—no coworkers with crushes, no bodyguards, no crazy stalkers. Completely alone.

I heard the click of the door and Hudson came up behind me. I felt it then—the crackle of energy that always existed between us. It kicked up to a high buzz, as if someone had just turned on a switch, and all my lingering fatigue and anxiety instantly left me, replaced with an intense, immediate need for him.

It wasn't just me that felt it. In one swift movement, Hudson had me turned around, one hand on my ass, the other pinning both of mine behind my back as he kissed me frantically. Mercilessly. His tongue tangled with mine, twisting in a dance that was new and consuming. He backed me up as he held his lock on me, leading me somewhere, leading me I-didn't-care-where. The only place I wanted to be was in his arms, in his mouth, in this bubble of frozen space and time that only contained me and him.

God, I was lost—Hudson's lips sent me spiraling into a haze of lust and desire. Then his hands were under my bodycon dress, gathering the material and shimmying it up my thighs and up over my breasts, over my head until I was free from the garment. He tossed it aside and pushed me against one of the log pillars. Again, he pinned my hands, this time over my head. His other hand stroked my skin at my hip. He broke away from my lips and lowered his mouth to my breast. He nipped through my bra, sending an electric shock through my body. The rough wood against my back, his teeth biting my sensitive flesh—it was a mix of such strong sensations, sending my nerves into full alert.

His fingers trailed along the skin at the top of my panties, then slipped inside to find my clit, already swollen and wanting. His hand slid lower through my folds. "Ah, you're so wet. I want to lick your lips clean. But I want to be inside you."

"Hudson." I wriggled against the post. "I need. My hands." I couldn't speak in full sentences. "Need to touch you. Need you naked."

His mouth returned to mine. He bit my lower lip and followed it with a soothing suck. Then he let my arms free. "Okay," he said.

He shrugged out of his jacket while I began on the buttons of his shirt. My hands worked so frantically, so urgently, that I popped a button. I paused. "Whoops."

With a groan, Hudson pulled at the material, popping all the remaining buttons. It was impressive. And hot. My hands flew to his chest. I pressed my palms along the smooth planes and down over the ridges of his abs. His skin felt like fire, the solidness of his flesh such a stark contrast to the softness of mine.

As I explored his torso, he explored mine. He pushed the cups of my bra down and plumped my breasts with strong, sturdy hands. My nipples stood at avid attention. A brush of his thumbs across them set my knees to buckle and my thighs to press together.

With another groan, Hudson let go of me and took a step back. "Fuck, you're so gorgeous like that. Your breasts standing up for me. Your legs begging for me to push my way between them."

I moved toward him, unable to bear the absence of his heat. As I reached him, though, he surprised me by picking me up and throwing me over his shoulder. "Time for a change of scenery," he said.

He spoke as we walked. "Mini tour. Kitchen's there. Bathroom. And here's the master bedroom."

I craned my neck to peek at each of the rooms as we passed, not really caring about them, but curious as to our destination. In the master, he plopped me onto the bed. "Though I plan to mark you in every room of this house, we'll be spending most of our time here."

I wasn't even tempted to glance around. I sat, propped on my elbows behind me with my eyes pinned on him while he undid his belt and pushed off his pants. His hard, thick cock poked from the top of his briefs. My mouth watered as I waited for him to take them off, too.

But he didn't. Not yet. "Turn around," he ordered.

I rolled to my stomach, my body obeying before my head could register his command.

"Up. On your hands and knees."

God, when he got dominant, I got insane. My limbs shook with anticipation as I pushed up to my knees, my head away from him. With his hands clutched at my hips, he tugged me to the edge of the bed and pulled my panties down until they were at my knees. He leaned over my body and undid my bra. The straps fell down around my elbows. I left it there, not wanting to move, enjoying the feel of his body pressed against my backside. His bare cock poked against my ass—he must have removed his underwear while I turned around. Instinctively, I spread my knees as far as my panties would allow them.

Hudson squeezed my breasts and slipped his cock between my legs, rubbing his hard length against my pussy. I moaned as he knocked against my clit, each jab sending me higher and higher. Yet he wasn't where I really wanted him—not yet.

"Hudson." It was half plea, half cry. "Please. I need you."

He continued rocking against my folds. "I know, precious. I know what you need."

And yet he wouldn't give it. I squirmed against his cock pulsing between my legs. "Need you. Inside."

"Say it again and I'll make you wait even longer."

"Please, Hudson." I couldn't help myself. The words tumbled out without my permission.

He pulled off of me. "I told you not to ask again." He slapped my ass. Hard.

A trickle of moisture pooled between my legs. He slapped me again on the other cheek, and I cried out from the pleasant sting. He rubbed away the burn with wide circular passes of his palms. If he spanked me again I thought I just might come right there.

But he didn't. His hands left me. My body shuddered from the absence of his warmth and the jolt of the strikes and the unease of not knowing what would happen next.

Then suddenly he was where I wanted him, inside me—not his cock, but his tongue. I cried out at the sweetness of it. I looked down between my legs and found his face there, his mouth poised over my hole as he plunged in and out with long, velvety strokes. His fingers came up to swirl across my clit. I squirmed, absolutely in love with what he was doing to me, at the same time desperate for him to fill me with his erection instead.

The torment drove me mad. It also made me come, hard and fast, a breathy cry escaping from my lips. I was still coming when he—*finally*—entered me. He thrust in, grunting as he pushed through the clenching of my orgasm. "Ah, Jesus, you're so goddammed tight."

Quickly he pulled himself out to the tip and bore into me again. I loosened around him as I settled down. He dug his fingers into my hips and hammered into me, pulling my whole body to his with each drive. My hands curled into the bedspread, another orgasm already beginning to gather in my belly like a storm.

With a frenetic pace, he continued to drill into me. "I. Can't. Get. Deep. Enough," he grunted a word in between each thrust. "I need. To be. Deeper."

Fuck, he was already so deep, each merciless jab hitting me in just the right place. Every exhale was a whimper, my hands and knees shaking as he assaulted me with enormous jolts of pleasure.

He withdrew again to his tip and paused as he flipped me to my back. Pushing my knees back into the bed, he leaned into me and resumed pounding into me with a fevered pace. "Come with me, precious." It wasn't a request. He meant for me to obey. "I'm going to go soon. Tell me you're coming with me."

"Yes," I panted. "Yes. Yes."

"Good." He pushed on the underside of my thighs, tilting my hips up, and bucked into me, hard and deep. Deeper than he'd ever been; I'd swear he'd never been that far inside of me. My orgasm began surging through me. "Wait, Alayna."

I widened my eyes, gasping in shallow breaths as I tried to hold on.

"Wait. Wait. Wait." His command matched the rhythm of his thrusts. "Wait." Then, "Now!"

At his permission, I succumbed to the force that had built inside, letting it rip through me with lightning speed. My pussy clenched around his cock as Hudson pressed into me with a long, deep drive. "Fuuuccck!" He elongated the word as he knocked against my pelvis, spilling into me fiercely.

He collapsed onto the bed next to me, his chest rising and falling in tandem with my own. "Well," he said after a few minutes. "That was…"

Holy, wow, I thought.

Hudson finished the sentence, stealing one of my other favorite terms. "…amazeballs."

***

We spent the evening in the bedroom, only leaving to make sandwiches from the supplies that the property manager had dropped off before we'd arrived. We made love late into the night and woke with a morning round as well.

Though we were in the middle of nowhere, I discovered we still had wi-fi. It was almost a disappointment—part of the beauty of the cabin was the remoteness of it. Yet it was nice for listening to music. After a breakfast of yogurt and fresh berries, I set up Spotify on Hudson's laptop, logging in as me, and turned on one of my favorite playlists. We lounged naked on the sofa, my head at one end, his at the other while he massaged my feet.

Phillip Phillip's *So Easy* came on. I hummed along for a bit, occasionally singing some of the words.

Hudson watched me with admiration. "You have a nice voice."

I blushed. It was funny to realize that I hadn't ever sung in front of him. Oh, the firsts we still had between us. Since I was already embarrassed, I admitted, "This song makes me think of you."

His nose wrinkled in surprise. "You have a song that makes you think of me?"

"Several. A whole soundtrack." We were listening to the playlist I had titled *H*, after all.

"Hmm. I didn't know that." He tilted his head and I could tell he was trying to catch the words.

I sang along, helping him hear the important parts, getting louder at the chorus where Phillip sang about making it so easy to fall so hard.

It was Hudson's turn to be embarrassed. He looked down at his hands working the sole of my foot, a small smile playing at his lips. The song ended, and he moved to my other foot. "How about a shower?"

I stretched my arms over my head and pointed my toes, noting the soreness of muscles that I didn't even know I had. "Yes. Definitely." A hot shower sounded good. But I didn't make a move to get up. Not moving sounded good too.

"Do you have any specific plans for the day? Besides the shower."

I groaned as his thumb worked at the knot in the ball of my foot. "You have me kidnapped in the mountains—I think I'm kind of at your mercy."

"That you are. In which case, I was thinking I'd like to spend the day inside you as much as possible."

I grinned. "I'm totally okay with that. Anything else you have planned?"

"I'd like to take you for a walk around the property. And perhaps some online jewelry shopping. I believe a new necklace or earrings for Mira's event might be nice."

Instead of automatically arguing about the idea of a gift like I usually did, I weighed the idea in my head. "That might not be bad. I don't have anything nice, and I have been through the wringer lately. Maybe I deserve a present of some sort." I smiled coyly.

"Alayna!" Hudson exclaimed. "I've never heard you care about any of that before."

I stared at my hands and shrugged, wishing I hadn't said anything.

Hudson abandoned my feet, crawled up to my face, and covered my body with his. "I'm very pleased. And a whole lot aroused."

Well, he was somewhat aroused. The new position made it evident.

"Why does my acting like a greedy bitch turn you on?"

"Because I love giving you things. It's something that I'm good at. I wish I could give you more but you never seem interested." He ran his fingers through my hair. "So anything you want, I'll give it to you. A shopping spree? A week in Nevis? A car?"

I rolled my eyes and tried to push him off of me. "You're making fun of me now."

He held his ground, both physically and conversationally. "I'm dead serious. Do you want me to buy you a company? Or an island?"

"Stop it."

"No. I won't." He tilted my chin up to meet his eyes. "Anything you want, Alayna. It's yours. And since you don't seem to know that, I'll have to work even harder to make sure you take advantage of my wealth."

Again, I tried to push him away. "I don't want or need to take advantage—"

"Now stop." He moved his hand to caress my cheek. "I know you don't. You never have. But I've told you before that you own me. Whether you take advantage of it or not, I'm yours."

I started to protest again, but he continued. "And thereby, all I own is yours." He met my eyes with stone-cold sincerity. "There are contracts that can guarantee that, you know."

I swallowed. Gulped, actually. The kind of contracts he was talking about…joint ownership…those were hints at wedding bells if I'd ever heard them. Petrified and a little bit thrilled, I tested the waters. "That's some pretty serious stuff you're implying."

"I'll do more than imply if you let me." His voice was quiet but genuine.

My heart pounded in my chest. He couldn't say I love you, but he could promise me the moon? He got intimidated when I expressed my feelings through a song, but he could offer a lifetime?

We weren't ready for that. I wasn't. He wasn't, even if he thought he was. "I think I'll just take a nice piece of jewelry for now," I whispered.

I waited with bated breath for his response, hoping I hadn't hurt his feelings.

It took a second, but he smiled. "Then it's yours."

Wanting to lighten the mood more, I added, "Also, some more books. And did you really say a car?"

He shook his head in disbelief. "You don't want a car. You don't like to drive."

It was true that I wasn't fond of being behind the wheel of a car. But there were other places that driving occurred. "No, I like to drive. You just never let me."

He narrowed his eyes. "You're not talking about cars anymore, are you?"

"Nope." I reached my hand down to circle his cock that was still semi-aroused. I stroked him, once, twice.

He groaned and flipped me so that I was on top of him. "How about you drive right now?"

I straddled him, positioned myself over his cock and slid down. "It kind of seems like I already am."

Chapter Eleven

We returned to the city Sunday evening, rested and deliciously sore. At least, I was. I was also more excited than ever about our relationship. Still, as eager as I was to get back to our home and our lives, a sadness accompanied our arrival. Hudson and I had made great strides at connecting while we were alone. Could we hold onto our progress back in the real world?

I worried that the answer was no. Especially when, after setting the suitcase in our bedroom, Hudson headed straight to the library to get some work done. I was asleep when he went to bed, and he didn't wake me. Just like that, our vacation was over and we were back to life.

The next morning, I woke before Hudson left for the day. I sat up against the headboard, watching him as he laced his belt through his slacks. "I'm glad I caught you."

He lifted a brow. "You caught me? I was under the impression that I'd caught you."

I tossed a pillow at him. "I mean right now. I'm glad I caught you before you left."

He put his jacket on and turned to give me his full attention. "Why? Do you need to talk to me?"

"I don't *need* to. My days are just better when they start off seeing you."

His lips slid into a smile. He came to the bed, placing one knee into the mattress and pulling me into him. "I feel the same way. Completely."

I wrapped my arms around his neck and played with the hair at the back of his neck. "Let's try to make sure we start it that way more often, okay? And when we go to bed, the same thing."

He leaned his forehead into mine. "I didn't want to wake you, precious."

"We never want to wake each other. Let's get over that. I'd rather lose sleep than lose what I have with you. And sometimes I feel like with our work and day-to-day lives, we slip away from each other. This weekend reminded me how good it feels to be the center of your world."

His expression grew warm. "You're always the center of my world."

I melted. Would he always be able to make me feel this good? I had a feeling the answer was yes. As long as he took the time to tell me. As long as I took the time to listen. "Well, then wake me up and tell me that before you go from now on."

"Done." He captured my mouth, kissing me sweetly. "You're the center of my world, precious. Every minute of every day. Even when I'm not with you." He brushed his lips against mine. *"You make it so easy to fall so hard."*

He remembered the words of the song I sang him! My heart flipped in my chest and my eyes grew misty. I clutched onto him. "God, I love you."

He lingered another moment, his gaze fixed on mine.

A rush of...*something*...swept through my body. It was impossible to pinpoint the exact emotion, and I suspected it was a combination of a whole lot of stuff—melancholy and lust and love and adoration.

But, even with all the good stuff, under all that, there was a steady pulse of dread.

He narrowed his eyes, studying me. "What is it, precious?"

"I don't know." How could I explain this unwarranted feeling that the beautiful thing we had was right on the edge of shattering? I brushed my hand across his cheek. "Sometimes, when you go, I'm left feeling off kilter."

"Trust me, precious, the feeling is mutual."

I thought about his response long after he'd left, wondering what he'd meant. Maybe he hadn't realized that my statement wasn't exactly a compliment.

Or maybe I had him just as off balance as he had me.

***

Mira tugged at the waistband of the blue floral A-line I was wearing. I couldn't see myself in the mirror from where I was standing in the dressing room, but from what I could see, it looked pretty damn good.

"Turn," she demanded.

I spun half-heartedly. I was tired of spinning, frankly. It was nearly three and after trying on dozens of outfits, we still hadn't found the perfect one for her reopening. Scratch that. *Mira* hadn't found the perfect outfit. I'd found several.

"Hmm." She studied me with narrow eyes. "I love this one, but it's not as good on you as I thought it would be."

I swallowed back my sigh. "Maybe I'm not a very good model." I suddenly had a ton of appreciation for those who modeled for a living. I loved clothes. I loved trying new clothes on. I did not, it turned out, love being poked and prodded and scrutinized by a feisty fashion expert.

Mira shook her head. "That's the thing. You're too gorgeous and this dress dulls you."

Dulls me? That was a new one.

"There's too much material," she went on. "It's like I'm trying to hide beauty."

"Whatever."

"There's got to be something else." She rifled through the dresses on the rack that I had yet to try on, which was not many. "All of these have the same problem. We need a perfect balance between the dress and you. We need one that shows more skin."

"Don't make it too skimpy or Hudson will kill you. Or me. Or both of us." Thoughts of Hudson were never far away when I was in Mira's shop. We'd had amazing sex right in that very dressing room— my hands pressed against the mirror, his cock thrusting in from behind—

"Hudson can bite my ass."

Leave it to Mira to bring me back to reality. Sharply. Except now I was thinking about Hudson biting my ass…

Mira pulled a dress from the rack, looking it over. "Did you figure out if Hudson has any plans for Celia?"

"Unfortunately, I think he doesn't." That was what my heart was truly telling me. It was probably also why he wanted me out of town. "And did you see Celia was there at the restaurant last week?"

Mira whipped toward me. "Oh my god! She was? I didn't see her. With Mom and everything, I guess I was distracted. Did she say anything to you?"

"Nope." She'd skirted past the Sophia incident, so I took that as a sign she didn't really want to talk about it.

"Thank goodness for that." She turned to put the dress back in its place and began shuffling through the outfits we'd already been through. "I can't believe she has time to dedicate to that. I mean, she doesn't need the money, but she has a job. Does she just ignore her clients?"

I'd actually lost jobs in the past due to my own obsessions. But for once, I didn't want to compare. I decided to go for a lighter approach. "I know, right? Maybe she pays an assistant to do all her work."

Mira laughed. "Or she canceled all her projects this month."

"And put up a sign in her office that says: *Closed for Stalking*." We were both laughing now. The release felt good. It broke the ever-present tension sort of in the same way sex did. If I couldn't spend all my days in bed, I definitely should spend more of it laughing.

"Well, at least we can find the humor." Mira moved behind me, apparently giving up on the clothes rack. "But there's no humor in this horrid dress. Let's get you out of this lousy thing." She loosened the ties that threaded across my back, then started removing the pins she'd put in to tighten the dress at my waist.

There was a tap at the dressing room door. Stacy entered without waiting for an invitation. "Here's some for that one." She handed a pair of cherry red heels toward her boss.

I hadn't seen much of Stacy that afternoon. She'd stayed relatively busy with another customer, but as soon as she was finished, she had popped her head in. Mira had sent her on errand after errand, asking for a different bra, another box of pins, and so on.

But even just seeing her sporadically, it was enough to send my mind back to the video she'd offered to show me. I'd told Hudson I didn't need to see it—and I didn't—but that didn't stop me from being slightly curious. Okay, more than slightly.

Mira waved the shoes away. "We're scrapping this one. It's not quite right." Her eyes lit up. "You know what? We should try the Furstenberg piece. The new one. What do you think, Stacy?"

Stacy tilted her head and examined me, perhaps trying to picture me in the dress they were talking about. "It would look great with her skin tone. And the fit is meant to accentuate the bust line, which works with her body type. Is it still in the backroom?"

"Yes."

Stacy turned to leave.

"No, wait." Mira stopped her. "I pulled it for Misty to try on and then she chose something different." Her brow pinched. "Crap. I don't know where it is now."

"I can look around," Stacy offered.

"Let me go. I don't expect you to figure out where my hormone-influenced brain left it. Will you help her out of this one?" Mira handed the pin box to Stacy.

Maybe it was my imagination, but Stacy's expression didn't seem too pleased. "Certainly." And her voice was tight.

Mira didn't seem to notice. "Thanks. Be back shortly!" Under her breath, she added, "Hopefully."

Stacy kept her head down while she moved behind me, as though she were deliberately avoiding looking me in the eye. Waves of hostility rolled off her body. She'd been cold in the past, but this was different. More angry. Was she mad that I'd refused to see her video? How petty was that?

I debated whether I wanted to break the tension or not. Finally, I decided to try. "Are you excited for the renovation celebration?"

"Sure." Again, her response was curt.

And not a lot to work off of. "I imagine it will bring new business. Will you be hiring more help?"

"Probably."

Yeah, definitely some rage going on. I felt the waistband loosening as she removed the last pins.

"Lift."

I raised my arms for Stacy to pull the dress over my head. She was rough as she did, and when my hair got caught, she muttered an unconvincing apology. Then she turned to hang up the outfit on the rack.

I wrapped my arms around myself, feeling odd in my panties and strapless bra in front of a woman I barely knew. A woman who apparently was not very happy with me.

I considered letting it go.

But letting things go had never been one of my strong points.

Stacy remained turned away as she worked, so I had to address her back. "Are you mad at me?" She didn't say anything so I clarified. "Mad that I didn't want to see your video?"

"Don't be ridiculous," she huffed. Then, after a beat, "That's not why I'm mad."

"But you *are* mad?" *I knew it!* My paranoia wasn't always off-base. "Why?"

"Seriously?" She flew back around to face me. "I offered that video as a gesture of kindness. One woman to another—we're supposed to look out for each other. At least we are in my book."

I was completely lost. "I have no idea—"

She cut me off. "I told you Hudson didn't know that I had it. And then you went ahead and told him about it anyway. That was just…just low."

My head swam. "Wait, wait. I'm confused."

"What exactly is confusing about it? I went out of my way to help you and you pretty much betrayed my confidence." She leaned against the dressing room wall, throwing her gaze up. "I don't know what I expected. He's Hudson Pierce, after all. He gets everybody's panties in a wad with just a glance." Her head shot back toward me. "Hey, he didn't trick you into telling him about it, did he?"

"No. No, he didn't trick me." Things were starting to fall in place, but not enough of them. I took a step toward her. "Look, I'm sorry that—"

"Don't bother." She practically spit. God, she was mad.

"Please!" I put my hand up either to prevent her from stopping me or to shield me from any further assault. "Please let me finish."

I don't know why I waited for her permission, but she gave it to me. "Fine."

"I'm sorry I told Hudson, and that it betrayed your confidence." Honestly, it hadn't occurred to me that she wouldn't want me to tell him. Now that I thought about it, perhaps it hadn't been in good taste. "I wasn't trying to…hurt you…or piss you off in any way. I was just trying to be honest with my boyfriend. And I didn't tell him what it was, obviously, because I didn't know. I asked if he knew what you might have and he said he had no idea. End of discussion."

She started to open her mouth to say something, but I spoke before she could. "Wait, one more thing—" *The most important thing.* "How do *you* know that I told him?"

She tapped her finger against her thigh as though considering whether or not she wanted to tell me. "He's emailed," she said after a beat. "And called me, asking about it."

"Emailed...?" *Hudson had emailed Stacy about the video?*

"And called. Every day last week, in fact."

The color drained from my face, and I had to sit down on the dressing room bench. "But why would he do that? What did he say?"

"His email said he learned that I had a video with him in it, and he wanted to talk to me about it. He mentioned a bunch of legal things about privacy and libel and all that crap. Then he asked if I'd send it to him. His phone messages said the same."

"What did you say?"

"I didn't actually talk to him. He kept calling, though, so I finally sent it Thursday. There was really no point keeping it from him. He knows I saw what's on the video, even if he didn't know about the video itself."

If she sent it on Thursday, then Hudson had most likely already seen it himself. Was that what he'd been referring to the other morning? His *secrets*?

"Then he emailed me today and asked me if we could talk about what he'd need to do in order to ensure the video was gone forever." Her voice was thick with disgust. "Like I could be bribed."

"I don't understand." My eyes rested on my lap, my words for myself, not Stacy. "He said there was nothing you could possibly have that would interest me. He wasn't concerned about it. Why would he...?"

"Because he's lying to you, Alayna!"

Stacy's emphatic statement drew my focus back to her.

"That's exactly my point about him. You can't trust him or anything he says. He'll string you along, make you think he's interested, make you think he's available. But he's not. I don't know what the hell game he's playing, but he's good at it."

A game. Was that what the whole thing was about? Had Stacy been one of his victims? It would explain why he'd been so protective about the material.

I felt sick.

Though I knew about the things he'd done to people, it didn't mean I was comfortable with it. Didn't mean I wanted to have to meet face-to-face with the people he'd hurt.

And what if that wasn't what this was about at all? If he'd scammed Stacy, I could deal with that. It wasn't new information.

If it was something different…

I made a choice. One that I didn't know if I'd necessarily be proud of later, but the only one that would protect my sanity. "What's on the video, Stacy?"

"Uh-uh." She turned back to the dressing rack, busying herself with straightening the clothing. "I'm not playing this game. You didn't want to see it."

I still wasn't sure that I wanted to see it. But now I had to. "I was wrong. I shouldn't have…I don't know…dismissed it so easily. You have to understand—I was trying to trust him because…" Why was I trying to explain the details of Hudson's and my relationship? It didn't matter why I hadn't wanted to see it. What mattered was that I'd changed my mind.

I stood and stepped toward her. "Look, you wanted me to see it to warn me about him. Don't you think I need the warning even more now? Woman to woman. Please." I was desperate—grasping at whatever would speak to her. It was manipulative, perhaps, but I'd been learning from the best.

Stacy's face softened. "I'm off at four. Give me your email and I'll send it to you as soon as I get home."

"Thank you. Thank you." I dove for my purse on the floor where I kept my business cards.

"But I'm done. I'm destroying the damn thing like he asked and then no more. Whatever you decide about the man, you're on your own."

"Of course." I found the item I was looking for and handed it to Stacy. "Here's my card. The email is my home and work."

She took the card from me and tucked it in her pocket.

"Thank you, Stacy. And, again, I'm sorry. If I can make it up to you…"

"Found it!"

Mira's return interrupted me. I was grateful, actually. The sooner she had a dress chosen for me and her event, the sooner I'd be on my way home. And Stacy would be off soon. Maybe her video would even be in my inbox by the time I booted up my laptop at the penthouse.

As I put the latest outfit on and posed and smiled and succumbed to Mira's primping and ecstatic cries of "This is the one," I felt more comfortable with myself than I had in a while. Lauren was right—some things would always be in my nature. Needing to know everything didn't say anything about my levels of trust or distrust in Hudson. It was all about me and my compulsions. The things I could and couldn't live with.

And when it came to secrets, I would always have to uncover them eventually.

Chapter Twelve

The drive back to the penthouse was the longest I'd ever been on.

I'd left Mirabelle's at the same time Stacy had. Once again, she'd said she'd email me the file and once again I thanked her. Then she headed toward the subway and I slipped into the back of the Maybach. My hands were sweaty as I fastened my seat belt, but my heart was also beating with anticipation.

It didn't escape me that I was reacting like an addict getting her first fix in months. And wasn't that exactly what I was doing? The romantic obsessive girl about to indulge in compulsive snooping?

It was only Jordan and me in the car—Reynold had the afternoon off—and I'd intended to go back to the club for a while after Mira's. But I knew I'd be too consumed with the video to work. And watching it in a private location seemed like the best move.

Four p.m. on Monday in NYC, though, is rush hour. Getting from Greenwich Village to Uptown was a nightmare. I busied myself with trying to figure out how to set my email up on my phone—why hadn't I thought that was a good idea before now? But I couldn't focus enough on the steps to make it happen.

Instead, my mind buzzed with questions. So many questions beyond what was on the video. Like, how had Stacy happened to make a video in the first place? If it had been made with her phone, wouldn't she have been able to send it by phone? Was she carrying around a video camera and then just happened to tape this…this…*whatever* it was? Why did she think this particular moment was even worthy of preserving?

Which led to the question, what about the video made Hudson want it destroyed? That was a big one, the reason I'd ended up pursuing getting a copy for myself.

And then there was Stacy's comment about Hudson wooing people. She'd said it as if he had wooed her. Hudson had sworn they'd only had the one date. It was this detail that intrigued me the most. Because even if all the video ended up being was proof that his relationship with Stacy had been one of his scams, he'd at the very least lied to me about the extent of his interaction with her. That pardoned me from whatever trust of his I was about to break, didn't it?

I hadn't promised I wouldn't see the video, I reasoned. I'd told him I didn't have to. Well, things had changed. And now I did have to. No promise broken, simply a new set of circumstances.

That's what I convinced myself, anyway.

At the penthouse, I was out of the car before Jordan could open my door. "Remember to set the alarm," he called after me. That was the arrangement. When I was at the penthouse alone, Jordan or Reynold would wait outside until I'd set the security system. Then they'd get an automatic text showing a secured status and they'd leave. At the moment, Celia was the least of my concerns, but in general, it was nice knowing that even though I was protected, I still had some semblance of privacy.

Once inside, I set the alarm, ran to the library to get my laptop, and settled in on the couch. I muttered to myself as my email seemed to take longer than usual to load, and then held my breath while I scanned my inbox.

There it was. My only unread message. From *StacySBrighton.*

I clicked the email open.

There was a short paragraph above the video attachment. Eager as I was, I began the download then returned to read it.

Alayna,

As I said, I'm done with this now. Take or leave this information as you wish. In case you want to know the circumstances of the footage, I'll tell you this: Hudson had asked me to meet him for coffee. I'd shown up and found him like this. I shot them with my phone before he saw me. Later, I transferred it to my computer and I got a new phone, which was why I couldn't send it to you that way.

Anyway. Here it is.

Stacy

At least she'd answered one of my questions. But Hudson asking to meet her for coffee? More and more I was sure what I was going to find—Hudson playing a game on his sister's assistant. It was heartbreaking. For Hudson, for Stacy...and what about Mira? I wondered what she knew about it all.

My computer popped up with a message that my download was complete. My hand paused above my keyboard as, for half a second, I considered not watching. Once I saw it, I could never un-see it. What if it was something that embarrassed him? Was it fair that I see the worst of him? What if Hudson had learned *my* deepest darkest mistakes? How would that make me feel?

But he already *had* learned them. He'd gone behind my back before he'd ever really spoken to me, read my police record, done his own research. And in the end, he was still with me. How was this any different?

I wouldn't know until I saw it.

My finger clicked the file open. I enlarged the picture to full-screen. Then I sat back and watched.

The video swept across a building as it moved to focus on its subjects. Then it settled on the back of a head. It didn't matter that I only could see hair and shoulders—I knew that hair. Knew the color and the texture by heart. I even knew that suit jacket. A dark blue Ralph Lauren. Not one of my favorites but definitely familiar.

Hudson's head swiveled slightly one way then the other. He was kissing someone—making out with her. His body completely hid the other person. All I could see of the woman were her small hands wrapped around his neck.

Jealousy wracked my body. I couldn't help it. Sure, it was before I knew him, but this was my man, my love, kissing someone else. If Stacy had come to meet him, thinking they were about to go on a date—well, that explained why she'd been upset.

Then the kiss ended. And for a moment I was thrilled.

But he moved away, and there she was—her face flushed, her lips plump from the kiss, her blonde hair wrapped tightly into the chignon that was typical of her style.

I felt the blood drain from my face. Hudson and Celia. I'd thought about the possibility before, but seeing it for real was much worse than I could have ever imagined. So much worse.

The video kept on. Celia reached out to straighten Hudson's tie. He shooed her away, turning more fully to the camera. Now I could focus on his face. His expression made my gut wrench—he was smiling, laughing almost. Something he'd done so rarely before he'd met me. At least, that's what I'd come to believe about him. It was that happy, carefree expression that made it impossible for me to excuse the kiss as being one-sided. They'd both been into it.

Then, when she started to walk away, he pulled her back into another kiss. Slower, sweeter.

The video ended there.

Thankfully. Because any more and I was going to throw up. Except that didn't stop me from pushing play again.

I pulled my legs up to my chest as I watched this time. Each second of their kiss, my chest tightened in anguish. It would have been cliché to say my heart was breaking. As if it could actually tear apart from emotional pain and still allow a person to live. How trite.

Besides, it didn't feel like that. It felt like a vise-grip. Constricting. Like someone had taken the organ from my chest and squeezed.

All the times I'd asked, all the times he'd denied...

But if it had been a scam, a scam on Stacy—my hopes lifted for a moment as I reasoned that scenario. Maybe the kiss wasn't real. Maybe it had all been Celia and Hudson playing a game together. He'd never said he'd involved Celia in his charades, but knowing that she was also a player, wasn't it a good possibility?

It was marginally better. They'd still been kissing, but it meant he hadn't lied to me about their relationship. It meant they'd never truly been together.

It took the third time viewing the video before I realized the flaw in that theory. When I'd seen it enough to be able to catch the details and not just be focused on the kiss. Hudson had said his scheming had been over for some time before he met me. That he'd been in therapy and had been on the wagon, so to say.

But the sign on the building behind them—it was for the Stern Symposium. That had been the night of my presentation. The night Hudson saw me for the first time. The night he said he knew that I was special.

The night that began everything for me and Hudson, he'd been kissing Celia Werner.

Either he was still scheming when he met me or he'd been dating her. Either way, he'd lied.

Having an alcoholic parent, I'd chosen to never use liquor to settle my emotions. My addictions were of a totally different nature. But the emotions boiling inside of me needed something stronger. I went to the library bar and reached for a shot glass and a bottle of tequila.

***

"Here you are."

When Hudson found me almost an hour later, I was outside on the balcony, looking out over the railing. I'd intended to be shit-faced by the time he got home, but had only managed four shots. For me that was enough to make me impaired.

But it hadn't been enough to stop the throbbing ache in my chest.

I glanced at him over my shoulder. I'd prepared several speeches, but at the sight of him, they all left me. "I didn't realize you were home."

I turned back to the view. It was far less devastating than looking at the man who'd betrayed me.

"I am." In my periphery, I saw him move up beside me. "You don't come out here very often."

I shrugged. "It scares me." I was cold to him—my tone, my entire demeanor. There was no way he missed it.

Tentatively, he attempted to figure it out. "You're afraid of heights?"

"Not really. It's falling that scares me." I gave a small laugh as I realized the relation of the fear to the feeling I was experiencing at the moment. "It's actually thrilling to be out here. Being so high up, feeling so untouchable, the wind rushing at you from below. I can see why so many people are intrigued by the idea of flying. Problem is, no matter how good the flight, you always have to come back down eventually. And lots of times, that return is a free fall."

"You're waxing poetic tonight." His frown was apparent in his voice.

"Am I?" I gathered up my strength and turned to look at him. "I suppose so."

Hudson smiled and took a step in my direction, his arms reaching for me.

I stepped away, or more like stumbled away.

He grabbed my arm to catch me. My eyes latched on to where his hand grasped. It felt like my skin was burning under his touch, and not in the amazing way that it usually burned, but in a way that left me wondering if I'd be scarred for life. Hell, he'd touched me everywhere in our time together—would all of my body be scarred?

At least my outside would match my inside.

Hudson leaned in to help me steady. He smelled it then, how could he not? "Have you been drinking?"

I pulled my arm away. "Is that a problem?"

"Of course not. You just don't usually drink. You're full of all sorts of surprises this evening."

"Ah. Surprises. It's certainly a day for that."

"Have there been others?"

"There have." I brushed past him to get inside. I was done with the small talk. There were things to be said, and saying them outside wasn't my preference.

He followed me in.

I waited until I heard the door shut behind me before I turned to face him. I'd planned to hit him straight up with the news that I'd seen his video. But those weren't the words that came out. "Hudson, why don't you ever tell me that you love me?"

"Where did that come from?" He looked like I'd slapped him. Considering that I wanted to, it was a pleasing outcome.

However, it wasn't the response I wanted. Not in the least. And I had enough liquor in my system to keep me pursuing the answer I wanted. "It's a valid question."

"Is it? My methods of emotional expression haven't seemed to bother you before—why now?"

"Hasn't bothered me?" I was incredulous. Did he really not know how desperate I was to hear it? "It's always bothered me. I've been patient, that's all. Letting you settle into our relationship. I realize it's all new for you—you've never let me forget it. But it's new for me too. I've bared all my heart to you. And you can't give me this one thing—three things, actually. Three little words."

"You know how I feel about you." He turned away from me and headed toward the dining room bar.

It was my turn to chase after him. "But why can't you say it?"

"Why do I need to?" He poured himself a Scotch. "If you understand, there's no point."

"Sometimes it helps to hear it."

"Helps what?"

He was so controlled, so even-mannered—it drove me insane. I raised my voice. "Helps everything! Helps deal with insecurity. With doubts."

He set the bottle on the counter and pivoted toward me. "What are you doubting? Us? What we have? I asked you to live with me. I changed my entire life to be with you. What is there to doubt?"

"Your reasons. Your motives."

"My reasons for wanting you with me are *I want you with me*. What more do you need to know? You want words? They can be changed and manipulated and misconstrued. But my actions—they speak everything that you need to know."

His words were calm and soothing and, at another time, would have melted me. There were many actions he'd shown that backed up what he was saying. Too many to do an inventory of in the space of a few seconds.

But there were other actions—the ones that were ambiguous and hard-to-interpret. Lunch meetings with Norma Anders. Purchasing the club for me before he'd even known me. And there was the video.

I wrapped my arms around myself, suddenly cold. "If I'm going by your actions, then right now what I know is that I've been lied to."

He took a swallow of his drink, his jaw moving the liquid around his mouth before he swallowed. "What are you talking about?"

I straightened my back for the moment of confrontation. "I saw it, Hudson. I saw the video."

"What vid—"

I punched my fist onto the dining room table. "Don't even fucking pretend you don't know what video I'm referring to, because after everything we've been through, I don't deserve the runaround."

His eyes were locked on mine, so I saw the brief flare of panic.

And then I saw the moment he resumed control.

"Okay. I won't run you around then." He wiped his mouth with the back of his hand. "Where did you get it? Stacy?"

Where did I get it? "Does it matter?"

"I suppose not." His tone was straight.

My gut clenched. I'd expected immediate denial or reassurance that it wasn't what it looked like. I'd expected answers. Not this. Not complete indifference.

"You were kissing Celia."

"I saw."

"Do you want to explain?"

"Does it matter?" He threw back my own words at me.

"Yes!" My composure was gone. Only he could fix me and he wasn't even trying.

He moved back to the bar and refilled his drink. "It was before I met you, Alayna. I haven't asked you to explain your actions before we met. I shouldn't be expected to either."

I gaped for a moment while he threw back his liquor. Of all the responses I'd imagined he'd give, downplaying wasn't one of them.

"But this is different," I finally managed. "Because you've already offered an explanation. You said there was never anything between you and Celia."

"There wasn't."

"I'm supposed to believe that after seeing what I saw?"

"Looks can be deceiving." His voice was a low rumble. The only indicator of emotion since I'd brought up the video.

It incited me. "That's all you got?"

"You've told me there's nothing between you and David, yet there's been many a time that it has looked like there was."

"It only looked that way because you were paranoid and jealous. You never saw me lip-locked with him. Believe me, seeing it is worse than you can imagine."

He placed his fingertips on the back of a chair and leaned toward me. "I'm sure if I went and looked at old security tapes I might see exactly that."

His words were cold and harsh and spiteful. It was times like these that Hudson's gift to manipulate showed itself. It was frustrating and unfair how he could mold a situation to his favor, but I understood that it was a part of him. He wasn't trying to play me.

Knowing that didn't make it any easier to deal with. "Yes. Once upon a time I was with David. I've told you that."

"After you let it slip and I figured it out."

"Jesus! Will I always have to pay for that mistake?" He didn't answer, but I didn't give him time. "Okay, I wasn't forthcoming. I kept things from you. But only because I didn't want to hurt you, and I admitted it when you confronted me. But this—you outright lied about this, Hudson. You told me there was nothing to see on Stacy's video. You told me I didn't need to go looking."

"And you went looking anyway."

"No. I didn't. I stayed away. Until I found out that you were deliberately trying to hide it from me—yes, Stacy told me you'd asked her for it. Was I supposed to keep trusting you then?"

He shrugged it away. "I didn't know what she had. I asked because I was curious. I wasn't deliberately hiding anything."

"You were deliberately hiding a whole fucking relationship with someone who you swore was never anything but a friend! And even now that I've figured out you and Celia were together, even now that I have proof, you still can't admit it." My eyes stung and my hands shook from the surge of frustration running through me.

Hudson pinned his eyes to mine. "I'm not admitting anything," he hissed. "You haven't figured out anything, Alayna."

"Then clear things up for me. Tell me what I can't seem to understand. What's going on in that video?"

"Nothing," he spit out. "Nothing's going on."

"Hudson!" My voice caught on the lump in my throat, but I kept on. "You're kissing her. Kissing her deeply. Passionately. Oh yes, I watched it several times, I could reenact the whole thing for you by now if you wanted."

Shaking his head, he started for the living room.

I was on his heels. "Not to mention that you were supposed to be meeting Stacy right then. And it didn't escape me on what night this whole thing took place."

He spun toward me. "*Meeting Stacy*? Is that what she told you? What else did she say?"

If he could withhold information, so could I. "That really doesn't have any bearing on this conversation."

"Well, as far as I'm concerned, this conversation is over." He headed for the library.

I stood stunned for a beat before following after. "It is not. I have questions and you've given me zero answers."

"I have no answers to give you. This subject is closed."

His dismissal infuriated me, and more, it left me feeling helpless. "Are you kidding me? You're not going to talk about this?"

"No, I'm not." He sat at his desk, reinforcing his refusal to speak further on the matter.

"Hudson, this is so not fair." I moved around to his side of the desk, not wanting this physical barrier between us. "We've said we needed to be honest with each other—that we needed to form a relationship built on trust. We agreed to be open. But you're hiding something with this. You lied! And not talking about it? How are we supposed to move forward when you're keeping such a big secret?"

He flew up from his chair and grabbed my arm with a tight grip. "Have I done anything to betray your trust before this?"

I was too surprised to try to pull away. "You went behind my back to transfer David…"

He yanked me closer to him. "That was *for us*." His eyes widened as he emphasized the last two words. "Have I done anything that makes you think I don't have our relationship's best interests in mind? Have I done anything to make you believe that I don't want to be with you? That I don't…" His voice cracked and he swallowed before continuing. "That I don't *care*…for you with everything I have?"

I shook my head, unable to speak.

He relaxed his grasp on me, but didn't let go. "Everything I've done since we've been together has been for you and me. Trust me when I tell you this isn't important." With his free hand, he brushed my hair off my shoulder. "This doesn't affect us."

"How can it not affect us? This was the night of the Stern Symposium. The night you said you first saw me."

"Yes, it was the night I first saw you." His voice was softer. Soothing as he cupped my neck. "But this was before that. Separate. You need to forget about this."

Separate. I held onto that word, absorbing it, searching for its meaning. But how could it be separate? It was the same night.

Looking into his eyes didn't clear up anything either. All I saw there was him pleading and begging to lay this video to rest.

But that wasn't the person that I was. He'd told me once that he would always be manipulative and domineering, even when he wasn't playing games. It was who he was.

Me, I would always be obsessive. I'd always question. Even when I was healthy. Asking to forget about this was defying my nature.

I swallowed. "What if I can't let it go?"

His expression filled with disappointment. "Then it means you don't trust me." He let me go, straightening his back. "And I don't know how we can continue on with our relationship without trust."

My knees buckled and I put my hand out on his desk to steady myself. "Are you saying that I have to choose? Trust you about this or we're over?"

"Of course not." His confidence was missing from his words. "But I have nothing else that I can say. Whether you can live with that or not is the choice you have to make."

I brushed my fingertips across my eyebrows and down my face. The situation felt so surreal, it was almost as if I had to be sure I was still physically there. How had I gone from a question about Hudson's past to an ultimatum about our future?

And even if I could bring myself to live with his terms, what kind of a future could we possibly have?

I shook my head. "That's a trap, Hudson. How could anyone live with that? How can we ever move forward when everywhere I turn there's a wall?"

"There are no walls." His jaw tensed and his voice tightened. "I'm here with you. I share everything with you."

"Except your past."

"Except this *one thing* in my past."

"No. There's more." My throat and eyes burned. "It's not just the video, Hudson. It's your secrets, the things you can't say. You can't tell me what that night was about. You can't tell me how you feel about me. You can't tell me what the true nature of your relationship is with Celia, with Norma—even with Sophia!"

"Jesus Christ, Alayna. I've told you exactly the true nature of my relationships and you—" he pointed a finger into his desk for emphasis, "refuse to believe what I've said."

"Because there's proof over and over again that says otherwise." I slammed my hand against my thigh each time I said *over*. "And if

I'm missing the whole picture, than maybe you should stop leaving all the vital parts out."

He closed his eyes briefly. Then he stepped closer to grasp my forearms. "Nothing of what I've kept from you is vital to our relationship." His voice was low and sincere. "It has nothing to do with us."

I threw my arms in the air. "It does! It has everything to do with us."

Hudson slammed past me to the other side of his desk, but he didn't go far. He rocked on his feet, his back to me, and I felt he was deciding. Deciding what, I didn't know.

I circled after him until I was within an arm's length. I could reach out to touch him with my hands, but I kept them at my side. "Don't you see, Hudson? I want to know everything about you. I want to be everything with you. How can I when you don't let me in?"

"I've let you in further than any other human being I've known. You know things about me that I never planned to share with anyone." He turned his head to look at me. "Doesn't that count for something?"

"It does." I reached out to caress his cheek and he moved the rest of the way to face me. "It counts for so much. But see," I dropped my hand to my side, "that's where we're stuck. Because you're asking me to give up so much of who I am in order for you to keep your secrets, and that will tear me apart. I can't do it. I can't function. I obsess, Hudson. I've never kept that from you. Now, I've had a history of obsessing over things that weren't valid, but this time, it's not in my head. There are real things you're hiding and can you not see how I'm going crazy over it? Everything you fixed about me is unraveling and I don't know what to do." I took a deep breath. "And I'm not even sure you care."

"I care, Alayna." He brushed a tear off my cheek—funny, I hadn't even noticed I was crying. "I care more than I can stand it, and I will do anything to make this better."

He braced his hand behind my neck and leaned his forehead against mine. It would be so easy—so easy to lean up and let him kiss away my pain and insecurity. His lips on mine could erase all darkness, could soothe any pain. Until that afternoon, I'd believed that like some people believed in their religion—Hudson could fix me, every time.

Except this time he was the problem.

And it wasn't his touch that would fix me. It was words. Words he wasn't willing to give. "Then tell me what I need to know," I whispered.

He straightened and took a step away from me. "No. I won't."

He turned away, heading back toward the living room.

Once again, I chased after him. "Were you together? Did you fuck her? Did you fuck her that night? The night you met me?"

He paced the room. "No. No. No. And no. I've told you this before and if those words aren't enough, why should I believe that any others would be any different?"

"Because those words aren't the words I need. I don't need denials. I need truths. What happened, Hudson? What is she to you?"

"Alayna, leave it alone."

"I can't!"

He stopped suddenly. After a beat, he said, "Then I need to leave."

"What's that supposed to mean?" I swallowed. "Like leave to cool down?"

He shook his head. "It means that we need to take some time apart."

"What? No!" I'd thought my heart had hit rock bottom before. Apparently there was a whole chasm left for it to fall into—a chasm so dark that it obliterated my previous notion of darkness. And the cold and the ache of that place made every pain I'd ever felt pale in comparison. The death of my parents, my journey from crazy to sanity, even the betrayal from Hudson when he didn't choose me over Celia—those were flesh wounds next to this.

"It's for the best," he said as he retrieved his jacket from across the back of the couch.

It seemed I needed to say something—anything—to make him stay. But I couldn't figure out what that would be. All I could hear were his words repeating over in my head—*time apart*. Because why? Because I'd needed him to be honest?

This couldn't be happening. "You tell me you care about me more than you can stand and now you want to break up with me?"

He glanced over at me, his eyes filled with sadness. "No, not break up, precious. Just take some time apart. Time to figure out how we want to deal with this."

His words were compassionate and sweet, but they weren't enough to mollify my hurt and anger. "You mean time for me to get my shit together."

"Both of us, Alayna."

I swiped the tears from my face with the back of my hand. "I don't know where you get your definitions, but that sure sounds like breaking up to me."

"If that's what you want to call it."

"I don't want to call it anything. I don't want it to happen!"

"I hope it will be temporary." He swept past me, careful not to touch me as he did. He grabbed his briefcase from the hall then patted his pockets, apparently satisfied that he had what he needed.

Oh my god. He was really leaving. Really, really leaving. "Hudson!"

When he turned to me, I rushed to him. "Don't go. Please don't go." I clutched at him.

His body remained cold and impassive, his eyes not meeting mine. "I'm doing this for you, Alayna. For both of us." His words were warm, though he still wouldn't look at me or touch me. "I can't bear that I'm hurting you, and it will destroy me if I lose you. But there are some things that I can never tell you. And now we're at an impasse, as you said. Because you say you can't go on not knowing and I can't go on without your trust."

"I do trust you. I'll learn to live with this if I have to. I'll figure it out. I just can't lose you!" I was desperate, making promises there was no way I could keep.

Finally, he connected his eyes with mine. "You're not losing me. We're simply stepping away. Maybe I can…"

He trailed off and I grasped onto whatever alternative he might be offering. "Maybe you can…what?"

But he had none to offer. "I don't know. I need time." Gently, he unwrapped my fingers from his clothing and pushed me away.

"But where are you going? This is your home."

"It's your home too. I'll stay at the loft."

Without looking at me, he stepped toward the elevator.

"Hudson! Don't do this. Don't leave."

He reached out as if he were going to touch me then pulled his hand back. "This isn't forever, precious. But I can't watch you like this."

"Like, what? Like crazy?" While I'd always feared that Hudson wouldn't be able to take me at my worst, I'd begun to think he'd be with me always. Like he promised so many times.

I'd been wrong. Again. "Yeah, I'm crazy. This is who I really am, Hudson. You see it now. Here I am, exposed. It always scares people away, but I never thought it would scare you. Yet here you are running. No wonder you think I can't handle your secrets. Because you probably think I'd react just like you are now. But I'm not a coward, Hudson. I can take it. I won't run from you."

His face fell. "I'm not running from you, Alayna. I'm saving you."

"From what?"

"From me!" We stood in silence as his exclamation rung through the foyer. Then he hit the elevator button. "I'll talk to you later. Tomorrow, maybe."

"Hudson!"

"I...I can't, Alayna."

He stepped inside the elevator, his focus fastened to the floor as the doors closed.

Then he was gone.

Chapter Thirteen

After Hudson left, I cried so long and so hard that it seemed like I should have passed out from exhaustion. But I didn't. I tried curling up in bed, but it felt too big. And no matter how many blankets I had, I felt cold. Eventually, I wandered out to the library where I had a few more shots of tequila to warm up and turned on a movie from my AFI's Greatest Films collection. I chose *Titanic*. I was already heartbroken, after all—might as well wallow in it.

Sometime before the ship sunk, I passed out on the couch. I woke the next day with swollen eyes and a splitting headache. My first thought was that I needed caffeine. But there was no smell of brewing coffee in the penthouse, and that's when I remembered that Hudson wasn't there. Every day before he left for work, he set the Keurig to brew for me. This simple missing gesture threatened to start a new round of tears.

But maybe he'd called.

I fumbled around for my phone and found it buried in the cushions. *Fuck.* It was dead. I'd been too consumed with grief to charge it for the night. After setting it up at the library charging station, I made my own coffee and found some Ibuprofen in the bathroom cabinet.

I showered then, hoping the warm water would relieve the swelling of my eyes. Perhaps it did, but I didn't feel any better. Afterward, I stood with a towel wrapped around myself and stared into the steam-clouded mirror. This was what it was like to see Hudson now—through this fog, knowing that something more lay underneath. If only it were as simple as stretching my hand out and wiping away the condensation to see the man beneath. If only he'd let me in, maybe it would be that easy. Maybe then my touch could finally bring him into focus.

But it wasn't that simple. Instead, all I could hope for was a message or a missed call. I dressed and settled back on the couch to power up my cell.

There was nothing.

So I sent one to him: *Come home.*

When I didn't have a response after five minutes, I considered sending another. He was at work. I shouldn't bother him. But I was supposed to be important. If he still cared at all, he'd answer me.

I battled with myself over it. In my past, obsessive texting and calling had been my biggest weakness. For more than a year after I started therapy, I didn't even allow myself to have a phone. The temptation was too great. In the height of my obsessing, I could fill a voicemail box within an hour. Paul Kresh had to change his number after I texted him nonstop for three days straight.

Even with Hudson, I carefully weighed each message I sent him. I didn't send everything I was thinking. It was hard, but I had managed to stay in control.

Today, I didn't give a fuck about control.

I typed a new message: *Are you going to avoid me now?*

Five minutes later, I sent again: *The least you can do is talk to me.*

I sent several more, delaying each by a span of three to five minutes:

You said I was everything to you.

Talk to me.

I won't ask about it if you don't want to.

This isn't fair. Shouldn't I be the one who's mad?

I was about to start another when my phone vibrated in my hand with a received text. It was from him: *I'm not mad. I'm not avoiding you. I don't know what to say.*

Hudson at a loss for words was the craziest thing I'd heard in the last two days. He always knew what to say, always knew what to do. If our separation had him so out of character, why were we apart?

My fingers could barely enter a response fast enough. *Don't say anything. Just come home.*

I can't. Not yet. We need time.

I had hoped the new morning would bring clarity. But I still wasn't even sure what I was supposed to be doing with the time that he insisted we needed. *I don't need time. I need you.*

We'll talk later.

You don't understand. I have to talk now. I'll keep texting you. I can't help myself.

And I'll read every one.

I almost smiled at his last message. After all the years of being ignored and called crazy, Hudson embraced my whacked out tendencies.

But one sweet little text wasn't enough to erase the hollow ache in my chest. I started to type out another message.

Then I stopped myself.

What the hell was I doing? Never mind old habits and what was healthy and what wasn't—why was I chasing after this man so desperately when he'd already clearly indicated it would have no effect on him? Besides, he'd said over and over that he liked my obsessing over him. It made him feel loved.

Well, fuck that.

If Hudson wanted to feel loved, he could come home and work things out. Yes, we had troubled pasts and were inexperienced with relationships. Still, sooner or later we had to grow up and take responsibility for our actions. More than anything in the world, I wanted to do that with Hudson. But if he wasn't ready, it didn't matter how much I loved him. I couldn't be the only one fighting. He had to fight too.

In one of the strongest moments of my adult life, I set down my phone and walked away.

Since I wasn't insane enough to believe my strength would last, I decided to get out of the house. And I needed a run.

I called Jordan. "Hey, you're a runner right?"

"Ms. Withers?"

"You were Special Ops. You had to stay in shape for that, right?" The idea had crossed my mind before, but since Hudson had been so opposed, I'd never pursued it. But now Hudson wasn't around. "And I imagine that makes you a fairly good runner."

"Yes, I suppose so."

"Good. I want to go for a run and Hudson won't let me go without a bodyguard. I'll be ready in fifteen."

He hesitated for only half a beat. "Be there in ten, Ms. Withers."

"Thank you." It had been surprisingly easier than I'd expected. Might as well see what else I could get. "And, oh my god, Jordan, please call me Laynie. Please, please, please. I know you're not supposed to, but I don't care about Hudson's stupid rules. I'm having a bad day and I could use a friend. Even if you aren't really my friend, pretend. Please."

"You should know me well enough to know that I'm not much good at pretending." The phone jostled as if he were getting ready while he talked to me. "But I am an excellent runner. Be ready to have your ass handed to you. Laynie."

I was almost grinning when I met him in the lobby. This was new for me—life actually going on in the midst of heartache. Who knew it was possible?

***

True to his word, Jordan handed me my ass on our run. The six miles we did around Central Park barely seemed to faze him, while I nearly had to be carried back to the penthouse. The physical discomfort was welcomed—it matched my sullen mood. The adrenaline and endorphin rush did little to improve my spirits, but it did make the act of living seem just a bit more bearable.

Back at the penthouse, I showered and got dressed. Then I did go to my phone. I scrolled through my texts looking for another from Hudson. The disappointment at finding none was hard to swallow. Even though he'd said he wouldn't respond, I had hoped. Wasn't it just the morning before that he'd said I was the center of his world? Was there any way he could still mean it?

I couldn't think about the answer. The evidence wasn't in my favor and it hurt too much to face.

Needing another distraction from reaching out to Hudson, I called Brian. We chatted for over an hour—a record for us. After that, I called Liesl. We were both working that night, which provided a perfect excuse for shopping and dinner beforehand. My heart wasn't in it, but I could fake it with the best of them. And being with Liesl helped keep the tears at bay.

It had already been a full day by the time Jordan dropped us off at The Sky Launch. "My shift's over, Laynie," Jordan said as he shut the car door behind me. "Reynold's waiting for you up there."

Sure enough, I spotted Reynold by the club's employee entrance.

Though I'd never done it before, I felt the urge to hug Jordan. So I did. "Thank you," I said, my throat tightening. "I needed you and you were there."

Jordan looked at me compassionately. "It's not my place, but you should know—Mr. Pierce is a complicated man."

"Yeah, yeah, I know." I wasn't interested in anyone defending Hudson at the moment.

Jordan continued anyway. "But no matter how complex the situation may be, it's easy to see how he feels about you."

I stuck my chin out, defiantly. "Is it?" I'd thought it was, but now all bets were off.

My driver patted my upper arm. "Perhaps not to you. But to me, it's obvious. I pray that he'll figure out how to show you before you're gone for good."

I watched Jordan as he got in the car and drove away.

Me, gone for good? It had been Hudson who'd left. Hudson who'd broken the promise he'd made to stand by my side through everything. Hudson who'd dropped not so subtle hints at a long-lasting future and yet he was now nowhere by my side.

With a sinking horror, I feared that Jordan was right—Hudson's feelings for me *were* obvious. Obviously gone.

I bit my lip to curtail any crying that latest thought might bring on.

Liesl wrapped her arm around mine and directed me toward the door. "Do you get sick of the bodyguard stuff?" She was excellent at deflecting. "I mean, I wouldn't get sick of that Jordan dude—he's hot."

"And gay."

"Figures. But maybe he's also experimental."

I laughed. "Not likely." My laughter quickly faded into a frown—it felt too strange to be amused when my heart was so heavy. "I don't usually mind having bodyguards around, though I do like my independence. And I don't really get why I need to have someone here while I'm at the club." An idea surfaced. "In fact—"

We'd reached Reynold by then. "Hey, stranger," I said in greeting. "Guess what. I'm giving you the night off."

He chuckled.

"I'm serious. Hudson is probably the only one who has the power to give you the night off, but here's the thing—Hudson's not around. And I'll be here at the club all night. We have security guards on staff and bouncers. I'm going to be fine."

I couldn't say why it was so important for me to send Reynold away, but it suddenly was. Perhaps it was an act of defiance. If Hudson wasn't willing to give in our relationship, then I wasn't willing either. Or not as willing as I had been, anyway. I was too pissed. Wasn't that a phase of grief?

Besides, I felt strong. I didn't need someone following me around. And Celia hadn't been around in several days—maybe she was bored with the game.

"So I'll see you when I'm off later. Okay?"

Reynold seemed dumbfounded. "Uh, sure. At three. I'll, uh, be here at three."

"Awesome."

The victory with Reynold bolstered me. I hadn't known how I'd be able to get through the night at work. Now I thought I might actually be able to do it. I hadn't forgotten my pain—more thoughts than not had been filled with Hudson—but the misery was almost tolerable.

The time with Liesl had been the most helpful. We hadn't seen much of each other recently, and there was a lot to catch up on. I told her everything that had been going on, including Celia's stalking and Hudson's secretive behavior. It was depressing but also therapeutic.

"Maybe Hudson is really, like, a CIA guy," Liesl said as I handed her a cash drawer for the bar. "And Celia's his partner. And he's abandoned his mission—defected, or whatever they call that, and she's trying to reel him back in."

Her crazy ideas were almost entertaining. "That one's definitely it."

She nudged me aside with her hip to take her place in front of the register. "I wish you'd be serious about this. I know I'm right."

I forced a smile. "Excuse me for being—what do they call it? Oh, yeah—based in reality."

. Liesl ran a hand through her purple tresses and laughed. "Reality is so overrated."

"Isn't it?"

We got lost in the hustle and bustle of the night after that. David had trained with Gwen the night before, but it was the first shift that

I really got to see her in action. She'd worked enough now that she knew what she was doing. I watched her as she managed the upper floor, keeping on top of change orders and unruly customers, not once missing a beat. She was good, and I'd never felt better about my decision to hire her. Especially now that my whole future at The Sky Launch felt in limbo.

With a shudder, I swallowed the sob forming in my throat. I couldn't think about that. Not here. Not now. In perhaps the same delusional manner I'd used in my days of Paul Kresh or David Lindt, I focused on convincing myself that Hudson and I were fine. This was just a blip. We'd recover and life would go on together.

Somehow it had been easier in the past. I hoped that said more about the current state of my mental health and less about my future with Hudson.

It was still early in the night, only a little past eleven, when I saw Celia.

I'd just come down from the upstairs to check in with the bartenders on the main floor. They were busy but not slammed. I slid behind the bar where Liesl was working and scanned the club, not looking for anything in particular—just getting a general sense of the scene.

The center of the club was surrounded by bunches of seating areas. They usually filled early in the evening. They were the best tables to get since they were right off the dance floor. She was the only one at her table, which was odd for a Saturday night, and that drew my attention. No one sat alone at The Sky Launch.

But there Celia was—alone, wearing tight jeans and a tight tank, her hair down around her shoulders. It was so uncharacteristic of her usual prim and proper look that I wasn't sure it was her. Then she caught my stare, and the wicked grin she gave me confirmed it.

I grabbed Liesl's forearm. "Oh my god."

"What? What is it? Did I fuck up the last order?" Her eyes were wide and alarmed.

"No. She's here. Celia!" I nodded toward the woman who still had her eyes locked on mine.

Liesl followed my gaze. "The stalker chick? Should I kick her ass?"

"No." Though the thought of the tall Amazon at my side kicking the ass of my now arch-nemesis was pretty entertaining.

Liesl squinted as she continued to study Celia. "No offense, but she's a knockout. Not like you're not a knockout, but I'd do her." She bumped me affectionately with her shoulder. "I'd do you harder, though. Of course."

"Wow. I can't believe she actually came here." *Maybe I should call Reynold to come back.* I instantly dismissed the idea. With everyone around, what could she do to me? Even her constant watch was nothing more than annoying.

Rows of goose bumps lined my arms despite my attempts to remain nonplussed. Well, I'd made it over three hours at work before having an emotional breakdown. That was something, right?

"What's going on?" David asked.

I turned to find Gwen and David had joined us. Which meant it was time to get back to the job. "Nothing." I certainly wasn't sharing my Celia story with my ex-boyfriend and an employee I barely knew.

Apparently, Liesl felt differently. "That girl over there is Laynie's crazy stalker."

"Liesl!" I smacked her shoulder with the back of my hand.

"I'm not going to stand by as the only one who knows about this. You need some backup. What if she does something to you? You know, roofies your drink or something."

"Right. 'Cause I'm drinking openly tonight." She was my closest friend, but sometimes she lacked in the intelligence department.

Gwen raised an eyebrow. "You have a stalker? You're cooler than I thought."

I rolled my eyes. "She's not...it's not...I don't even know why she's..." I let out an exasperated breath. "It's complicated. I'm going in the back room if you all need me."

Without looking back, I headed to the employee lounge behind the bar. Seeing Celia had thrown me, and in the shape I was in, that was enough to send me over the edge. I paced the room, trying to get a hold of the composure I'd had earlier in the evening.

Gwen and David followed.

I considered telling them I wanted to be alone. But I wasn't sure I did.

"Are you okay, Laynie?" David's voice was tentative and tender.

"No. Yes. I'm fine. I'm just..." I shook my head, unable to finish the thought. My chest was tight and my head felt like it was going to explode.

"Well, tell us something about her. Your stalker." Gwen genuinely seemed like she wanted to be helpful. "A name. How you know her. Anything."

"Her name's Celia Werner." I was surprised at my willingness to share, yet even more, I needed to talk.

"As in Werner Media?" David kept abreast of the who's who in the business world. Of course he'd recognize her name.

"That's the one," I confirmed.

David stepped closer to me, concern on his face.

"It's nothing to worry about, David. She's just not happy about me being with Hudson."

"Is she the ex?" Gwen asked.

"Yeah." When I'd said that in therapy, it was because it was easier. Now after the video, it was what I truly believed. "She is." For the millionth time, my mind went to thoughts of her kissing Hudson. What else had they done? How close had they been? Had he slept with her?

I swallowed the bile that threatened to come up. "So now she's trying to scare me by showing up where I am. Sending me messages. Stuff like that."

"Do you want us to kick her out? I can call Sorenson up from the door." Unlike Hudson, David's protective mode was subtle, but I recognized it in his face all the same.

"She's not going to hurt me."

"Are you sure?" David put a hand on my shoulder.

"No." I stepped casually out of his grasp. Despite its innocence, his touch felt like a betrayal to Hudson. "But I don't want her to win."

"Fair enough." His body language told me that my brush-off had stung. Another reason it was good he was leaving.

Gwen turned a plastic chair around and straddled it. "It's creepy how she just stares at you like she does."

"Isn't it?" I was still trying to decide how I felt about Gwen knowing about my private life.

"We could spike her drink."

Now this sounded interesting. "With what?"

"I don't know. Spit."

I didn't laugh, but I managed a genuine smile. Okay, Gwen was officially cool. And maybe I needed more people involved in my life—more than just Hudson and his family. The phone call with Brian, the run with Jordan, the day with Liesl—all of it reminded me that there was a whole world outside the one I'd been living in. A world with friends and interests that I'd forgotten about recently.

Whether or not Hudson and I had a future together, I had a future of my own. I couldn't ignore the people that belonged in that future anymore and just hope that they'd still be there when I needed them. And Gwen was now a part of The Sky Launch. That made her family. It was time to embrace her as such.

But just because they were family didn't mean I had to talk about everything with them. And talking wasn't calming me down anyway.

"You know what? I'm fine," I lied. "Don't worry about me. Let's get back out there where we can at least keep an eye on her."

With Gwen in the lead, we stepped back into the club, the flashing lights and thumping beat washing over me with a familiar comfort.

I ran into Gwen's back when she stopped short. "Ah," she said. "She knows we were talking about her. She's calling in reinforcements." She lifted her chin toward Celia. "See?"

I looked toward my stalker and saw she had her cell to her ear.

Just then Liesl walked over to me with the bar phone in her hand, the cord stretched almost to its max distance. "There you are, Laynie, phone call."

"Oh, shit." Gwen's eyes were wide, and I imagined they mirrored my own.

Was Celia calling me?

"Let me take it," David offered.

"And say what?" I shook my head decisively. "I've got it." What was she going to say to me, anyway?

I took the receiver from Liesl's hand, my own hand surprisingly steady. "Hello?"

"Alayna, where is your bodyguard?"

The voice on the line shocked me more than if it had been Celia. "Hudson." I said his name out loud, looking around at my coworkers so they'd know who it was. "Hello to you, too."

A mixture of disappointment and elation swept over me. I'd almost wanted the call to be from Celia—more and more, I was eager to confront her.

But on the other hand, it was Hudson on the phone. *Hudson!* I'd longed for his voice all day. I didn't even care about the circumstances for his call—*he'd called,* that was the point.

"Ah, it's not even her," Gwen said. "That was some mind fuck."

David agreed. "I think she must have been checking messages. I never saw her mouth move."

I looked back at Celia, who was, sure enough, pocketing her phone.

"Could you answer the question, please?" Hudson's voice in my ear drew my attention back to him.

It took me a second to remember what he'd asked—oh, about my bodyguard. As glad as I was to hear from him, I wasn't about to make things easy. "Why do you care?"

"Goddammit, Alayna!"

His voice was so loud that I had to lean my ear away from the receiver. Well, what had I expected? That Reynold wouldn't tell him? "I sent him home. I figured I didn't really need him at the club."

"How's that working out for you?" His sarcasm was lined with frustration.

"I'm fine! With the security guards and cameras and the bouncers..." It took a second for me to realize what his statement meant. "How do you know she's here?"

"Because I'm outside."

"You're outside? Why are you outside?" My heart sped up. He hadn't just called, he was here. I covered the mouthpiece with my hand. "Liesl, hurry, grab the cordless."

Hudson continued. "Thank god your bodyguard works for me and not for you. You don't have the authority to send him home."

Don't have the authority...? "Jesus Christ."

"And when he noticed Celia..."

Liesl handed me the cordless. "Thank you," I whispered.

"Alayna, are you listening to me?"

"Yes. I'm working here too, you know." I punched the talk button on the cordless and handed the other phone to Liesl. "Go on." Then, I bee-lined for the front of the club. If Hudson was there, I wanted to see him, wanted to see the look in his eyes and in his face. See if I could read the emotion that I needed to see from him.

"When he saw Celia entering The Sky Launch, he contacted me, as he's supposed to do, and asked me if he should go in as well since you didn't want him on the premises. I told him yes. So Reynold will be there whether you want him to be or not."

"Fine." I didn't really care anymore. "Send him on in."

"I already did."

"Of course you did." I was almost at the bottom of the ramp now. The club was picking up for the night, and I was fighting against traffic. "But why are you here? You could have arranged all that over the phone." Had he wanted to see me as much as I wanted to see him?

He paused. "I wanted to be sure you were okay." His tone was softer. It tugged at my chest.

"I'm okay." Well, since Hudson was still sleeping in another apartment, maybe that wasn't the right word. "I'm safe, anyway."

"Good." He cleared his throat. "Then I'll talk to you later."

"Hudson, wait!" I was at the front door now, the night air cool compared to the warmth of the club. Not wanting to be seen, I stayed tucked behind the doorman.

"What is it, Alayna?"

I scanned the circle drive in front of the club. There he was standing next to his Mercedes, the emergency lights flashing as he paced the sidewalk next to the car. He was in another three-piece suit. It was late, why was he still dressed for work? And had he really driven all the way out to the club just to leave without seeing me face-to-face?

My next words bubbled with the hurt I'd carried all day. "Is that all you have to say to me?"

"Right now, yes." He shoved his hand through his hair. "You're protected. That's what's important right now."

He'd been concerned—that much was obvious. His hair was tussled as if he'd ran his hand through it more than just the one time, and his agitation was present in his stride.

It wasn't enough. If he really cared, I'd be in his arms. He'd have come in and found me instead of the other way around. "Have you considered that if you just told Celia that you'd left me that she'd probably drop this whole thing?"

He shook his head, even though he had no idea I could see him. "I didn't leave you."

"It sure feels like you did."

He leaned his hand on the top of his car and looked toward the club entrance. "Is that what you want?"

"No!" *Never.* "No. I just want the truth. That's all." The doorman shifted, and my cover was blown. Hudson's eyes met mine.

We stared at each other, locked in our gaze, for several long moments. Even across the hundred feet of sidewalk, there was a current between us. An electric spark that ignited from so much more than chemistry or lust. It was an emotional charge that surged right from the heart of me. We were connected, so completely, that for the first time since he'd walked out of the penthouse the night before, I felt a flash of hope.

He broke the gaze first. He looked to the passenger window of the car, as if someone were inside, talking to him through the glass.

I stepped forward, squinting to see. "Oh my god, are you…?" My stomach fell. "Hudson, are you with Norma?"

Hudson threw his hands in the air. "Not now, Alayna."

I started toward him. "Are you fucking kidding me? One day gone and you're out with her?"

He circled around to the driver's side of the car. "It's for business!" The door slammed.

I picked up my pace, even knowing he'd be gone by the time I reached the curb. "At this time of night?" In a suit, by themselves. How fucking stupid did he think I was?

"It's…I can't get into this right now." He pulled out onto the road. "Why can't you ever just trust me?"

"Because you can never tell me the truth!" I watched the taillights of the car as they mixed in with the rest of the traffic. It was comical, really, to ask for his trust when I'd just witnessed him on what could be described no other way but as a date.

"I have to go. I can't talk to you while I'm driving."

I could hear Norma's voice in the background. I wanted his attention on me, not her. "Wait, don't—"

"Goodbye, Alayna."

"—hang up." The dial tone replaced his voice. "Dammit!" I screamed and threw the phone down on the sidewalk. Hard. It shattered into pieces. Seemed fitting, considering that's how I felt inside.

"Laynie, are you okay?" David's voice was neither surprising nor comforting. Of course he'd come after me. It was a nice gesture—I just wished he were somebody else.

"Yeah." Total lie. My entire body felt weak. Like I could just fall over there on the sidewalk, unable to walk or even crawl back to the club.

But I was strong. I could ignore the fact that I had died inside until I was alone at home. "Yeah, I'm fine," I said again. "I broke the phone." I bent down to collect the pieces off the sidewalk.

David squatted next to me to help. "It's technically Pierce's phone."

"Well, that makes me feel better." Marginally. "Funny, this is the second phone I've destroyed on account of that man."

"Maybe that means something."

"Maybe." I knew what David wanted it to mean. I didn't want to think about what it could mean for me.

When we'd gathered all the parts, David stood and held his hand out to help me stand. Reluctantly, I took it. He didn't let go right away, though. Worse, I didn't pull away.

David studied me with soft eyes. "I'm not going to ask because I know what you'll say. I'm just going to do."

"What?" Next thing I knew, I'd been pulled into his embrace. "Oh."

"It seemed like you could use a hug."

I hesitated for only a second. Then I gave in. For me, it was comfort from a friend, comfort that I needed. He may have taken it as more, but in that moment, my need outweighed his.

Except then he pulled me in tighter. And his arms felt strange and his scent was wrong. As gently as I could, I began to push away. "I think I better…"

David released me, his eyes pinned on the club door behind us. "Hey, look. She's leaving."

I turned to look. Celia was indeed leaving. She'd seen our hug, I was sure. It didn't matter. Even if she told Hudson, he'd been out with Norma Anders. I was certain his trumped mine in terms of disappointing a lover.

David's smile grew tight. "Man, I don't know anything about her, but that smile was wicked. What a bitch."

The pain and hurt of the past twenty-four hours subsided then, leaving in its wake a tidal wave of rage. I was angry, so angry. While a lot of my wrath was meant for Hudson, the greatest portion belonged to Celia. Without her, Hudson and I might be able to work through our differences. But how could we when she was always around, reminding us of our pasts, stirring up our distrust?

My hands balled into fists. "You know what? This is ridiculous. I'm confronting her."

"Laynie, I'm not so sure you should." But that was the extent to which David tried to stop me.

I'd covered more than half the distance between me and Celia when a figure stepped from out of the club and blocked my progression.

"Ms. Withers." Reynold put a gentle but firm hand up to stop me from proceeding. "Not a good idea."

He was right. As worked up as I was, I probably would have punched her. And though it would have felt good, it would be me with the restraining order then, not Celia.

Still, I had to wonder what my bodyguard's orders had been. Did Hudson mean to keep me from trouble, or was he worried if I talked to his ex that I'd learn things he didn't want me to know? "One question, Reynold. Are you protecting me from her? Or protecting her from me?"

"I don't catch your drift."

And even if he did, he likely wouldn't answer honestly. "Never mind."

By then, Celia had made it to the curb and was hailing a cab. Determined to not let her get away without some victory chalked in my square, I approached our doorman. "You see that woman? She's not to be let back in here. Permanently banned."

The doorman nodded. "Yes, ma'am."

"I'll hang her picture in the back room." I'd print something off the Internet. Maybe it wasn't a good move to let her know that she'd gotten to me, but honestly, I didn't care about her game. I simply wanted my life back. Kicking her out of my club was a good first step.

***

It was just past three when I crawled into bed. Though it still felt too big and lonely, I was pretty sure I was exhausted enough to sleep. It was worth a try anyway.

Even with my determination, I was still tossing and turning when four a.m. rolled around. My insomnia turned out to be a blessing. Otherwise, I may have missed his call.

"Alayna. I need you." The ache in Hudson's voice was new to me.

I sat up with a bolt. "What is it?"

"Mira. At the hospital." He couldn't even speak in full sentences. "The baby…"

I was throwing on my yoga pants and a t-shirt before he finished. "I'll be right there."

"Jordan's already on his way to get you."

Forever With You

Chapter Fourteen

Hudson was waiting for me outside the emergency room when Jordan dropped me off at the hospital. He'd obviously dressed in a hurry as well. He was wearing jeans and a wrinkled polo I didn't recognize.

Though he didn't smile, his eyes seemed to light up at the sight of me. "She's not in the ER anymore, but this is the only entrance open at this time of the morning." He was already heading toward the elevator.

I trotted to catch up. "Have you seen her? What's going on exactly?"

"All I know is that she's having contractions. Adam called as they were checking in and he texted me when they were moved to the OB ward." He pushed the up button on the call panel. "I didn't want to see her without you."

I reached out and grabbed his hand. He took it without hesitation.

He let go though, when the elevator arrived, gesturing for me to go in first. He followed and hit the floor button, then stuffed both hands in his pockets. He glanced at me sideways, and I felt his ache to touch me. It echoed my own yearning. Still, he didn't reach for me again.

The elevator began moving. "Alayna, about Norma…"

I shook my head. "You don't have to do this now." Didn't he know that I didn't care at the moment? In the past few weeks, I'd grown to love Mira too. If anything happened to her or her baby…

But Hudson went on. "I need you to know—this business deal." He ran a hand through his hair. "It's very important and I've had to be sneaky about the whole thing. Tonight was about that. Norma was able to arrange what looked like a chance meeting with the sellers at a charity gala. When Reynold called and said that you sent him away and that Celia was at the club..." He trailed off and I knew he was imagining the worst. "I didn't even think to arrange a ride home for Norma. I simply grabbed her and we left."

A pang of guilt burrowed through my gut. "Is the deal ruined?"

"No. And it wouldn't matter if it was." He turned to me and brushed his thumb across my cheek. "You're safe, precious. That's all I care about."

I closed my eyes, savoring his caress.

Then the door opened, and his hand fell to his side.

We followed the signs pointing to OB, eventually reaching a set of doors that required us to buzz to get in. "Will they let us in at this time of night?" I asked while we waited for a response.

"It's my impression that babies are born twenty-four hours a day," he said. "And we're on her list."

Mira was only six months along, though. Hopefully her baby wasn't coming any time soon.

"May I help you?" a voice said through the intercom.

"We're here to see Mirabelle Sitkin. Hudson Pierce and Alayna Withers."

Instead of an answer, the door simply opened automatically.

I smiled lightly. "I guess we've been approved."

Mira's room was easy to spot because Adam, Jack, Sophia and Chandler were standing in the hall outside. Hudson went straight to Sophia. He put his arm around her and bent to kiss her cheek. "Mother."

"Thanks for being here, Hudson." Sophia's hand was shaking as she hugged her son, and I couldn't help but wonder if she was emotional about Mira or simply in need of a drink. Either way, she was with it enough to throw a glare in my direction. "You brought her?" Her tone accentuated her disgust.

"Yes, and you'll not say another word about it." At least Hudson was still defending me to Sophia. That had to mean something.

Jack gave me a warm smile, reaching out to squeeze my hand. "It's good to see you, Laynie."

Neither Sophia's insult nor Jack's welcome registered very high on my interest level. I only cared about Mira—my friend.

I peeked around Jack past the open door and found Mira lying in the bed surrounded by two nurses. They looked calm enough. Hopefully that was a sign that things weren't dreadful.

Hudson wasn't the type to simply hope. "What's her status?" he asked Adam.

"She's fine. Now." Adam's expression looked tired and concerned, but his words were only slightly strained. "When we came in she was having contractions every three minutes. But they got her hooked up on an IV, got lots of fluids in her, and everything settled down. She hasn't had any contractions now for almost forty minutes. Her blood pressure is still a little high, though, so they want to keep her here a bit. Fortunately, they don't think it's pre-eclampsia, but they'll watch her at her visits."

"We can go back in as soon as the nurses are done," Jack said.

Chandler nudged Hudson with his elbow. "Mira said Mom and Dad were making her too tense. She sent us here for a timeout."

The twinkle in Adam's eye said he had found as much amusement in the statement as Chandler had. "She is a bit feisty at the moment."

The nurses came out then. One stopped to talk to us, or Adam, rather. "She's doing better, Dr. Sitkin. I'm sure she'll be out of here in the next couple of hours. When you go back in, try to keep things light and relaxed."

"Thanks." Adam gestured toward the door. "After you, Laynie. I know she'll be happy to see you here."

I nodded, surprised and touched that he thought I meant that much to his wife. I made my way inside. Hudson followed close behind me, but not so near that we were touching.

"Mira." I offered a warm smile.

"Hey! You came!" She tried to reach toward me, but the cuff on her arm kept her trapped.

"Of course we did. Don't be silly." I stepped aside for Hudson to slip in, eager for him to get a chance to connect with Mira as well. Hudson was family. I was only the girlfriend. And maybe I wasn't even that.

"Hudson." Mira smiled up at her brother. "Thank you for being here."

He nodded and it struck me that he was too overcome with emotion to speak. I remembered then how hard it was for him to say how he felt—not just with me but with everyone. Mira had once told me Hudson never gave out *I love you*s. Even to her. But the look in his eyes said he felt it for her in spades.

Was that the way he looked at me? I wanted to say yes, but it was hard to be objective.

Hudson patted his sister's hand then stepped away, turning his back to her momentarily. He was getting himself together. More than anything I wanted to go to him, to reassure him. But his body language so far had shown he didn't necessarily want it.

My eyes stung. Again and again he shut me out. Even with something as normal as sharing concern over his sister, he couldn't let me in. Didn't he know how much it killed me?

This wasn't the time to dwell on it. Forcing my smile in place, I stepped near Jack and gave my attention to Mira.

"I have to tell you," she said to no one in particular, "this whole incident has proven one thing—labor is going to be a bitch. Those contractions hurt like a mother and when they hooked me up to this thing—" She gestured to the monitor. "They barely registered."

Sophia sat in the armchair next to Mira. "Has this finally changed your mind about taking Lamaze?" Her condescension suggested this had been an ongoing battle.

Mira rolled her eyes. "It's changed my mind about wanting drugs. I'd like them as soon as I arrive, please." She hooked eyes with Adam, who had slipped in on the other side of her. "Can you add that to the birthing plan, honey?"

"Add them? I'm demanding them." He brushed her hair from her forehead. "Sorry, but you're not a nice person when you're in pain."

Mira's eyes flared. "You keep that up and I'll exclude you from the birthing room." Adam hadn't been kidding when he'd said she was feisty.

Chandler laughed. "I don't think she's joking."

"Do they know what caused this in the first place?" Hudson's question drew the room's attention back to him. Though he was engaging now in the conversation, he still wasn't huddling close like the rest of us.

Mira's gaze flicked from me to Hudson. "A combination of dehydration and stress. *Stress*. Do you all hear that?" She narrowed her eyes and scanned the room. "So you two right there—" She gestured to Sophia and Jack. "You need to get your shit together because you are hurting me and my baby."

Sophia's mouth tightened, but she refused to look at Jack who stared after her tenderly. Man, he really did love her.

"And you two—" This time Mira pointed to me and then Hudson. "Don't think I don't notice how you're standing apart. And you're barely looking at each other. I don't even want to know what the hell is going on with you right now. Go work it out." The cuff on Mira's arm began clicking as it tightened around her. She turned her attention to the numbers on the screen next to her.

I froze, not sure if she was actually sending us away or if she meant for us to work things out later.

Chandler seemed to get the sense that she meant now. "Are you kicking out Mom and Dad too?"

"No. Their crap is too messed up to fix on demand. But those two—" She sent us both scathing looks. "You better not be that messed up."

"Might as well get comfy then." Chandler settled on the couch and began playing on his phone.

I exchanged glances with Hudson. *Shit.* He wanted to be with Mira—and she was wrong, our crap was too big to solve quickly.

Hudson stepped toward his sister. "Mirabe—"

"I'm not kidding, Hudson. Leave. I don't want to see either of you until you've got that happy glow again." The machine next to her flashed a readout. "See? My blood pressure is spiking. Jesus."

"Mira," Adam said, "just take deep breaths. Settle down. Stop yelling at everyone."

"I'm not yelling at everyone. I'm yelling at them!"

Adam turned to me and Hudson, his expression apologetic.

"We're going." Hudson gestured for me to proceed in front of him. "But we'll be back," he said over his shoulder.

"Happy and glowing," Mira yelled after us.

We walked in silence toward the waiting room at the end of the hall. With each step, my heart grew heavier. This was wrong. I shouldn't be there at the hospital. Hudson should. As for working things out, it was going to take him opening up. And he was certainly not ready for that. His attitude to me since we'd arrived proved that.

At the waiting room, Hudson held the door open for me to go in first. It was a small room, completely enclosed with several couches and a counter with coffee supplies. It was empty, thankfully. Babies might be born at all hours, but no one was expecting one at the moment. At least that gave us privacy.

I turned to face Hudson as he shut the door behind him. "I know you want to be in there with your sister. I can leave. Or we can pretend things are all hunky-dory, if you'd rather. I'll under—"

Hudson cut me off. "Don't leave."

His desperation stunned me. Did that mean he *did* want me there? The man was a bunch of mixed signals. This signal I liked. I'd cling to it, if he'd let me. "Okay. I'll stay."

"For Mira."

My spirits plummeted. "For Mira. Of course." Not for him. He didn't want me to stay for him.

All of a sudden, I wasn't sure if I could do it anymore, if I could remain self-controlled around him. I turned away and made my way to a couch. With shaking knees, I took a seat.

Sitting was better. It made me feel stronger than I was. I thought about the reason we were there—the perky romantic sitting in the room nearby. Her faith and encouragement had been instrumental in reuniting me with Hudson. Even if she couldn't save us again, I owed her.

I lifted my chin and met Hudson's eyes. "Then we need to put everything else aside for right now and give Mira our happy face."

He held my gaze for only a second. "I agree."

There was plenty of room on the couch by me, but he took a seat in a chair instead. He couldn't even sit by me. The rejection rippled through me with excruciating pain. Every move he made, everything he said, hurt.

I wanted to do the same to him. Wanted to hurt him in all the ways he'd hurt me. My fists tightened into balls as I thought about ripping into him, telling him all the things that were barely under the surface of my composure.

But again, I remembered why we were there. Mira would be upset if we didn't walk back in her room together. The best thing I could do for her and myself was make a plan and get back to her.

Back to the comfort of people who made me feel good rather than sad.

Obviously this would require some acting. A lot of acting. "So any idea how to give Mira a happy face? Because she read right through us in there."

"She is very perceptive." Hudson leaned forward, his elbows on his thighs, his chin in his hands. "But I think if we wait here for a while, give us time to supposedly talk things out, then if we go back in there with smiles and...holding hands, she'll believe it." His pause said that even holding hands sounded uncomfortable for him. "She wants to believe it, so she will."

I made a gruff sound in the back of my throat. "Pretending we're a couple. Just like old times."

His head spun toward me. He fastened me with a piercing stare. "We aren't pretending we're a couple. We *are* a couple. We're pretending that we're...that we're not..." He moved his hand in the air as he tried to figure out how to finish his sentence.

When he didn't come up with an end, I pushed him. "That we're not...what? Not fighting? Not completely confused and heartbroken? Not miserable and lied to?" My voice cracked, and I refused to cry. Biting my lip, I crossed one leg over the other and put all my energy into jostling my knee up and down. It helped to focus my pain.

Hudson stared at the wall across from him, refusing to respond or look at me.

I should have dropped it, but I couldn't help myself. "I don't understand how you can say we're a couple when you're living in one place and I'm in another. When you're on dates with another woman."

"I told you what that was," he said quietly.

I ignored him. "When you won't even let me touch you without acting like it burns." I shook my head. I was getting too upset. "I

210

said I wouldn't do this here. I'm sorry." Except I really wasn't. "Sort of."

I wanted him to refute my words, wanted him to explain how things really were. But he didn't. Sure, it wasn't the time or place—I knew that in my head. My heart, on the other hand, didn't care. I was in so much pain, how could he not be? And if he wasn't, what did that mean?

It means he can compartmentalize, I told myself. That's all. God, what I'd give to believe that was all it was.

We sat in silence, the only sound the clicking of the seconds ticking by on the wall clock. Finally, Hudson spoke, his voice low and sincere. "Touching you only burns because it reminds me how much I want to touch you more."

A wave of optimism burst through me, so tangible and fierce that my whole chest felt on fire. "Then touch me more, H. Come home."

He raised a brow and his expression carried the same air of hope that I felt. "And you'll let the past lie?"

With everything in me I wanted to say yes. Yes, I'll live with it. Whatever it is. I'd find a way. I'd said that before, and I'd thought I meant it. But I'd been talking desperate. I couldn't live with it. There was no possible way.

Besides, I respected myself more than that. I respected our relationship more than that. Even if it meant losing him, I had to stand my ground on this. "No. I can't let it lie. But you can tell me what it is you're hiding."

With a shake of his head, he dismissed it.

There we were again—at our impasse. "We might as well be broken up, Hudson, if you can't believe that I'd love you beyond whatever this secret is."

And if we truly couldn't get past this, why were we even taking time apart? Weren't we just postponing the inevitable?

It wasn't something I could face. Not yet. Maybe the time apart was to help make that idea more bearable.

Apparently, Hudson felt the same way. "Let's not do this here."

"Let's not." *Let's not do this at all. Let's go back to where we were three days ago, lost and alone in the mountains.* Happy and glowing, as Mira put it.

If there were anything I'd ever wished for more, I didn't know what it was.

But wishing wouldn't get us through the next hour. I stood up and paced the room. "Okay. We'll go in there. We'll smile. We'll hold hands. We'll be happy and glowing. And Mira will never know the lie."

"Yes," Hudson said. "Thank you."

"What if she asks what our problem was?"

"She won't."

I wasn't so sure and the expression I shot him said exactly that.

"If she does ask, let me handle it."

"Yes, I'll do that." The venom I was trying to bite back slipped past my lips. "You are the master manipulator, after all."

He stared at me with sad eyes. I'd meant to hurt him, and it worked. But he didn't argue, didn't defend himself. He wouldn't even fight with me. Wouldn't fight *for* me.

It's not the place, I reminded myself. The reminder didn't change the hollow ache in my chest. I knew his indifference extended beyond the walls of the hospital.

Hudson stood. "Are you ready to go back?" He shoved his hands in his pockets, obviously keeping them from my reach.

Fucking asshole.

I didn't let him know how much his simple gesture felt like a knife in the gut. "You think she'll believe this was long enough?"

"Yes." He moved to the door and held it open for me. "If we convince her that all is well, then she won't focus on the timespan in the least. She'll have no reason to question what we're selling." He was so clinical about it. So proficient about the steps of pulling off a scheme.

And why wouldn't he be? "Tips from the expert," I said as I passed him.

"You're very good at lashing out, precious. It's interesting that I'm just learning this now." He was behind me, and he said it quietly, but I heard him all the same.

I held on to his endearment—*precious*—like it was gold. Like it was the last drop of water in a desert. Like it was a beacon in a dark storm. He couldn't still call me that and not feel something for me. Could he?

We hurried back to Mira's room, not speaking or looking at each other. Outside her door, Hudson paused. His hand hung at his side now. I placed mine in it automatically, as if it were the most natural thing in the world. Because it was that natural. The way it fit so snugly, so perfectly in his. As if we'd been made to lace our fingers in just that way.

He looked down at where we were joined, studying our hands for long seconds. There was sadness and yearning in his tone when he spoke. "Your hand fits so well in mine, doesn't it? Like it belongs."

I had to turn my head in order to fight the tears. He was so in sync with me. Why, why, why were we apart?

"I didn't mean to say that out loud," he said. "I apologize. Can you still do this?"

Forcing a smile on my face, I turned back to him. "Yep."

"Showtime, then." Hudson led us in, entering with much more zeal than he had earlier. "We're back." He headed straight for his sister, placing a sweet kiss on her forehead. "And everything's fine."

He was such an excellent liar. I'd known he had to be. I'd seen him pretend to his family about me before. Then I'd convinced myself that his acting was so good because he'd actually felt something for me. Seeing Hudson now, so easily falling into the charade—it stung. How much of the past had been a lie as well?

Mira narrowed her eyes. "I want to hear it from Laynie. I don't trust you." She swatted him aside.

Taking a deep breath, I pushed away my heartache and reminded myself this was for Mira. I gave her what I feared could only be taken as a fake grin and slid in closer to her. "Everything really is fine." I looked back at Hudson, hoping for a sign to make the lie easier. I received none. "Maybe not perfect, but things are definitely fine."

Mira frowned dubiously.

Damn. I needed to get my shit together.

Before I could, Hudson stepped in to save the farce. He wrapped his arms around me from behind, a major show of public affection for Hudson. "I don't know what you're talking about. Things are completely perfect."

He nuzzled his face against my hair and I shivered with an unwelcome tingle from head to toe. I sighed into him. How could I not? This was what I wanted—to be held by him, to be loved by him.

But this was fake. It had to be or he'd tell me what I needed to know. Right?

Either way, Mira bought it. She clapped her hands together. "Ah, see? The happy and glowing is back! Thank god." She cast her eyes around the room, stopping first at her mother beside her, then Adam and Chandler and Jack on the sofa, then to me and Hudson in front of her. "This is the best. Now my whole family's here."

I shifted, feeling a little uncomfortable at her declaration. I wasn't family. And at the moment, I was sure I never would be. The farce was going too far. I opened my mouth to protest.

Sophia beat me to it. "Well, not everyone here is family."

Mira glared at her mother. "She is. And right now I'd send you out before Laynie. Since I want all my family here, you can sit over there with your mouth shut and pretend you're shaking because you're cold and when you get home you can have the drink you wish was in that water bottle."

All eyes darted from Mira to Sophia to me. The tension was so thick and palpable. I felt I had to say something. "I should go, Mira. The sentiment is nice, but I'm not really family."

Jack met my eyes. "Yes. You are."

Hudson tightened his grasp around me. "Agreed."

I nodded, not daring to speak. My throat was thick and my eyes filled with tears. At least when Mira looked at me, she thought I was crying out of happiness. She had no idea she was watching my heart break even more.

Forever With You

Chapter Fifteen

Mira was released shortly after seven a.m. under strict orders to take it easy and drink more water. We all walked out together, Adam and Jack fussing over Mira as an attendant wheeled her to the front door. While I'd both hoped and feared that Hudson would drive me home himself, Jordan was waiting as we exited the main doors. Hudson must have texted him while I wasn't watching.

The others had to wait for the valet to bring their cars up, so I was the first to say goodbye. I bent to hug Mira. "Take care of yourself, sister. I don't want to be back at Lenox Hill until you're pushing out a baby—and that better be months from now."

"I couldn't agree more. Thanks for coming, Laynie."

"Anytime." I straightened. "Well, my ride's here." After all the talk of being part of the family, leaving by myself felt extra lonely. My mixed feelings were no longer mixed—I wanted Hudson to drive me home. Desperately.

"Your ride...?" Mira looked from me to Hudson, obviously questioning the different cars.

"We're off to separate places," Hudson said. "Alayna gets to go home and crawl in bed. I'm off to work." Always prepared with an answer, he was. Except when I was asking the questions.

Mira scowled. "You're going to work after no sleep? And I'm the one getting yelled at about working too hard."

Hudson waved his hand dismissively. "I got enough sleep." He walked me to the Maybach, opening the back door for me. "I should kiss you goodbye," he said quietly so that only I could hear.

"I suppose you should. Do you want to?" I held my breath, afraid of the answer. I didn't know the answer for myself. It was like what he said in the hospital waiting room—kissing him only reminded me how I wanted to kiss him more. And knowing that I wouldn't kiss him more anytime soon felt like razorblades to my chest.

His response only heightened my pain. "I've never kissed you just for show, precious. I'm not about to start now." But his actions said differently when he bent in to deliver a partially open-mouthed kiss, no tongue. The type of affection suitable for onlookers.

Without permission, my hand flew to the back of his neck. I held him there, locking our lips for much longer than I believe he'd intended. When I finally pulled away, I made sure I had the last word. "That would be easier to believe if your actions matched your words. But, let me guess—you're not about to start that now either, are you?"

I slipped in the car and slammed the door before he could respond.

***

After five hours of restless sleep, I woke up with another throbbing headache, swollen eyes, and a plan.

I made two phone calls, right off the bat. One of them was productive, earning me an appointment for the next day with someone who, hopefully, could shed some light on Hudson's recent behavior.

The other call got me nowhere. Mirabelle didn't go into work, of course, so it was Stacy that answered when I called the shop. That was fine. She was whom I wanted to talk to anyway. But even though I pleaded and put on my sweetest voice, she refused to talk any more about the video she'd sent.

"I told you, I'm done," she said and hung up.

I bounced my knee as I thought about what to do next. Then I made one more call. "Can you come over for a bit? I need your help with something."

"Um, sure." Liesl sounded groggy, as if I'd woken her up. It was just after one p.m. I probably *had* woken her. "I need, like, twenty. And coffee."

"Awesome. I'll send my driver to get you. With Starbucks."

I got off the phone, showered and dressed in record speed, and then dove into my project. Projects, I'd learned in therapy, even ridiculously unnecessary ones, were excellent forms of distraction. They helped keep me from doing the crazy things I tended to do when I was hurting. It was possible that this project in particular was as crazy as the things it kept me from doing, but I was ignoring that.

More than an hour later, Liesl and I sat on the floor of the library surrounded by books—the books that Hudson had ordered for me through Celia. While most of them hadn't been marked at all, we were pulling those that were. They were easy to find. All of them were bookmarked by Celia Werner's business card. I planned on burning the pile when we were finished.

"Here's another one." Liesl read the highlighted quote. "*'Don't cry, I'm sorry to have deceived you so much, but that's how life is.'* It's from *Lolita*."

I cringed. Nabokov. One of my favorites. "Put it in the to-go pile." On the notepad next to me I scribbled down the quote.

She stacked it with the others that had been highlighted—the books I planned to get rid of. "What do you think it means?"

I shook my head and looked over the list in my lap. There were several from my favorite books and some from books I'd never read:

"People could put up with being bitten by a wolf but what properly riled them was a bite from a sheep."— James Joyce, *Ulysses*

"He who controls the past controls the future. He who controls the present controls the past."— George Orwell, *1984*

"Blameless people are always the most exasperating." — George Eliot, *Middlemarch*

"Once a bitch always a bitch, what I say."— William Faulkner, *The Sound and the Fury*

"There ain't no sin and there ain't no virtue. There's just stuff people do."— John Steinbeck, *The Grapes of Wrath*

"It's not my fate to give up—I know it can't be."— Henry James, *The Portrait of a Lady*

"There is no harm in deceiving society as long as she does not find you out."— E.M. Forster, *A Passage to India*

There was another page, much of the same. If there was a hidden message, I couldn't find it. "I'm beginning to think none of them mean anything. They're simply ominous quotations intended to mess with my mind."

Liesl snatched the list from me. She scanned it quickly. "I think she's talking about herself. She doesn't think she's harming anyone, she's not going to give up, she thinks she controls stuff, and she's a bitch." She tossed the notepad to the ground and reached for another book. "So spill it. Why did you so badly want me here for this only mildly entertaining task?"

I twisted my lips. "I didn't. There's something else." With a deep breath, I spilled the plan that had occupied my mind since waking.

When I was finished, Liesl sat back against the couch, her forehead pinched. "So let me get this straight—you're going to obsess and stalk people on purpose?"

"Research," I corrected. "Research, dammit! Not stalk." Though the idea sounded much better in my head than when I said it out loud.

"You're obsessed with your boy toy's past. And you want to *track down* people to research whatever he's hiding from you. Right? Or did I miss something?"

"That's exactly it." I nodded more enthusiastically than necessary. "That's not stalking. That's talking to people. People who have insight into Hudson. If he won't tell me what I want to know, then I can ask them. Get a clearer picture."

Liesl shot me a disapproving glance.

"Why is this not an ideal plan?" I'd hoped she'd be more supportive. Especially since parts of the idea were already in action.

"Because you have a history of being, you know..." She clicked her tongue and circled a finger in the air next to her head, the universal sign for psycho. "I'll just say it. Cuckoo. You've been cuckoo. And I haven't been to that many of your group thingies, but I seem to remember that snooping and prying and digging into people's stuff are all on the no-no list."

I shut my eyes so I wouldn't be tempted to roll them. Liesl had been to a few of my meetings. I hadn't realized she'd actually paid attention. "This is different."

She nodded. "Yes, it is." Then she stopped nodding and raised a brow. "How exactly?"

Inwardly I groaned. To me, the difference was obvious. "The other times it was a compulsion. I couldn't help myself. This time, I'm choosing it. It makes it totally different."

"Uh-huh. Totally different." She didn't seem convinced. "And why am I here? 'Cause if you want me to tell you you're not crazy, that's not happening."

"Then, well, fine. Think I'm crazy." Liesl's version of sanity wasn't necessarily one for the textbooks anyway. "But I also need your help."

Her eyes lit up. "You want me to take down that Selina bitch?" She punched a fist into her palm a few times.

"*Celia*," I corrected. "What is with you and getting names wrong?"

"It's fun to watch you get all I-know-everything and correct me." She smacked her gum with a wide smile. "I really will take Ms. Celia Werner down if you want me to. I'll kick her ass so hard she'll lose that cute bubble butt of hers." Without any guilt she added, "Yeah, I checked out her behind. Sue me."

"Um, no. No ass kicking. Please." Liesl could do it, though. She was a brute when she wanted to be. And wouldn't that be awesome to see Celia with her pretty little face bruised and bloodied?

But that hadn't been the help I'd needed from Liesl. I had another plan in mind. Perching on the coffee table next to where she sat on the floor, I put on my puppy dog eyes. "I was hoping you could come with me to see someone."

"Oh, Jesus. You're trying to convert me to stalking too?"

"There's no stalking." It wasn't in the plan, anyway. "I just need to talk to a lady that doesn't want to talk to me. I'm hoping if I'm not alone, she might be more amicable."

Liesl grinned, obviously flattered with the request. "You think I'm intimidating, don't you? You want me to intimidate the fuck out of her."

"Yeah. Sure."

Her smile widened.

Then it fell. "God, I don't know, I don't know!" She stood up and began walking in a circle. "The whole thing seems really fun. And I want to be a good friend. But I'm not sure if I should be supporting you or putting up a big fat stop sign in your path." She brought her hands to her forehead, massaging her temples. "What to do, what to do? Maybe we should call Brian."

I flew up from the table. "You should be *supporting me*. Please! And we don't need to call Brian." I heaved a lungful of air out, trying to calm down. My plan could work without Liesl's help, but I needed her to understand, at least. Needed her to realize how close to the edge I was, how, as far as I was concerned, this was my last chance. My last chance at sanity.

"Okay. You might be right—this might not be the healthiest of ideas." I waited until Liesl's eyes were on mine before continuing.

"But here's the thing—if I don't take some control over this limbo state that my relationship is in, then I'm going to end up doing the stalking and obsessing and all of that anyway. I'm being proactive. I'm taking a stand for once instead of letting a guy walk all over me. Because if not this, I only have two other choices—let Hudson and me stay in this '*time apart*' mode, which is asinine and unproductive and really leaves me as a doormat. Or break up. And I'm not ready to lose him." My lip trembled with the raw honesty. "And I don't think he's ready to lose me. Or he would have ended things already."

Liesl's eyes grew compassionate. But also concerned. "You are so overthinking this, Laynie."

I threw my hands emphatically to the side. "No! I'm not. I'm *fighting* for the guy I love." My eyes stung with the tears that seemed to be ever-present as of late. "Yes, I'm pissed that he's not fighting for me, but maybe he doesn't know how to fight for anyone. Maybe he needs me to show him."

If Liesl still had reservations, she hid them. "All right, I'm in. What else am I going to do with my afternoon, anyway?"

"Really? Thank you. Thank you!" I hugged her. Though her company wasn't crucial, I was desperate for it. Her presence helped with the unending loneliness that occupied my heart since Hudson had walked out the door.

When I let her go, she shrugged dismissively. "It's all good. Besides, this book project is pretty much done."

I looked around at the mess. There were still a few unmarked stacks that needed to be shelved. That could be done later. "Then I'm ready to go if you are."

"Yup." She grabbed her backpack from the couch. "Where we headed, anyway?"

"Greenwich Village."

I'd told Jordan that I'd be leaving later. I texted him now and found he was already waiting in the parking garage. After grabbing my purse and my cell phone, we stepped in the elevator.

We stood next to each other, leaning against the back wall. Liesl nudged my shoulder. "Have you considered that you might not like what you uncover with all this?"

The sinking feeling in my chest wasn't just from the descent of the elevator. "I'm pretty certain that whatever it is, it might kill me." That was the bitch about the situation—Hudson had confessed pretty shitty stuff already. If he couldn't tell me this, it had to be bad.

So why was I so desperate to find out?

Because that's who I was. And whatever this was, it was who he was too. "It might kill me, but I need to know. And then I can move on, preferably with Hudson."

It didn't fix the bigger problem—Hudson wasn't being honest with me. But maybe if he realized that I really would love him no matter what, he'd be able to let his last walls come down and we could finally start working on rebuilding our relationship together.

***

Since neither of us had eaten, we stopped to grab souvlakia from a food cart nearby before heading to the Village. By the time we got to Mirabelle's, it was nearly four. I wasn't positive that Stacy would still be there, or that she'd be available to talk. Or that she'd answer the bell when I rang. Their clients could only come by appointment. If she wasn't expecting anyone, would she open the door?

Maybe showing up unannounced was a long shot, but when she'd hung up on me, this was the only way I could think of to get a few questions answered.

At the door, a sudden flashback of the first time I'd been there flooded my memory. I'd been so nervous, standing there waiting with Hudson for his sister to answer. It had been our first outing as a couple—as a *pretend* couple. The fear that I'd mess up the charade had been immense, but more than that, the sizzling energy between me and the man that stood at my side had threatened to light me on fire. Threatened to consume me.

In the end, it *had* consumed me, and that was why I was there now—burned and blistered and broken.

Before ringing, I turned to Liesl. "This is where I need you. There's a peephole. If Stacy looks through it and sees me, I'm not sure she'll open the door."

"Cool. I got this."

I moved to the side of the building and made myself flush with the wall. At my nod, she rang the bell. The door opened almost immediately.

"Hi. Vanessa Vanderhal?" Stacy asked Liesl.

She must have been waiting for a client. Before Liesl could answer, I stepped into view.

"Oh, no. Not you." Stacy began to shut the door.

But Liesl wedged her shoulder in the entrance before the opening got too narrow. "Hey, she only has a few questions. Nothing that's going to take more than a few minutes. You're the only one she can ask. Can't you help a girl out? Woman to woman?"

I'd known Liesl could be intimidating. I didn't realize she could also be charming.

Stacy narrowed her eyes, considering. Considering was better than I'd expected, to be honest.

I looked to Liesl, mentally sending her signals to lay on more charm since it seemed to be working.

She apparently wasn't on the same wavelength. "If you aren't interested in doing this the easy way, I'm willing to go another route. I'll introduce myself—I'm Liesl. I have a triple black belt in karate and I do competitive boxing on the side. So come on. Let us in."

The extent of Liesl's fighting skills was kickboxing at a nearby gym. But Stacy didn't know that.

Stacy groaned. "Oh, all right. Come on in. But make it quick. I have a client in fifteen."

I was more relieved than I realized I would be. There were too many questions about the video that could only be answered by three people. And I wasn't about to ask Celia. "Thank you, Stacy. We'll be in and out. I promise."

She widened the door for us to come in. "Yeah, yeah." To herself, she muttered, "I knew there wouldn't be an end to this." As soon as we were in, she let the door slam and crossed her arms over her chest. "What is it you want to know? I didn't stage the video, if that's what he's convinced you."

Obviously we were having our conversation in the front entry of the store. At least she'd let us in.

"No, he didn't." I supposed he deserved credit for that—for not denying that the kiss had taken place. By avoiding telling me anything, he'd avoided making up a lie. Was that an effort to remain true to our promise to be honest with each other? If so, didn't he realize that concealment was just another form of lie?

"Actually," I said, "he won't tell me anything about the video at all."

"Ah, I see." Stacy rubbed her gloss-shined lips together. "And so you're asking me instead."

The judgment and superiority lacing her words irked me to no end. I wanted to shake the woman by her thin shoulders and tell her she didn't know. That she couldn't understand.

But I was trying to play nice. And why would she understand anyway? My best friend was having a hard time figuring out why it was so important to me to uncover Hudson's secrets, why would a practical stranger get it?

She wouldn't.

I gritted my teeth. "Yes, that's exactly what I'm doing. I'm going behind his back and asking you instead. It's definitely not one of my finer moments."

Stacy stared at me hard for several seconds. "Well, we've all experienced some of those, I suppose." Her shoulders relaxed ever so slightly. "So he doesn't know you're here?"

I shook my head.

"And you're not planning to tell him?"

"No." Guilt shuddered through me like a cold chill. Hudson hadn't asked me not to talk to Stacy again, but I'd promised to be open and truthful with him. Not telling him felt secretive. Sure, he wasn't living up to his promise, and he'd called for a fucking break—those facts probably excused me from the open-door policy. But I'd said I was done keeping secrets. Period. Either I meant it or I wasn't worthy of him in the first place. And if I wasn't worthy of being with him, why did this whole detective scheme matter?

I changed my answer. "Actually, that's a lie. I will tell him." If I ever actually had a chance to speak to him again. "I told you before—we're working on honesty. I can't betray him." Even if he'd betrayed me by not being forthcoming.

My transparency had likely cost me Stacy's cooperation, but my only other option was to lie to her. And that seemed shitty too.

She pursed her lips, her eyes darting back and forth between me and Liesl. Finally, she sighed, leaning back on the counter behind her. "What do you want to know?"

Knowing our time was short, I jumped right in. "Why did you film Hudson and Celia kissing? I mean, what did you plan to do with the video in the first place?"

"Prove he was lying." She said it matter-of-factly, as if I'd understand with just that much. When she realized I didn't, she expounded. "I was supposed to meet him that night. For coffee—I think I told you that before. As I was walking up, I saw him with *her*. He'd protested so much about them being a couple that I knew he'd deny it again. So I filmed it. As proof."

My chest tightened. Oh, how the protest story sounded familiar. Still, there were holes. "But you never showed it to him."

She shook her head. "I didn't end up needing to. I walked up to them right after I filmed it. While they were still...like that." She cringed as if the memory of seeing them kissing hurt her.

I knew how that felt. And it hurt doubly that Stacy was upset about it. She obviously had something with him, even though he'd denied it. How many women had he been with that he'd told me he hadn't? Was Norma also on that list?

Well, that I'd find out tomorrow, if all went as planned.

Stacy brushed a strand of golden hair off her face. "I'd filmed them in case they stopped before I got there. In case he denied it. But he didn't."

No, denial wasn't Hudson's thing—redirection was. And avoidance.

Or maybe that was just with me. "What did he do when he saw you?"

Stacy's nose crinkled as she recalled the scene. "He acted surprised, even though I was supposed to be meeting him. Or maybe it was because he'd lost track of time or forgotten he was meeting me. I don't know. Celia apologized first, which was strange because I didn't realize she knew anything about me. Then Hudson apologized. Most of the explaining came from Celia. I guess he was shocked to have been caught or something. I really didn't listen to most of what she said. I was shocked as well. And too busy feeling stupid."

"Feeling stupid?" This was where I needed clarification. Hudson had seemed honestly perplexed when I'd mentioned Stacy had been there to meet him.

"Yes, stupid. He'd made me feel like he liked me, you know?" She seemed to be recalling an old ache that hadn't healed entirely. "And all the time he was with her. Why would he do that? "

"Why do any men cheat on their women?" Liesl asked then returned to biting the nail she'd been working on since we'd arrived.

I frowned. Of all the negative traits I was realizing about my lover, I sure hoped cheating wasn't one I had to add to the list.

Stacy protested the logic in that. "He asked me to meet him, though. Hudson Pierce doesn't seem like the type to mix up his dates. If anyone could successfully pull off an affair, that man could."

That's exactly why Norma scared me. But, like Stacy was saying, if Hudson were really with Norma—or back then, with Celia—wouldn't he be better at covering his tracks? That was the part that didn't make sense.

Maybe Stacy had misread his intentions. "How did he make you feel like he liked you? I thought you only accompanied him to that charity event last year." Taking a stab in the dark, I added, "I didn't realize you were together."

Stacy lowered her eyes. "We weren't. Not really." She ran her hands along the counter behind her. "After that charity event he never asked me out again. But we talked a lot—by email. He flirted. Sent me flowers a couple of times. That's why I thought there was a possibility. That night on the video was the first time he'd offered to see me in person again."

"Maybe they were dicking with you together." Liesl wiped her freshly "manicured" hand on her jeans. "You know. Like maybe the emails weren't from him."

"You mean Celia sent them?" I considered it. I'd certainly learned Celia wasn't to be trusted, that she'd manipulate information for her benefit. "Yeah, she could have." And I liked that scenario better than some of the others.

Stacy, on the other hand, didn't like the idea at all. She straightened up to her full height and narrowed her eyes in my direction. "Are you saying that you think Hudson couldn't possibly like me? That's pretty nervy to assume. What, you don't think I'm good enough for him?"

Man, that woman had claws. It wasn't even me who'd suggested the idea.

I put my hands up in an attempt to calm her. "No. That's not it at all. There's just details that don't add up. Like you said he seemed surprised to see you there. And when I mentioned you being there to meet him, he had no idea what I was talking about. Total deer in the headlights. Maybe he was faking his reaction—I'm not denying that's a possibility. But that's exactly why I wanted to talk to you. I'm trying to figure it out for myself."

Liesl poked me with her elbow. "And tell her about Celia WerWhore."

I ignored her jab though it inwardly made me smile. "That's the other thing, Stacy. Celia tried to pull a scam on me recently. And now she's messing with me in other ways. I may not be the first of Hudson's interests to get that treatment."

Stacy's posture didn't change, but her expression said she was pondering the new information. "So when he took me to the charity event, I showed up on her radar?"

"Possibly." I hoped that was it. Otherwise Hudson was lying to me about his relationship with Stacy. "And possibly not." That was the problem with secrets—anything was potentially the truth.

Stacy's eyes grew dim, as if the idea that all of it had been a hoax disappointed her more than catching the guy she liked with another woman. I got that. She'd wanted Hudson Pierce to be interested in her. Simply by being a woman, I could relate to crushing on a guy. Being me, I could relate to crushing on Hudson. If I'd discovered he'd faked being into me…well, that would have been more devastating than the current situation I was in.

I decided to give her some compassion. "But even if it wasn't Hudson who wrote those emails, Celia obviously thought you were a threat. That has to mean he showed some interest in you in front of her."

Stacy blew out a stream of air. "It's actually an interesting theory. It fits in some ways."

"Do tell." Liesl was as eager now for the information as I was.

"Like I said, he did act strange when I came up to him. And whenever he came in the shop, he ignored me. As if he hadn't said all the beautiful things he'd said to me online. He was very poetic. His emails were like long letters."

"I'm not claiming to know who the actual author was," I started tentatively, afraid of hurting Stacy's feelings more, "but from what I know of Hudson, he's not much of a letter writer. And Celia does seem to be comfortable around the literary world." The quotes she'd picked to highlight in my books indicated as such, anyway.

"What was the email address he sent from?" Occasionally Liesl came up with things I should have asked.

Stacy wrinkled her brow. "H.Pierce@gmail.com, I think."

I was already shaking my head when Liesl asked, "Is that his email?"

"I only know of his Pierce Industries account. He uses it for both business and personal, but he rarely sends personal emails." Or if he did, I wasn't aware.

The bell rang, announcing Stacy's next client. She looked to the door then back to us, as if she was torn.

I felt the same way. There was more to potentially uncover, but I'd promised we'd be in and out. Besides, there probably wasn't anything else I could know without reading the actual emails and that seemed like too much to ask from Stacy unless she offered. "Thanks again, for your time and your answers. I know you're busy now."

She nodded as she crossed in front of us to open the door. With her hand on the knob, she paused. "I should be thanking you too, I suppose. You've enlightened the situation." She opened the door before I could respond. "Vanessa? Welcome to Mirabelle's. Come on in."

Stacy's client walked in and we headed out.

"If I think of anything else," Stacy called after me. "I'll contact you."

It was a hopeful ending to the conversation. If she was anything like me—and very few people were, but it was possible—she'd go home and reread all the emails "Hudson" sent with the new scenario in mind. Maybe she'd find something there and send me a note.

I texted Jordan and discovered he'd found a meter down the block. He waved, letting us know his location.

Liesl linked her arm in mine as we walked toward the Maybach. "Do you think you learned anything?"

I shrugged. "I'd like to believe it was all a scam on Celia's part. But that doesn't answer why Hudson was kissing her or why he won't tell me the truth about it."

"Maybe she asked him to play along. Would he do that? Or he was in on it all along."

I bit my lip. "All of those options are possible." I thought he'd been well at the time he'd met me, but maybe he had still been playing people. Was that what Hudson didn't want me to know? That so recently, he hadn't been well?

Or was it Celia he was protecting? Yet again.

***

The club was already open to the public when I showed up for work that night, so instead of using the employee entrance, I went through the front doors. If I hadn't, I wouldn't have seen Celia waiting in line. So much for her being bored with the game.

The doorman asked before I had a chance to remind him. "Not her, right?"

"Right." I looked out toward the blonde once more. It was somewhat comforting to know she was still interested in tormenting me. To my sick mind, it proved that she thought I was still important to Hudson. Even if it wasn't true any longer, at least she hadn't gotten the memo.

As I stared at her, she waved. "Hi, Laynie." It was the first time she'd talked to me since she'd begun her stalking.

I didn't respond with words, but I did smile before going into the club. In about two minutes she was going to be turned down at the door. That was definitely something to grin about.

It was the last time I smiled for the remainder of the night. My shift was ho-hum and I worked my ass off keeping on top of the summer crowd, but the constant ache of missing Hudson ate at me. Everywhere I looked, I saw him—in the bubble rooms, in the office, at the bar.

By three a.m. when my shift was over, the idea of going back to the lonely penthouse had me in tears. I considered going somewhere else instead—Liesl's, a hotel. The loft. *I could go to the loft and see him.* Be with the man I wanted to be with.

But why would I want to be with someone who didn't want to be with me? That was proof that I wasn't the person I'd once been— the person who would have gone anywhere to be with the man she was into, whether he wanted her or not.

So I ended up at the penthouse. Alone. I managed not to cry as Reynold drove me there, but the tears started before I exited the elevator. They continued while I got ready for bed, and while I checked my phone that I'd left at home during the night. Then they turned to sobs when I read the one text message I had:

Sleep tight, precious.

Tomorrow, I thought as I cried myself to sleep for the fourth time in a row. *Maybe tomorrow I'll wake up from this horrible nightmare.*

Forever With You

Chapter Sixteen

"Jordan, I need to go to Pierce Industries?" I asked when I got in the car the next afternoon. I paused, wondering if I should say that I wanted to see Hudson. It wasn't really a lie—I did want to see him. He just wasn't whom I *intended* to see.

"Certainly, Ms…Laynie." He corrected himself before I had to. After a moment he added, "I'm sure he'll enjoy the surprise."

I smiled and nodded as his eyes met mine in the rearview mirror. It bothered me that he knew enough about my life and my day-to-day schedule to know that Hudson didn't expect me. Had Hudson told Jordan he didn't want me to come by? Then he probably wouldn't agree to take me. But then I'd find my own way to his office—Hudson had to know that about me by now. Perhaps my driver was simply informed of my daily plans. Though it wasn't by me, so how accurate did he expect that information to be? I wasn't Hudson's prisoner, after all.

Whatever knowledge the two—three, if I included Reynold—shared about me, I was convinced that Hudson was always apprised of my whereabouts. Jordan would likely text Hudson the minute I got out of the car, telling him I was on my way up.

I couldn't stop my bodyguard from telling on me—it would risk his job. But I could buy some time. When we pulled in front of the Pierce Industries building, I leaned toward the front seat. "Give me a few minutes before you report me, will you? I don't want to ruin the surprise."

He didn't verbally agree, but Jordan's smile said he'd play along.

"Thank you." I kissed my driver on the cheek, surprising both him and me with the affection, and stepped out of the car.

Considering how destroyed my heart was, my spirits were actually almost good as I hit the elevator button for Hudson's floor. The talk with Stacy had gone well, and that boosted my confidence that today's appointment would follow suit. Even without Liesl accompanying me, I felt capable of accomplishment. And if all went well, I'd have answers.

Hopefully they wouldn't be answers that destroyed me more.

I panicked only briefly as the elevator opened on Hudson's floor. I peeked through the glass walls to Hudson's waiting room. Except for Trish at her desk, the room was empty. Hudson's office door was closed. If Jordan had already sent a text about me, Hudson either hadn't read it yet or wasn't in the building. Either way, it was good news for me.

I escaped down the hall free and clear.

Norma Ander's office was easy to find. There were only top executives on that floor so there weren't many to look through. I could tell from the outside that hers was smaller than Hudson's and didn't have a corner view. For some reason, that made me feel good. God, was I really such a spiteful bitch? No, I was simply a woman scorned.

I'd scheduled my appointment with Norma's assistant so I already knew I'd find a male at the desk outside her door. What I didn't know from his voice was how attractive he was. Not attractive in the dominating powerful way that Hudson was, but in the cute, nerdy way that was trendy lately. He seemed about my age or possibly a year or two older. His hair was light brown and unruly and his blue eyes were bright despite being hidden behind dark framed glasses.

How lucky was Norma to be surrounded by hotties? Maybe I needed to take a job at Pierce Industries after all so I could enjoy the view.

Like I cared about any guy besides Hudson. If I could just have that view back, I'd be happy.

The nameplate indicated his name was Boyd. I stepped up and introduced myself. "Alayna Withers to see Norma Anders."

"Let me just buzz her to see if she's ready for you. Please feel free to take a seat."

The idea of sitting made me want to puke—I was much too nervous. "No, I'll stand. Thank you." I circled the small waiting area, pretending to study the art on the walls while stealing glances into Norma's office. Despite her door being open, I couldn't see her desk, and the more time I had to myself, the more I thought I'd chicken out. The meeting with her could very well backfire, after all. She may not get the whole woman-to-woman thing. The possibility of security or Hudson being phoned was quite high. Both those scenarios were unattractive.

For good or bad, I didn't chicken out and Norma didn't keep me waiting. "Alayna, please come in." She stood aside to let me pass her and gestured for me to take a seat in front of her desk.

As she shut the door behind me I heard her say, "Stop it. You're being bad." At least that's what it sounded like she said.

I turned back to her before sitting. "Excuse me?"

"Oh, nothing. I was talking to my assistant."

As she crossed around to her side of the desk, I took in her space. Not only was it simpler and smaller than Hudson's, it also lacked any aesthetic form. The room consisted of a desk, three chairs, two bookcases, and several file cabinets. Apparently Celia Werner hadn't been hired to design all the offices—just Hudson's.

Norma cleared her throat. Since I hadn't initiated the conversation, it seemed she would. "I was surprised by your request to meet with me. I assume it's about Gwen?"

When Boyd had asked the reason for my appointment with Norma, I'd simply said, *"It's personal. I'm her sister's boss."* The implication was clear.

Also, it was totally misleading.

I sat up taller in my chair. It was lower than Norma's and I supposed that was a tactic to make her clients feel beneath her. I wouldn't let it affect my confidence. "No, I'm not here about Gwen. Though I may have led your assistant to believe that's what it was about. I apologize for that deception."

Norma blinked once. "Now my interest is piqued. Go on."

I leveled my eyes with hers. "I'm here to ask you about Hudson."

"Hudson?" She actually jolted in her chair from the surprise. "You couldn't have shocked me more if you said you were here to talk about the pope. Why on earth would you be asking me about your boyfriend?"

It was the most words she'd ever spoken to me directly. It occurred to me that I knew absolutely nothing about this woman— whether she was fun or serious or compassionate or mean. She'd always acted as though she disapproved of me or I disinterested her. Was that simply because I was with Hudson? She was a woman with authority—she'd likely learned over time how to be tough, learned to thicken her skin. Was there a girl beneath her exterior that I could appeal to with my jealousies and insecurities?

I hoped so. "I'm interested in your relationship with him. With Hudson."

Her mouth curled up on one side. "Call me a bitch, but why aren't you asking him?"

I'd already called her a bitch many times in my head, but I recognized the title hadn't been validated. Yet. And, just as when Stacy had judged me, I felt the urge to be defensive. That would get me nowhere though. "I have asked him. He's answered. I'd like your clarification."

She nodded, accepting my answer easily. "I have a business relationship with him. He's my boss. I'm his lead financial officer."

"Business only?"

"Business only."

I'd feared her answer wouldn't convince me, and it didn't. He signed her paychecks—for that reason alone, why would she disclose information to me? And if he had been her lover, or still was her lover, then she had doubly the reason not to be honest with me.

Still, I hoped that proceeding with the conversation would teach me something. Maybe she'd slip, or I'd see it in her face—anything. "You obviously find him attractive. You don't hide it when you look at him." She stared at him like he was Adonis.

Then again, wasn't he?

Norma let out a small laugh. "He's a very attractive man." *Well, duh.* "But I'm not interested in him that way."

There was no way that was true. Besides what I'd seen from her, Hudson had confirmed her interest. "He said you approached him about having a relationship."

Her eyes widened in surprise. "Did he?"

My heart thundered in my chest. *Why would he lie about that?*

But then Norma conceded. "Well, I did. Quite a while ago. I'm simply surprised it meant enough to mention. Things have changed now."

I tilted my head, trying to read her. Very few of my crushes had simply disappeared with time. Generally it took a new man to end my interest. But I obsessed, so I didn't have an accurate point of reference.

Hudson, however, believed she still liked him. "He doesn't seem to think things have changed."

She stared for two solid seconds before she narrowed her eyes and grinned. "Maybe I don't want him to think so."

I wrung my hands in my lap, determined not to slap the smugness off her face no matter how tempting it was. Instead, I pinned her with my eyes, hoping that my persistence would deliver.

After a brief stare-off, I won. Sort of. She offered an answer, albeit not a completely satisfactory one. "He's my boss. It pays to flatter him."

I leaned back in my chair. "There's more than that. What are you not saying?"

Her eyes flickered briefly with rage or panic. I wasn't sure which, but neither would get me what I wanted.

I backed down and tried another tactic—appealing to her sense of compassion. "I'm sorry. It's none of my business, I know. But I'm desperate for information. It would mean a lot to me. And with Gwen at the club now, I thought maybe we could find some sort of a bond."

Now her eyes definitely showed rage—and not just a flicker. "Are you threatening Gwen's job security if I don't answer your questions?"

Fuck! "No! God, no. I love Gwen." *Not exactly true.* "Or, I like her anyway. A lot. She's good at the job. Perfect for what I was looking for." Jesus, I was flustered.

I took a deep breath and centered myself. "I mean that I think of everyone at The Sky Launch as family. Gwen's moving her way into that category quite nicely. Even though she's sometimes blunt and overly anxious to speak her mind."

Norma chuckled. "That's Gwen for you." It was her turn to tilt her head and study me. "I appreciate you getting her the job, by the way. I thanked Hudson, but he says it's really you who hired her. She needed out of Eighty-Eighth. In many ways, she was as desperate as you say you are now."

She swept her tongue across her teeth and narrowed her eyes, considering. "And for that reason—because of what you did for Gwen—I'll share something with you." She pushed a button on her phone. "Boyd, can you come in here?"

Boyd's voice filled the room. "Certainly."

Norma focused her attention on her closed door. I turned in my seat and followed suit, curious and anxious about what her assistant could offer to my situation. Was this who would drag me out of the building?

Boyd rapped on the door and then opened it without waiting for a response. "May I help you?"

Damn, his grin was that of a schoolboy's, all sweet and contagious.

Norma's smile almost matched his. Definitely contagious. "Boyd, Ms. Withers wants to know if I'm having an affair with Hudson Pierce."

Boyd's mouth dropped open and his eyes flitted from me to Norma to me to Norma. He wiped his hand on his suit pants, suddenly nervous.

"It's okay, dear. Answer honestly. As honestly as you like." Her tone suggested an inside secret.

Did Boyd schedule trysts for his boss? I braced myself for his response.

At Norma's encouragement, he relaxed and met my eyes. "She is not."

The answer should have been comforting. But I was a cynical girl. "How can you be certain? Are you there when she has her meetings with him?"

"I am not. But I know that she isn't." He looked one more time to Norma for permission to continue. Seeming to believe he'd received it, he went on. "She wouldn't do that to the person she's involved with." He moved his focus from me back to Norma. "She's very loyal."

"Thank you, Boyd. That's all."

He nodded once and left.

The door wasn't yet shut when I spun back to Norma. "You're involved with someone?" The blush on her cheekbones said it all. "Oh my god, it's Boyd!"

Her blush and her smile deepened. Damn, the woman had it bad. "Now do you really think I would fool around with someone else in the office when my lover is right outside my door?"

I was speechless. "Why didn't Hudson just tell me you were involved?" It would have eased my mind. Of course, affairs could still happen, but her having a boyfriend diminished the likelihood. Especially knowing how gaga he was over Boyd.

At the mention of Hudson, though, Norma's giddiness evaporated.

"Hudson doesn't know," I realized. "Why? Is it a big secret or something?"

"Corporate policy is no dating within the same department. Boyd would be transferred. I don't want to lose him. He's worked for me for two years; we've been together for half that time. He's the best assistant I've ever had. In more ways than one."

"And perpetuating the idea that you're still into Hudson is to throw him off track." I was slow but catching on. "Gotcha." The woman wasn't a bitch—she was simply nervous her secret would be found out.

A wave of guilt rolled over me. "I feel like an idiot. I'm sorry to have assumed. And don't worry—your secret is safe with me."

She shrugged. "Thanks. It's actually fun to tell someone." Her smile reappeared.

"I'm sure." The true nature of my relationship with Hudson had started as a secret. I'd been busting to tell someone—anyone—what was really going on. I certainly could relate.

Plus, talking about being in love was one of the highlights of the emotion.

Despite my paranoid nature, Norma convinced me she only had eyes for her assistant. But that didn't explain all the time she was spending with my boyfriend. "So if there isn't any romantic interest, why are you with Hudson so much?" I was keen to hear if Norma would say it was a business deal as well, and if so, if she'd expand.

Norma's forehead furrowed. "He hasn't told you?"

I shook my head, and she took that in. "Well, maybe I understand." This seemed to be more for her than myself. To me, she

242

explained, "It's a very complicated idea he's working on. He owns stock in a company but wants to purchase enough to have a controlling interest. But he doesn't want the board members to be aware that he has the controlling interest. So he's in the process of buying out another company that has enough stock in the first company to equal controlling interest when combined with the shares he already owns. Since he's doing this all under the radar, we've had to be covert about the purchase. It's all been like a game. Chess moves. We move, they move. I've had to research financial laws and tactics I've never encountered before. It will be a miracle if it goes through, but I'm beginning to believe in miracles."

Her eyes lit up as she talked about the deal and I realized it wasn't Hudson that turned her on as much as it was the work.

She paused, thinking perhaps that she'd gotten carried away. "Hudson's methods have been brilliant," she concluded. "He's a fascinating man to watch in action."

"It's obvious you love your job, Norma." I waited as she nodded. "Hudson's mind is certainly one of the most creative I've ever encountered. It must be a real thrill to get to work with him so closely." I loved it when he let me work with him. It was a real turn-on both mentally and physically. "And I'm not insinuating anything by that."

"I understood what you meant. And yes, it is." Her face grew serious. "By the way, I meant it when I said that I think you're a much better match for him than that Werner girl. She made him miserable. You make him almost happy."

I'd heard Norma insinuate that Hudson had been with Celia before. He'd dismissed it, saying she was as snowed as everyone, that he'd used the misconception to avoid Norma's advances.

Now that I'd seen the video, I wondered if there wasn't more to Norma's notion. "Why do you believe he was with Celia? Did he ever tell you he was? Did you see them together?"

She frowned as she recalled. "He never said they were. She accompanied him to many of the office functions. I simply assumed. Were they not?"

I ignored her question, eager for more information. "Did you ever see them intimate together? You know, holding hands? Kissing?"

"No, I didn't." She thought about it a moment, as if realizing that it was strange. "That's part of what seemed miserable about them as a couple—they were so unaffectionate when they were together. There was never the shine in his eyes like there is when he's with you. Even when he talks about you, he glows."

This surprised me. "He talks about me?"

"All the time." She said it as if it were the most matter-of-fact thing in the world.

My heart flip-flopped. "Hmm. I never knew."

***

I left Norma's office feeling lighter than when I'd arrived. She'd assuaged my doubts about Hudson's fidelity and had even given some insight on his relationship with Celia. More and more, the video seemed to be a sham.

Walking to the elevator, my better mood quickly quieted as I remembered I had to get past Hudson's office again. If Jordan *had* texted him, he'd certainly be on the lookout for me. I wasn't sure if I wanted to bump into him or not. If I saw him, I'd have to explain why I was there.

But I'd see him. And that sounded both glorious and painful.

I walked cautiously down his hall, trying my best to keep my heels quiet on the marble floor, all the while keeping my eyes pinned on his closed office door. Which was why I didn't notice he was standing in front of me until I bumped into him.

"Alayna."

There it was, the sound I loved above all others—my name on the tongue of the man I loved. The way he said it, reverent like a hymn, like a lullaby—it kindled the emotions I'd been attempting to bury deep inside. Goose bumps scattered down my arms and my chest grew tight. So tight, so ready to burst.

I started to say something, but my voice was gone.

Hudson wrapped his arm around mine. "Let's talk in private, shall we?" He led me to his office. "Hold my calls," he said over his shoulder to Trish. Then he shut and locked the door behind us.

If the circumstances had been different, the whole dominating alpha mood he was in would have been hot. Okay, it was still hot. No matter the circumstances. And I'd been a bad girl—going behind his back and speaking with his employee. Maybe if I was lucky, I'd get spanked.

Wow, wasn't I feeling optimistic?

"Well, hello, H."

He released my arm. "What are you doing here, Alayna?" He looked and sounded tired. His eyes were bloodshot and rimmed with dark circles. Was he losing sleep over me? Or were work and an unfamiliar bed the more likely cause?

Even with the bags, he looked delicious. I'd wondered many times if I'd ever get bored of his devastatingly good looks. If so, it wasn't today. His simple presence affected me—aroused me, flustered me. Pissed me off. The combination of attraction, frustration and desperation put me in an odd mood—a cross between flirty and feisty with a whole lot of bitter on top.

"What am I doing here in your office? You dragged me in here, remember." I walked away from him, dragging my hand along the top of the couch.

"Don't be cute." Though I sensed a smile behind his straight-man routine. "I meant in the building."

I peered at him over my shoulder. "Maybe I came to see you. I tend to stalk when I feel dismissed by a man." It could happen. It had happened before. With him, even.

Hudson heaved a sigh. "You didn't come to see me. You arrived on this floor over half an hour ago and are just now coming by my office."

I spun toward him. "How the fuck do you know everything I do? Jordan? Your security cameras?" I knew it was my bodyguards, but I wanted his confirmation. And saying it out loud, I realized how much the situation ticked me off—if he was watching my every move, I didn't feel so bad digging into his life. As far as shitty behavior went, the two were on par in my book.

"I'm not going to feel guilty for the lengths I go to in order to protect what's mine." He crossed his arms over his chest, his already broad shoulders expanding.

And I didn't miss his words. I might have licked my lips.

"Alayna?"

I tore my eyes away from him, breaking the hypnotic trance he had me in. "Yours, huh? Don't make me laugh." I seemed to be back at the angry phase of grief. It was an interesting and a thrilling change to the constant pain I'd been experiencing.

My rage spurred Hudson's. "Jesus, how many times do I have to go through this with you?"

"I don't know." I shrugged dramatically. "Maybe a couple hundred more times. Because I'm obviously not getting it."

He turned his back to me, running his hand through his hair. When he faced me again, he was relatively calmer. "Why. Are. You. Here?"

I battled over telling the truth and keeping it to myself just to spite him. My bitchy mood was voting for spite.

But I was fighting *for* him, not against him. Honesty it was. "I came to see Norma."

His brows rose. "About Gwen?"

I covered my face with my hands then dropped them. "About you, you dummy. I don't give a shit about anything but you." My throat tightened with the truthfulness of my declaration. "Jesus, how many times do I have to go through this with you?" I threw his words back at him. Guess the spite was coming along with the fight. It helped keep away the tears.

"You came to talk to *my* employee about *me*?" His eye twitched and his jaw was tense. From my experience, that meant he was pissed. Beyond pissed.

And I'd been going for romantic.

I threw more of his words back. "Don't guilt me for protecting what's mine."

His eyes sparked. That remark hit him—in a good way. In a way I didn't know I could anymore. As if he were moved by my possessiveness.

I took advantage of his surprise and softened my approach. "I only wanted to see for myself if she was into you. If you had something going with her."

Bitterness crept back in. With a pointed finger, I said, "And don't you dare talk to me about trust because you know I get jealous about her, and you aren't around to help reassure me."

Every other word I said was pointed and harsh. I'd hated feeling so distraught. This new temperament wasn't any better, but at least I was getting it out. It was like shedding my skin and underneath was nothing but raw and rugged emotion.

Hudson leaned his hip against the couch, regarding me closely. When he spoke, he was calm and controlled. As always. "Did you get what you came for?"

"I did."

"And?"

I bit my lip, not wanting to give away any ground. Carefully, reluctantly, I answered. "She thinks a lot of you. She respects you and admires you and she recognizes you're physically attractive—don't let that go to your head."

"But..."

"But she's not into you anymore. I can see it in her eyes." It was a fair way to avoid spilling Norma's secret. Besides, I *could* see it in her eyes.

"Good. Then you believe the things I've told you." He appeared pleased.

"It was never the things you've told me that were the issue. It's the things you haven't told me."

"They aren't your things to know," he snapped back.

The sliver of composure I was maintaining disappeared. "What the ever living fuck?" I was infuriated. Enraged. Out of my mind with exasperation. "I could say the same thing about you—spying on me, digging into my history before you'd even met me—maybe I think those aren't your things to know. Still, you did and do whatever the hell you want with no regard to boundaries or personal space."

I squared my shoulders and faced him head on. "And while that's out there, let me be clear—since you aren't able to explain things to me, I'm digging on my own."

Concern flashed through his eyes.

It fueled me. I wanted him off kilter. Wanted him where he always had me—flustered and imbalanced. "That's right. I've been through all of the books Celia sent. I've been to see Stacy. And Norma. I'm collecting my own facts. Don't you think it would be better to tell me your secrets than have me find them out on my own?"

"Alayna, stop digging." He took a step toward me, his voice even but strained.

Why, why, why couldn't he just tell me what I'd find? "You're protecting Celia again, aren't you?"

"Celia's not who I'm protecting."

"Who then? Yourself?" I was yelling, not even caring if his doors were solid enough to absorb the sound. "Me?"

He reached for me, grabbing me at the elbow. "You need to leave, now."

With those five words the anger disappeared and the hurt returned full force. The air left my lungs. My chest constricted. My eyes filled. He wanted me to leave, wanted me gone. And the last thing I wanted was to leave.

We were at such odds. All there was between us lately was struggle. There was never any progress.

I wiped a renegade tear from my cheek. "Shutting me out again. Like you always do. Hiding behind your thick walls. What's the point of me even fighting for you if you're never, never going to let me in? Who are you protecting, Hudson? Who?"

His grip on me tightened. "Yes, you, dammit! I'm protecting you. Always you."

Before I could blink his mouth was on mine, crushing into my lips, bruising me with his abrasive kiss. He tasted of the same neediness that I felt deep in my own belly—of lonely desperation. Of lust and affection that had been bottled for far too long.

My tears halted and my hands flew to his lapels, pulling him to me. I lifted my leg around his, my skirt bunching around my upper thighs. Pressing against him, I tilted my hips, rubbing my core against his erection. He groaned in frustration and I echoed the sound, eager to be even closer, not able to get close enough.

In a blur, he spun me toward the couch. I grasped the back as he removed my panties. He growled when his fingers dipped into my hole and found me wet—soaking wet. Next, I heard the sound of his belt, then his zipper. His palms settled on my ass. Then he drove into me, deep and hard, again and again. He grunted with each thrust, his balls slapping against my ass, his fingers curled around my hips like a vise-grip.

He was fucking me, bent over his couch, and it felt so good and I needed him like that so much. But I couldn't see his face—not in that position—couldn't look into his eyes. I knew that he was doing that on purpose, trying to avoid that extra level of intimacy, hoping to make the act just about sex and nothing else.

But it was never just sex with us. It was always something more—a complete and total union of him and me, where we became whole and healed and brilliant. I couldn't let him succeed in making it less.

Twisting my torso, I reached my hand back to his chest and clutched onto his shirt. His lids had been squeezed shut, but at my grasp, they popped open. I locked my gaze on his. With the contact of my eyes, his drive steadied—still fast, but no longer frenzied. It was the connection I needed. My pussy clenched and I began my ascent. The friction increased as I tightened around him, but he continued at his even pace through the tension until he was spilling his seed with a long stroke and spilling my name on a low groan.

As his orgasm tore through him it spurred mine to higher heights until my head was spinning and my vision blinded. I fell forward on the couch, panting and euphoric. Hudson collapsed on top of me, holding me tight for several beautiful moments while our breathing became regular.

The minute he pulled off and out of me, I straightened and turned into his arms. He welcomed me, tilting my mouth to his. He locked my upper lip in a hard kiss, holding me in place with his hand behind my head. It was different from any kiss we'd shared—our mouths not moving, our bodies held together in a desperate union, as we breathed in and out in tandem.

When we finally broke apart, I wrapped my hands tightly around his neck and kissed along his jaw. "Oh god, I miss you. I miss you so much."

"*Précieux…mon amour…ma chérie…*" He ran his hands down my face, caressing my skin with sweet sweeps of his thumb.

250

He was tender and perfect, and though I was afraid to break the moment, I was more afraid to miss out on the power of our junction. Barely above a whisper, I voiced the question I desperately needed to ask. "When are you coming home?"

He leaned his forehead against mine with a sigh and settled his hands at my neck. "I have to go to L.A. for the weekend." He tilted his wrist to glance at his watch. "I'm set to leave in about twenty minutes, in fact."

If it was possible to be both elated and disappointed at once, that's what I was. He wasn't pushing me away as he had been the last few days, but if he was coming back, it wouldn't be tonight.

I proceeded with caution, pressing him to let me in without scaring him off. "Part of your big business thing? With Norma?"

It wouldn't bother me if she were going. Well, not as much as it would have before I'd spoken to her. I just needed to know the answer.

Hudson stroked my nose with the tip of his. "Yes, with Norma. And after this, if all goes well, we'll be done."

I closed my eyes and inhaled him. So close…we were so close to working everything out…I felt it in my heart, felt it in my bones. Would we lose it all because he was leaving now?

Invite me to go with you. I willed him to say the words, *Come with me.*

He didn't.

With what felt like great reluctance, he pushed me away. He tucked himself in, zipped up his pants, and stood to face me, his fist on his hip as if trying to decide what to do about a problem that had arose unexpectedly.

It was surprising that I could still be hurt when I was already in so much pain. Wasn't there a limit? Where the ache would become so unbearable and my spirit would simply cease to go on? If there was a threshold, I hadn't met it yet. Because that look on his face—it pushed me further into the depth of the hell that I was in. It crushed me.

I didn't want to be his *problem*. I wanted to be his *life*. After all, he was mine.

Then, all of a sudden, everything changed. He dropped his hand to his side and his expression melted and transformed, and for the first time in days, the look in his eyes said I was the center of his world again. The crux of his universe. The core of his existence.

He reached for me, and instantly I was back in his arms. He clutched me tightly to him, with determined devotion. "God, Alayna, I can't do this anymore." It was almost a sob. "I can't bear to be apart from you. I miss you so terribly."

"You do?" I leaned back to look into his eyes, to see if they told the same story.

He settled his hand at my jaw, his thumb tracing the line of my lower lip. "Of course, I do, precious." His tone was uneven but sincere. "You're my everything. I love you. I love you so much."

My heart thudded in my ears and the world closed in around me as if there were only Hudson and me and nothing else.

He'd said it. He'd said it *twice*. Said it, and meant it. I felt the sincerity in every cell of my body.

And with just those three little words, the darkness scattered and the sky cleared. The heaviness that had cocooned me for days fell away, and I was left new and beautiful in its place. It was he who'd finally taken the step, had metamorphosed enough to deliver what I needed to hear, but it was me who was now the butterfly—me who could finally soar.

And still, as I was already flying, I needed to be sure. "W-w-what?"

His lips fell into an easy smile. "You heard me."

"I want to hear it again." I held my breath, afraid that if I stirred at all that the spell would be broken and I'd be alone in our bed at the penthouse, that all of this would be a dream.

But it wasn't a dream. And I wasn't alone. And I was in the arms of the man who was saying once again, "I love you."

"You love me?"

He brushed his lips over mine. "I love you, precious. I've always loved you. From the moment I first saw you. I knew before you did, I think." He tilted my chin to meet his eyes. "But there are things—things in my past—that have kept me from being able to tell you. And now…I have to do this…this thing. Finish this deal. Then, when I get back, we'll talk."

"We'll talk?" I felt like a parrot, repeating his last words, but I was delirious, my mind hazy with happiness. It was all I could manage.

"I'll tell you anything you want to know. And if you still want me, I'll come home." He swept a strand of my hair behind my ear, seeming to need to keep touching me as badly as I needed to be touched.

God, he's such an idiot! "Yes, I want you home. Of course I do. We belong there together. There's nothing you could say that would make me stop loving you. *Nothing*. I stick, remember?"

He sighed into me. "Oh, precious. I hope that's true."

"It is." It was the truest thing I knew, like the way the sun knew to rise in the morning, the way a rosebud knew to blossom in the spring. He was in my veins, in the innermost recesses of my heart and soul. I'd love him until I died—through death, even. Through fire, through hell. I'd love him through eternity.

And now I believed he might love me that way too.

I dug my fingers into his jacket and shook him softly. "Say it again."

"You're such a spoiled girl." He circled my nose with his. "And I love…spoiling you."

I leaned back and smacked his chest.

"And I love you." He pulled me back toward his mouth. "I love you, I love you. I love you."

Forever With You

Chapter Seventeen

Hudson and I kissed and cuddled right until the moment he was supposed to leave, neither of us wanting to end our reunion. Hand in hand, we walked out of the building together. He invited me to ride with him in the limo to the airport. I considered it, but Norma was accompanying him, and the look in Hudson's eyes said he'd have his way with me, no matter who was present.

We did get a chance for a goodbye kiss. "I'll miss you," he mumbled against my lips.

If he wasn't going to say it, I would. "You could ask me to come to L.A."

"Someone keeps reminding me about a club that she has to run…" He ran a hand down my bare arm, sending chills down my spine. "And I'm going to be swamped. Though I'd love you there, you'd be ignored."

Briefly I wondered if he had an ulterior reason for not wanting me to go with him, but I didn't let the thought stay. He was right. I had responsibilities at home. His recognition of that was a big step on his part.

But I pouted all the same.

Hudson kissed my forehead. "Don't pout. Stay here, go to David's going away party on Sunday, I'll be back by Monday."

"Back to the penthouse?" I wanted his reassurance once more. I could bear a few more days if he'd come home for good.

"Back to our house, yes." He brushed one more kiss against my lips then got in the limo and rode away.

Though Hudson and I were still apart in the literal sense, the fact that we were a couple again made all the difference in our distance. Finally, we were happy and in love. Happy and in love like we'd never been before. I fluttered around work all shift like I had wings. Gwen introduced herself to me, claiming we'd never met. David, on the other hand, spent the evening being glum. He blamed it on his impending move, but I knew it was me. He'd been hoping Hudson and I were over. Thank god we weren't.

Even across the miles, Hudson showed me things were different. He had flowers sent to work—a bouquet of wildflowers that looked exactly like the patches we'd seen in the Poconos. He also texted me, something he rarely initiated. I'd received several before I had the chance to look at my phone.

Just landed in L.A.

Did you get my flowers?

I had some sent to my room too, so I could think of you.

Are you avoiding me now?

I laughed at his repeat of what I'd said when he hadn't responded to my texts. Then I sent: *Not avoiding you, working. Thnx for the flowers. Keep texting. I'll read every one.*

His next message came immediately, as though he'd been sitting with his phone in his hand, waiting for it to buzz. *If that's a challenge, I accept.*

He continued texting me throughout the evening. I responded when I could between the busy Friday nightclub scene. Our messages varied from romantic to sexual to sweet to funny. We acted like a couple in that slaphappy, I-can't-get-enough-of-you phase that happened at the beginning of relationships. With our untraditional start, we'd never really experienced that. Then we'd had too many walls. But now they were all down—or nearly all down.

On Saturday, more flowers arrived at the penthouse. Then late that afternoon, he did more than text. He called.

I answered on the second ring. "I can't believe you're calling me." Hudson called as rarely as he texted. He was a no-nonsense type of guy. To him, chit-chat was a waste of time.

Now though, he was acting like I was anything but a waste of time.

"I wanted to hear your voice. Digital letters weren't cutting it any longer."

Talk about wanting to hear a voice…

His low tenor stirred butterflies to dance in my stomach. "I love hearing you too." I stretched on the bedroom floor, my legs raised to rest against the bed. "Did you sleep well last night?"

"I did not. I've slept horribly every night that I haven't fallen asleep inside you."

I couldn't hide my grin from showing in my voice. "So you're horny."

"No, Alayna. If I were simply horny, I could take care of myself."

That's something I wouldn't mind watching.

"It has nothing to do with sex—" He paused. "Well, it only has some to do with sex. It's connecting with you that I miss."

Damn, now I was horny. "I get it. I feel the same. When you come back, we'll connect for hours, how does that sound?" Knowing Hudson, it would be literally hours. We had lots of reconnecting to do.

"It sounds wonderful, precious." His tone grew serious. "But we still have to talk."

"We'll talk. We can connect first and then talk. And then connect some more." I shook my head as I listened to myself. Usually it was Hudson who was all about the sex.

"You're insatiable." He didn't sound like he minded. "You forget that you may not want to connect after we talk."

I waggled my eyebrows even though he couldn't see me. "Another reason to connect before. But I'm not worried about it. Just your willingness to talk is enough." That wasn't quite true. "Okay, not exactly enough, but it pleases me. A lot." And even though I knew whatever he had to say would likely rock me, I was sure that we'd get through it.

Hudson still didn't believe that. "Hmm," he said, and I knew he doubted the strength of my love.

Part of me wished he'd just spill his secrets now, over the phone. I was eager to hear what they were, but more than that, I was eager to put him at ease—to prove that I'd stick around.

But I had to start getting ready for work soon. There wasn't time. And I had the feeling we'd need *connecting* after his revelation, in whatever form that took.

We sat silently for several seconds, and I worried he was fretting. "What are you thinking about, H?"

"You. Bent over the couch in my office."

I laughed. "No, you aren't."

"Actually, I am. The sounds you made…the way you looked at me…your eyes when I made you come…God, Alayna, do you have any idea how beautiful and sexy you are?"

My face warmed and my toes curled into the comforter. How could he make me blush over the phone? "If I am, it's because you make me that way."

"That's a lie. I never want to hear you say that I'm responsible for your beauty again. I can't take an ounce of credit for your perfection."

"But you can take every ounce of credit for my happiness, and that's much more important to me than beauty."

He was silent again, and I feared I'd scared him. "What is it, Hudson?"

"I was just wondering what I did to deserve the responsibility of your happiness. I hope that I can live up to the honor."

Perhaps it had been an ill-timed remark since he'd so recently made me miserable. That was the fact of the matter though—Hudson had the power to lift me to heights I'd never imagined, and that meant he also had the ability to absolutely obliterate me.

Maybe it was a lot of pressure, but it was part of the romantic relationship package. "You deserve the honor just for loving me," I said softly.

"And love you, I do." He barely let a beat pass before switching gears. "What are you wearing?"

"Black lacy panties and a camisole." I pulled the phone from my face to check the time. *Shit*, I needed to wrap things up soon. "I was just about to jump in the shower when you called." I rolled to my knees and stood.

Hudson's next words were a gruff command. "Take off your panties."

"Oh my god, Hudson, I don't have time for this." Though, I was already stripping. For the shower, not for him.

"You have to undress anyway."

Such a man of reason. "For that alone, they're off. And now I'm getting off the phone. You're too distracting for me at the moment." I walked to the bathroom as I spoke.

"Fine." Tenderly, he added, "I miss you."

"I miss you, I love you."

"I love you first."

I held on to the handle of the shower door and closed my eyes, relishing his words, breathing them in. "I *said* it first," I teased.

"But I meant it first," he said with finality. "Get in the shower. Don't touch yourself unless you're thinking of me."

"Whom else would I think of, you silly man?" My nipples were already standing at full attention, and even though I was naked, it wasn't because I was chilled. "I'm letting you know now that I plan to text you throughout the night. Wicked, dirty things. You'll be desperate for me when you get back."

"I'm desperate for you now," he groaned. "Go, before I make you touch yourself with me on the phone."

With a reluctant sigh, I said goodbye and hung up, catching my face in the mirror as I did. The woman I saw was quite a contrast to the one who'd stood there only the day before. And there would only be one more day—maybe two—before Hudson would be home. I couldn't wait to see the woman in the mirror then.

***

By late afternoon on Sunday, I was stir-crazy. Minutes passed like they were wading in molasses. Every time I looked at the clock, it seemed the time hadn't changed at all. Normally in these situations, I could entertain myself with a movie or a book. But I was too anxious, too ready for Hudson to be home. His texts and calls had occupied the days before, but he'd texted while I was sleeping that he would be in meetings the entire day and unreachable.

I'd already put a run in on the treadmill, and though I considered doing some window shopping, it was Reynold on duty and he was not my favorite companion. At five, I was already completely ready for David's going away party—two hours early—and couldn't think of a single thing to distract me from my boredom.

I decided to fuck it.

Grabbing my laptop bag, I set the alarm to *away* and slipped down to the lobby. I knew a text went out to my bodyguards when I set the alarm to *home*, but I wasn't sure if it did anything when I left. I stood outside The Bowery for several minutes, waiting to see if Reynold would show up or message me. He didn't. I scanned my surroundings. Seeing no pesky blondes lurking in the area, I set off for the French bakery on the corner of the block.

Being out on my own felt absolutely amazeballs. It wasn't that I minded having Jordan and Reynold in tow; it was simply such a pain to arrange outings that spontaneity had lost its place in my routine. The whole need to be protected was Hudson's idea, anyway. Celia didn't scare me.

Okay, she scared me, but there was no reason why she should. What the hell could she do to me anyway?

The bakery had very few customers when I arrived. Though I would have liked to sit at one of the outdoor tables, I took my iced tea and a pesto panini and settled in a seat near the side door. If I wasn't going to have my bodyguard, then I should at least take some additional precautions. Sitting inside was my version of precaution.

After finishing my food, I set up my computer and opened up my email. There were a few items regarding the club, a random e-card from my brother, and an unread message from Stacy. Ignoring everything else, I opened Stacy's email and scanned it.

I'm still not sure who wrote the emails. Maybe if you looked at one, it would help. Here's one of the longer ones.

Below her short note was a forwarded message from the H.Pierce email she'd told me about. Other women might have decided that reading the message wasn't necessary when Hudson was planning a tell-all.

I have never been other women. I read eagerly.

Before finishing the first paragraph, I was convinced the message wasn't from Hudson. It was too poetic, too flowery. Hudson avoided analogies and figurative language. Even when he was romantic—something he swore he never was—his phrasing was direct and to-the-point.

This letter was composed of everything Hudson wasn't. There were references to nature and popular music and relatives. The author spoke of his mother as *the rock of the family* and his father as a *compassionate patriarch.* Definitely not the Pierces I knew.

It was a section midway through the letter that confirmed without a doubt that the email was not written by Hudson. The paragraph read:

I've studied and learned about the world from books and tour packages arranged by and for the discontented rich, but I'd prefer to one day leave all my life and responsibility behind and travel the earth by whim. Right now, I can say that I love Paris and Vienna, but what do I truly know of these cities when I haven't lived *in them,* participated *in their culture? Words without experience are meaningless.*

I read the last line again. "*Words without experience are meaningless.*" It was a quote from *Lolita*. There were other lines that seemed familiar, certainly more quips from other literary classics. Hudson Pierce did not read the classics. His library had no books before I'd moved in. Celia, on the other hand…

A flash of movement out the window drew my attention.

I peered out to find that a couple sitting on the other side of the glass was leaving. What kept my focus was the woman at the table behind them.

Goddamn, speak of the devil.

As my eye caught hers, Celia smiled—the same old bitchy smile she always delivered.

I chewed on my lip, deciding what to do. I could continue sitting in the bakery and text Reynold for a ride. Or I could leave and see if she'd follow.

Or I could talk to her.

There wasn't anything I burned to say to the woman. I knew that any request I made to be left alone would only result in more harassment. And asking her reasons for her actions wouldn't get me anywhere. Anything she said to me couldn't be trusted, so what was the point in conversation?

The point was that I was curious. Curious what she'd try to convince me of, what her body language would say.

Before I could talk myself out of it, I threw my bag over my shoulder, grabbed my computer and walked out to the patio.

To her credit, Celia didn't blink when I sat across from her.

"By all means, Laynie, sit," she said, her tone pleasant and condescending and a little bit eager, as though she was looking forward to a confrontation. She probably was.

Without any preamble, I turned my laptop to face her and pointed to the email still on the screen. "This is you, isn't it?"

She scanned a few lines, recognition flashing in her eyes. "I don't know for the life of me what you're talking about, Laynie."

She liked to say my name a lot—it was a trick I'd learned in grad school. When said in the right tone, it made a person feel patronized. She certainly knew the tools of basic manipulation.

But so did I. "That email, Celia. You're the one who sent it to Stacy. I recognize your choice of literary quotes."

"Why, that's crazy." Her inflection was exaggerated. "This says it's from Hudson. Did you hack into his email? I hear that's typical of women with your condition. In fact, Laynie, should you really be sitting with me? I could still file that restraining order."

I tilted my head, studying her. She wanted me to threaten a restraining order of my own. But we were playing this conversation on my terms. "What I don't understand is how you got Hudson to go along."

"Go along with what?" She blinked innocently.

"The kiss." I turned the screen back to face me and loaded the video. I pushed play and spun it toward her. "This."

She watched silently, giving nothing away. When it was finished, she raised her eyes to meet mine, her expression suddenly serious. "So you've discovered our little secret."

She wanted me to assume the kiss was real. I didn't believe it was. "That you played together? Yes."

She laughed. "Is that what he told you? I suppose he wouldn't want you to know what we really meant to each other."

"Ha ha. I don't buy it."

"That I was Hudson's lover? Suit yourself." She pursed her lips. "It lasted beyond that, you know. Why do you think I had a key to his place? And when I picked him up at the Hamptons—there was no business trip."

Lies, lies, lies.

I didn't have any doubt that every word was meant to instigate me. "You've fucked with me too many times to believe anything that comes out of your mouth." I closed my computer and began stuffing it in my bag. There was nothing to learn from her after all.

Celia shrugged. "I could give you proof, if I wanted to. I know all his bedroom moves. Does he dominate you completely? Does he have a nickname for you? *Precious,* perhaps?"

Unwittingly, my eyes popped up at Hudson's pet name. How the hell did she know about that? Hudson had promised me it was private.

She caught my reaction. "He does, doesn't he? Don't you know that he calls all his lovers *precious*? Did you think it was just for you? He called me that when he plowed into me over and over on his office desk. '*My precious, my precious,*' he'd say. I'm sure he simply says it now out of habit."

It didn't matter if she was telling the truth or lying. Either way, she'd tainted something sacred. Something that meant a great deal to me. That combined with all the other shit she'd pulled?

I snapped.

"Maybe it wasn't just for me. But this is just for you." My hand curled into a fist and flew at her face before she could see it coming. From the cracking sound that accompanied my punch, I guessed that her nose was broken.

"You fucking bitch!" she screamed, her hands holding her nose.

"I was thinking the same about you. Though cunt would have been my choice of noun."

Blood oozed out from between Celia's hands. "You want a noun? Try *lawsuit.*"

That was the last I heard before I darted out the patio gate. Afraid Celia would find someone to come after me, I headed straight for the subway.

A lawsuit, huh? Well, it was fucking worth it.

Forever With You

Chapter Eighteen

I jumped on the first train that was available and found an empty seat in the back, my hands shaking and my heart pounding.

God, what had I done?

I couldn't decide if I was scared or exhilarated. Probably an equal combination of both. Because, *damn*. I'd punched Celia Werner. And probably broke her cute little nose. That was surely going to get a cop or two knocking on my door. And, with her power and money, they'd take her charge seriously. I'd had trouble with the law in the past. Having another incident on my record was not something I was looking forward to.

On the other hand—I punched Celia *fucking* Werner. And holy fuck did it feel good.

I had to do something, tell someone. I considered my options—Brian had always been my go-to person for getting me out of sticky situations. That had been hard on our relationship, and now that we were getting along, involving him wasn't my ideal choice.

That put Hudson at the top of my list. He was better suited to go up against the Werners. While I was pretty sure that he would be one hundred percent supportive and take care of anything I needed, calling him with the news promised to be embarrassing. Especially since I'd ditched my bodyguard. He wouldn't be pleased with that.

Cell service was spotty underground, but I managed to get through. Unfortunately, I reached his voicemail. I tried a couple of times with the same result. Hudson had said he had meetings all day. I was sure that was where he was. I chose not to leave a message. Instead, I texted him to call me ASAP and hoped to heaven I got to him before Celia did.

Because she would try to contact him too. Of that I was certain.

And what about what she'd told me? As much as I didn't want to let her get to me, I couldn't help but think about the things she'd said. I didn't automatically believe her—why would I?

But her proof…

I shook off the idea. Somehow she found out about Hudson's name for me. That had to be it. There was no way he'd called her that too. And, yes, he was dominating in bed, but anyone who knew him would assume that.

The only reason it continued to nag at me was that I still hadn't heard Hudson's confession. Was this what he meant to tell me all along? That he'd been with Celia? That he'd slept with her while with me?

I didn't think so. I didn't *want* to think so. It was too easy, too predictable. Hudson was never predictable.

Except if that wasn't it…

The alternate possibility that had started to form in my mind was worse than what Celia had suggested. Much worse. Like, it would shatter my world to discover it were true. I couldn't entertain the idea long enough to work through it, even to try and discount it.

So I didn't think about it at all. Buried it until I had to deal with it. *If* I had to deal with it.

Meanwhile, I needed someone to give me some advice. Besides Brian, who would know how police handled battery charges? I considered David and Liesl. Mira and Jack were even possibilities. Finally, I settled on someone who I was sure would be able to handle the situation the best.

Jordan answered on the first ring.

"Hey, I know your shift doesn't start for a bit, but I'm sort of in a situation and I need your help."

"I can be at the penthouse in twenty-five."

He was already about to hang up when I stopped him. "Actually, I'm not there. I'm just walking off the subway at Grand Central Station."

There was only a minor pause before he asked, "Reynold's not with you?"

"No." I should have been more regretful, but I wasn't. "I'll explain when I see you. Can you come meet me?"

"Yep. In fact, if you're at Grand Central, I can be there in ten."

We agreed on a place to meet. Then I hung up and waited for him to show.

True to his word, Jordan was indeed only ten minutes away. *He must live nearby.* Funny how little I knew about the man.

We found an empty bench and talked without leaving the station. I caught him up quickly, leaving nothing out. Well, very little out. I didn't mention what it was exactly Celia had said to cause my fist to fly.

Jordan seemed neither surprised nor judgmental of my story. "Have you called Hudson?"

"I tried. I got voicemail." I'd tried again while waiting for Jordan with the same result.

"That's fine. It's really not urgent. Here's what's probably going to happen: Celia will likely have gone to the ER. Because of who she is and the pull she has, I'd assume she'd get the police to take her complaint there. With a simple one-swing hit, the cops will often forget the whole thing. They won't because she's a Werner."

"Could I be arrested?" It was the question most pressing on my mind.

He shook his head. "They'll track you down and give you a court date. No warrants, no arrests. There will be plenty of time for Mr. Pierce to get the whole thing dropped—which he will. You know that, right?"

"I do." I wrung my hands in my lap. "At least, I think I do. I also feel shitty about being a burden."

Jordan laughed—I'd never heard him outright laugh. He was nearly as serious and on-task as Hudson. "That man could never think of you as a burden, Laynie. He turned mountains over to get your last charge completely expunged. And the deal he's working on now has been much more problematic than it will be for him to get rid of any charge from Celia."

I'd known Hudson had buried my restraining order violation, but Jordan's last words were news to me. "What does the deal he's working on now have to do with me?"

He studied me carefully. "I'm sorry, Laynie. That's going to have to come from him. My point is that you're not his burden. You're his reason."

I savored Jordan's words. I needed them right then. Especially with Hudson out of reach, I needed the reminder that he was still there for me. "Thank you, Jordan. I appreciate that more than you can understand. Do you know when he'll be back?"

Jordan's mouth tightened, and I knew he was being careful how much he said. "Depends on how his meetings go today."

Why did it feel like everyone knew some big secret about this business deal that I didn't? Hudson, Norma, even Jordan. From what I'd gathered, it wasn't anything bad. Then why was I not allowed to know?

Hudson had promised me I could find out anything I wanted to know when we talked. This was definitely going on the list. I'd rather hear things from him than my bodyguard anyway, so I didn't press.

I checked the clock on my phone. There was only a little over an hour before David's shindig. Maybe I should just head there. Unless that was going to be a problem. "The club is closed on Sundays, but we're having a party for my coworker who's going away. Do you think the police will show up there? I don't want to ruin anything."

"Nah. They'll either show up at the penthouse or wait until normal business hours to find you at work. You'll be fine."

"I know I have to face them eventually, but I'd rather not today." Shit, I was such a coward.

If Jordan agreed with my assessment of myself, he didn't indicate as such. "Let's do this: we can take the train back uptown. I'll leave you at The Sky Launch—I don't expect Ms. Werner to show up and bother you tonight."

"No. Not likely." Though, I wouldn't mind seeing how much damage I'd actually incurred. Just thinking about it brought a smile to my face.

"The car is parked at the penthouse. I'll go and get it and come back to the club. Then we can leave whenever you want." Jordan casually watched the subway passengers as they walked past us. Or it appeared casual. The more I learned about him, the more I realized nothing he did was casual.

And he was always thinking. "I bet that the police will stop by tomorrow morning, Laynie. If you prefer to stay away from them until Mr. Pierce gets back, I could take you to the loft tonight after the party instead."

"That's not a bad idea. I'll consider it." Except I hoped that when I finally reached Hudson, he'd take care of things for me so I wouldn't have to hide out anywhere.

But even if Hudson could get rid of a battery charge, he couldn't protect us from her forever. He hadn't been able to stop her stalking. Surely now she'd up her game. I thought of Jack's advice from our lunch—*the only way to get rid of her was to let her think she'd won.* Punching her in the face definitely wasn't letting her win. By striking against her, had I made the worst move possible? More than ever I feared that Celia Werner would be a permanent fixture in my future. Could Hudson and I survive that?

***

The problem with holing up at The Sky Launch was that I wasn't in the mood to be there. Fortunately, I didn't have to do anything for the party except open the doors for the caterers. Hudson had arranged the whole thing, including an open bar. It was beyond generous on his part—probably his way of apologizing for the circumstances in which David was leaving.

Everyone on staff had been allowed a plus one. With David's friends and the few regulars that had been invited, the total guest list numbered around a hundred. It was a true party. The whole thing might have been fun if my plus one was there. But he wasn't. And by ten, I still hadn't heard from him.

"Put the fucking phone down and boogie with me," Liesl urged. I'd filled her in on the day's events when she arrived. Her feeling was that if I was going to face policemen tomorrow, I should party harder tonight.

She and I were definitely different people.

"Laynie, I love you and I'm here for you if you truly need me. But you seem to have moping down on your own so I'm going to leave you to it and go have a good time." She tugged at a strand of my hair. "Forgive me?"

"Totally forgive you. Go. Have fun."

She gave me a peck on the lips and joined a raucous group in the center of the floor. I tried not to feel abandoned. It wasn't Liesl I wanted anyway.

Determined to not spoil the evening for anyone else, I sat curled up on one of the sofas that lined the main floor and nursed my champagne while I watched the crowd dance and mingle in front of me. It was probably a good idea for me to sit out anyway. Most of them were my employees, after all. There should be a level of separation and respect.

I wondered how much respect I'd get if they all watched me get dragged out in handcuffs.

Stop it, I scolded myself. Jordan said there'd be no arrests, and Hudson would fix everything before it came to a head, though it wouldn't surprise me if Celia reported my assault to the media.

God, the media!

I closed my eyes, wincing at the thought. *Please, Hudson, call me. Please!*

"Mind if I join you?" a voice shouted over the pulsing beat.

Opening my eyes, I found Gwen in front of me.

She was already taking a seat before I answered. "By all means, join me." I scanned the room again. Though not everyone was dancing, I appeared to be the only loner. Was that why Gwen had come over?

Fuck, I hoped not. I wasn't in the mood to be jollied up. Might as well let her know that right off the bat. "Why aren't you out there?" Maybe she'd get the hint and join the crowd on the dance floor.

She furrowed her brow and I realized that the drink in her hand had not been her first. If she wasn't drunk already, she was on her way. "I'm not really into…" She trailed off as if forgetting what she was saying.

I finished for her. "Dancing?"

"Actually, I was going to say *people*." She added an amendment. "Besides, they're our employees. It doesn't seem right to party hard with them tonight when I might be writing them up tomorrow."

Damn, she was a good manager. "Gwen? I'm starting to like you. What's up with that?"

She almost laughed. "I'm sure it won't last. Give it time." Her words were heavy, as if she had a sad story to back them up. Or perhaps she was simply a somber drunk.

If she wasn't outright going to share, I wasn't going to ask. I had my own problems. For the tenth time in fifteen minutes I hit the screen of my phone, checking for a missed call or text.

Nothing.

Jordan had already returned with the car and was now hanging out in the employee lounge watching something on PBS. I shot him a message: *Any word from Hudson?*

His reply came fast. *Nope. West coast is 3 hours behind. It's only six there. Give him time.*

It had already been five hours since I first texted Hudson to call me. How much time did he need?

Gwen interrupted my thoughts. "You keep checking that thing. Are you expecting a better offer?"

With a sigh, I stuffed my phone in my bra. "Just waiting for Hudson to call. He's in L.A. for a couple of days. I hadn't realized I'd been so obvious."

She groaned. "God, you're so lovesick, it's disgusting."

I tilted my head. "Do you not approve of me with Hudson?"

Gwen shrugged. "I don't give a flying fig about you and Hudson. It's love I don't approve of. I get it enough with Nor—" She stopped, catching herself before she finished her sister's name. "Anyway. Seems there's love all around. I'm over it."

She didn't know I was already aware of Norma and Boyd's fling. I didn't bother to tell her. It was her anti-romance attitude that intrigued me. Did she feel abandoned by her sister since she'd started fooling around with her assistant? Knowing almost nothing about Gwen, it was hard to say.

Then it hit me. "Ooh, Gwen's got a heartache story." Things were clicking in place. For the first time that evening, I felt slightly interested in something other than myself. "Is that why you were so eager to leave Eighty-Eighth Floor?"

Her eyes glossed over, whether from memory or alcohol, I wasn't sure. She opened her mouth to say something. Then her focus returned. "Nice try. I'm drunk, but I'm not that drunk." She took another swallow of her Wild Turkey and glanced at my half-full glass of champagne. "Speaking of which, why don't you join me on the intoxicatrain?"

"Not much of a drinker." With my low tolerance, I was already feeling a little tipsy, and I planned on being sober when I talked to Hudson.

"Hmm." She looked me over as if sizing me up. Then her attention went to the crowd tearing it up on the dance floor. She took another swallow of her drink. "I heard you saying something about addiction to Liesl. Are you a former alky?"

I laughed. She was as curious about me as I was about her. Perhaps if I spilled my story, she'd spill hers. Except at the moment, bonding wasn't exactly on my priority list. "Uh-uh. Not happening. You have your secrets, I have mine."

Gwen smiled. "I'm good with that."

"So this is where the party is." David leaned over the back of the sofa between our heads.

"Ha ha. Sarcasm. Nice." Gwen finished off her glass and set it on the table next to her.

David ignored Gwen and turned his attention to me. "This night is supposed to be my last chance with my favorite people. And my most favorite people is over here moping. What's up with that?"

His reference to me as his *favorite people* made me tense only slightly. He was on his way out of town. No need to worry about his intentions.

And he was right. This night was about him, not me. "Shit, I'm sorry, David. This is supposed to be a party, and I'm crashing it with my bad mood."

He crossed around in front of the sofa and sat on the low table in front of us. "Why are you in a bad mood, anyway? You were so...*peppy*...the last two days." His brows lifted, hopeful. "Trouble in paradise?"

It was sweet how he never stopped trying. "I hate to disappoint you, but I don't think so." Though telling Hudson about my lapse in self-control might alter that.

Why hadn't he called yet? And did Jordan really know how the NYC legal system worked?

I bit my lip with worry. "There is the fact that I could be arrested soon." It was easier to let info slip with David than Gwen.

David glanced questioningly at Gwen. "Don't look at me," she said with a shrug. "She doesn't tell me jack shit."

He wrapped his hands around the edges of the table on either side of him. "I think I need to hear more."

For half a second I considered spilling it all. But that wasn't fair to David. He'd been a good manager and a good friend. Was this any way to send him off?

"No, you really don't need to hear more. Forget I said anything. Please. I'm being melodramatic." *Hopefully.*

"Let me know if I can do anything?" That was David. Never the type to push or pry. At one time, I'd fooled myself into thinking that could be enough for me. That he'd be safer. That he was the guy that would keep me sane.

Now I knew differently. Though Hudson pushed and pried and drove me crazy, he was the nearest thing to clarity I knew.

That was why I needed him so desperately at the moment.

But sitting around lamenting his absence wasn't going to bring him to me. And it was a hell of a lousy way to say goodbye to my friend.

Putting on the happiest face I could muster, I set my glass down. "You know what you can do, David? You can cheer me up." I stood up and nodded toward the floor. "Let's dance, shall we?"

"I thought you'd never ask."

Instead of joining the rest of the crowd in the center of the floor, we stuck to an empty corner. A few minutes into the dance mix of David Guetta's *Titanium*, I felt better. It had been forever since I'd let myself loose, since I'd stopped worrying and fretting and just lived in the moment. I closed my eyes and let the beat overtake me, let my feet and hips move as they liked. Sweat gathered at my brow and my breath got short, but I was alive—alive in the way that only the club made me. Soon my anxiousness dissolved and all I was thinking about was the present—the music, the lights flashing around us, the friend standing in front of me. It was exactly what I needed.

I wasn't sure how long we'd been dancing or how many songs had played before the DJ faded into a slow song. The club never played slow songs. I looked to David, my brow raised.

"Someone must have requested it." He held his hand out for me. "Let's not waste it, shall we?"

A voice in my head nagged that it was a bad idea. If David had asked for the song to be played—and I was certain he had—then he'd meant it for me. He'd meant it as a means to get me in his arms. It would be wrong—I had a boyfriend that I loved with my entire being. Hudson wouldn't like it, and that was reason enough to not engage. Every impulse in my body said to walk away.

Except there was a flicker of emotion in my chest that I couldn't ignore—a need for closure, perhaps, or a touch of melancholy for what once was or what could have been. Or maybe it was simply the alcohol and the adrenaline and the need for someone to hold me after all the stress and anxiety of the day.

And Hudson wasn't there, so what could one dance hurt?

Without another thought, I took David's hand and let him pull me into his arms. He was warm in a way that I'd forgotten. Like a giant teddy bear. He wasn't nearly as cut or as trim as Hudson, but he was strong and easy to fall into.

I rested my head on his shoulder as we swayed together. Closing my eyes, I listened to the words of the song and relaxed into our final embrace. The singer was familiar, but I couldn't remember his name. He sang to his love, telling her that she was in his veins, that he could not get her out.

They were words that made me think of Hudson. He was so deeply imprinted on me that he'd seeped through my skin and into my veins. He was my life force, each pulse of my heart sending another shock of love through my body.

Was this how David felt about me?

A strange mixture of panic and sorrow and a little bit of contentment washed over me as I realized that it was exactly how David felt about me. If I had any doubt, it was cleared when he began singing the words at my ear. "*I cannot get you out.*"

I stopped moving with him and leaned back to look at his eyes. He knew, right? Knew that this was wrong, that I was spoken for? That I didn't feel the same way about him?

If he did know, he didn't care. He pressed forward, taking my lips in his before I knew what was happening. His kiss was shocking and unwelcomed. Immediately I pushed him away.

The sadness in David's eyes pierced through me. I knew that depth of heartache. It tore me up to know I was the cause of his.

There was nothing I could do for it but shake my head and bite back tears.

David started to speak—to apologize maybe, or to try to persuade me to give him a chance. Before he said anything, though, his eyes moved upward to a point behind me, his expression stricken with alarm.

I knew without looking who was standing behind me. Wasn't it fate's sick way of paying me back for all the shit I'd pulled in my lifetime? Put the person who I wanted most in the situation I wanted him in the least? That's why he hadn't returned my call, why I couldn't reach him—he'd been coming home.

Slowly, I turned toward him. His jacket was off, his shirt wrinkled from traveling. He'd loosened his tie and his jaw had a layer of end-of-day scruff. It was his face that I focused on, though. The pain in David's eyes was nothing compared to what I found in Hudson's. The anguish there was unbearable, his expression filled with so much pain I wondered if there could be any balm to soothe it.

For the second time that night I asked myself, *god, what have I done?*

278

Forever With You

Chapter Nineteen

I swallowed back the panic that surged through me. I could fix this. I *had* to be able to fix this.

"Hudson." I took a step toward him. "It's not what it looks like." I didn't actually know what it looked like, having no idea how long he'd been standing there. Did he see that I'd pushed David away?

His face was stone. "Maybe we should discuss this in a more private setting."

"Okay." It was more a squeak than a word. But I headed toward the employee office and assumed he'd follow.

He did.

We took the stairs without speaking. I didn't feel his eyes on me as I walked. He didn't even want to look at me. Despair washed over me. I'd been so desperate for him, and now I'd fucked it up. Again.

I didn't turn to face him again until he'd shut the door behind us in the office. When I did, I almost wished I hadn't. The forlorn look I'd seen downstairs was even worse than I'd remembered. Was there really anything I could say to erase that?

With feeble words, I tried. "*He* kissed me, Hudson. I didn't kiss him. And when he did, I pushed him away." It was the truth. If he'd been there long enough, he'd have seen it.

"Why were you in his arms in the first place?" His tone was low and gravelly. It was more emotion than he generally displayed, and it killed me.

A tear trickled down my face. "We were dancing. It was a party."

His eyes flared. "You were in his arms, Alayna. In the arms of someone who has made no secret of his feelings for you. What did you think he'd do?"

He was right on many counts. I'd known it was dangerous, felt the wrongness of the embrace from the minute David put his arms around me.

But *my* intentions had not been to lead him on. It was a goodbye dance. My thoughts had been focused on Hudson the whole time. "It was innocent," I insisted. "I needed someone. He was here. And you weren't."

The memory of the anxiousness that had driven me to David's arms in the first place turned my tears bitter. "Where were you today, anyway? When I needed you?"

He matched my bitterness plus some. "What was it you needed, Alayna? Someone to keep you warm?"

I pressed my lips together, hoping to squelch the sob threatening to escape. "That hurts."

"What I just witnessed hurts."

That wasn't news, but hearing him say it twisted my heart all the same. I'd experienced that same hurt—when I'd seen him kissing Celia on the video, then again earlier today, when she'd suggested they'd had an affair. Perhaps it wasn't fair to compare her probable lies with what he'd witnessed in person, but he had to see where I was coming from. "Yeah, I know how it feels."

"Do you?" Even that tiny phrase was filled with enough venom to smart.

It triggered more of my own snark. "Yeah, I do. Let me see if I can explain it. It feels like your gut has been wrenched out of your body. At least that's what it felt like when Celia told me that you'd been *fucking her* for most of the time we've been together."

"What?" He seemed truly surprised, and not in the *I've-been-caught* way, but in the *what-the-eff-is-she-talking-about* way. It was the same expression he'd had when I'd mentioned him having more of an involvement with Stacy. "When did she say that?"

"Today," I grumbled, already regretting bringing Celia up this way.

"You saw her today?" His eyes narrowed. "Does this have something to do with the phone message she left me?"

"I *knew* she'd call you!" And if she had, why hadn't he called me? "What did she say?"

He shook his head dismissively. "She was raving nonsense. Something about you and her lawyer. I figured it was more of her shit from before so I deleted it."

Hudson took a step toward me, and I noticed his eyes had softened, that instead of pain the predominant feature was now worry. "What happened with her? Was she following you again? What did she do? And why didn't Reynold call me?"

I leaned on the desk behind me. "He didn't know." Guilt pressed on my chest, not only for ditching my bodyguard, but for Hudson's willingness to set aside his ache out of concern for me.

The expression on his face magnified my shame. "Please don't look at me like that. I'm sorry. I was stir-crazy so I grabbed my computer and went for coffee. I thought when I set the alarm to *away* that Reynold might notice, but I guess it didn't inform him."

Hudson's mouth tightened. "It only texts when you set it for *home*."

I was a little surprised that he hadn't set the system to monitor all my comings and goings. It wasn't like him. At a more appropriate time, I'd try to remember to be impressed. "Anyway, I just went to the bakery down the street. And Celia showed up. And I was sick of it. So I approached her."

"*You* approached *her*?" Not only was his eye twitching and his jaw tense, but his hand was shaking as well. I hadn't seen that from him before. Was he that angry?

"I did. It was stupid. I know it was stupid. But Stacy had sent me one of the emails that you had supposedly sent her, and I was reading it, and I could tell it wasn't from you. I recognized one of the quotes used from one of the books Celia highlighted, and I knew the email was from her. So I confronted her about it. About writing the email." The story spilled out in babble that I wasn't even sure he could comprehend.

Apparently he did. "And she told you then that I was with her? Just out of the blue?"

I cringed. He wouldn't like what I had to say next, but it was best to get it all out. "First, I showed her Stacy's video." After checking for his reaction, which I couldn't read, I went on. "Then she said that you were together. That you were a couple. That you fucked her that night and it wasn't the first time and it wasn't the last."

If Hudson's face grew any redder, steam would come out of his ears. "And you believed her?"

I squared my shoulders. "It pissed me off enough that I punched her." Yeah, I admit it, I sounded proud.

"You *punched* her?" There went the steam.

That hadn't been the reaction I'd wanted. "You know what? Keep acting like this is an interrogation and I'm out of here."

Hudson paced the room, pushing his hands through his hair. When he stopped to focus on me again, he'd regained some composure, though his shoulders were still tight and his voice strained. "I'm sorry if I sound a bit tense, Alayna. I assure you it's only out of concern for you."

I studied him for several seconds. It was out of concern—I saw it now. His eyes were pinned on me, his shaking wasn't out of anger; it was fear. Fear for me. The extent that he cared for me was limitless. It was as obvious as the color of his eyes.

The realization calmed me. I pulled back every ounce of snark and venom and gave him raw honesty in its place. "Yes, I punched her. I think I broke her nose. So I'm probably going to get some sort of assault charge for that. *That's* why I needed you."

"Alayna." His eyes radiated with love. "Why didn't you call me?"

"I did! Your phone was off. I could have left a message, but I didn't want to say all that over voicemail, and I didn't want to interrupt your meeting because I knew it was important."

"Not as important as you." He wanted to come to me—the urge was palpable. But there was still that other thing hanging in between us—the moment he'd walked in on—and so he sat on the arm of the couch instead, his hands playing with the bunched fabric of his slacks. "Have the police contacted you?"

I shook my head. "I was afraid to go back to the house so I came here to wait for your call."

His eyes settled on his shoes. "I got your text when I was already in flight. I didn't call because I knew I'd end up telling you I was on my way home, and I wanted it to be a surprise." He laughed gruffly. "I took a nap instead. I should have called."

Now it was my eyes that studied the floor. "I should have kept my cool."

"I'll take care of everything. Don't worry about it in the least. She's not going to bother you again."

He said it with such conviction that I had no choice but to believe him. He'd find a way to protect me from Celia. I simply had to comply with the parameters he set to keep me safe. If I'd done that to begin with, she wouldn't have had the opportunity to push me, and Hudson wouldn't have to bail me out of my mess.

Gratitude and relief swept through me, along with a twinge of regret. "Thank you."

And then a whole bunch more regret followed. If I hadn't punched Celia, would I have ended up in David's arms? Something told me probably not. Either way, the weight of what Hudson had witnessed was immensely heavy. "Hudson," my voice trembled. "I'm sorry."

"Don't be. Good for you, actually. She deserves worse." He even managed to smile as he said the last part.

I wanted to smile with him. But I couldn't. Not yet. "I mean, I'm sorry about David."

"Oh." His face grew grim and the pain from earlier resurfaced. His next words were careful and precise and burdened. "Tell me one thing—do you still feel anything for him?"

"No. No, I don't. Nothing. I've told you that before, and I meant it, though I'm sure it doesn't seem like it seeing me tonight. But the whole time he was holding me, it felt wrong. All I could think about was you. I was missing you, H. Needing you. So much. And I didn't think about what I was doing. I'm so, so, sor—"

He flew to me before I could finish, wrapping his arms around me.

Yes, that was how it was supposed to feel, that was what I'd been longing for.

He buried his face in my hair. "I missed you too, precious. Needed you. I was trying to get back here—"

"And I ruined your surprise." I nuzzled further into his chest. "I'm so sorry."

"I don't care. It hurts, but I've hurt you. And as long as you swear that he means nothing—"

"Nothing. I swear with every fiber of my body, it's only you." I tilted my head up to kiss along his jaw. "How about you—" The question threatened to stick in my throat, but I forced it out. "Do you still feel anything for Celia?"

His body stiffened. Leaning back to meet my eyes, he said softly, "Alayna...I've never felt anything for Celia."

"You mean, it was just sex?" They were things I had to ask, even if the answers were already clear.

He shook his head slowly. "I've never been with her at all."

"She was lying." It wasn't a question. I'd already suspected she'd made it up.

He confirmed anyway. "She was lying."

"That's what I thought." It should have been a relief. Why did my acceptance of this only bring a pit of dread?

Because if that wasn't what he had to confess to me about the video, then there was still a truth I had to learn. Something told me I already knew. The alternative explanation that I'd managed to tuck away earlier returned to niggle at me. And this time it wouldn't let go until I explored it fully.

Gently—reluctantly—I pushed my way out of his arms. "But here's the thing—I sort of wish it were true."

He raised a questioning brow.

"Not that you were sleeping with her while we were together—not that part. But the rest of it—that you were really with her when Stacy saw you. If that was the truth, I could accept it. Don't get me wrong—the idea of you with her, fucking her—it torments me. It really does." Like, actually produced bile in my mouth. "But I think I always knew you were never with her. It's in your eyes—both now and in that video."

Hudson's Adam's apple bobbed as he swallowed. "I wasn't. I was never with her."

I continued to stare at his neck. It was easier than looking at his eyes where dark storms were beginning to gather. "And that means that the thing with Stacy was a scam. Of course it was. I wanted to think it was just Celia in on it, and you were protecting her. But you said you weren't and you did go along enough to stage that kiss. You were part of it."

I paused, letting what I'd said sink into my consciousness, tasting the truth of the words that still lingered in my mouth. "I thought for a minute that might be your secret. Except it's not it. I mean, yeah, that's shitty that you did that to her, but I knew you had those things in your past. And *you* knew that I knew those things. If that were all there was to learn from that video, you would have told me. There had to be more you were hiding."

Finally, with great effort, I raised my eyes to his. "It's because of what night it was, the night of the symposium, isn't it? I considered that you didn't want me to know that you were still manipulating people for fun that recently, but now I don't think that's all of it either."

"Alayna…" Even though only a whisper, there was weight to his single word. It was cautionary, it was pleading. It said, *don't go here*, even though we were always headed there, from the second he first laid eyes on me. It was fated that we'd arrive at this moment, and whether we wanted to face it or not, here it was.

"It's not the video itself. It's what happened after." I spoke as if I was just figuring it out, but really, it had always been there, buried in my subconscious where I didn't have to deal with it. I knew. I'd always known what I was only now able to admit.

Hudson repeated my name, calling for my attention, but I was no longer focused on him.

"If Celia was there with you outside the symposium…then doesn't it make sense that she went in with you? And if she went in with you, she was there when you first saw me. And if you were still playing people together…"

My skin broke out in goose bumps as a chill ran down my spine and a wave of nausea wracked through my body. A ringing began in my ears, and somewhere behind that I could hear Hudson still speaking.

"I was going to tell you," he seemed to be saying. "I came back to tell you."

I searched his face, barely registering his fragmented explanation as the truth settled over me.

"It's my worst mistake, Alayna." He stepped toward me, his face twisted in anguish, his voice desperate. "The most horrible of all the things I've done. My biggest regret, although it's what gave me you and for that I'm forever grateful. But I never knew what I'd feel for you. I never knew that I could hurt you that much, and that I would care that I did. Please, Alayna, you have to understand."

I was beginning to understand. With shocking clarity. "That's what I was, wasn't I?" I wasn't really asking anyone. "A game. Your game. Together." My legs went weak and I fell to the floor. "Oh god. Oh god, oh god."

"Alayna—" Hudson fell to his knees and reached for me.

I scrambled away, my entire body shaking. "Don't touch me!" I screamed. I couldn't tell if he'd stopped moving toward me or not— my vision was blinded with fury and pain. My stomach twisted as though I might vomit and my head—my head couldn't process, couldn't think.

It didn't help that Hudson refused to let me have a minute to hear my own thoughts. "It wasn't what you think, Alayna. Yes, it started as a game. As Celia's game. But I only went along because it was you. Because I was so enamored with you."

I stared at him, blinking until my vision cleared. Then it was as if I were seeing him for the first time. I'd known this was his M.O. How could I have ignored that this exact situation was a possibility? Our beginning had been strange and unusual. He'd bought the club. Then he'd hired me to break up his engagement—an engagement that wasn't ever a real thing. Why had I not questioned the bizarreness of it before?

And now he was trying to reason with me. My stomach wrenched tighter and I began to dry heave.

"Alayna, let me—"

I held a hand out to stop him from coming toward me. "I don't want your help," I said when the heaving subsided. With the back of my hand, I wiped the spit from my mouth. "I want fucking answers."

"Anything. I told you I'd tell you anything." His words tumbled out as if he thought that answers might benefit him.

I already knew there was nothing he could say to fix this. That every answer would likely be more painful than the last. Still I had to know everything.

I bent my fingers into the carpet, trying to grasp onto something to give me strength. "You were enamored with me?" The phrase was sour on my tongue. "So you decided to fuck with me?"

"No." He sat back on his haunches and shoved both hands through his hair. "No, I wanted to get near you, and her plan was an excuse."

"And what was her plan? '*That girl presenting now. Make her fall in love with you and*'…what?"

He shook his head fiercely, emphatically. "No, it didn't happen like that. It wasn't like that."

I slammed a fist into the floor. "Then what was it like? Tell me!"

He clambered to find his words. I'd never seen him so lost, so off-balance, so miserable. "I saw you, like I've told you, and I was drawn to you. Completely drawn to you. I've never lied about that."

"Drawn to me so you decided to destroy me." And it had worked, hadn't it? Because here I was, completely destroyed.

Hudson shook his head again. "This isn't how I wanted to tell you. It's not coming out right at all."

"You mean if you told it another way, you could manipulate it to make it sound better." I was shaking so badly, my teeth chattered as I spoke.

He winced as if I'd slapped him across the face. "I deserve that. But that's not what I meant." He inched closer, then stilled when my expression told him not to dare move nearer. "Let me tell it the way it was. Please. It won't be better. It will still be awful, but it will be accurate."

I leaned my back against the desk front, not wanting to hear more, needing to hear it all. "I'm waiting."

He ran his tongue along his lips. "I saw you. And Celia noticed, I think. Noticed me noticing you. A few days later, she showed up with information about you."

"*She* showed up with information?" My interruption shook him from what I'd guessed was a memorized script. Too goddammed bad. I wasn't about to let any of it be easy for him.

"Yes, Celia had investigated you. It wasn't me. She had your police record and the restraining order, plus a copy of your mental health record."

Another wave of nausea rippled through me as I thought about Celia being the one to uncover my secrets. As I pictured her running to Hudson with the information of my worst sins.

He seemed to read my disgust, seemed to want to ease it. "It was in complete opposition to what I'd seen of you, Alayna. Everything she'd gathered—that wasn't the strong, confident woman we'd seen at the symposium. It was obvious those things existed in your past. You were better. I saw that."

"I was better." I said it defiantly, even though it was exactly what he'd just said. "I was."

"Yes. You were. It was evident." He took a breath. "Her theory, though, was that you could be broken again." His eyes flared. "*I didn't agree.*"

He let those words hang in the air, waiting for them to sink in.

But what did he expect that I'd do? Stand up and give him a fucking medal because he'd wagered on my side? Because he'd assumed that he *couldn't* break me?

He'd still tried!

Anyway, he'd been wrong. He had gone beyond breaking me. He'd shattered me.

He kept talking, my brain barely computing his words. "That was the bet. She made up the whole idea to have you break up our nonexistent engagement. After a time, I was to end things with you, naturally. Say that the farce was no longer necessary. Then we'd wait and see what happened." He paused to find his words. "But I didn't ever feel—"

I cut him off. "So all of it was a scam. Every single part of us was a lie." My speech was labored as I forced out words that I could never have imagined saying.

"No!" He was animated, passionate. "Even in the beginning, it was never about the game. Not for me. I wasn't supposed to seduce you. I wasn't supposed to fall in love with you. And I did both before you'd even agreed to play along."

I tilted my chin up, the only challenge I could muster besides my heated words. "But you didn't fall in love with me. There's no way, because you don't do shit like that to people you love!"

"I'd never been in love, Alayna! I didn't understand what I was feeling. I only knew I had to be with you and this was the way to do it." His voice cracked. "I'm not excusing what I did, but I'm explaining. I'm pleading for you to try to…to try and…"

"And what? See it from your point of view? Forgive you?" Bitterness dripped from me. There wasn't anything else inside me. I couldn't even cry.

I cocked my head and met his eyes, making certain my next words were clearly understood no matter how I stuttered to get them out. "This is unforgiveable, Hudson! There is no moving forward from this."

"Don't say that. Don't ever say that." His tone was urgent and remorseful. Pained.

I didn't fucking care. Let him hurt. I was glad for it, if that's even how he really felt. I'd hurt him further if I could. I did my best to try. "What is it exactly that you don't want to hear, Hudson? That I can't forgive you? I can't. I can't forgive this. Ever."

"Alayna, please!" He started for me again.

I kicked at him, managing to connect a foot with his upper arm. "We're over. Over! Don't you get it? There's no fucking way to ever trust you again after this!"

He sat back again. He could have easily overcome me if he'd kept trying. Even when I was upset and pumped with adrenaline, he was stronger than me. I couldn't even gather an ounce of gratefulness for it though. He owed me that. He owed me more.

I didn't trust that he wouldn't try once more, and the last thing I wanted was his touch. In fact, I couldn't even look at him. I had to go. Placing a hand in front of me, I pushed myself up to stand. "I'm leaving now. Don't try to stop me. Don't come after me." It took great effort, but finally I was on my feet. "We're done."

Hudson followed me up. "We aren't done, Alayna. This isn't over. We've rebuilt trust after you've broken—"

I spun toward him. "Don't even fucking compare what I've done to this! My mistakes are not even in the same category. This is the worst thing. The *worst* thing you could...I can't even...I can't breathe..." I leaned over, placing my palms on my thighs, trying to get air into my lungs.

He settled a hand on my back, leaning in to check on my breathing.

I shrugged him off. "Don't," I seethed with what air I could find. "Don't ever again. Don't touch me. Don't call. Don't try to reach out to me. This is over, Hudson. *Over*! I can't see you anymore." I'd been numb before, but now I felt volcanic, explosive. Everything inside—I wanted it out. Wanted to retch up every single speck of emotion I had about Hudson, good and bad. I yearned to be free of it all.

And yet the feeling went on. Endless and deep and unbearable.

"Don't say that, Alayna. Tell me how to fix this. Please." Hudson's despair echoed my own. "I'll do anything. There has to be a way."

I reached my hand out to the desk for support. "How? Tell me how there could possibly be a way to go on together after this?" I wasn't even sure I'd be able to go on at all after this.

"I don't have all the answers yet. But we can work on it together. We fix each other, remember?" Hudson curled his hands into fists, straightened them, then curled them again. "I love you, Alayna. I love you—that has to mean something."

For so long I'd waited to hear him talk of his love. Now, he said it freely, and it felt like a complete mockery of everything I'd yearned for him to express. "Right now it really doesn't."

"Please. You can't mean that." He reached for me yet again, his grasp circling my wrist.

With a scream, I yanked my arm away. "Get your fucking hands off me!"

He put his hands up in the air, in surrender. Then he let them fall to his side. He took a step backward. "You said," he paused, "you said you could love me through anything..."

I'd been waiting for him to throw that back at me. Honestly, I was surprised he hadn't mentioned it earlier. "Since everything you said turned out to be a lie, I don't feel like I'm obligated to honor my promise either."

Obligated or not, I did still love him. If I didn't, then I wouldn't feel this way. Every molecule in my body wouldn't be consumed in despair. That was the joke of the whole thing—I'd kept my promise. I did still love him through this horrible, fucked up thing he'd done to me.

But it didn't matter. Not anymore. Not when everything that my love was based upon was a sham.

There was a short knock followed by the opening of the office door. David stuck his head in. "Are you okay, Laynie?"

Had he heard me screaming a moment before? Or had he simply decided enough time had passed that he should check on me? Either way, I'd never been more grateful for the sight of him. "No. I'm not okay."

David looked from me to Hudson, not sure what to do.

Hudson tried once more. "Alayna..."

I had no more words for him. Nothing left to say, nothing left to give. I simply shook my head once. I was done. That was all.

He continued to plead with his eyes for long seconds. After a while, he lowered his head. "I'll leave." Hudson turned to David. "I'm sorry to put a damper on your party. Thank you for looking out for her."

He turned to look one last time at me, his expression filled with sorrow, regret, and longing. I knew he believed that I'd run to David after he left, and that the idea pained him even further. He was making a huge sacrifice leaving me with David alone.

But his sacrifice was a classic example of too little, too late.

So he was hurt? Too fucking bad. I was destroyed.

I turned away, not able to look at him any longer. I knew he was gone when David put his arms around me. I let him hug me for a moment, but contrary to what Hudson believed I'd do, I wasn't interested in seeking comfort from David. All I wanted to do was go somewhere and cry until the pain in my chest, in my head, in my bones, didn't threaten to pull me under anymore.

I wasn't sure it was even possible. I suspected that in reality I'd hurt—hurt hard—for a very, very long time.

"What can I do?" David asked as I pulled away.

I wiped a stream of tears from my face. "Get Liesl, please."

Forever With You

Chapter Twenty

Liesl was an angel.

She calmed me down enough to get me out of the building without drawing attention from the employees. I barely had the strength to walk, and she let me lean on her as we went to the curb and got into the cab that David hailed for us. She didn't make any jabs about being pulled away early from the party, nor did she try to get me to talk about what happened. Instead, she pulled my head into her lap and smoothed my hair while I cried all the way to her apartment in Brooklyn.

Once inside her place, Liesl tucked me into her bed with a glass of straight tequila. Though she had a futon in her living room, she stayed with me all night. She spooned behind me, and when I woke up from the little bouts of sleep I managed to get, her warm presence calmed my screams to sobs. I hadn't grieved and mourned that much since the death of my parents. Even then, I hadn't known the level of betrayal that I felt now.

That was the worst part of it, the betrayal. If I'd heard the story earlier from Hudson, at a point in our relationship where I hadn't put everything on the line, then I may have been able to survive it. I'd still have left him—I couldn't possibly be with him after that—but it would have been so much easier to survive. Leaving it as long as he did, especially when we'd talked at end about honesty and transparency—that was the ultimate betrayal. That was the deepest cut.

But the loss of the man I loved so desperately came as a close second.

The first two days were a blur. Liesl cooked for me and forced food down my throat. She listened to my story as I told it, in spurts, piecing it together as best she could, again without pressing. Throughout it all, she refilled my glass any time I asked. In a rare moment where I managed to focus on something other than my heartache, it occurred to me to wonder if that was why my father had spent his life drinking—had he been trying to block out some sort of pain? What had hurt him? Wasn't it sad that I'd never know?

The rest of my thoughts were mismatches of memories and realizations. Sweet recollections turned sour with the new information layered on top. I relived every conversation that I'd had with Hudson a dozen times. Sometimes all I could do was cry. At other moments, I became angry. I broke more than one glass throwing it in rage.

Once even, I considered taking a broken piece and slitting it across my skin. Maybe not too deep.

Or maybe exactly too deep.

Thankfully Liesl was there to clean up the fragments before I managed to steal any away. Besides, I didn't really want to end things—I just wanted to end the pain.

Eventually, I began trying to piece things together. Tried to figure out what was real and what wasn't. Imagined how and where Celia had fit into my relationship with Hudson. Like the way he'd condoned my jealousies, the way he supported my snooping. *Encourage her obsession*, I imagined Celia saying. *Don't get mad or upset if she shows any of her crazy traits.*

And the way she knew to throw his pet name in my face. Had that been her idea as well? *Give her a pet name. Something like* angel *or* precious.

I remembered Sophia's birthday—Hudson had spoken with Celia then, and when we came home he'd been distant. Had she reminded him of the game then? What he was really supposed to be doing with me?

To his credit, Hudson hadn't lied. His exact words came back to me with full force: "*I will be saying and doing things—romantic things, perhaps—that are not genuine. I need you to remember that. Out of the public eye, I will seduce you. That will be genuine, but it can never be misconstrued as love."*

When had that changed? When had his false romancing become true? Had it ever? Was he at this very moment celebrating with his partner in crime—toasting to the complete and utter destruction of my soul?

That was the crux of my heartache—I'd never know. There was nothing to hold on to with fondness because the authenticity of every moment we'd spent together was up for debate. I couldn't believe anything he'd said or did. He'd so expertly administered his manipulation it was impossible to see the real story underneath the formulated one.

That plain and utter truth was what kept me refilling my glass.

By Tuesday night, I sobered up enough to acknowledge some of my responsibilities. I propped myself against the headboard of Liesl's bed and called her from the kitchen into her room. "The club…" I started to say.

She leaned her head against the doorframe. "I already called in sick for you."

God, she was amazing.

She'd told the truth. I could barely get out of bed, let alone leave the apartment. And I'd cried so hard that I'd thrown up more than once. That had to count as sick.

Knowing that burden was off my plate, I considered resuming my drinking and sleeping. But as I scratched an itch at the top of my head, I discovered my hair was matted and dirty—I really needed a shower. And a change of clothes. Did I care? Yeah, I kind of did. That was progress, right?

But I had nothing of mine at Liesl's apartment. "Do you have something I can wear if I take a shower?"

She nodded encouragingly. "Anything in my closet's yours." Cleaning up would be as much to her benefit as mine. I smelled pretty rank.

The shower hurt as much as it helped. Though it made me feel better, it cleared my mind enough to worry about the future. Where was I going to live? Where was I going to work? Could I go back to The Sky Launch? I'd had the club before Hudson had come into my life—I didn't want to give that up. But even if he let me work there, could I be there anymore?

Maybe. Maybe not.

First things first. I couldn't stay holed up in Liesl's room. I moved to the futon that night.

"My bed is yours, babe," she said as I pulled the mattress into a prone position.

It was tempting to take her up on that. But I stayed surprisingly strong. "I already feel bad about overtaking your place. Besides, I need to start trying to function a little bit on my own. Even if that only means being in my own bed."

"Suit yourself." She threw me a pillow from her closet. "And you're welcome here as long as you want."

I wrapped my arms around the pillow and fell onto the futon. "I think it's going to be a while, Liesl. Are you sure about the offer?"

"Yep."

At least that took care of living arrangements for a bit. I'd have to arrange to pick up my things from the penthouse at some point. I didn't have much, but I needed my clothes. Not the items that had been bought by him—I didn't want those—but the rest of my stuff.

And I needed to get a new phone. My current one also came from Hudson. I didn't want anything to do with it. I'd already given it to Liesl and asked her to hang on to it for me. If Hudson had decided to ignore my request and call, I wouldn't even know. I didn't want to know.

Then there was Celia's possible lawsuit…

I sat up. "Have the police been looking for me?" Hudson had said he'd take care of it, but I didn't trust a word he said anymore.

Liesl sat down at the foot of the futon. "Nope, and they won't be." She answered my questioning look. "Hudson called me on my cell yesterday morning. He wanted me to tell you that he'd gotten the whole battery charge dismissed."

So he knows where I am. Of course he did. It wasn't that hard to figure out where I'd go. And I had the feeling Hudson wasn't the kind of guy you could hide from very easily.

 I couldn't help myself. I had to know. "Did he say anything else?"

"He said lots of things. I decided you weren't interested in hearing any of it."

"Good thinking. I wasn't." I leaned back on my elbows. "But I am now. What did he say?"

"That he wanted to give you your space, but that he's anxious to talk to you when—*if*—you want to. That he'll do anything you want him to for the club, even if that includes doing nothing. That you're welcome to come back to the penthouse—he's staying at his other place."

"The loft." The offer of the penthouse was a waste of his breath. I had no desire to be anywhere I'd been with him. Except maybe the club. I still hadn't decided about that yet.

"Yeah, the loft." She lowered her eyes. "He also insisted that I tell you he loves you."

"I don't want to hear that." Even knowing it was a lie, it still had impact. My stomach tightened and my eyes watered. And some stupid little spot in my chest flickered with a spark of...I don't know...hope, maybe? It surprised me. Disgusted me. After everything, how could there be any part of me that still wanted his love to be true?

Liesl grinned. "That's what I told him." Her mouth straightened to a tight line. "He said it didn't make it any less true."

That night when I cried myself to sleep, it wasn't the betrayal that kept the tears coming—it was the loneliness. My lips burned for Hudson's mouth, my breasts ached for his touch, my entire body pulsed with isolation. And instead of wishing I'd never met the man, that I'd never heard his name, I wished I'd never found out the truth. Ignorance, it turned out, truly could be bliss.

***

"I told you it sucks," Gwen said when I called in sick on Wednesday.

I didn't follow. "What sucks?" I should have had Liesl call in for me again. This talking to people thing was harder than I'd comprehended.

Gwen delivered her response in sing-song voice. "Love, darling. L-o-v-e, love. Worst thing ever."

Guess my claim of the flu wasn't fooling her. "Yeah. It really does."

***

Thursday I almost seemed like a real person again. A broken, distraught person, but that was better than the sobbing lump that I'd been the days before. Now I could feed myself and I even managed to drink something other than alcohol.

Liesl had seemed to think I was ready to be pushed further. "You need a distraction. A release. Like maybe you should pet the pussy. I could loan you my vibrator while I'm at work tonight."

I cringed. "Um, no thanks."

"Then we could drive to Atlantic City this weekend and check out David's new place. You know he'd fuck your brains out if you asked."

"First of all, David doesn't fuck anyone's brains out." Though I'd never slept with him, I'd been with him enough in a sexual sense to know he was a total puppy dog.

"Secondly, I don't ever want to have sex with anyone ever again." Hudson had ruined sex for me—there would never be anyone better, no one more serving and demanding and fulfilling. It had been the place where things had been real for us—even now, with all the lies, I believed that. Anyone who tried to come in after would be a sorry comparison.

And there was a third thing—Saturday was the day of Mira's Grand Reopening. I couldn't go, of course. That would be ridiculous to even consider. But telling her was going to be hard. Since it was already Thursday, I probably couldn't put it off any longer.

With a deep breath, I held my hand out to Liesl. "Speaking of the weekend—can I borrow your phone? I need to call Mira."

She handed me her cell. I looked up Mirabelle's Boutique and pressed the button to dial. This would be a true test of my strength. Mira had been so pro-Alayna-and-Hudson that she was likely as devastated as I was. Well, not quite that devastated, but nearly. And knowing her and her love-conquers-all attitude, she'd probably try to convince me we could work things out.

Maybe I didn't want to call her after all.

"Mirabelle's. This is Mira." Too late to hang up now.

"Hey, Mira."

"Laynie!" she exclaimed with her usual bubbly, happy tone. "I was going to call you and check in. Great minds. I have your dress altered and ready for you—do you want to pick it up before Saturday or change here that day? Or I could have it sent to you by courier."

Dammit. Hudson hadn't told her the news of our breakup. What the fuck?

I definitely didn't want to be the one to tell her that. But now I kind of had to.

"I…Mira…" I was having trouble finding the words. I decided to start somewhere else. "I can't do your event. I'm sorry. I called to cancel." Then, after a swallow, "Hudson and I…we broke up." Why did it hurt so much more to say it out loud?

I swallowed again, bracing myself for Mira's reaction.

"I know," she said softly. Then she immediately perked up again. "Which is why I banned him from the store on Saturday. I don't give a shit if he makes it to my event. But you—Laynie, I have to have you here. Please say you'll still come. It would mean so much to me."

My mouth went dry. I was not emotionally equipped to handle shock. Or anyone being nice to me. "Mira, no," I floundered. "That's not right. You can't keep your own brother from your special day."

"Yes, I can," she insisted. "He doesn't care about fashion. He does care about me. And you."

Ah, there was the Mira I'd been expecting.

I clamped my eyes shut to ward off a new set of tears. "Please, don't say that. I don't want to hear about his supposed emotions."

"Okay, okay. That's fine. I wasn't trying to meddle. I was simply trying to tell you that he already offered to not come before I banned him. He said he wanted me and you to be happy and so he was bowing out. Yes, I'd rather have you both there. Of course I would. But if it comes to you or him, I definitely choose you. You're one of my models, and more importantly, you're my friend. You're like a sister, Laynie."

I warred with my options. When I called, there'd been no way in hell that I planned to go to Mira's event. I couldn't be there with him. It would be impossible to be a model under those circumstances.

But her speech…

We had become friends, and I had hoped that we'd one day be sisters. She'd done a lot for me and Hudson, but truly, she'd also done a lot for just me. And maybe doing this for her would help me with closure.

"All right. I'll do it." *Did I really fucking just say that?* "But you better swear to god that he will not be there. And this better not be a trick to get us together."

"I swear he will not be there. Swear on my baby." She paused. "Though that tricking you to get you together idea..."

"Mira—"

"I'm just kidding." Her smile was evident in her voice. "Yay! Thank you, Laynie."

"You're welcome." *Sort of.* "But don't expect a cheery model."

"You can do the serious/somber thing. I'm totes okay with that." She lowered her voice. "And for the record, I don't know what that fucker did to mess things up with the two of you, but he's a miserable wreck about it. I mean, completely and utterly broken up."

For half a second, I actually felt joy. Was it because I was happy the asshole was as miserable as I was or because I thought his misery said something about how he felt for me?

It would kill me if I kept wondering about the validity of any of his emotions. I had to stop thinking about it. "Mira, if you're going to keep telling me about him, I'm going to cancel."

"No! Don't do that." She sounded panicked. "Just had to get that out there. I'm done now."

"Okay, but no more." *Please, no more.* Another deep breath. "I'll change there on Saturday."

She squealed. "I'm so excited! See you then."

I almost smiled as I hung up.

"Well, look at that," Liesl said as I handed her phone back. "You have some color in your cheeks."

"It's not possible." I scrubbed my hands over my face. God, mourning was exhausting. And boring as hell. I had to find a way to move on. Mira's event was a good first step. But I needed to take some other steps.

Like figure out what to do with the rest of my life.

Just thinking the thought seemed overwhelming. A tear rolled down my cheek. Seriously? Wasn't I about fucking cried out yet?

But it had to be done. I grabbed a Kleenex and dabbed at my eye. "I, um, I want to go to work."

Liesl cleared her throat. "Are you sure?" My tears probably had her unconvinced.

"Not tonight. But tomorrow, yeah. I need to see if I can be there. I don't think I can make a good decision about my future at the club without trying a shift out."

Through all my struggles with obsessive love addiction, The Sky Launch had been my sanity. It had been the only thing to ground me when I'd been free falling. Now, as I was falling again, couldn't it be the place to save me again?

If not, I had to find out what could. Because already, I was getting that restless feeling in the pit of my stomach—that anxious tickle that marked me as an addict no matter how healthy I was. It was another sign that it was time to start figuring out my future.

When Liesl went into work that night, I forced myself to find something to do other than sleep and cry. Something other than remember. I turned on Spotify and found something to download on my Kindle app since Liesl had no books in her apartment.

But I couldn't get into the novel. And nothing else on the Internet or on TV was enough to occupy my mind. I couldn't stop thinking, and as I moved through the grieving process, my thoughts turned obsessive, as they always did when I was hurting. Some of them weren't even clearly formed but were instead only rough impulses. The urge to see him, for example. Not to talk to him, but to look at him from a distance. The urge to smell him again. The urge to hear his voice.

The yearning drove me mad.

And it pissed me off.

Because I was stronger than this. I was stronger than Hudson Pierce and Celia Werner. I would not let them pull me down to the person that I once was.

She thought she could destroy me?

Well, fuck that. I'd survived heartache before. I could survive it again.

Adrenaline surged through me, and I suddenly felt invincible. Or capable at least—invincible was going a bit too far. But "Roar" by Katy Perry came on my playlist, and I did jump around the room singing at the top of my lungs.

It felt good. Invigorating. Energizing.

Then "So Easy" by Phillip Phillips came on, and immediately my strength disappeared. *"You make it so easy…"* he sang, and all I heard was Hudson saying it to me.

And it was all a lie.

I dissolved into a mess of snot and ugly tears. Well, another night of crying wasn't the worst thing in the world. There was always tomorrow to be strong.

Forever With You

Chapter Twenty-One

The next day, I didn't feel stronger, but I did feel resolved.

Planning the future still seemed overwhelming, but I could handle today. *Baby steps.* It's what I'd learned in therapy. It was something I knew how to do.

On paper and in pencil, I broke down the hours. It helped to look at it written down so it didn't feel bigger than it was. I started at the bottom of the page since I'd already decided to go to the club.

8 p.m. to 3 a.m. work, I wrote.

Before that I'd go to a group meeting. I looked online and found one at six that evening. *Perfect.* I filled it in above my work shift.

At the top of the page I wrote in: *breakfast, shower, dress.*

Then: *sneak over to the penthouse to get some clothes.*

Even writing the last thing had been hard. To say it sounded daunting was an understatement. The Bowery had been the place where Hudson and I had really begun sharing our life. It would be filled with painful reminders.

But going through the memories, dealing with them—that was part of healing.

Getting through the first line of items was easier than I'd expected. Breakfast actually stayed down, and I managed to find a pair of drawstring shorts in Liesl's drawer that didn't fall off my waist.

"Do you want me to go with you?" Liesl offered around a bite of a bagel.

"No. I need to do this by myself." I threw my still wet hair into a ponytail. "I'll need you for the next time—when I get all my stuff. But this time, I'm just going to run in and pack a bag to get me through a few days. It'll feel good to finally wear panties again."

I stood up and looked at my bare feet. "Shit. I only have my heels from the party."

"I'll loan you some shoes."

"We don't have the same size feet." Liesl was much taller than me, with a larger frame. If it weren't for the drawstring, I'd be drowning in her shorts.

She kicked off the flip-flops she was wearing. "You can wear these. They're like one-size-fits-many."

"Fine." I slid my feet into them. They'd do. "Okay. I'm off. Wish me luck."

"You don't need luck. You got this." She pulled me in for a hug. "You're sure he won't be there?"

"Positive." I'd called Norma for that. She'd checked with Hudson's secretary and reported back that he had a meeting in his office all afternoon. And he'd told Liesl he wasn't staying at the penthouse. If I believed him, which I didn't necessarily, then he wouldn't be there no matter what. It was possible that he hadn't even been back there after L.A. I guess I'd find out soon enough.

Since it was still early in the day, I took my time getting to the penthouse. I took the subway instead of a cab and didn't rush to meet the connecting train. But as much as I dillydallied, I eventually arrived at my destination.

The memories started before I made it inside the building. I stood outside staring at the letters engraved on the stone above the door. *The Bowery.* In many ways it felt like the first time I'd been there, when I was nervous and anxious and unaware of what waited for me inside. Then though, my stomach fluttered with butterflies. Today it was filled with rolling stones. Though both had my tummy in motion, there was a definite difference in gravity. One feeling lifted me up. The other pulled me down, anchored me to my dismal reality.

With a final breath of fresh air, I headed in.

On the elevator ride up, I decided I'd be no-nonsense about my task. As soon as the door opened inside the penthouse, I headed straight to my closet. I put on some underwear and changed into a dress and shoes suitable for work. Then I packed a duffel bag with a few items to get me through the next week. I was done and ready to go in less than fifteen minutes.

But a sudden wave of nostalgia kept me from leaving without doing a final look around. I told myself it was the smart thing to do—in case I found something that I wanted to take with me.

Yeah, that was it.

The place was almost exactly the way I'd left it, except the cleaning lady had been through. The trashcans and dishwasher had been emptied. The only sign of disarray was the books I'd left out in the library. All clean and immaculate like that, the apartment felt empty, abandoned. Lonely. The warmth that had once filled it was gone. It seemed staged. Like a model home that no one really lived in. Like nothing special or beautiful had ever happened there.

It could be anyone's home. Nothing reflected us. How had I never noticed this before?

It was fitting, I supposed, to feel so empty.

Except it deepened my sorrow. I'd been prepared to walk in and be met with the ghosts of our past. That they weren't there rocked me.

Suddenly, I felt desperate to find a sign of us somewhere—anywhere. I set down my bag and ran back to our bedroom. I threw myself onto the made bed and buried my face in a pillow. It smelled clean. The bedding had been changed since we'd last slept there together. In Hudson's closet, I found only rows of clean clothes and an empty hamper. Finally, in the bathroom, I found a bottle of his body wash. I opened it and breathed in the scent.

My knees buckled. God, it was him and not him all at once. The smell permeated into my skin, reawakening every memory of him, rekindling feelings that I wanted to forget.

In that moment, though, I didn't want to forget. I wanted to embrace everything I had left of him. And this scent wasn't enough. It was missing the most important part. I wanted more, all of it. And I couldn't find it here.

I recognized the emotion immediately—the desperate urge. I could make it go away if I tried hard enough, if I refocused, if I concentrated on my substitute list.

But I didn't want to do that. I wanted to follow the urge, to let it lead me where I needed to go. For once, I wanted to give in to it instead of constantly fighting it. Wanted to fall into the comfort of the old pattern and let it swallow me.

Maybe, just today, I could let it take me away. I could go to the loft, slip in while Hudson was in his meetings, and feel him in the place that he'd been living. Look for traces of his existence. Smell him and sense him.

It wasn't healthy, but it would only be one time. One time wouldn't destroy me. And after that, I could move on. I'd go to my group meeting and get back on track and my new life—my life without Hudson—could really begin.

It sounded divine. Like a guilty pleasure. No worse than eating a whole tub of Ben and Jerry's straight from the carton. Without any more thought, I decided to do it. Then I flagged down a cab and headed to the Pierce Industries building before I could change my mind.

I was grateful that Norma had told me about Hudson's afternoon meeting. It made the chance of bumping into him not an issue. He'd be wrapped up in his business whatnot, never knowing I was right above him. It added to the appeal.

As soon as I opened the front door of the loft, I felt it. The thing I'd been missing—Hudson's presence. It lingered in the air, not just his scent, but the warmth of him. It made the hair stand up on my arms and made my skin tingle. It was exactly what I'd longed for.

Setting my duffel by the front door, I explored further, remembering and putting to memory the place where we'd shared our first time. I trailed my hand along the back of his leather couch as I passed. Then I trailed my other hand over the papers on his desk as I went deeper into the loft. At the back, I found the private elevator. It led to one place only—down to his office. That's how close he was. I placed my palm on the cool metal.

How close. How far away.

In the kitchen, I lingered over a half empty mug of coffee on the counter. *He drank from this.* His lips had touched the rim. I lifted the cup to my face, pressing it against my cheek. It was cold, but I could imagine it hot. Imagine him sipping at it gently, carefully.

I knew I was acting crazy, but I didn't care. I couldn't stop myself even if I did care.

Soon, I made it to the bedroom. The room he'd first taken me in. He'd been both amazing and overwhelming. I'd felt out of my league, and yet, I couldn't help but try to fit into his world in the way he'd wanted me.

My eyes glanced toward the bathroom. If I went in there now, would the scent of clean Hudson still be lingering from his morning shower? I'd go there next.

But first, the bed…

I fell across the mattress. This time when I inhaled, he was there in abundance. I wrapped my arms tight around his pillow and closed my eyes, breathing him in and out and in. And out. The scent soothed me, calmed me. The ache in my chest released ever so slightly. The tension behind my temples abated. For the first time in days, I felt okay.

Closing my eyes, I let the fantasy wash over me. Let myself forget the hurt and betrayal and pretended Hudson and I could be together again in all the ways we used to be. I imagined his lips on me—phantom kisses along my neck and down my torso that sent shivers down my spine and caused my toes to curl. Then his hands, caressing and kneading my body, reawakening my skin with his simple touch. Adoring me physically but with so much concentration and attention that the effort had to come from true and pure love.

I was still lying on the bed, lost in my daydream, when the private elevator arrived in the next room.

My eyes flew open. Had I imagined it?

Then Hudson's voice filled the air.

Fuck!

And he was talking to someone—he wasn't alone.

I scrambled off the bed and crouched by the floor considering what to do next. It sounded like he was still in the back of the loft, near the kitchen. I crawled to the wall next to the doorframe. There I could peek out and get a better idea of the situation and still stay hidden from the living area. As long as they didn't come in the bedroom, I'd be fine.

But if they did come in the bedroom…

Gathering my courage, I peeked out and saw Hudson standing in front of the open refrigerator. He grabbed a bottle of water and turned toward his guest—toward me.

I pulled my head back around the corner. *Did he see me?* No, I didn't think so.

Shit, shit, shit. All I could do was swear. And pray.

And eavesdrop.

"I haven't been here in a while." I hadn't gotten a chance to look at his visitor, but I knew who it was from her voice. "I'd forgotten what a good job I'd done with the place." *Celia Werner.*

My chest tightened and my eyes began to water.

I was gone barely a week, and he was bringing her to his loft? Why? To celebrate the slaughter of my soul? To plan their next game?

To *connect?*

314

Each possibility was worse than the last. This was heartache on top of heartache. Salt on the wound. A lesson to teach me not to give into my urges again.

Celia's heels clicked on the cement floor.

Where was she going? I held my breath, my heart pounding. Maybe I should hide out in the bathroom. Then they wouldn't see me if they came this way. But then I couldn't hear what they were saying. And, besides, if they did need the bed…

God, I couldn't think about that.

"Remember how I had to convince you to go with the leather couch?" she asked.

She was in the living area. If they stayed right there, I could pull this off.

"We're not here for a walk down memory lane." Hudson's voice was cold.

Her footsteps paused. "Why *are* we here?"

Yes, Hudson, do tell. Though I wasn't sure I wanted to know.

"Because we have some things to talk about, and they aren't suitable for my office."

"Then I can't help but think of old times. Other conversations that weren't appropriate for your office." Her heels clicked again and then stopped. Then the leather of the sofa creaked as she took a seat.

I let out the breath I'd been holding.

Now Hudson's shoes sounded on the floor. "If you want to relive those times, then do it on your own." His voice got nearer.

Shit, fuck, dammit! He was headed my way.

But then I heard the rattling of ice in a glass. Slowly, I turned my head to the side. He was there—not ten feet away, fixing himself a drink at the bar. If he looked over and down, he'd see me.

I froze, not blinking, not even breathing; willing myself to fade into the wall. My heart thudded so loudly, I was certain he could hear it.

Except he didn't. He finished making his drink, then turned back to face Celia.

"Come on, Huds." Her tone was playful, cajoling, in complete opposition to his. "You act like we never had any fun together."

"That was a lifetime ago, Celia." Though he was still merely steps away, his words were distant. "It's time to move on."

Celia laughed. "Because of her?"

"Who? Alayna?" A chill ran through my body. Jesus, even when he said my name to someone else, it had the same effect as when he said it to me. "Yes. And no." He paused. "We aren't together anymore."

And hearing him say that—it was as painful as when I'd said it to Mira. The verbalization of it made it so real. So final.

Celia seemed overjoyed with the news. "Am I supposed to be sad?"

"Why would I expect that? That was your intended outcome, after all." He moved forward, out of my sightline. Then there was another creak of furniture. He'd sat in the chair across from her, I guessed.

I struggled with listening to them talk as I debated with myself—should I scurry to the other side of the doorframe? If he came back to the bar, I'd be better hidden. But if one of them went to the guest bathroom, then I'd be easily seen.

"No," Celia said, "my intended outcome was that she'd go crazy after your break-up and end up back in her psycho obsession mode."

I decided to stay put.

"Well, that's not happening. She's stronger than you thought."

And yet, there I was, hiding in Hudson's bedroom because I'd done exactly as predicted and gone stalker. It crushed me that he could believe otherwise—that he had no understanding of how much he could break me. Did he not get what he'd meant to me?

If he didn't understand, Celia did. Perhaps it was a female thing. "Maybe. I'm not sure I agree. How long ago was this breakup?"

"A few days now."

"Oh, give it time. She'll be back. That girl was head over heels for you. She's not walking away that easily. Not that type."

I cringed at the accuracy with which she was describing me. It would fuel me to be strong, I decided. Otherwise, she'd win. Technically, she'd already won—I was here, after all. But if she didn't know, then she couldn't take it as a victory, right?

"Celia, stop it." Hudson's sharp command drew my attention.

"Are you still sticking to the story that you're in love with her?"

Her question made my hair stand on end. *He'd told her that he loved me*...did that mean there'd really been some truth to it?

He didn't answer her verbally, but his expression must have been in the affirmative because Celia scoffed. "That's ridiculous, Hudson. You've never loved anyone. It's not in your nature. You're fascinated with her for some godforsaken reason. But it's not love."

"What do you know about love?" He'd never spoke so harshly in my presence.

She laughed again. "Everything you taught me—it's a fleeting emotion that can be manipulated and fabricated. It's not real. It's never real."

"It's time you found another teacher. I no longer believe any of that."

I drew my knees into my chest. He believed in love now—because of me? The discovery tugged at my heart, begging me to reexamine the status of our relationship. Oh, how I wanted to fasten myself to his love. Wanted to turn it into a chance for us to be together.

But I couldn't. His deceit was too great. It didn't matter that he fell in love. It was deserved. His just rewards. His karma.

"Maybe I should be the teacher for a while," Celia suggested. "It's time to change up the game anyway."

There was a sound of ice rattling—Hudson shaking his glass, perhaps. Then a pause while he swallowed. "I don't want to play anymore, Celia."

"You said that before with Stacy. And you ended up coming around."

"That was all your game. I gave you a make-out session. That's all. And it wasn't for you, it was for her. I don't know the extent you played with her, but it was time you were done. I knew that the kiss would end it."

"Are you trying to convince me you had feelings for Stacy too?"

"You were using my name to fuck with my sister's assistant. It was going to come back and bite me in the ass eventually. And she was a nice girl. She didn't deserve it."

Their words had come fast, one statement on top of another.

Now they paused as Hudson perhaps took another swallow of his drink. Then he said, "Those are the only reasons I resorted to helping you with that."

His words hung in the air. They sunk over me slowly. They pissed me off. I didn't want to think of him as the hero of that situation, of any situation. So he'd participated in the scam to help Stacy. There were other ways he could have helped her. It wasn't enough to redeem him.

I heard the creak of the couch—maybe just Celia leaning forward, but I tensed, afraid she was on the move again.

But there wasn't any sound of footsteps, just her speaking, "And why did you agree to the Alayna game? Don't tell me that was an excuse to be with her."

Hudson must have nodded, because next she said, "Liar. You're you. Hudson Pierce. You would have found a way to be with her anyway."

"The minute I showed her any interest, you did too. Going along with your game was the only way to protect her."

"Whatever," Celia echoed my thoughts. "If it's true that your interest was what attracted me, then the way for you to *protect her* would have been to run from her. Far and fast. I don't buy it. You wanted to play."

I hated to admit she and I were on the same page, but we were.

It was Hudson's answer that surprised me. "You're right. I should have run. I couldn't. So I did the next best thing."

A memory flashed into my mind of the first time I'd seen Hudson at the bar of the club. I'd known immediately that he was someone I should run from. The words *far and fast* had even occurred to me. Against my own conscience, knowing my faults and my weaknesses, I'd gone after him anyway.

Could I blame him for doing the same?

"I didn't want to play the game with her," he said next. "And I don't want to play ever again."

More movement. Then Hudson returned to the bar.

I should have moved. I should have moved! My pulse accelerated, and again, I held my breath.

"You don't mean that, Hudson." Celia stood as well. Her heels gave her away.

God, please don't let her join him. Hudson was at least focused on his glass. She'd see me for sure.

Thankfully, she stayed where she was.

"Remember what it's like?" she asked him. "The adrenaline rush? To stage a situation, knowing exactly how it will play out because you studied the characters so well you understand what they'll do. There's nothing like it."

"You're destroying people's lives!"

"*You* taught me!"

"Then learn this next lesson well—it was wrong. I. Was. Wrong."

Their words flew back and forth again. My heart continued to thud in my chest as they sparred. It was thrilling, exhilarating to hear him fight her.

Did that mean I thought of her as a worse enemy than him? Because I wanted him to defeat her?

Until that afternoon, I'd thought of them as a pair. Two of a kind. Now, my feelings were changing ever so slightly.

Hudson turned again to face her. "And of all the lives I've destroyed, Celia, I'm most regretful for what I've done to yours. But I can't be responsible for that anymore. You have to decide now who you're going to be. This is not who I'm going to be."

Damn tears at my eyes again. Not wanting to move while I was still in his sightline, I let them fall freely. If it was true—if he really was done with his games—well, it made me proud.

Why the fuck I even cared, I couldn't say.

"Then you're out," Celia said, resigned. "That's fine. I'm not. And I'm not done with the Alayna Withers experiment."

My stomach sunk. My break-up with Hudson should have won me a reprieve from her games. I'd never be away from her, would I?

Hudson thought I would. "Oh yes, you are done with Alayna." He stepped further into the room, again out of my sight. "And don't give me the line that you play to win. I can think of some times that you've lost. You've lost big, if I recall."

"That's cruel." She actually sounded hurt. I hadn't realized the woman had feelings.

"Ah, but isn't that one of the requirements to playing the game?" His awful, caustic tone both frightened and elated me. It was scary to think Hudson had it in him, but it was delightful that he used it on my nemesis.

"Tell me, I'm curious," Hudson began now, "what exactly was your plan with Alayna, anyway? After I dropped out and refused to break up with her, you created your befriend-and-frame scheme.

When that failed, then what? The books with the quotes, the stalking—what was that supposed to do?"

I swear I heard her shrug. "I don't know. Push her over the edge. Make her doubt you. Drive you apart."

Hudson chuckled. "It seemed like random flailing to me. Guesswork. That's not how we played."

"It worked, didn't it? You're not together anymore."

Oh, how I wanted to knock the glee out of her voice. It was another one of the worst parts of breaking up with Hudson—Celia took it as a victory.

He wouldn't let her take the credit, though. "Believe it or not, that has nothing to do with anything you did."

"Really? I thought for sure telling her we were lovers had been the final nail in the coffin. Especially when I gave her proof."

"What proof could you possibly give for something that never happened?"

Though he'd said they'd never been together, I'd still had lingering doubts. His word no longer meant anything. But now…now I knew for sure. They'd never been romantic together. At least there was that.

"I told her you called me the same pet name you called her. Tore. Her. Up."

"From the looks of it, it seems she tore you up."

"Battle scars," she said dismissively.

Her face! I'd almost forgotten. Damn, I wished I could see the results of my attack.

"What pet name are you talking about, anyway?"

His question alone meant he'd never told her. I turned my head toward the opening, eager to hear how this proceeded.

"*Precious*," she said.

"How the hell did you know about that?" He was furious.

So it *had* been only ours. Finally, I had something to hold onto. That—his name for me—that would be the memory I'd take away as pure and true.

"I borrowed her phone one day when we'd had lunch. I saw text messages between the two of you. You called her precious."

Such a fucking cunt. I wanted to stand up and shout it across the room. It was almost worth revealing myself.

Almost.

Hudson's expression must have indicated he wasn't happy about the information because Celia said, "Oh, come on. It was a good play. A fucking good play. And you're telling me that had no bearing on your breakup?"

"No. I think she could have survived that, honestly." *Yes, we could have survived that.* "It was the truth that did us in."

"The truth? You told her—?"

He cut her off. "Everything."

"That's against the ru—"

Again he broke her off. "There are no fucking rules anymore, Celia. It's over! I'm not playing. And I'm not discussing Alayna with you for another minute." He spoke with finality.

I pictured what he must look like—his shoulders broad and squared, his face stern and unmoving. There was no way to refute him when he looked like that.

Her heels clicked again.

I tensed.

Then the sound of the couch creaking. "Is that why you brought me here? To tell me that you're quitting?" Though she was trying to sound bored, I heard the disappointment in her voice.

"I haven't even really played in years. Except to be your pawn." Hudson's steps then movement as he sat in his chair. "But no, that's not why you're here. I'm telling you that *you're* quitting. You're done, Celia. No more games."

"You're joking, right? You can't decide that for me."

While I appreciated that Hudson believed he could simply talk Celia out of her ways, I recognized her fortitude. She was not one to give up easily. Or at all. Even if Hudson asked her nicely.

"You're right that I can't monitor you in every facet of your life," Hudson said, "nor do I have any intention, but I can tell you that you will not be messing with me or my family or my employees and definitely not Alayna."

There, again. The sound of my name from his lips. Said so carefully, so reverently, like carrying something fragile and precious. *Ah...precious.* His care for me was...it was deep. I couldn't deny that.

And the realization only hurt that much more.

Celia's response kept me from spiraling into a fit of sobs. "That's hilarious that you think you have any control over me in any measure. And your declaration is only begging for me to prove you wrong. Plus, even though I agreed to not press charges, I'm not finished with this Alayna game."

"You *are* finished, Celia." Again, he spoke with authority. "While I'd hoped you'd give it up for the sake of our friendship—or whatever it is that we once had—I had a feeling that you'd disagree. So I've attained some insurance."

"I'm intrigued."

So am I.

"Let me tell you about a company that I just bought." There was unusual pep in Hudson's tone. "Actually, I'll show you the paperwork."

Once more my heart raced as Hudson stood and moved. But he sounded like he was walking away. Then a shuffle of papers—he was at his desk. Then back to where he'd been—again, the chair creaked. I heard another shuffle and then individual paper movement as though someone was flipping through a packet and periodic silence as they paused to read. I could picture it—her French-tipped nails turning one page after another.

What was it? I itched to know. Though there was no way I'd be able to see what she was reading, I couldn't take it anymore—I had to peek. If they were buried in papers, they wouldn't notice me. I moved to my knees and peered around the door.

She sat, as I'd imagined, on the couch, a manila folder in hand, her brow furrowed. Her hair was up, as usual, and her nose was bandaged. Black and blue bruises extended underneath the tape.

I couldn't help but smile at her injury.

Her eyes widened and her head shot up to look at Hudson whose back was to me. I sat down quickly, not wanting to be seen.

"How did you…?" she asked.

"Very sneakily." He was proud; I could hear it in the edges of his even tone. "I'll admit, it wasn't easy. I had to convince another company to purchase a portion of the stock, and then I bought out that company—you don't really want the details, do you?"

The deal he'd been working on. It had to do with Celia?

"The contracts are signed now," he continued. "That's all that matters. I'm officially the majority owner of Werner Media Corporation."

I gasped, then slapped my hand over my mouth too late. *Fuck!* Had they heard my gasp? Had they heard my slap? And now my heart was beating louder than it had the whole time I'd been trapped in his bedroom—surely they could hear that?

But if they did, they gave no indication.

"And you said you'd quit playing the game." Celia's words were low and heavy.

"I had one final move to make," he said.

And what a move it was. Werner Media Corporation—Celia's family's business—Hudson had bought it? This was…this was *big*.

She let out a long, slow hiss of air—or I guessed it was her, I couldn't see for sure. "It's checkmate, is it then?" she asked.

"You tell me." Triumph hung in the texture of his words.

"What are your plans for Werner Media?" She fought to the end. Some people might be impressed with her dedication.

I imagined, once upon a time, that Hudson had been one of those people.

For me, it was Hudson that impressed me.

"At the moment, I have no plans. The company's doing well as it is. Warren Werner is definitely the right man to be in charge. However, if there were any reason that I felt his presence was no longer needed…" He let his threat trail off.

"He'd be devastated," Celia said softly.

"I imagine he'd be devastated just to learn he no longer holds controlling interest. For now, the fact is still hidden. He has no idea that he's no longer in charge. Would you like that to change?"

"No," she said.

"Do you plan on doing anything that might cause me to alter my current business plan?"

Defeat clung to her simple one-word answer. "No."

"Then yes, it's checkmate."

We sat silently, all of us, for several minutes after the game was declared finished. My skin tingled as Hudson's victory settled in the air. A smile graced my lips and a mixture of many, many emotions swept up and over me, very few of them sinking in with enough clarity to cling on to for long. Some, I could name—surprise, gratitude, relief, triumph. Others were more difficult to discern through the blanket of heartache that still covered me from head to toe. Was there some forgiveness toward Hudson in there? A touch of hopefulness, perhaps?

Love, there was love. There was always love.

"I guess it's time for me to go," Celia said eventually.

"It is. I'll walk you out."

They weren't going back through the office. The realization sent another stab of panic through me—was Hudson not leaving? And my duffel—it was at the door.

Once again, I held my breath as they crossed the floor. I heard the door open. If they were at the entrance, their backs would be toward me. I had to see what was going on.

I moved up to my knees again and peered around the frame. Hudson was holding the door open as Celia walked past. He started to shut it behind her—*dammit, he was staying*—then his gaze fell on my bag.

He paused there for half a second. Then his eyes rose to scan the room.

I didn't move—did I want him to find me?

He did.

Our eyes locked, and the intensity of his expression—it was all-consuming. Maybe I couldn't read all of my own emotions, but in his gaze I saw three with clarity. Surprise, elation. And, clear as day, I saw love.

If he came to me at that moment, I was certain I'd fall back into him.

But he didn't.

"Hold the elevator," he said to Celia without looking away. His lip ticked ever so slightly, delivering me a half-smile. Then he left, shutting the door behind him.

Chapter Twenty-Two

Nine in the morning came awfully early after working until three a.m. I peeked from under my lids at the sun that suddenly filled the room.

"Hey," I groaned. "I had the curtains shut for a reason."

"Too bad. You got your fashionything." Liesl poked at my foot sticking off the bottom of the futon. "Get up."

"But, Mom, I don't wanna." I rubbed my eyes and sat up. I glanced at the time. It was actually after nine. I must have pushed the snooze button on the alarm clock a couple of times. "Why are you awake anyway?"

I'd worked a short shift but Liesl had stayed until close. That meant she'd probably only been home a couple of hours. Funny, she hadn't woken me when she came in.

Then I realized, her coming in was what *had* woken me.

"Got a ride from one of the regulars." She waggled her brows. "And when I say ride, I don't mean in a car."

Sex looked good on Liesl. Her cheeks were rosy and her eyes bright. Part of me had always been jealous of her ability to sleep with random people and not get attached. This morning, thinking about sex just made me sad.

My face must have given away my thoughts because next thing I knew, Liesl had crawled onto the bed and wrapped her arms around me in a giant girlfriend hug.

I sighed into her embrace. It felt so good to be touched, to be cared for.

She kissed my temple. "Are you going to be okay today?"

I shrugged against her arms. "Hudson's not supposed to be at the show. So yeah." Saying his name made my heart simultaneously flip and sink. After he'd left the loft, I'd expected him to come into the club during my shift. Or to call. Find me somehow. There was so much to say after all I'd witnessed. Maybe he wasn't interested.

Liesl released me and bopped me on the nose with her finger. "What's that frown about then? You're wishing he was coming, aren't you?"

Did I wish that? "I don't know." While I didn't want to see him, I wanted *him* to want to see me, if that made any sense.

I hugged my knees to my chest. "Why do you think he hasn't tried to talk to me?"

"Maybe he's respecting your space."

Memories washed over me, times Hudson had bullied his way into my life when I'd tried to push him away. "Hudson's never been one to respect my space." Maybe that hadn't been the real Hudson Pierce. It was preferable to think that than to believe he'd really given up on me so easily. "I guess I thought he'd fight for me. Especially after what he did yesterday. After he saw me."

Liesl tilted her head. "Wanna hear what I think?"

"Probably not, but I'm sure you're going to tell me anyway."

"I am." She tucked her legs underneath her. "I think that it's probably still too soon to figure out whether he's going to fight for you or whether you even want him to."

"I don't want him fighting for me." Except I sort of did.

She wagged a finger at me. "Uh-uh. Too soon."

Maybe she was right. A myriad of emotions had enveloped me in the past week. Which of them would endure? In a month from now, which feeling would dominate? In a year? Betrayal? Pain? Or would it be love?

Liesl *was* right. It was too soon to know.

She reached her hand out to squeeze mine. "I'm proud of you though. You made it through this week. And through work last night. And you're going to his sister's thingamabob. And you only had one obsessive breakdown. I think you've done pretty good."

It was amazing how she made just living sound like an accomplishment. Truthfully, it did feel like a success. A little bit of pride filled my chest.

But that ever-present ache didn't go away. I bit my lip. "I miss him."

Liesl leaned forward and kissed my hair. "I know. That might get worse before better."

"Yeah."

***

Mirabelle's Boutique was crazed when I arrived, even though the event wasn't due to start for more than another two hours. The place swarmed with florists and caterers and models and new employees. It took me a while to find anyone I knew in the crowd, but eventually I spotted Adam sampling—or stealing rather— a chocolate-covered strawberry from a Saran-wrapped food tray.

He paused to finish chewing. "Laynie, good to see you."

He gave me a hug, which was a little weird since he'd never been affectionate with me.

"I'm so glad you're here. Please, get Mira to stop running around, will you? She needs to sit and put her feet up. I swear to god, after today, if she doesn't start taking it easy, I'm going to chain her to the bed."

"That sounds a little personal," I teased. "Where is she now?"

Adam directed me to the workroom in the back. There I found even more models, more employees, and Mira fussing over everyone.

"You're here!" she exclaimed when she saw me. Though her expression and smile were bright, the bags under her eyes gave away her exhaustion. "I was afraid you'd bow out at the last minute."

I'd been a little afraid of the same thing. "Nope. I'm here. Do you have time to give me a tour?" Maybe getting her distracted would keep her blood pressure from spiking while she worried about the details of the event. "Or would you prefer I get dressed first?" I wouldn't want her stressing about that either.

"Get dressed first and then it's on."

The dress she'd chosen for me looked stunning with the alterations she'd had done. Looking at myself in the mirror of the dressing room, I couldn't help but remember when I'd first tried it on. It was the day Stacy had sent me the video. That had been the beginning of the end, hadn't it? If only I hadn't let my curiosity get the better of me.

I shook my head, tossing the thought aside. Today, I wouldn't be sad. It was Mira's day, and I didn't want to ruin it for her. Even though I had waterproof mascara on, crying didn't go well with makeup.

Besides, I couldn't wish for anything to be different. Sure, I'd been happy with Hudson, but it had been a lie. The truth would have come out eventually. Better now than later.

When I was dressed, I found Mira, this time seated in a chair as she yelled at people. Adam must have forced her to sit.

She jumped up when she saw me, though, her eyes wide. "Oh my god, you're so beautiful! You are definitely going to be the finale. Dammit, I wish Hudson could see you." She clapped her hand over her mouth before I could scold her. "Sorry. It slipped out. It's going to take a while to get used to the new situation."

"Yeah, I get that." I was still adjusting myself.

She wrapped her arm around mine. "Let me show you my baby. Well, one of my babies." The new addition was beautiful but simple. There was more space to display clothing, a few more dressing rooms, a bigger workroom for the staff and a small runway.

"The stage is where we'll do today's show. In the future it will be for private fashion selection," Mira explained as we finished up. "Some of these rich bitches are too lazy to try on their own clothes so we have models hired to do it for them."

I laughed. Mira was a Pierce—she was probably richer than any of her clients, and she was neither lazy nor a bitch. I could certainly see her mother being one of the women she was referring to, though.

"Speaking of Sophia," I said, looking around the shop, "where is she? Isn't she coming?"

"Um, no." She bent to pick a piece of lint off my skirt. "I banned her along with Hudson."

"What?" Not that I was disappointed about Sophia's absence. With as out-of-control drunk as she'd been the last time I saw her in a public situation, it was probably a good idea she wasn't here.

Mira straightened but kept her eyes down. "I took your advice. We staged an intervention."

"Oh, my god, Mira!" I reached my hand out to touch her arm.

She slid my hand into hers instead. "It was hard, but Hudson and Chandler and Adam and even Dad were there. We all sat her down and told her she needed to get help." She met my eyes and flashed a somewhat forced smile.

I squeezed her hand. "When did this happen?" *And how is Hudson handling it?*

"Last night. She didn't want to hear it, of course. But when I told her she couldn't be a part of my life anymore if she didn't get help, then she agreed. She checked into a long-term facility upstate this morning. Hudson, Dad, and Chandler drove her out."

"Wow." My chest ached in a way that was different from the past several days. Instead of hurting because of Hudson, I hurt *for* him.

"You know, I've never seen my mother sober—she might still be a bitch. But at least I could trust her not to drop my baby."

I pushed thoughts of Hudson out of my mind yet again and studied the beautiful woman in front of me. Though I was twenty-six to her twenty-four years of age, she struck me as the most genuine, mature person I knew. Such a contradiction to her brother. Such a contradiction to myself.

She blushed under my stare. "What?"

"I'm just really amazed by you. That's hard to stand up like that for someone you love and today you have your event...how are you dealing with all of this?"

"Honestly, except for being tired, I feel really good." It was her turn to squeeze my hand. "The only thing I'm worrying about now is you and my brother."

I pulled my hand away from hers. "I'm miserable enough without the guilt trip, thanks." I studied my shoes, afraid that any more show of emotion might wreck me.

"He told us what he did to you."

My eyes flew back up to meet hers. "What?"

"During mom's intervention. He said that if we had any hope of being a family, then we needed to face our flaws and own up to our mistakes. He went back to therapy this week, and I think his doctor encouraged him to be open with us. So he owned up to what he did to you." Her expression grew serious and sad. "I'm sorry he did that to you, Laynie. Really sorry. I'm not going to defend him. But I will say that he is full of regret."

"I'm..." My throat tightened. "Dammit, Mira, you're making me cry."

She grasped my upper arms. "Don't cry! Then I'll cry and that will be a disaster. No more serious talk, except to say I love you. Thank you for being here."

"I wouldn't miss it for the world."

***

There was a little more to the modeling gig than standing and smiling. I also had to walk down the short runway, pose, and return. While the place seemed to be crawling with models, there were only seven of us in the show. We were able to run through it enough times in rehearsal that by the time the actual event started, I wasn't so nervous that I couldn't perform.

Frankly, I was happy for an emotion other than grief. I clung to it. Wrapped it around me like a blanket.

At two, the doors were opened and the event began. It wasn't a big hurrah like the charity fashion show Sophia Pierce had hosted, but was elegant and important in its own way. Mira was a beautiful bird, floating around the room, talking to big name fashion designers and top clients that had been invited.

Then there was the press—they'd been limited to invitation only and were sequestered in an area near the stage, which made them less intimidating. I never got close enough to them to be hounded with their questions. If they wanted to know about me and Hudson, they'd have to ask him.

Would they even ask? When the next girl showed up on his arm in the limelight, would they ask what happened to that nightclub manager the same way they asked about Celia in front of me?

There were so many awful things about that scenario that I had to block it out with a glass of champagne.

At a quarter to three, I lined up with the other models along the horizontal length of the stage. This is where we stood while each person walked the runway. My placement as last in the show made me wish we were walking on from offstage instead of waiting there the whole time. It felt like hours that I had to stand still and smile while the other women walked and posed. Stacy described each item, crediting the designer and then explaining the individual alterations done by the boutique to make the outfit perfect for the wearer.

Finally it was my turn. I walked to the end of the runway with a smile that was surprisingly authentic. Butterflies stirred in my stomach as I stood at the end while Stacy talked about my dress. Photographers were flashing bulbs at me, but the room wasn't dark as in a typical fashion show, and I could actually see the faces of the onlookers as I cast my gaze around the room.

That's how I spotted Hudson so easily.

There, in the back, leaning against the wall. His hair was mussed and he was underdressed in a t-shirt and jeans. His eyes were pinned on me—hell, the whole room's focus was on me—but his were the only eyes I felt. Even across that distance I could sense that electrical current, the simmer in my belly that spurred the butterflies to dance more frantically than before.

Our gazes locked and without thinking to let it happen, my smile widened.

God, it was good to see him.

Then Stacy finished her speech, the crowd applauded, and it was time to turn around and walk back to my place along the back of the stage. With my back to him, the momentary elation disappeared, and all the shit rumbled back over me like a Mack truck. The deceit, the hurt, the garbage—and he wasn't supposed to be there!

Though I was the final model, I had to remain on stage while Stacy introduced Mira, and then while Mira spoke about her renovations and made her acknowledgements. I was still in the limelight, but I couldn't stop fidgeting and wiping my sweaty palms along my skirt.

He's here, he's here. What do I do?

I tried to keep my attention on Mira, but my eyes kept darting back to Hudson. Every time, he was already looking at me. It wouldn't be easy to escape. Especially because I couldn't just run out—my purse and belongings were still in the back. I could leave my clothes, but I needed money for a cab or my subway card. He was across the room, though, and there were lots of people—perhaps I could sneak away before he got to me.

The minute the final applause began, I took off. As discreetly as possible, I slipped off the stage and to the back hall, hoping Hudson didn't see me and follow.

Or hoping he *did* follow. I couldn't quite decide.

Of course my stuff was in the last dressing room in the hall, but I made it there without anyone behind me. My hands were shaking as I gathered my clothes from the floor where I'd left them. Looking around, I realized I had nothing to carry them in. *Shit.*

I could change. Or get them later.

Later.

I should have at least folded them, but there wasn't time for that. Instead, I set them on the dressing room chair, grabbed my purse from the corner of the room where I'd stowed it under my clothing, and turned to go.

But there he was, filling the doorframe.

My shoulders sagged, but my stupid heart did a little dance.

Dammit, feelings were confusing.

He looked even better up close. Was it possible he'd gotten more attractive in our time apart? His blue-gray t-shirt hugged his muscles, which seemed more pronounced than I'd remembered. His faded dark jeans hung low around his trim hips. His eyes were soft and sad with bags underneath them that matched his sister's. Matched mine.

And the way he looked at me...as if I were more than a silly, emotional, broken girl. As if I were someone who mattered. As if I were someone he loved.

"Hey," he said softly. His voice was like the pied piper, calling goose bumps to the surface of my skin with just one word. Did he even know he had that effect on me?

The way his hands were stuffed in his pockets, making him look so boyish and innocent, I had to think he had no idea.

Except, no matter how he looked, he wasn't innocent. Not at all. It was even manipulative that he'd shown up here.

I folded my arms over my chest, as if that could protect me from his piercing gaze. "You're not supposed to be here, Hudson. Mira promised you wouldn't be."

He pursed his lips. "Mira had nothing to do with me coming."

I started to say something snarky, and then softened as I remembered where he *was* supposed to be. "Weren't you taking Sophia to rehab?"

God, that was blunt.

I wanted to say something more comforting, something to let him know I was feeling for him, but I was afraid my compassion might be construed as something else. So I left it at that.

"Already done. I hurried back." He took a step into the room. "So I could talk to you."

His quiet tone was so un-Hudson-like, it put me off-balance.

Or his presence in general put me off-balance.

I sighed, rocking from one foot to the other. I should leave. But there were things I wanted to hear him say, whether I could trust them or not. "If you wanted to talk to me so badly, why did you leave yesterday?"

"I had to be at my parents' for the intervention. If I stayed, I wouldn't have been able to leave. It was hard enough to leave as it was." He tilted his head. "And I thought perhaps it was best to let you have your space."

If he kept saying all the right things, I was screwed.

What am I thinking? I'm screwed anyway.

I leaned against the wall behind me. "But you're here now." *When he'd promised he wouldn't be.* "How is that letting me have space?"

Do I really want space?

It was hard to answer that question. On the one hand, the walls of the dressing room felt like they were closing in around me. On the other hand, the distance between Hudson and me seemed wider than the Mississippi.

"I couldn't stay away anymore." As far away as he was, his words found their destination, piercing through the ice around my heart. "Why were you at the loft?"

I couldn't stay away anymore. "Because I'm weaker than you give me credit for."

He stared at the blank wall to the side of us as he scratched the back of his neck. "I was hoping it wasn't weakness, but a sign that you still cared." His eyes swung back to me, searching for my reaction.

I almost laughed. "Of course I still care, you asshole. I'm in love with you. You shattered my fucking heart."

His eyes closed in a long blink. "Alayna, let me fix it."

"You can't."

"Let me try."

"How?" It was a rhetorical question because there was no answer for it. "Even if I can figure out how to forgive you, I can't trust you again. I could never believe that you were with me for any reason other than to continue your sick game."

He flinched only slightly. "I quit all that. You heard me."

I shrugged. "Maybe it was all a set-up. Maybe you knew I was there the whole time." He hadn't known I was there—his expression of surprise when he saw me was genuine. But there were still pounds of bitterness inside me that I had yet to expunge.

"You don't believe that."

I made a disapproving sound in the back of my throat. "It's hard to believe anything after being so totally lied to."

"For the record," he bent to catch my eyes with his, "I didn't lie to you about us. Everything I ever said and did with you was honest."

"The whole circumstance of our *pretend to be my girlfriend* sham was a lie."

"Yes, but that's all. Every touch, every kiss, every moment between you and me, precious…none of that was pretend. I didn't *want* to pretend with you. I wanted every experience with you, every moment to be completely genuine. You're the first person I have ever let in, the first person who's ever seen the real me through all

337

the bullshit." His voice narrowed to a point. "You're the first person I've ever loved, Alayna. And I know you'll be the last."

His words hurt. They were everything I'd ever wanted to hear from him and more. But what was the saying? *Fool me twice, shame on me.*

"I don't know." I pressed my fingertips to my forehead. "I don't know, I don't know. I don't know how I can ever believe that you really feel the way you say you do."

He took another step toward me. "I'm sure that's true. But I thought of a way to prove that I'm devoted to you." Another step, and we were now only a handful of feet apart. "Alayna, marry me."

My gaze flipped up. "What?"

"Marry me. Right now. My plane's already ready and waiting on the tarmac. All you have to do is say yes and we're on our way to Vegas."

"What?" I was in too much shock to say anything else.

"I know you deserve a long engagement and a proper wedding—and we can do that again, whenever you want—but I know right now you need reassurance."

His hands were all over the place as he talked, totally out of character. Was he high? Nervous? Insane?

"You need confirmation that I am committed to you, Alayna, and there's no better way I can think of showing you that than to marry you. To declare in a written contract that I'm yours and that I promise to love you forever."

I settled on insane. "Hudson, you're crazy."

"And no prenup either." He wiped his palms on his jeans. Was he sweating? I sure was. "I'm ready to give you everything I have, to make myself vulnerable, just like you made yourself to me time after time."

"No prenup? Now I definitely know you're crazy." And I was crazy for simply continuing the conversation.

"I am crazy. Crazy without you in my life." He pushed his hands through his hair. "You're the only one who's ever made me better. And you have me by the balls now, Alayna, in so many ways. Because if you say no, if you turn me away, then I've lost everything that means anything in my pathetic excuse for a life. But if you say yes, I have to be the one to trust *you*—you could scam me if you wanted to. You could simply marry me now, divorce me later and half of all I have would be yours."

As if his money meant anything to me. "I have no interest in your—"

He cut me off. "I know. I know that you would never take advantage of me like that. But the point is you could." He paced the small room. "This is the only way I can think of to show you that I'm willing to be vulnerable to you. That I trust you." He turned to face me again. "And that, even though I don't deserve it, I'm determined to fight to earn back *your* trust. Even if it takes the rest of my life."

I was in shock. So many thoughts and emotions swarmed over me that I had no idea what to feel or think. Out of the plethora of reactions brimming to escape, I picked one at random. "Some romantic proposal—marry me so that I can prove you can trust me."

"No, Alayna," his voice deepened. "Marry me because I love you. More than life itself." He squared himself to me. "Marry me *today,* so I can prove I mean it."

"Hudson, this is insane." He didn't even have a ring. "You destroyed everything we had together. You can't just fix it by asking me to marry you out of the blue."

"Why not?" He was desperate, both his tone and his body language gave him away. "Why not?" He shook his hands in front of him for emphasis. "We belong together. For all the wrongs we've done—*I've* done—you can't deny that we make each other better." He shifted his weight to one hip. "You admit you love me. And I love you. What's keeping us apart? The fact that we hurt each other?

Can you honestly say that you feel less hurt without me around? You came by the loft, Alayna. I know you're still thinking about me." He put his hands together, steepling his index fingers. "The only logical reason you can give for not being with me is that you don't trust that I'm really in it for love. Marry me and you'll have no doubt."

His voice lowered as he asked one more time, his eyes begging. "Please, marry me."

I'd thought about it. More than once. Thought about a forever with Hudson Pierce. And he'd hinted at it before. If I really believed him when he said that the majority of our relationship had been real, then his proposal wouldn't seem completely out of the blue.

And I did believe that most of it had been real. Not just because I wanted to, but because it had been real to *me*. The way I loved him didn't happen in a one-sided relationship. That was the false attraction I'd felt for men in the past, I knew the difference. No, this kind of love only grew from reciprocation. Whatever had been false between us, our love hadn't been.

But despite what I'd thought about and what we'd felt, there was more between us that hadn't had time to settle. More that hadn't healed. Falling into anything with Hudson again, let alone marriage—*marriage!*—would be like lying out in the sun while still recovering from a bad burn.

Baby steps.

Marriage was not baby steps. And, honestly, I didn't even know yet if the steps I wanted to take were in that direction. In his direction.

He was waiting for my answer.

I gave it. "No."

"No?" His expression was more confused than disappointed.

Hudson rarely heard the word no. It was likely shocking to hear it when he most wanted a different answer.

"No," I repeated. "No." I straightened. "You think you can fix everything between us by asking me to elope with you? It's hard for me to even look at you right now. Why would you think I would consider marrying you?"

He opened his mouth and I put my hand up in the air to shush him. "Don't talk. I don't want an answer. I need to say some things. Yes, I came to the loft because I missed you. Missed you desperately. But if I'd had any inkling you'd be there, I would have found a way to resist. I'm glad I was there because I found out some things that I needed to know. I'm grateful for what you did. But it doesn't change you and me. It just makes it easier for me to maybe one day find some closure."

"Don't say closure, Alay—" He stopped himself, realizing I wasn't finished. "Sorry. Go on."

His willingness to submit to me almost did me in. That had to be hard for him to give me the floor. He got a point for that one.

But he was so behind on the score that a measly point made little difference.

I took a breath and went on. "Even if I could trust you, Hudson, I wouldn't want to marry a guy just because he scammed me and now he feels bad. And not in Vegas. I'd want my brother and Mira and Adam and Jack. And even Sophia."

His expression turned hopeful. "You want my family at your wedding? Does that mean I have a shot at being the groom?"

"Once, you did. But now…" *Oh, this was hard to say.* "Now I can't see how."

Though it hurt for me to say the words, it was Hudson who appeared crushed. He closed his eyes and his jaw twitched as his entire body sagged. It struck me that the tables had completely been turned. Wasn't it usually he who had the emotional control while I was left floundering? He who was even and strong while I fell apart?

Strangely, it didn't feel any better to be on this side. Because though it seemed like I was in control, inside I was a mess.

Was this what it felt like to be Hudson Pierce?

I couldn't think about it anymore. None of it. It was time to get off the emotional roller coaster and move the fuck on.

There was no way to the doorway except through him. "I have to leave now, Hudson."

He made no effort to move. "Alayna, let's talk about this more. If not this plan, maybe we can talk about something else. Or no plan at all. Just talking to you is nice."

"I can't. I need to go." I was done.

"Alayna…"

"Please," my voice cracked, "let me go."

Slowly, reluctantly, he stepped out of my pathway. But just as I was about to step through the door, he slipped in front of me. He put his hands on each side of the frame, not touching me, but blocking my way. "No, I'm not ever letting you go." His words were raw with emotion. "I'll let you leave here right now, but I'm not giving up on you. I'll pursue you like I've never pursued anything in my life. I'll fight until you have no choice but to believe that I love you with everything I am."

He was so close. I could smell him, breathe him in the same way I had his pillow at the loft. But this was so much better because it was really him. Warmth rolled off him, calling me to his arms. If I simply leaned forward, I'd fall into him.

And the things he was saying—his vow to fight for me—it was hard to resist.

Then Liesl's advice from that morning came back to me. It was too soon. I needed more time. "Hudson," I kept my eyes down, unable to meet his gaze. "Let me go."

He waited a beat, but then he did step back and I slid past, careful not to touch him, though every cell in my body yearned to do just that.

I managed to hold my head high as I walked away from him, even when he called after me. "I'm never giving up, Alayna. I'll prove myself. You'll see."

Forever With You

Chapter Twenty-Three

I went into work that night to find a package with my name on it waiting in the office. "What's this?" I asked Gwen.

"Beats me. A courier left it for you about half an hour ago. No message." She went back to counting the money in the safe.

No way to know unless I opened it. Inside, I found a brand new Kindle. I'd never had an e-reader, but I'd used the Kindle app on my computer. I turned it on and found the device was filled with books. Flipping through them, I recognized the titles as the ones on my bookshelves in Hudson's library. I picked up the wrapping, searching for a card, and finally found one—a simple note, handwritten:

In case you're missing your books as much as I'm missing you.
– H

I stared at the card for several minutes while I tried to quiet my pulse. He was really going to fight for me, then. The realization thrilled me. Gifts weren't going to cut it though. I couldn't give a shit about material items. The note—that I'd cherish.

Gwen swung the safe door shut and came to glance over my shoulder. "Ah, so lover boy's trying to win you back."

"Supposedly." I tucked the note in my bra and waited for her traditional love sucks speech.

It didn't come. "There could be worse things," she said with more than a hint of melancholy.

It was possible she was right.

Sunday, a delivery service showed up at Liesl's with a new futon mattress, much thicker and of higher quality than the old one. The card this time read: *You should be sleeping well even though I'm not.* *– H*

I glared at Liesl. "How does he know I'm sleeping on a futon?"

She shrugged. "Maybe I said something in one of our texts."

"You're texting him?" Wasn't she supposed to be on my side?

"He had your phone charger delivered the other night to the club. Guess he figured that's why you hadn't been responding to him. So I plugged it in and holy Jesus, Laynie, that thing was filled with texts." She pulled her long hair over one shoulder. "Some of them made me feel a little bad for the guy. I texted him back."

I swatted her shoulder—or more like shoved. "What the fuck?"

"I told him it was me and not you." As if that were the reason I was pissed.

"That's private, Liesl."

Again she shrugged. "Someone should be reading them. That's all I'm saying." She turned to the deliveryman, who just walked up with his clipboard looking for a signature. She signed then looked back at me. "It's plugged in on top of the fridge if you're interested."

It was much later, when I couldn't sleep despite the comfortable new mattress, that I pulled my phone down from its hiding place. There were more than a hundred unread texts, plus a handful that had been marked read that I hadn't seen. Apparently Liesl had only viewed some of them.

I curled up on the new futon and began reading. Like the notes he'd been sending, most were sweet, but some were sexy, others desperate. I took my time absorbing each one, intermittently crying and smiling and sometimes even laughing.

Even though I'd responded to none of them so far, each was written as if I would. I rolled my eyes at one sent earlier that day.

I ordered a futon for me as well. Maybe sleeping on it will make me feel closer to you.

And then later, after eleven p.m., he sent several in a row:

God, this sucks shit. I wasn't sleeping before but at least I was comfortable.

I'll continue to endeavor, though. If this is how you're sleeping, I shall as well.

You know, we could both be together in the bed at the penthouse. If I remember correctly, the lack of sleep we got had nothing to do with the comfort of the mattress. ;)

Before I could stop myself, I shot a text back:

Hudson Pierce using an emoticon…will wonders never cease?

It was two in the morning and he responded immediately. He really *wasn't* sleeping.

I'm hoping they don't cease. If I ever have you in my arms again, that will certainly be a wonder. Goodnight, precious.

That night I slept with the phone next to me. Though I didn't often reply, I read the texts he sent from then on. Each and every one.

***

The gifts continued through the week with jewelry, tickets to the symphony, and a new laptop. On the days I worked at the club, the packages would be waiting there. Obviously Hudson was still monitoring my schedule, which was both irritating and sort of a turn-on.

Thursday, though, there was nothing on my desk when I arrived. I told myself it was silly to be disappointed. He didn't have to give me something every day to prove he was thinking about me. And I didn't want him thinking about me all the time anyway, did I?

I was still mulling around the question, still thinking about *him*, when the club opened for the evening. Since one of the bartenders had called in sick, I stepped in to help at the upstairs bar. We were hopping before the clock even hit eleven, so I was somewhat distracted when Liesl bent near me. "Did you see the suit at the end of the bar?"

"No," I said with a scowl. If she thought I would be interested in ogling man candy, she was wrong.

She winked. "Well, check him out then."

I finished topping the beer mug in my hand and, against my better judgment, shot a glance to the end of the counter.

He was sitting in the same seat that he'd been in the first time I saw him, wearing the same suit, if I wasn't mistaken.

And the way he stared at me? His eyes held the same heat as they had that night before my graduation. That burn that was more than lust, more than desire, it was possession.

Was it wrong that I smiled?

When I could finally tear myself away from Hudson's magnetic stare, I made a Scotch, neat, and delivered it to him.

"The service here is excellent," he said when I handed him his glass. As he took it from me, he brushed his fingers against mine.

Or had that been me that had done that?

Either way, the contact sent goose bumps running down my arms and warmth spreading through my chest. It had been so long since I'd touched him in any form. My body yearned for more while my head sent warning bells to run, run, run.

And my heart played some sort of Switzerland in the whole transaction, deciding not to make its desires clear.

With the war going on inside, I didn't know what to do or say. I stood frozen, my gaze locked on his. It felt so good—so *right*—to do nothing but get lost in his grays. Couldn't I find a way to do this every day of my life?

"Order!" a waitress called from down the counter.

I blinked, recovering from the trance Hudson had me in. "I have to go." Silly to explain. I didn't owe him anything. "Um, will you be wanting another when you've finished?"

"No, just the one. But I might sit here for a while, if you don't mind." His eyes moved down my body. "The view is stunning."

I turned before he could see my blush.

When he left, over an hour later, he settled his bill with Liesl. I only noticed he was leaving when she handed me an envelope. "This is from the suit."

I opened it and found a hundred dollar bill and a certificate to his spa in Poughkeepsie—the same gifts he'd given me that night in May.

"Liesl, I'll, um, I'll be right back." Maybe it was because I was disappointed to see him go, but I came up with an excuse to run after him.

"Hudson!" I yelled when I found him outside headed toward the parking garage.

He stopped and waited for me to catch up.

I held the envelope out toward him. "I can't accept this. I'm in charge here. I can't leave for a week to go to a spa."

It suddenly occurred to me that we hadn't talked about my job since our break-up. "Unless you'd rather I wasn't working here."

"Don't ever think that." His tone was harsh, final. "If you think you can't work with me as your owner, I'll give you the club." He would too, knowing him.

And that was definitely not a gift I could accept. "I just want to keep my job, thank you."

He softened. "It's yours as long as you want it." He pushed my hand that still held the envelope back toward me. "And the certificate—keep it. You can use it anytime you want. There's no expiration." His fingers lingered on mine.

Was this what we'd been reduced to? Stealing touches at any opportunity possible? Making up reasons to talk?

I pulled my hand—and the envelope—away from his. "Fine. Whatever."

A chill ran through me, though the night was warm. Frantically, I searched for something else to say. "There's another thing." I took a deep breath. There really was something I'd been avoiding. "I need to get my stuff from the penthouse."

His mouth tightened. "I wish you wouldn't do that."

I ignored him. It was the easiest way to deal with statements like that. Especially when I so liked the way they sounded on his lips. "I want to come get the rest of my things Monday."

"I can have it packed and moved for you, if you'd like."

"I'd rather pack it myself." If he packed, I'd end up with all sorts of things that didn't belong to me—things he wanted me to have. As sweet as it might be, I didn't want his gifts. I also didn't have any room for them in the apartment with Liesl. Even if we got a two-bedroom place together as we'd been talking about doing, we couldn't afford anything that big.

"At least let me arrange a truck." His tone was insistent, but his eyes were pleading. It was hard to resist.

So I didn't. "Okay. You can do that." Only because it was going to be a pain to do it myself. And he did owe me.

"It's done." His lip curled up at the edge. "This doesn't mean I'm done trying to win you back."

"I didn't think for a second that it did." Though I bit back a smile, my pleasure at his declaration showed in my voice.

Hudson tilted his head to study me. "You say that as if you almost enjoy my groveling."

I rolled my eyes and turned toward the club with a wave. But I couldn't resist calling back over my shoulder, "I couldn't say, H. I haven't really seen you grovel yet."

***

Friday and Saturday saw more gifts delivered—a coffee table book of pictures from the Poconos and concert tickets to Phillip Phillips.

"He's, like, recalling your entire relationship with this stuff, isn't he?" Liesl said on Sunday as I opened the box that had arrived that morning. "I hate to say it, but he's kinda good."

I wadded up the brown packaging paper from the box and tossed it at her. "Shut up."

"What's this one?"

"I don't know yet." I pulled out the John Legend CD I found inside and read the song list on back. I knew of the artist but had never listened to any of his music. The case wasn't sealed so I opened it easily and found Hudson's note.

This is the song that makes me think of you. Track 6. - H

R&B. Huh. Hudson rarely listened to music around me. When he did, he deferred to me to choose. I didn't even know what style he liked. Was this it?

I looked back at the song list and found track six. "*All of Me,*" I read out loud. "I don't know it. Do you?"

"Never heard of it. Let's stick it in." She grinned and added her own, "That's what she said."

Shaking my head at her, I pulled out my new laptop, put in the disc and pushed play on the track Hudson had indicated. I leaned my head back against the futon and listened.

The song started with a haunting piano line. Then a tenor voice crooned about a beautiful woman with a smart mouth who had the singer distracted and spinning. He was a mess, but it was all good, because no matter how crazy she made him, she was still everything to him.

It was the chorus that had me in tears, when he sang about "*all of me*" loving "*all of you*" and offered to give all of himself to her in exchange for the same.

Sure, it was just a song, but if it really held the message that Hudson meant for me to hear, well, I couldn't help but hear it loud and clear. If he could really give all of himself to me—no more walls, no more secrets—then what was left holding us back? The past?

But my own history was imperfect. I'd even shown him my flaws on more than one occasion. He'd forgiven and stuck around. Fixed me and found me and made me whole.

And now…

Not saying a word when I set the song to repeat, Liesl sat next to me and pulled me to her shoulder.

"Liesl, I don't care anymore," I sobbed into her shirt. "Even if I shouldn't be with him, I can't live without him. He makes me feel better about me. I don't care anymore about what he did in the past. I only care that he's around in my future."

She rocked me back and forth. "No one's telling you what you should or shouldn't do here. Either way, you got my support."

"Good, because I think I'm going to give him another chance." I wasn't quite sure what that chance would be yet—dinner? A date? Lots of dates?

That was a decision for tomorrow.

***

Though I didn't have a lot to pack up from the penthouse, I wanted to get started on it early enough in the day that we'd be long gone before Hudson arrived home from work. Getting Liesl anywhere before noon, however, proved difficult.

"Maybe I could join you later," she said, burying her head in her pillow at my first attempt to drag her out of bed.

"But I need you the whole time," I whined. "Please?"

The pleading worked, but she tried again to get out of going as we were getting in the cab. Then at The Bowery, she suggested that she make a coffee run and join me later.

"There's a beautiful Keurig inside. Best coffee ever. I'll make you as many mugs as you want." Maybe Liesl wasn't really big on packing.

"Fine."

It was much easier to go inside the building with Liesl along. As we went up in the elevator, I wrapped my arm around hers, grateful for the support. Though I hadn't been living there for two weeks, moving out was big. It reeked of finality. And with my recent decision to let Hudson back in my life in some way, I wasn't quite looking for finality. I needed Liesl to talk me out of anything stupid.

Like deciding to leave my stuff there and not move out.

When the door opened to the apartment, I waited for Liesl to step out first. She didn't move so I went ahead of her. I turned around and put my hand on the side to keep the elevator open. "Aren't you coming?"

"Uh…" her eyes grew wide. Then she pushed my arm out of the door and pressed a button on the call panel. "Don't hate me!" she called as the doors shut.

What the fuck? I heaved a frustrated air of breath out of my lungs and closed my eyes. Either Liesl had somewhere else she wanted to be or she had something up her sleeve. And if it was the latter, there was no doubt Hudson was involved.

Might as well find out what was up.

I opened my eyes and peered around the corner of the foyer toward the living area. It was empty. Not just empty as in no Hudson, but empty as in no furniture. None. I wandered into the room to be sure I wasn't going crazy.

Well, if I were going crazy, the delusion I was having was of an apartment with no furniture. I glanced at the dining room. Also empty. Strangely, the place didn't feel any more cold and lonely than it had when I'd been there the last time. But the emptiness put me off. I couldn't understand what it meant. Was my stuff gone as well?

I backtracked and pushed the door open to the library. This room was only mostly empty. The sofa and desk and all the rest of the furniture were gone, but the shelves still contained all my books and movies. The books I'd pulled that Celia had marked were gone from the floor, but several boxes were stacked against the wall.

I walked toward the stack, intending to peek in and see if the books were there, but it was sealed.

"Those are new books."

Ah, there he is.

I turned slightly to find Hudson leaning in the doorframe. Again he was wearing jeans and a t-shirt. Dammit, he hadn't even planned on going to work if he was dressed like that. And he looked extra yummy. Somehow he had arranged that as well, I was sure of it.

He nodded again at the box I was still touching. "They're for you. To replace the ones that had been damaged."

"Oh," I said. Then I frowned.

"What is it?"

"I have nowhere to put all these." I hadn't intended to take them. They were beautiful and I loved them, but in New York City, that many books were a luxury.

He sighed softly and I could tell the rejection of his gift hurt, no matter what the reason. But all he said was, "I'll keep them for as long as you want me to."

"Thank you." I caught myself scanning his body. It was impossible not to. He was so good-looking, and I missed him so much. Though I'd planned my move on a day that he wouldn't be around, I was happy to see him. Elated, actually.

I wondered if he could see that in my smile. "I didn't expect you to be here." *I'm so glad you are.*

"You didn't say I couldn't be."

"It was implied," I teased.

He caught my eyes with his. "You don't seem that horribly pissed to see me."

God, the butterflies were stirring in my belly. Not the tug of fixation that used to make me act crazy, but the twitters I felt only with Hudson. It had confused me when I first felt it those months ago, but now I recognized it for what it was—a combination of nerves and excitement and attraction and anticipation. It was such a gloriously delicious feeling.

Surprisingly, it eclipsed the still fresh wounds from his betrayal.

Still, I was scared. And I didn't know what he was up to. His stuff was gone from the apartment. I didn't like what that had to mean. What *did* it mean? "Where is everything?"

His lips drew tight. "Your stuff is still all here."

"But where's your stuff?"

With another deep breath, he threw his eyes to the window then brought them back to me. "I can't live here without you, Alayna."

"So you're moving out?" I didn't know how I felt about that.

Strike that, I did know. I didn't like it. At all. The penthouse was where our real relationship had taken place. I hated the idea of someone else being in our space.

And Hudson moving out because I wasn't there—that meant he didn't really believe I'd ever be back.

I was too late. He was giving up on me.

But his next words tossed everything up in the air again. "Actually, I hope I'm moving in."

The twists and turns of this interaction had me flustered and on edge. I had to call an emotional timeout before I broke down. "H, you confuse me enough without you trying to be confusing. Could you say something I can understand?"

"I confuse you?" His eyes sparkled with satisfaction.

"Is this a surprise?"

He shrugged.

"So you're moving in?" I prompted. Dammit, why did he have to be so difficult?

Seeming to sense I was on my last nerve, he answered. "One day. I hope." He rubbed his lips together—ah, I missed those sweet lips. "But for now, I want you to live here."

"What?" One day a proposal, another *live in my million dollar penthouse without me.* The man certainly knew how to keep me on my toes.

He also had no idea what I really wanted or needed from him.

Hudson's expression grew serious again. "I can't live here without you, precious." His words were soft and low, but I could hear him clearly. "But I don't want to sell it, because I love being here with you. Someday, you and I will be here again. While I'm waiting for you—scratch that—while I'm groveling for your forgiveness, it's a shame to let it sit empty. You and Liesl should move in."

"I can't accept that, H." My eyes felt watery. But at least he'd said he wasn't giving up on me.

"I had a feeling you'd say that." He sighed, giving up much more easily than was characteristic. "Then it will have to sit."

I bit back the urge to say we could live here together and offered instead, "You could rent it out."

His brows rose. "I could rent it out to you."

I laughed.

"Best rent in town—only cost you a weekly dinner with the landlord."

"Stop it." I was still smiling.

"Biweekly then. I'm not above bargaining."

"Hudson." He had no idea that he already had me sold. Not on moving in, but on the dates.

"Fine, monthly. I'll take whatever scraps you're willing to give me." He studied me. "You're considering giving me scraps now, aren't you?"

"Maybe." How did he read me so easily? And why was it so easy to be with him when he'd hurt me so deeply?

The question scared me, so I skirted the issue. "Seriously, though, where's all your stuff? Did you get another place?" All his furniture wouldn't fit in the loft.

He shook his head. "I gave it all to a charity fundraiser."

"Lifestyles of the rich and famous." Though I couldn't say I'd miss any of it. It was beautiful furniture, but Celia had chosen it all. I was quite happy with the thought of the less fortunate benefitting from it.

It seemed Hudson felt the same. "I wasn't attached to any of it." He straightened and walked into the room, gesturing to the empty space. "This entire apartment was perfectly designed to my tastes and style, but it never felt like a home." He stopped a couple feet from me. "Not until you, Alayna. You made it come alive. The things that were here—they were chosen for me by someone I want completely removed from my life. Right now, the things here are the only things that made this house a place I'd want to live. Your things. You."

"I…" My throat was too tight to speak.

"And when I move back in, we can refurnish this place from scratch. Together. You and I."

I took in a shuddering breath. "You're so sure that one day I'll take you back." The outlook was getting better and better.

"I'm hopeful." He smiled mischievously. "Would you like to see how hopeful I am?"

"Sure." Really, all I wanted was for him to pull me into his arms. I was almost certain that was where we'd end up. But the game we were playing to get there was intriguing.

Hudson dug in his pocket and pulled out something small and silver. "I bought this."

He held the object by the jewel so I couldn't really see all of it at first, but when I realized what it was, my breath caught. Because it was a ring. *The ring.*

He dropped it in my palm for me to examine. It wasn't silver after all—it was platinum, if I guessed right. And the jewel was surrounded by two tapered baguette stones that led the eye to a round, brilliantly cut diamond in the center. It was at least two and half carats, maybe three. Maybe even four, for all I knew.

Tears gathered in my eyes and bewilderment muddled my brain. He'd handed it to me—it wasn't a proposal. What was this then? A way to mess with me?

"There's an inscription," Hudson said softly, as though he could read my confusion.

I blinked to clear my vision enough to read: *I give you all of me.*

Then he bent down on one knee.

It *was* a proposal.

I couldn't speak, couldn't think, couldn't even breathe.

"I realized something about the last time I asked this," he said from his place on the floor in front of me. "I did it wrong. First, I didn't have a ring, and second, I should have gotten on one knee. But more importantly, I didn't give you the right thing. I offered you everything I had, thinking that was the way to win your heart. That wasn't what you wanted at all. The only thing you ever asked for, the only thing I would never give you, was me."

A sob escaped my throat, but for the first time in days, it wasn't a sorrowful sob.

"But now I do." Hudson threw his arms out to the side. "Here I am, precious. I give myself freely. All of me, Alayna. No more walls or secrets or games or lies. I give you all of me, honestly. For forever, if you'll take it."

He took the ring from my grasp. With hands that were so steady compared to my shaky one, he slipped it on my finger.

I stared at it, shining brilliantly on my hand like a beacon in the darkness I'd been living in. Was he really asking me to marry him? Not elope, but marriage? Was this really something I could actually consider?

My plan to let him back into my life had been much simpler and less drastic—like a dinner and a movie type of thing. Not a proposal.

But that had always been Hudson. He moved fast and furiously, but when he truly wanted something, he committed with everything he had. If I said no, if I turned him away, I knew without a doubt he'd ask again and again. And again.

That wasn't a reason to accept a marriage proposal.

The reason to accept was because I loved Hudson Pierce with every fiber of my being. Even his flaws and imperfections attracted me to him. They made him who he was. And I wanted all of him. I wanted to give him all of me.

And he had a lot of making up to do to me. Forever might just be the only way he'd get it covered.

"Alayna, I love you." He drew my gaze from the ring to his eyes—his wildly intense, passionate eyes that shown brighter than the diamond on my hand. "Will you marry me? Not today, and not in Vegas, but in a church if you like, or at Mabel Shores in the Hamptons—"

Somehow I found my voice. "Or the Brooklyn Botanic Gardens during the cherry blossom season?"

"Yes, there." His eyes widened. "Is that a—"

"Yes," I nodded. "It's a yes."

Hudson pulled me onto his knee and into his arms faster than I could blink. "Say it again."

"Yes," I whispered, placing my hand on his cheek. "Yes, I'll marry you."

His lips found mine, and it was like a first kiss—soft and tentative. Then our mouths parted and our tongues met and the kiss gathered from a fragile breeze into a raging storm. One of his hands tangled in my hair, the other cupped my face, holding me as if he feared I wouldn't stay, as if I might disappear.

And the way I held him was the same. I wrapped my arms around his neck, clutching onto him with all my strength. When our kiss began to metamorphosis into something bigger, something that required more of our body to be touching, and less of our clothing to be on, he grabbed his hand around my thigh, lifting it around his waist as he stood. I threw my other leg around him, hooking my ankles together at his backside and bucked my hips, rubbing against his crotch.

Damn, I'd missed this. Missed him—all of him. His touch was searing, his kiss burned me to my core. And the solidness of his body, his strong arms, his muscled chest—he was my foundation. Sturdy and fixed. Permanent.

Permanently mine.

We were halfway down the hall, our lips still locked when I realized I had no idea where he was taking me. If the house was empty, did it matter that we made it to the bedroom?

Asking, though, would require me to let go of his tongue, and the growl he made as I sucked on it made that not an option I wanted to consider.

I got my answer soon enough anyway. Hudson pushed into our bedroom and in my peripheral vision I saw on the floor, minus the bedframe, our mattress.

He toed his shoes off and then dropped with me onto the bed.

"You left the mattress?" I asked while he pulled my shirt over my head.

His shirt disappeared quickly after. "I picked it out myself. Besides, I couldn't bear to part with it. It has too many memories."

Yes, it does.

And more to be made. A lifetime of them, in fact. *Oh my god, a lifetime with Hudson.*

He bent down to nip my breast through my bra, bringing me sharply back to the present.

I moaned breathily. "Are you sure you weren't simply—" I moaned again as he nipped my other breast. "—being prepared for me to say yes?"

His mouth returned to mine. "There may have been a little bit of that," he said against my lips, his hands reaching behind me to undo the clasp of my bra.

"You know me so well, don't you?"

He grinned and lowered his gaze to my breasts newly released from captivity. "I want to know you better." He licked around one taut nipple. "I want to know you better right now. God, I've missed your gorgeous body."

And god, how I'd missed the things he did to it. Was there a manual somewhere entitled *How to Please Alayna*? If so, Hudson had surely memorized the thing. More likely, he'd written it. He knew how to please me better than I knew how to please myself.

As he teased and taunted my breasts, making me dizzy with desire, I reached down to cup his erection through his jeans. The warmth of it, the hardness, even through the thick denim material, had a geyser going off in my panties.

I stroked along the length of his imprisoned cock. "I remember this."

"Uh-uh. First we're focusing on you." He already had a hand traveling beneath the band of my yoga pants, determined to prove his point.

"But I like this." I petted him again. "There should definitely be some of this."

"Oh, there will be a whole lot of this." He bucked into my palm then turned his attention back to what his hand was doing. What his hand was doing so well. His thumb had settled on my clit, swirling across it with expert pressure.

I wiggled underneath him, wishing I was naked and that he was naked and that we were to the next part where he was inside me. I was desperate for that.

But Hudson made me wait. He dipped a finger inside me and I gasped.

"Jesus, Alayna. You're so wet. Do you know how hard that makes me? You're so wet and juicy that I'm tempted to lick you clean. But I'm anxious and missing you and I need my cock inside you as soon as possible. Tasting you will have to wait until the next round."

"Next round?" I was a bit delirious with the awesomeness of this round.

He added a second finger, bending them so that they rubbed against that magic spot that only Hudson ever knew how to find. Quickly my belly tightened and my legs began to quiver.

"You're so turned on—you're going to come fast, aren't you, precious?"

That was all it took to push me over. Pleasure washed over me in a tidal wave, and I let out a moan, digging my fingers into his back as he continued to rub me and finger me until the last spasm trembled through me.

Hudson sucked the lobe of my ear and then praised me. "Good girl. You're so fucking sexy when you come. It makes me so hard my cock throbs."

Fuck, his mouth alone was going to send me over again.

Hudson removed his hand from my pussy and pulled off my pants and underwear. "Remember our first night in the Hamptons? When I made love to you so many times that you were sore the next day?"

"How could I forget?" I watched in a haze as he stripped out of his jeans and briefs. His cock sprung free, harder and thicker than I'd ever remembered it being.

Hudson Pierce naked.

I had to swallow. Twice. There wasn't any sight on Earth that compared to the mouth-watering deliciousness in front of me.

And it was all mine. *Forever.*

Hudson climbed on top of me, covering me with his body. "That night is going to pale in comparison to today, precious. Today, I'm going to make love to you sweetly and tenderly. Then I'm going to fuck you so long and hard, your beautiful pussy is going to be raw. You won't be able to stand, let alone walk. After that, I'm going to go down on you until you're shivering and coming all over my tongue. And then we'll do it all again."

My pussy clenched at the promises being made. "You're such a big talker."

"I sure hope that wasn't a challenge," he said, settling between my thighs. "Because if it was, game on."

Now that was a game I didn't mind that he played.

I wrapped my legs around Hudson, ready for him to enter me. But he paused, his tip grazing my opening.

"Hurry." I tilted my hips up, prodding him. "I want you inside."

He ran a hand through my hair and laid a kiss on the tip of my nose. "Patience, precious. We have time, and I need to feel you."

He slid into me then, slowly and with great patience. I cried out at the agonizing sweetness as he filled me and stretched me and buried his cock inside of me. When I thought he couldn't possibly go any further, he bent my thighs up toward my chest and pushed in more.

Ah, he *was* throbbing. I could feel him pulse against my walls as he sank deeper, deeper.

"You feel so good, precious." He pulled out ever so slightly and thrust back in with a circle of his hips. "Rough, gentle—how do you want me?"

"You're giving me a say?" I blinked up at him.

His lip curled up slightly at the edge. "This time."

I loved him every way he gave himself to me. The only thing that mattered was that he did. "You decide. I trust you."

And I did trust him. Maybe not at the level that I could or once did, but we were a work in progress. We had time.

He seemed to like that answer. His eyes melted and his face softened. As he moved inside me, he clasped my hands in his and leaned his forehead against mine. "I love you, Alayna. My precious. My love."

We danced together, enjoying each other, loving each other as we took each other higher and higher. Pleasing each other in the ways we'd learned in the past and in new ways as well. It wasn't exactly sweet and it wasn't exactly rough and it wasn't exactly frenzied or passionate or gentle even—but it was all of that, rolled together. It was everything. And it was exactly perfect.

Forever With You

Epilogue

April

She's the most beautiful bride that's ever graced the Brooklyn Botanic Gardens. Hell, she's the most beautiful bride that's ever graced the Earth. I can't keep my eyes off her. Her dress hugs her gorgeous tits and her slim hips then trains out behind her. And the corset style in the back is fuck hot. I can't wait to undress her later. Though, when I finally get the chance, I have a feeling those ties will be more frustrating than sexy.

Though sometimes the frustration is half the fun.

And it's necessary. "Without struggle there is no progress," Alayna loves to tell me. It's a quote she learned in her counseling that she feels suits us fairly frequently. She's said it so many times in the last nine months that I was almost surprised it wasn't embroidered on our wedding napkins.

Honestly, the truth that lies in that simple statement is astounding. Though I am a man of commitment, a man who doesn't walk away from a challenge, I am the first to admit that the road from our engagement to our wedding was paved with boulders and potholes. Even though she said yes on that day back in August, there were many times I'm sure she was tempted to break it off afterward. Moments when I shut down and forgot how to let her in. Days when I pushed her away because I believed that I could never be worthy of her love.

Then there was the biggest issue of all—trust. I'd shattered every ounce of trust that existed between us, and rebuilding it took time. And therapy. Not just for myself, but for us as a couple. I'd thought working out my own problems was hard. Adding another person to the mix added a whole new dimension of struggle.

There was so much healing to be done, wounds that threatened to never scar over. Embracing Alayna's obsessive tendencies was natural for me, but I have had to learn how to not overly attach myself to her jealousies and insecurities. It can become enabling and as much as it's a turn-on to have her need me, I love her all the more when she's whole on her own. When she's strong and confident.

My healing has been much more tenuous. Abandoning the game I'd played for a lifetime proved the easiest part. With Alayna in my life, I have no desire to be cruel and heartless like that again. But my inclination to manipulate and master runs deeper. I don't even recognize when I'm molding a situation to my whims. Alayna, kind and forgiving woman that she is, often doesn't point out when I'm wielding and dominating. A great deal of the time, she even likes it. But she also doesn't wish to give too much power to my weaknesses. So she calls me on it more and more, and I in turn attempt to let go. To let things run their natural course.

That has been the most difficult part for me, the hardest component of recovery.

But the progress has been amazing. We wouldn't be here today if it hadn't been for the steps we took together to strengthen our relationship. And while I'm sure the struggle isn't over simply because I've slipped a ring on her finger, we know that we're worth the fight.

She's worth the fight.

Look what my reward has been? Even without our wedding vows, she's mine. And I'm hers. Completely and absolutely.

The ceremony was simple—that's how she wanted it, and her wish is my command. Mirabelle and Liesl and Gwen, who has become a surprisingly good friend to Alayna, stood as her bridesmaids. Their pale pink dresses exactly matched the blossoms on Alayna's veil and in the garden. How Mirabelle managed that, I'll never know. I'll thank her later for her contributions to my wife's day.

My wife.

I'll never get tired of saying that—*wife.* Who would have believed that I'd ever have one of those? I'd never been a man who intended to marry. My mother and father didn't present a pretty picture of matrimony, and I had no understanding of the concept of romantic love. It took Alayna to teach it to me. She's been the best teacher possible—patient and forgiving beyond what I deserve.

She hates it when I say that about myself—that I'm undeserving, and I suppose it's the same way I feel when she talks destructively about her own past. The difference, of course, is that her weaknesses and imperfections didn't almost destroy us as mine did. There are days it's hard to live with myself because of the lie that I wrapped her in. She soothes me then, fixing me with her love. *"We would never have found each other if it weren't for your game,"* she tells me.

I don't believe that, though. I would have always found her.

Always. Without a doubt.

It's not an exaggeration when I say I fell for her at first sight. If anything, I downplay. Not on purpose. The effect she had on me is simply beyond words, and when I attempt to voice it, the true experience becomes abridged and reduced. In all honesty, the woman who stood on that stage left me speechless. Her business ideas were only part of it. They were sound and innovative, but really, there are bright, intelligent up-and-comers around every corner. This went beyond that. I can't even pinpoint if it was her mannerisms or her pattern of speaking or the shocking depth to her chocolate brown eyes. Whatever it was, there was a definite recognition of her soul by mine. An awareness of something greater that tied us to each other upon first acquaintance. As if some part of me had always known she was out there, had been waiting for her to come and bring me to life.

It took me quite some time to label that as love. At first, I didn't know what it was. And now that I do, I still hesitate to call it that since the word fails to express the multi-dimensional way I feel for her. But it's the nearest thing I have, and I say it to her now as often as I can. Then I try to tell her what I really mean by that simple four-letter verb. That not only does my world revolve around her, but she is my world. That she's not just my reason for breathing, she's air itself. That she's the meaning behind every one of my thoughts, every thrum of my pulse, every whisper of my conscience. She's my entire everything. It's as simple and as complex as that.

I don't know that she'll ever understand, but I'll happily spend my lifetime trying to show her.

I gaze around the crowd of people that have shown up to celebrate our special day and think it's funny how, now that I know what it means to love and be loved, I see it everywhere. In the way that Adam tends to the baby and tags along behind Mirabelle as she flits from one person to another. In the way my father held my mother's hand during the ceremony. In the tender look that Brian had for his younger sister when he gave her to me to wed. Has there always been all this love in the world? How have I never seen it before Alayna Withers showed up in my life?

Alayna Pierce now. Doesn't that have a nice ring?

She's coming to me now, and my grin widens. I haven't stopped smiling since she walked down that aisle. I'm sure I look ridiculous.

"Hey, handsome," she says in that lusty voice of hers that makes my cock twitch. "It's time for the first dance."

I let her lead me to the center of the Esplanade. It's impressive how fast the crew we hired transposed the ceremony arrangement to a reception area. We could have moved to the Atrium or another venue all together as our wedding planner suggested, but Alayna wanted the whole event to be outdoors among the blossoms. It was a good decision. The Brooklyn Botanic Society doesn't usually rent out the whole garden for weddings. It's amazing what they'll do for a large donation.

The emcee announces our first dance as I pull my bride into my arms. "What will our first dance be to, Mrs. Pierce?"

I know nothing she has planned for the reception. Alayna took care of all the wedding details. I offered to help, but she preferred to surprise me. The tables will be turned when I get her on the plane to our honeymoon destination. She has no idea that we'll be staying in a private cabana in the Maldives Islands for three weeks. I'd considered Italy or Greece—both locations that she's mentioned wanting to visit—but out of my own selfishness, I chose a tropical setting. It will be easier to keep her naked on a private beach than at the site of an ancient ruin or in an art museum.

"Patience, Mr. Pierce." She's always so good at throwing my own lines back to me.

The music starts and I smile. *All of Me.* Of course.

She snuggles into my arms and I bury my head in her neck, breathing in the scent of her. Her cherry body wash mingles with the blossoms in the air, but none of it can completely cover up the delicious aroma of Alayna's skin—a combination of salt and sweet that I can't describe but would recognize anywhere.

Though I want to hold her and enjoy her in this tender first dance as a married couple, I feel that I've had so little chance to talk to her today, and I can't stop myself from doing so now. "It's a beautiful wedding, Alayna. You did an excellent job."

I feel her cheek tug into a smile at my shoulder. "Thank you. I had a lot of help, thanks to your money."

"*Our* money," I correct. As I'd promised the first time I asked her to marry me, I demanded no prenup. What's mine is hers, openly and without question. I wonder if she'll ever get used to it.

"*Our* money," she concedes. "And it's going well, I think."

"Very well." *Very well, indeed.*

"Did you notice Chandler's been following Gwen around like a lost puppy?"

I had noticed. Though there's too much lust in his eye for me to understand the puppy comparison. "She doesn't seem to mind." Gwen's gaze also holds a degree of desire. Can Alayna see it?

"No, she doesn't." Alayna giggles. *She does see it, then.* "And everyone seems happy."

"Everyone does at that." *And I'm the happiest.*

She places a kiss on my neck that sends a jolt to my cock. "Even your mother has managed to remain polite."

The mention of my mother has me limp. "She does seem slightly more in control of herself now that she's sober." Sophia's only been home from upstate since January. She missed Mirabelle's baby's birth, something that I believe she regrets deeply, but she's better now than she was, and I believe even Sophia thinks the sacrifice is worth it. "She still is a nasty old bitch, though, isn't she?"

Alayna laughs, her hair tickling my neck with the movement, the sound tickling my heart with its purity. "You said it, not me."

I hold her tighter and kiss her temple. This is everything I ever needed and never knew I wanted, wrapped up in the most beautiful of packages. Well, not quite everything. There's still one thing left on the list.

I broach the subject I've been avoiding in a passive way. Perhaps it's manipulative, but it's who I am. "I saw you with Arin Marise, earlier. You're so good with her."

Arin Marise Sitkin is Adam and Mirabelle's baby. My sister insists that she gave her daughter a name that couldn't be shortened so that I'll call her what everyone else calls her. But I've taken to calling her Arin Marise just to rile her up. She's five and a half months old now, all cheeks and grins. Arin's petite like her mother but feisty. You only notice her small stature in comparison to Braden, Alayna's nephew who's only four months old, but almost twice as big as Arin.

Alayna and I have never talked about children, not about our children, anyway. I've seen her with Arin and Braden and fallen in love with her all over again with the care and gentleness she gives them, but I've never brought up the actual topic. Perhaps it scared me, but it doesn't scare me now. Not now that I know she's mine truly and deeply no matter how this conversation goes.

I pull back from our embrace to look in her eyes, thinking I should probably put this off until a more appropriate time, but unable to wait another second to ask. "Do you…" I begin then start over. "Have you thought about children of your own?"

She leans forward to kiss my throat then, with her eyes cast down, says tentatively, "I'd probably fuck them up."

That had always been my fear, and if it weighs too heavily on her, I'll abandon the whole idea. I kiss her head again and then ask outright, "Would you like to fuck them up with me?"

She laughs again and meets my gaze, her eyes misty and her face aglow. "Yes," she says without any hesitation or trace of doubt. "I'd love to."

"Good." I draw her closer and spin her around. "We can get started tonight in the plane. Or right now, if you prefer. I saw a rather large oak in one of the smaller gardens. I'm almost certain we could hide there, even with this dress of yours."

"I'd love to see how you plan to get at me with all this material in the way."

I nip at her ear. "Oh, precious, I'm very resourceful. Need I remind you that I'm a man who gets what he wants?" Again I lean back to look in her eyes. "And anyone who ever doubted that only needs to look at me right now to know it's true. Everything I want is here, in my arms."

"I love you," she murmurs.

"I love you first." *And last. And everything in between.*

I kiss her, sweetly, chastely enough for our onlookers, but with just enough bite that she knows I mean it. Then our dance is over and it's time for her to dance with her brother and me with Sophia.

Reluctantly, I let her go. I can bear these few minutes apart. I have her for a lifetime.

THE END

Gwen Anders left her job as a top manager at Eighty-Eighth Floor to come work at The Sky Launch. She left suddenly and without warning. She hasn't told any of her new coworkers anything about her past or why she left.

Gwen Anders has a story of her own.

FREE ME

COMING SOON

ACKNOWLEDGMENTS

Here we are at the hard part. Seriously, writing 110,000 words is easy compared to writing the couple thousand that makes up the thank yous. I know I'll leave several people out. Please don't think that means I've forgotten you in my heart. Just my mind is a little fried.

First, as always, to my husband, Tom—I love you first. And last. And everything in between.

To my children who thought that mom writing full-time would mean they'd see me more—thank you for your patience and understanding. I love and adore you, even when I'm yelling at you to get out of my office.

To my Mom—thank you for raising me to be a person who goes after her dreams yet still thinks about others. I, too, hope I never change.

To Gennifer Albin for my covers and for understanding me in ways that many people never will. For sure, 2014 is your year.

To Bethany Taylor for editing and book-fairying and even a little for the moping because it makes me feel better about the amount of time I spend moping. And for teaching me so much about stick-to-it-ness and kindness (yes, I said that, you faux-blackhearted woman, you).

To Kayti McGee for being my plot partner and an excellent submissive. I fully recognize that I dominate all our conversations. Thank you so much for your ear and your suggestions. I will drive to Boulder/Longmont to see you even though the laws have changed; I swear it!

To my critique partners and beta readers. My, God! I would not have made it through this without you, especially when I was so behind. Thank you all for reading and suggesting so quickly. Specifically, thank you Lisa Otto for making time for me in your busy schedule and telling me how it is. To Tristina Wright for knowing my characters better than me and correcting their behavior. To Jackie Felger for always making me feel like I'm a better writer than I am while catching more comma errors than a person should possibly be able to catch. To Melissa B. King for always letting me know that the steamy scenes were working. To Jenna Tyler for last minute edits, even when I didn't ask—you are an amazing find of a friend. To Angela McLain for your passion and support—you're such a beautiful person to know. To Lisa Mauer for your enthusiasm and genuine love of my series; sometimes I felt like I was writing more for you than anyone. To Beta Goddess, you know who you are, but will never understand how grateful I am for "fixing" my book. I looked forward to your notes with a mixture of trepidation and excitement because I always knew you'd be hard, and that would make the story better. THANK YOU!!

To the people who make things happen for me: my agent, Bob DiForio; my formatter, Caitlin Greer; Julie at AToMR Book Blog Tours; my publicists at Inkslinger, Shanyn Day, and K.P. Simmons—both of you are amazeballs; Melanie Lowery and Jolinda Bivins for making me awesome swag; to my "other" editors Holly Atkinson, who has taught me to be mindful of comma splices, and Eileen Rothschild who is supportive of all my works and not just the one she bought.

To my FANTASTIC assistants, Lisa Otto, Amy McAvoy, and Taryn Maj. How did I get so lucky to have all of you working with me this past year? In many ways it's been the best part of the job.

To my soulmates and bandmates, The NAturals—Sierra, Gennifer, Melanie, Kayti, and Tamara. I honestly don't know what I'd do without you women. You love who I love, hate who I hate— you're my touchstones. I think Mel said this first, but I'm stealing it: If anyone had told me three years ago that I could love people I met on the internet more than people I knew in real life, I'd never believe it. But then I met you. Love and boobs to you always.

To Joe, last year was our year. So how much cooler will we be by this time next year?

To the authors who have helped out the newbie and inspired me with beautiful writing and so much amazing advice, especially Kristen Proby, Lauren Blakely, and Gennifer Albin. I'm really honored to know you all. Thank you for sharing your words and wisdom.

To the WrAHMs and the Babes of the Scribes—I can't wait to meet you at WrAHMpage and to hug the fuck out of all of you.

To the Book Bloggers and reviewers who have so enthusiastically shared my books. I can never hope to mention you all, but there are some of you I wouldn't dare miss: Aestas at Aestas Book Blog; Amy, Jesse, and Tricia at Schmexy Girls; The Rock Stars of Romance; Angie at Angie's Dreamy Reads; Lisa and Brooke at True Story Book Blog; Kari and Cara at A Book Whore's Obsession; Angie and Jenna at Fan Girl Book Blog; Jennifer Wolfel at Wolfel's World of Books. Though we have a symbiotic working relationship, I also truly think of you as friends. Thank you for your love and support.

To the Readers who make it possible for me to work full time as a writer and take care of my family with what I earn. I am so appreciative to you that I get choked up thinking about it. I know you have so many choices when it comes to picking up a book—thank you so, so much for picking up mine.

To my Creator who has given me more than I deserve—may I continue to understand what your role is for me in this life and to accept it with humility.

Did you know leaving a review helps authors get seen more on sites like Amazon?

If you liked *Forever with You*, please consider leaving a review.

You can sign up for my email newsletter to receive new book release info at www.laurelinpaige.com. You can also connect with me on Twitter @laurelinpaige and on Facebook at www.facebook.com/laurelinpaige.

Also by Laurelin Paige:
Fixed on You (Fixed #1)
Found in You (Fixed #2)

Coming Soon by Laurelin Paige:
Free Me
Find Me
Take Two
Star Struck

Lights, Camera…

TAKE TWO

Coming February 4, 2014 from Samhain Publishing
Available for preorder at <u>Amazon</u>, <u>Barnes & Noble</u>, and <u>iTunes</u>

On the night of her graduation from film school, straight-laced Maddie Bauers fell completely out of character for an oh-my-god make-out session with a perfect stranger. Complete with the big O.

Seven years later, that romantic interlude is still fresh in her mind. That stranger is now a rich and famous actor. And she's one very distracted camera assistant working on his latest production. She might consider another tryst…if he even remembers her.

Micah Preston does indeed remember Maddie. Too bad he's sworn off Hollywood relationships. He allows himself as much sex as he likes—and oh, he does like—but anything more is asking for trouble. For the woman, not for him. Yet knowing Maddie could want more than a movie-set fling doesn't stop him from pursuing her like a moth drawn to hot stage lights.

But as the shoot nears its end, it's decision time. Is it time to call, "Cut!" on their affair, or is there enough material for a sequel?

Here's a preview from TAKE TWO by Laurelin Paige.
Copyright Samhain Publishing, 2014.

Chapter One

A nightclub would have been bad enough, but when Maddie Bauers heard the stereo pulsing loudly outside the Woodland Hills house, she froze, and prepared to march full stomp back to her car.

"Oh, come on." Bree flashed her puppy-dog eyes, the ones that usually got her anything and anyone.

Maddie pursed her full lips. "You said one drink, Bree. This is not one drink. This is a noise violation and disorderly conduct ticket waiting to happen."

"This is fun waiting to happen." Bree tossed her long blonde hair behind her shoulder. "I know you're frigid and anti-good times, but one fucking party isn't going to kill you. As your best friend, it's my duty to tell you that you need to chillax. Have a good time." Bree leaned closer to Maddie. "And I heard from someone who heard from someone else that the cast and crew of the latest Davenport indie might show up. That means hot celebrities." She raised her hands triumphantly above her head. "Woo hoo!"

"First of all, I couldn't care less about celebrities. Secondly, how do you know they're hot?"

Bree waggled her eyebrows. "Let's just say I heard some rumors."

Maddie groaned. "I'm so leaving."

"Come on. Don't you want to celebrate your graduation even a little bit?"

"I am perfectly happy to celebrate on our couch with a glass of red wine."

"Maddie, I hate to tell you this, but for twenty-two, you are old."

Bree had a point. Maddie had always been serious, probably too serious for her own good. But it paid off. While the rest of the students in her film class partied and fumbled their way through college, she'd graduated with several completed independent films under her belt and landed a summer internship with the Oscar-winning filmmaker Joss Beaumont. Maddie was headed for a lifelong career in the film biz and she rarely let parties or men distract her.

Bree was another story. Maddie believed the petite buxom blonde would try to sleep her way into a starring film role—a goal bound to get her into trouble sooner or later. Parties like this one could bring that trouble sooner rather than later, and leaving Bree there alone was probably not such a good idea.

Maddie sighed. "Okay, okay, I'll stay." Before Bree could squeal with happiness, Maddie gave conditions. "But you have to promise not to abandon me in some corner like you usually do. And whoever you decide to randomly hook up with, promise me you'll use a condom."

"You act like I'm such a slut." Bree pulled Maddie toward the front door. "But yes, I do have a condom. In fact, I brought two."

"Are you planning to get lucky twice?"

"No, I was planning for you."

Bree didn't abandon Maddie in the first five minutes as she usually did at parties. She waited nearly ten. Then she excused herself to find a drink. Bree being Bree, Maddie knew it'd be awhile before they met up again.

Maddie snagged a seat on the living room sofa and busied herself with picking at her nails. She assumed a don't-bother-me posture, more out of habit than on purpose. After an hour that felt like three, she wondered if it was too soon to hunt down her roommate and declare the night over. Was she really so much of a fuddy-duddy that she wanted to leave a graduation party before midnight? Yes, she was. But it was Bree's graduation night too and she deserved to celebrate so Maddie determined to hold out a little longer.

Taking a deep breath, she stood up, tugged the straps of her pink tank top into place and smoothed down her knee-length black cotton skirt. *Might as well try to enjoy myself.* She pushed through the crowd and found an open cooler with beer near the patio doors. She grabbed a Corona, leaned against the open sliding door and peered into the backyard. Though the party extended there as well, there seemed to be more breathing room.

Once she got around the crowd surrounding the doors, Maddie saw that most of the partygoers congregated in and around the pool and hot tub, many sans swimsuit. Definitely a scene she wanted to avoid. She stuck to the side of the house, steering clear of the pool area all together.

On the other side of the backyard, she spied a couple making out on a porch swing. She watched as the man's deft fingers traveled up and under the woman's thin chemise. Even in the darkness, Maddie could see her shiver. She let out a moan of longing and Maddie's belly ached with unexpected jealousy. It had been awhile since she'd been kissed that way. Too long.

It didn't have to be too long, she reminded herself. That had been her choice. She could choose differently. What if she were audacious and uninhibited like Bree?

Then she wouldn't be on her way to a promising film career, *that's what.*

She shook off her arousal and fancies of unbridled passion and searched for a place to hole up unbothered. She spotted a concrete sitting area with an unlit fire pit against the yard's back wall. It was dark and in shadows, and looked deserted. She moved to claim it for herself.

Excited voices near the pool caught her attention when she'd nearly made it to the sanctuary. She peered over, seeking the cause of the excitement. A drunken woman, clothed only in a shirt and panties, stepped out from the center of the spectators and onto the diving board, twirling her discarded skirt in the air.

Maddie stopped short as she made out the face of the woman. Her stomach tightened. She knew that stripper. It was Bree.

Bree sang some current popular hit at the top of her lungs, basking in the attention her display earned. Soon she began inching her shirt up, teasing her audience, until the clothing was abandoned in the pool below and Bree stood simply in a black demi-cup bra and matching panties. The crowd cheered as she bent over provocatively, shimmying her petite behind.

"What the hell are you doing?" Maddie softly asked herself, willing the question to penetrate the distance between them and stop the antics of her wild friend.

"I'd say she's having a good time," a male voice said behind her. "Giving one as well."

Maddie jolted and put her hand over her heart. She turned to find her sitting area wasn't deserted as she'd hoped. In the shadows on the stone bench behind her sat a male figure. She couldn't make out his face, but moonlight fell on his lower body and taut, lean muscles pressed against his tight jeans.

"Sorry. Didn't mean to startle you." He leaned forward, appearing out of the shadows.

She took a quick breath as her gaze met his. His dark hair, thick and tousled, framed his smooth chiseled face. Deep-set eyes peered under intense eyebrows. She couldn't be sure in the darkness, but she guessed his eyes were blue. Whatever color, they were piercing and her knees weakened under his stare.

"No problem," she managed. "I didn't realize there was anyone out here."

"Clearly." He grinned. "I mean, the whole allure of this area is the seclusion, right?" His smooth words combined with the slightest hint of a drawl sent an unexpected ripple of desire south of her belly.

"Right." Maddie turned back to Bree, hoping to hide the heat that was rising in her cheeks. What was wrong with her? She never reacted this way to guys, let alone ones she'd just met. Perhaps the couple she'd witnessed making out had aroused her more than she'd realized.

"She'll be fine." The man mistook Maddie's withdrawal as concern about her stripping friend. "She has plenty of people looking out for her."

"That's what I'm afraid of." But this stranger had the right idea. It was no good worrying about Bree when she got herself in these situations. Maddie knew from experience the best course of action was to just wait it out. Bree would summon when she could no longer handle herself.

Maddie took a swig of her Corona and turned back to the piercing eyes. Despite the nearby striptease, his gaze was fixed directly on her. "She doesn't seem to have captured your attention."

The man shrugged. "I prefer private shows."

An image of the kind of show Maddie could give him flashed through her mind. She quickly took another swallow of her beer, clearing her head of the inappropriate thoughts. Seriously, what had come over her?

The stranger tilted his head, as if trying to interpret her silence. "You're welcome to sit."

Her insides twisted at the thought of being close to him, wanting an accidental brush against his strong body. She dismissed her usual tendency to over-think and walked toward the stone seating. "You were looking to be alone—I wouldn't want to intrude."

"I was looking for seclusion, not necessarily to be alone."

His words possessed a teasing tone that made her shiver. She tensed as he looked her over, fully aware that he was checking her out. She'd been gifted with pretty brown eyes and nice features, and she took care of her figure, but she didn't pay attention to whether or not she was attractive to men. This man seemed pleased, though, giving her a look that would usually turn her on her heels. She didn't flirt with strangers—didn't flirt much period—which was one of the reasons she avoided social gatherings such as this one.

But this man compelled her, his body drawing her like a magnet. He was so incredibly attractive, and hell, didn't she deserve a little fun on her graduation night?

"I'll take you up on the offer. To sit, I mean."

"Ah, I hadn't offered anything else." He let out a slow breath. "Yet."

Her heart raced at the implications as she sat beside him on the bench, closer than she imagined she'd ever dare. Her skirt rose as she crossed one long leg over the other and she fought the impulse to adjust it, feeling the intensity of his eyes on her thigh.

She flushed again under his gaze and she needed to calm the fire kindling between her legs. Seeing he held a Coors Light, she lifted her bottle in a toast. "To privacy."

He smiled, his face lighting up as he did, causing another stir in Maddie's nether parts. "To privacy." He clinked her bottle then took a sip of his own. She watched as his mouth parted around the tip of the bottle and found herself imagining the feel of his full, firm lips, wondering what he'd taste like. Her tongue darted across her teeth at the thought.

"Tell me," he said, setting his bottle down on the ground next to him. "What's a hot, I mean, attractive woman like you doing at a party like this if you're looking to be alone?"

Her heart raced at his shameless remark. "One could ask the same of you."

"Yes, they could. It's the question on everyone's mind. But I asked first."

"You aren't full of yourself at all."

He feigned seriousness. "No, not at all. If I was full of myself, we would be talking about me, but I'm trying to find out about you, so you should answer the question."

Hot and charming. Delish.

"Well…" She wished she had some witty comeback. She settled on simply answering his question. "I was dragged here with Miss Bare-It-All over there." She nodded toward Bree, who now only wore panties. "It's supposed to be our graduation party."

The man stiffened. "Graduation?"

She laughed. "From film school. Were you worried you were coming on to a teenager?"

He leaned back, distancing himself from Maddie. "Oh, you thought I was coming on to you?"

Crap! Had the teasing only been in her mind? She opened her mouth to speak, but she stuttered. "Uh…"

He chuckled. "Relax. I was totally coming on to you."

She raised a brow. "Really? Or are you just keeping me from being completely humiliated?"

"No, I really was hitting on you. Come on, it was incredibly obvious."

"Yes, it was. Are you still hitting on me now? Or has the moment passed?"

"Oh, no, the moment hasn't passed." He cocked his head and his eyes travelled down her body again, lingering at her low neckline. "So…film school," he said after a heat-filled moment. "What's your area of interest?"

"Uh, uh, uh." Maddie barely kept herself from a fit of nervous giggles. "You never told me why you were here."

"That's boring."

"Impossible."

"Okay, you really want to know? I was also dragged here. By some of the guys I work with." He craned his neck, looking around the party. "I have no idea where they are. Nor would I tell you if I saw them because they might be more attractive than I am and I wouldn't want to give myself unnecessary competition."

Maddie let her own eyes explore his body. His casual white-and-black button-down shirt opened to mid-sternum and she could see serious pecs underneath. The bottom buttons also remained open and when he stretched his arms above his head—on purpose, no doubt—a patch of tight abs and a trail of hair peeked out. Yum, yum, and yum. "You don't need to worry about competition."

"Seriously? Then I'm doing okay?"

"You're doing just fine." She locked eyes with him, and thoughts of him naked above her flashed through her mind. Blushing, she looked away.

"So…" she said, raising her eyebrows. Was she really flirting like this with a stranger?

"So, you never told me what area of film you studied."

As a rule, Maddie stayed away from this conversation with people she'd just met. Saying you graduated from film school in L.A. was like saying you had breakfast. It was a dull, overdone topic. But this subject was safer than her fantasy thoughts and the man's assertiveness easily drew the answer out. "Screenwriting."

He nodded.

"And directing."

He raised his eyebrows. "Hmm, now that would be fun."

"Directing?"

"Being directed by you."

Her eyes widened. She quickly finished off her Corona, attempting to calm her nerves. How on earth did this stranger manage to fluster her like that? Turn her inside out so easily?

She played with the label of her empty bottle as she fought to stay on solid ground, steering away from his innuendo. "Yeah, so directing is my thing. But, of course, it's difficult to break into that biz, so I'm interested in all things film at the moment. Sound, camera, you name it. Screenwriting just fell in the mix because when you're a kid growing up wanting to direct, you had to have material to direct so you could practice. I've got three full-length films under my belt—indies—but still…and I start an internship with an amazing film crew on Monday." She stopped, realizing she was babbling.

"I'm intrigued." He took the bottle from her and set it on the grass next to his.

Without the bottle in her hands, she felt vulnerable. And was he sitting closer than he was a moment ago? She returned to her jabber, unable to organize her thoughts. "It's really not that interesting. I'll be a production assistant, the lowest of—"

"That's not what I'm intrigued with," he interrupted, his voice husky.

Maddie met his eyes and saw a flicker of desire. He wanted her—it was obvious. Why not? For one night, why not live carefree?

She tilted her head toward him and braved herself to tempt his seduction. "Then tell me, what is intriguing you?"

In one swift move, he had her pressed against the wall, his mouth hovering above her own. The rough stone behind her barely registered as she licked her lips in anticipation of the kiss she knew was coming.

But he didn't lean in. Instead, he brought his finger to her cheek and caressed it softly. She shuddered at the electric pulses that followed his light touch as he traced her jawline. When he reached her chin, he lifted her face up to within an inch of his mouth. She felt his breath, hot and sweet, on her skin. And then his mouth was on hers, tugging at her bottom lip, teasing her until she eagerly drew him in, wrapping her arms around his neck.

The kiss built, each stroke varying in pressure and intensity. Soft nips evolved into frenzied exploration, their tongues dancing, plunging deeply and hungrily. She savored his taste. A rush of pleasure rippled through her and she trembled under his attentive suckling.

His mouth released hers, traveled along her jaw and down her throat, his trail of kisses searing into her skin. She clung to a fistful of his thick hair while he alternately nibbled and nuzzled her neck, stoking the fire in her core. When he raised his head to reclaim her lips, she glimpsed a greedy longing in his eyes.

He pressed tighter against her and Maddie could feel the bulge of his erection against her hip. She drew in a sharp breath, and he grinned against her mouth before recapturing it in his.

Desperate to feel more of his body against her own, for him to touch her more intimately, she arched her back, pushing her chest deeper into him. He read her cue and brought his hand down over her shirt to cup her breast. He stroked his thumb firmly over her nipple until it stood under the contact.

"Damn," he said, his tone pleased.

For once, Maddie was grateful that her chest, though on the smaller side, was firm enough to wear built-in shelf tank tops without bras.

He continued his assault on her other breast. Maddie moaned, her hips rocking up, instinctively looking for something more, something her rational brain would have told her was inappropriate to seek from a man she'd just met. Hell, she didn't even know his name. But her rational thought was lost within the flood of passion brought on by his equally fervent ardor.

She raised her hips again, and this time he responded by moving his hand to the inside of her upper leg. Softly, he caressed her thigh, journeying up, up until he reached her panties. She gasped as his fingers moved underneath the elastic and found her taut bud. *Holy fuck!* She relaxed her legs to give him better access, letting him know she wanted more.

And, man, did he deliver. With the pad of his finger, he stroked and swirled her tender flesh. Expertly, he increased the pressure to her swollen bundle of nerves until she was lost in glorious sensation. His mouth recaptured hers, swallowing her cry of pleasure as wave after wave of ecstasy crashed through her, and she shuddered uncontrollably.

His kissing slowed, and when she had calmed enough to resume a modicum of control, he pulled his lips away and rested his forehead against hers. "Would you join me somewhere even more private?" he asked, his engorged shaft still pressing hot against her hip.

Yes, yes, a million times yes! Even in the afterglow of her release, she desired him, longed to bring him to his own climax. Still panting, she opened her mouth to answer when a not-too-far-off voice interrupted her.

"Maddie! Maddie? Is that you?"

Bree.

Maddie turned from the handsome stranger and saw her near-naked friend peering at her from a few feet away.

"It is you!" Bree squealed. "I'm so, so, so, so happy I found you. I really think you need to take me—"

Bree's sentence was cut off as she vomited all over the lawn.

The man shook his head. "I see you're needed…Maddie, is it?"

"I…I'm…" She felt torn between responsibility and recklessness. She wanted to leave Bree to figure out her own mess rather than give up this magnificent creature in her arms. Maybe it would teach her a lesson. But Bree was in no condition to handle herself. Maddie sighed with frustration.

"I totally understand." He released her from his embrace. "I won't say I'm not disappointed—very disappointed—but I understand."

"I'm sorry. Truly sorry." She stood, reluctantly, and glowered at Bree, now on her hands and knees sobbing. Maddie readjusted her skirt and took a step toward the pathetic creature.

"Wait." He grabbed her hand. "Can I see you sometime?"

Maddie tilted her head to stare back at him. "Really? You don't have to—"

"I know I don't. I want to."

She broke into a grin. "Give me your phone." He did and she typed her information into his contacts, then handed it back.

"Thanks." He nodded toward Bree. "Let me help you with her."

"No," Maddie said quickly. His questioning look prompted her to explain. "It's just, I'd rather remember you right there, not fumbling around with my idiot drunk friend." Plus she couldn't subject him to dealing with Bree, especially with the hard-on she knew he still sported.

"Got it." He adjusted himself. "Just as long as you are remembering me."

"Oh, I could never forget." She sighed to accent her point. He winked and she turned again to leave when a thought crossed her mind. She spun back to him. "Hey, I don't know—"

"Micah," he said, accurately predicting what she was going to say. "I'm Micah."

"Nice to meet you, Micah." She rolled the name off her lips, relishing its feel in her mouth. Then she gave him one last longing look before she left to help Bree.

THE AUTHOR

Laurelin Paige is the USA Today Bestselling author of the Fixed on You trilogy. She's a sucker for a good romance and gets giddy anytime there's kissing, much to the embarrassment of her three daughters. Her husband doesn't seem to complain, however. When she isn't reading or writing sexy stories, she's probably singing, watching Game of Thrones and the Walking Dead, or dreaming of Adam Levine. She is represented by Bob Diforio of D4EO Literary Agency.

Made in the USA
San Bernardino, CA
18 April 2014